NO ESCAPE

"Let's start over," he said.

Tess glared at him. *Fine with her.*

She shot off the wall and blew by him. This time he didn't try to stop her; he simply stood there with his hands on his hips. When she got past him, she found out why. In a flash of movement, a robot appeared, hovering about three feet off the floor in front of the main door. Tess skidded to a stop and stared. The metal monster stared back. His metal form was covered in panels and arms and lights that flashed just like Christmas tree lights—half a suit of armor that looked just human enough to scare the living daylights out of her.

Tess spun around to face Cohl. He appeared more annoyed now than amused. As if he were the one in trouble.

"I told you, don't bother." His voice was low and steely.

Tess stood as tall as her five-foot-four frame would take her and gathered her courage. Thrusting her chin out, she challenged, "I can swim."

He looked at her in puzzlement, then laughed aloud. Turning, he pressed a panel behind him. A huge section of the wall slid up, revealing endless black space and stars. In the center of the window hung one very brown, very alien-looking planet.

He smiled. "Yes, but can you fly?"

UNEARTHED

C. J. BARRY

LOVE SPELL   NEW YORK CITY

This book is dedicated to my wonderful family:
Ed, Rachel and Ryan.

LOVE SPELL®

May 2003

Published by

Dorchester Publishing Co., Inc.
276 Fifth Avenue
New York, NY 10001

ISBN 0-505-52540-2

The name "Love Spell" and its logo are trademarks of Dorchester Publishing Co., Inc.

Printed in the United States of America.

Visit us on the web at www.dorchesterpub.com.

ACKNOWLEDGMENTS

I owe my deepest gratitude to all those who believed in me: Christopher Keeslar—my terrific editor—and the great staff at Dorchester Publishing for making this book the best it could be; the Purple Pens for their unrelenting support, emotional fortitude and treasured friendship; the CNY Romance Writers for patience and guidance, with special thanks to Gayle Callen; my dedicated critique partners Lisa, Patti, Joyce, co-workers and cyberfriends; the ladies at the Chittenango Library for researching all my morbid questions without once calling the police; the kind souls in the Lollies, the FF&P chapter, and the Romance Writers of America; Susan Grant for clearing the way and fielding more newbie e-mails than any one person should have to; Maggie Shayne for her generous heart and paranormal wisdom; Adleen and the late John P. Barry; my siblings Tom G. Dishaw, Chris Walker and Cheri Revai; and my parents, Tom and Jean Dishaw, for their undying confidence and love.

And finally, my husband Ed for understanding when I leave Earth for hours at a time and always welcoming me back, my son Ryan for lending his spaceship models and action figures for choreography purposes, and my daughter Rachel for her joyful spirit and timely hugs.

Thank you all for helping me to reach the stars.

UNEARTHED

Chapter One

Earth, present day

Staring down the wrong end of the gun, Tess MacKenzie realized something she hadn't thought was possible: This lousy day *could* get worse.

"You heard me, lady. Hand over the cash. I know you just got paid."

Tess tore her eyes away from the gun to the face of the man pointing it at her. The back alley of Sonny's Bar and Grill was a stupid place to be alone at 3:00 A.M. on a Saturday night. Stupid, dark, and smelly. You never knew what kind of vermin you'd find crawling around. The two-legged variety she stared at now was proof-positive. She squinted at her assailant in the faint moonlight. All she could imagine was a beer keg on legs—and even that was a compliment. She wondered how he'd got so round eating with just those half-dozen teeth.

She forced a casual smile. "Sorry. Sonny said it was a slow

night. He couldn't pay me and the band until tomorrow."

Keg-on-legs snorted. "Nice try. I saw Sonny hand ya the money, honey. Now it's mine." His few teeth glinted as he smiled.

Tess glared at him. Damn it, she needed that three hundred bucks. The rent was due, the recording studio was holding her CD hostage for payment, and her car was on its last legs.

But hey, it could be worse. She could be getting mugged by a filthy little varmint in the back alley of the tackiest gin joint in upstate New York.

"Are you gonna hand it over nice-like, or am I gonna hafta come get it from you?"

Tess shuddered at the thought. There was just enough light to see the filthy hand holding the gun, and she didn't need that hand any closer.

Grumbling, she reached into her purse to get the cash from the night's gig and vowed that this was the last time her manager was going to book something in the middle of God's country. She didn't care how desperate they were for money; from now on, she was sticking to radio appearances and recording studios.

Her hand struck something hard and cold. Hair spray. She paused. It *could* work. All she needed were a few seconds to duck around the side of the building and head for the all-night diner across the street.

Slowly, she wrapped her fingers around the cold metal and found its top. She swallowed hard and yanked the canister out of her bag, pushing the nozzle and aiming for the mugger's head.

Keg-on-legs jumped back, grabbing at his face where the spray stung his eyes. Tess spun and ran wildly, with Keg-on-legs swearing and stumbling behind her. He recovered quickly and moved faster than she could have imagined on those stubby legs.

Damn. She'd thought she would have more time. *Oh God, don't shoot me.*

By now he was cursing behind her, calling out in precise, disgusting terms just how much trouble she was going to be in when he got his hands on her.

Tess rounded the corner of the building and ran right into a big man who caught her in his arms.

Yes! Help had arrived.

"He's got a gun!" she gasped as she glanced up into the stranger's face. If she hadn't been so pumped up with adrenaline, she would have fallen over. *Wow.* What good-looking cavalry. The man was tall and gorgeous with a killer smile.

Keg-on-legs rounded the corner right behind her and skidded to a halt, aiming his gun with both hands at first Tess, then the stranger. Breathing heavily, he shouted, "Don't move, I don't wanna kill nobody. I just want the money."

The stranger eyed him thoughtfully. Tess couldn't pull her gaze away from his shadowed face, so calm and relaxed. Didn't he realize there was a gun pointed at him? Her eyes widened. She'd almost forgotten—there was a gun pointed at her, too.

"Would you like me to neutralize him, sir?"

Tess jumped at the strange new voice emanating from the darkness. It sounded somehow both mechanical and human. It also sounded . . . well, bored. *Bored?*

"Please," the stranger drawled.

A beam of light flashed from somewhere behind him. It hit Keg-on-legs square in the chest, and the mugger crumpled quietly to a pile on the ground.

Tess gaped—first at the incapacitated man in the dirt and then up at her savior. The stranger's eyes narrowed, watching her every move. She backed away with feet of lead. That was when she saw the bizarre silver apparition behind him, hovering in midair. She didn't know what it was, but she knew

3

what it wasn't. It wasn't like anything she'd ever seen on Earth.

In detached horror, she watched as the thing turned its sights on her. Was it a robot? Her heart pounded painfully in her chest.

"I'd like you to come with me," the stranger said.

Tess's mouth went dry. Good Lord. Wasn't a mugging enough tonight? "If you don't mind, I think I'll pass."

The robot slipped closer, and with growing panic she added, "Just so you know, I can scream really well."

The stranger's smile faded. "I'm afraid that won't do." He turned and nodded to his metal monster.

The last thing Tess saw in the burst of light was the stranger's golden eyes.

Chapter Two

She wasn't at all what he had expected.

Cohl stretched his legs, propped his feet up on an examination table, and regarded his sleeping captive from across his starship's med center.

Was it really *her* voice he'd followed across the galaxy, *her* song broadcast out on the airwaves into space? He had listened to that song over and over again on his six-day journey to her planet. During those long nights, the picture of the woman he envisioned singing it had shifted and settled. With that pure voice, she would be an angel, fair and delicate; a gentle and innocent creature in need of protection.

Cohl crossed his arms over his chest. That's definitely not what he had found. Not exactly.

Any woman who would attempt to fend off a much larger attacker and a lethal weapon with nothing more than a can of compressed air was all fighter. He had seen the flash in her eyes just before Pitz stunned her—the quick turn from gratitude to betrayal to anger. He would have his hands full convincing her that she was the answer to his mission and the salvation of millions.

He dropped his feet to the floor and rested his elbows on his thighs. There was another problem. She was simply bewitching. Since yesterday, he'd spent far too many hours in this med center watching her.

He studied her face. There was . . . something about her, something familiar in the light auburn hair with its fiery red edge. Something comfortable about the petite, well-shaped body. Something exciting in those lively, green eyes that had gazed up at him in relief when she first saw him.

No, she wasn't what Cohl had expected at all. And that was the real problem.

Behind him, the med center door slid open and shut. He didn't turn to see who entered. The only crew member on board who didn't walk on the floor was Pitz. The robot clicked and whirred as it hovered to a halt behind him.

"Are you sure we have the right woman?" Cohl asked without taking his eyes off her.

Pitz gave the mechanical equivalent of a woeful sigh. "Yes, sir. I have checked the voice-match over one million times. This is the woman we seek."

Cohl turned and faced the machine he'd known his entire life. All the robot's systems appeared functioning at capacity: lights winked and blinked across Pitz's humanlike shape from his head to the metal skirt over his hips that covered his hover mechanism and turbo propulsion. Hidden within that metal body was a lethal assortment of weaponry and data-processing capabilities—all of which Cohl had seen in action. Pitz was a formidable ally and a loyal friend.

"Any sign of the Traka-Sou this time?"

"None. We must have lost them in that last set of maneuvers over Earth," Pitz responded. "An unorthodox use of the hyperspace, sir. Well done."

Cohl cast the robot a sharp glance. "Don't get too relaxed.

The Traka-Sou won't give up that easily. Especially if they find out we have *her*. This is no time to get sloppy."

"Yes, sir," Pitz replied. "I will notify the crew to remain on alert."

"Are we on schedule to meet with Zain?"

Pitz computed that. "Yes, we will be at the rendezvous point at the agreed-upon time. Will he?"

"Captain Zain Masters? Late? Never. Not unless he's dead."

"Pardon my doubt, sir, but do you really believe that he can find the location of the Demisian Amulet? Although it is a popular legend, there is no actual proof of its existence. And, Captain Masters *is* only human."

Cohl laughed aloud and shook his head. "Pitz, don't ever say that to him. If Zain says he knows where it is, then he does. Period."

He watched Tess, momentarily distracted by the gentle rise and fall of her breasts. "Were you able to access the computer networks back on Earth?"

"Of course," Pitz said haughtily. "Their artificial-intelligence systems are positively primordial."

"What did you find on her?"

Pitz settled into a monotone recital of statistics: "Her name is Tess Elisa MacKenzie. She is twenty-nine Earth years old, Earth years being approximate to our Standard years. She grew up in and resides in Marley Corners, a small town with a population of 5,326."

The robot paused. "Do you want her physical characteristics and dimensions?"

"I have eyes," Cohl muttered. He probably knew more about her physical statistics than Pitz did.

Indifferently, Pitz continued. "She lives alone and is un-mated. She worked in her parents' private enterprise until they were killed in a vehicle accident last year. Since their deaths, she has begun pursuing a singing and entertainment career with moderate success."

7

Cohl shook his head. "Moderate. Apparently, her own people don't know how unique her voice is."

"One is never fully appreciated by one's peers," Pitz complained.

Cohl eyed him warily and redirected the conversation before the robot could lapse into melodramatic self-indulgence. "What else?"

"Compared to the norm for her race, her financial situation is abysmal. She owns nothing of significant value and, in fact, owes more than she is worth."

Cohl narrowed his eyes. So *that* was the reason she'd fought off an armed attacker in a back alley—the man was after her credits. It burned Cohl that she might have gotten herself killed for something so insignificant.

"Would you care for a list of her possessions, sir?"

"No," Cohl decided. "You said she worked in her parents' enterprise. How long?"

"Since she was a child."

Cohl leaned back in his chair. "Any siblings?"

Pitz clicked softly. "She has a brother and a sister. They left Marley Corners to attend institutes of higher education and did not return. Both reside elsewhere."

"So she stayed and helped her parents," Cohl guessed, rubbing his chin. "A sense of duty and responsibility. That's good. It's just what I was hoping for."

"I do not see the association," Pitz commented. "What does that have to do with our mission?"

Cohl smiled. "Everything. When can we revive her?"

The robot whirred over to the med center console and plugged in. After a few seconds, he reported, "She has completed phase one and two of the language translation interface. Phase three is still running. Estimated completion time: two hours."

"Are you sure this won't harm her? We've never tried to interface our language patterns onto an Earth human before." Cohl glanced at the neural halo around Tess's head.

"Her subconscious can handle the interface. It is no different than learning a second language. The process is simply accelerated," Pitz answered. He added in a droll tone, "Although, she may have a slight headache from cerebral over-exertion."

"I can sympathize with that," Cohl muttered, rubbing his own head. "The English language is a mess. I may never recover from that interface."

"Just remember that she will only comprehend our fundamental language. Slang terms and proper names will still be a mystery to her."

"It goes both ways," Cohl reminded him.

Pitz snorted. "Not for me. I know everything."

Cohl chuckled. He'd consider Pitz arrogant if it weren't for the fact that the robot was right.

He stood up. "I'll be on the bridge. Contact me when you're ready to bring her around. We should move her to regular crew quarters. I don't want her waking up here."

He took one final look at Tess before walking out.

The first hint of consciousness floated through Tess like a warm, muzzy fog. Voices faded in and out. She didn't even try to understand them. Life was wonderful. No thoughts, no worries.

Someone said her name—a male voice, low and sexy. She hummed softly. He sounded good-looking. The term stuck in her mind. *Good-looking*. She had seen someone like that recently.

Reality invaded in a nightmarish rush.

The stranger. That voice. Those golden eyes.

Tess broke through the fog in a violent lunge. Lights blinded her. Hands held her down.

"Easy, Tess," a deep voice soothed.

She fought; but the hands were strong, the arms attached

to them powerful. Her eyes adjusted enough to concentrate on their owner: the stranger with the beautiful eyes. He had a beautiful smile, too.

"You!" she snapped. "What have you done to me? Where am I? And what the hell is going on?"

His smile widened, but his hands remained firm. "Pitz, I'd say she's recovered nicely," he said.

Tess tried to kick him where her mother had always told her to, but her legs wouldn't cooperate and her foot ended up glancing off the stranger's kneecap. He released her with a grunt. She leaped from the bed and stumbled toward a closed door. Her kick had the desired effect, but that effect lasted much less time than she'd have liked. The stranger grabbed her by the wrists and backed her against a wall, pinning her like a bug on a board.

"I told you to put the restraints on her, sir. Females are so unpredictable."

That bored mechanical voice stopped Tess cold. She recognized it as that of the metal monster from the alley; the one she'd hoped was nothing more than a bad dream. She struggled with renewed effort, her fear growing. "You shot me, you bucket of bolts!"

The creature answered with a surprisingly human snort. "Hardly. Just a small dose of charged particles. Enough to incapacitate you."

"You better hope I never get my hands on a can opener, pal," Tess muttered. She became painfully aware of her captor's strength, and her exhaustion from fighting him. All he had to do was stand there. Then she realized he wasn't trying to hurt her, only hold her still.

Relaxing slightly, she gazed back at his face just inches from hers. It was the face of a poet. The stranger had eyes the color of burnished gold and eyelashes she would have killed for. His hair was a tawny brown with golden highlights, slightly wavy and chin-length. Her eyes followed his straight nose down to full, strong lips. Lips that were grinning.

"You know, I rather prefer this method of restraint," he murmured.

He was watching her with amusement. Arrogant amusement. She would have slapped him if she could have freed her hands, but he held them on either side of her head. She tried again to yank them free, but the wiggling only increased her fatigue and got no results.

She gazed into her captor's golden eyes. They smoldered, and as she felt the brush of his hot breath on her skin, awareness rippled through her.

"Let me explain the situation here," the stranger said slowly. "You can't escape, so don't bother trying. I'd also think twice about attacking me again. It's been a while since I've seen this much action from a woman. Don't push your luck."

"Who are you?" she whispered.

"Cohl Travers."

"What do you want?"

He paused. "You promise to behave if I release you?"

Like hell. Tess nodded.

He freed her wrists and planted himself a few feet away.

Tess inhaled a full breath, pressing her back to the wall. She closed her eyes for a moment, trying to pretend none of this was happening. She opened them. No such luck. He was still there. Still smiling. She hated him.

He crossed his arms over his chest, strong muscles moving under the tight, ribbed crew shirt he wore. The dull silver fabric did nothing to hide the fact that he was in excellent physical condition. His pants were black, made of a material unlike any she recognized. Perhaps he was foreign: an unhappy thought. She'd never even been outside of New York State.

Tess surveyed the small room. It contained only the bed

and a few chairs. The walls and ceiling were some sort of blue-gray metal like on a boat, but there was no rocking. Must be a big boat.

There were no windows and, in her moment of freedom, she'd glimpsed a wide door—but her path to it was currently blocked by the big man. A second, smaller door was to her right. It was too small, probably for storage. She didn't need to get locked in a closet. The wider one held her only promise of escape.

"Let's start over," he was saying.

She glared at him. *Fine with me.* She had a good idea for a new beginning.

She shot off the wall and blew by him. This time he didn't try to stop her; he simply stood there with his hands on his hips. When she got past, she found out why. In a flash, the robot had moved; it now hovered about three feet off the floor in front of the main door. She skidded to a stop and stared at it. The metal monster stared back. Its metal form was covered in panels and circuits that flashed like Christmas tree lights—here was half a suit of armor that looked just human enough to scare the living daylights out of her.

Tess spun around to face the man named Cohl. He appeared more annoyed now than amused. As if he were the one in trouble.

"I told you, don't bother." His voice was low and steely.

Tess stood as tall as her five-foot-four frame would take her and gathered courage. Thrusting her chin out, she challenged, "I can swim."

He looked at her in puzzlement and then laughed aloud. Turning, he pressed a panel behind him. A huge section of one wall slid up, revealing nothing but endless black space and stars. In the center of the window hung one very brown, very alien-looking planet.

He smiled. "Yes, but can you fly?"

Chapter Three

Tess's mouth gaped open. *Holy cow.*

She backed against a wall, still staring at the planet while her heart hammered a painful, rapid tattoo inside her chest. The metal felt cold and foreign against her skin. This had to be an illusion, a trick, because if it wasn't, she was in big trouble. A small spacecraft floated lazily across the face of the planet. She blinked. Pretty good trick.

A trembling started deep inside her gut and worked its way out until her hands shook. This was bad, very bad. Where the hell was she? In the middle of space looking down onto a planet? Impossible. Then again, there was a talking robot floating around. *Danger, Will Robinson. Danger.*

And here she'd always thought all those sci-fi movies were silly, too absurd, too hard to believe. Too alien.

Her gaze shot back to Cohl, who was watching her the way a lion eyes its next morsel. An alien. Oh God, *he* was an alien. Idly, she admitted they looked better than she'd heard. Was he going to start sprouting horns and twelve arms?

"Who are you?" Much to her dismay, her voice cracked.

"Cohl Travers."

She shook her head slowly. "No, *what* are you?"

His eyes narrowed. "Just a normal man."

Tess gave a short, semihysterical laugh. "Oh, that's funny. That's what they say about serial killers, too. Where am I?"

"On board *Speculator*. My starship." He paused. "I need your help."

Tess's mouth dropped open. "You can't be serious."

"I generally don't go around abducting women if I don't have to," he said.

She almost believed him. "But you're so good at it. You and this, that . . ." She waved a hand at the robot.

"*That* is Pitz. My first officer."

Pitz floated forward. Tess cringed. "It's got a name?"

The robot stopped, then said huffily, "Of course. Delighted to meet you, Tess MacKenzie."

His greeting had an ironic tone, and the lights in his eye sockets flickered in a hypnotic pattern. He seemed terrifyingly intelligent, as if he were actually thinking, not just reacting. What kind of robot had a brain, a voice, and an attitude?

Then, something even worse dawned on her and her breath caught. "How do you know my name?"

The robot's head tilted slightly. "We know everything about you—your background, your family, your finances, your friends . . ."

Tess's eyes widened as she absorbed his words. Good Lord. What kind of mess was she in?

Cohl held up a hand to interrupt Pitz's monologue. "Thank you, Pitz. Why don't you head to the bridge and see if Zain has arrived? I can handle it from here."

The robot whirled to face him. "Are you certain you don't want some restraints?"

"They won't be necessary." Cohl shot Tess a warning look over Pitz's shoulder. "She can't go far."

Pitz hummed toward the door. "Actually, I was more concerned for your physical well-being."

Tess watched the door slide shut behind him and reluctantly turned back to her captor. He was regarding her with a single-mindedness that made her shiver down to her toes.

He folded his arms over his chest. "I have a problem that I believe you can help me with."

"No." Whatever he had in mind, Tess wasn't interested. This crazy adventure had gone on long enough. She wanted out. Out before they dissected her or bred her or did whatever aliens do to poor, defenseless Earthlings.

Cohl's eyebrows raised. "You haven't heard the problem yet."

"Take me home."

He frowned. "I can't do that."

"Can't or won't?" she demanded.

The frown deepened. "Won't."

Tess stepped forward and put her hands on her hips. "You have no right to do this. I am *not* having your alien baby."

His eyebrows shot up again and stayed. She felt a small sense of victory. He was obviously speechless.

Then he smirked. "Do you know that for certain?"

She took one giant step back. Okay. So he wasn't exactly speechless. His expression was arrogant but not menacing. Surely he wouldn't have done anything to her in the time she'd been unconscious.

"How long have I been here?" she gasped.

"Three days."

Three days. She looked down at herself. Nothing hurt, no marks, no extra appendages. Other than being a bit stiff, she felt fine. Unless, of course, he was serious about the conception thing.

Suddenly, she brightened. She'd been missing back home for three days. By now, someone would have noticed. Her landlady, her manager, her band . . .

She caught herself with a half laugh, half sob. What was she thinking? They couldn't come after her. Besides, no relatives were expecting her and her manager might think she'd just become a hermit to write songs. Her landlady would think she'd traveled to see her brother or sister. The band didn't have another gig until next Friday ni— *Oh no!*

She leaped forward and grabbed Cohl by the front of his shirt. "Turn around. Right now. I have to be back by Friday morning."

His golden eyes darkened. "We aren't turning around."

She yanked hard on his shirt but he didn't budge. "Look, I don't care what your problem is. I have a very important meeting on Friday. My whole singing career is on the line here. We've got a chance to be an opening band for, a six-month tour—"

Cohl gripped her wrists and held her away from him. "You'll miss it."

She stared at him in disbelief at his casual dismissal. "No. I have waited eight years for this chance. I put my life on hold long enough." She broke free from his grip and tapped her chest. "It's my turn. I earned this. I paid my dues. No one is going to take it away." The words tumbled out and over each other.

He didn't say anything. *Good.* Twice she'd left him speechless. The bastard. The alien bastard. Damned if she would allow him to stand in her way. The unfeeling, uncaring, tin-hearted . . .

He spoke softly. "I'm sorry. I have no choice. My father's life is at stake. They will kill him if I fail."

She watched him run a hand through his hair, the blond

highlights glistening. He looked back up at her with those amazing golden eyes. What was she supposed to say to that?

"Huh?"

He took a deep breath. "Sit down. I'll explain."

Tess rubbed her forehead, which had begun to throb. Then she looked back at him. His expression was sincere and patient, his eyes concerned. Maybe if she indulged him, he would leave her alone. Then she could concentrate on how to get herself out of here. She plunked down on the edge of the bed and folded her arms tightly over her chest.

Cohl started to pace as he talked. "My home planet, Yre Gault, is in another quadrant of your galaxy. I grew up there with my parents. It's a peaceful planet with nice people."

He stopped prowling and turned to her. "Ten days ago, my father was abducted by a group calling themselves the Traka-Nor. They occupy the northern hemisphere of the planet Trakas. The Traka-Sou occupy the southern hemisphere. The two sides are at war." His voice tightened, and his big fists clenched at his sides. "It's been bloody and violent with brutal fighting and heavy casualties. The opposing leaders are brothers. They hate each other enough to destroy their own people for their personal vendettas, putting weapons in the hands of farmers and children."

There was little emotion in his voice but his tense body spoke volumes. What amazed Tess was the ruthless and complete control he held over his anger. She'd bet he never got mad, never yelled, never threw anything in his life. That couldn't be good for you.

She watched in fascination as Cohl started to pace again. He moved like a panther, stealthy and silent for such a large man.

"The Traka-Nor leader, Rommol, discovered an old legend about an amulet. The Demisian Amulet is supposed to have the power of persuasion, the ability to control your enemy. Rommol believes it's the ultimate weapon to defeat his

17

brother and take control of the entire planet."

Tess blinked at him. "An amulet can do all that?"

Cohl shrugged. "According to the legend, whoever wears the amulet controls the power. For thousands of years, all the rulers of Demisie wielded the amulet and the planet thrived. Then something happened and the Demisians decimated themselves in a civil war. The amulet disappeared, hidden away in a secret chamber somewhere on Demisie."

Tess rubbed her temples with her fingertips. She was talking to an alien about a magic amulet that could take over planets. She needed an aspirin in the worst way.

"So, how does your father fit into all that?"

"The Traka-Nor are using him to get to me."

"I don't understand."

Cohl gave her a crooked smile. "I'm an adventurer, what you'd call a treasure hunter or salvager. Difficult acquisitions are my specialty. The Traka-Nor approached me several cycles ago to hire me to find the amulet, but I refused. I won't be an accomplice in a war that kills millions. So, they took my father and are holding him in exchange for the amulet. Now I have no choice."

Tess shook her head. "I'm sorry, but what does all this have to do with me?"

"The acquisition of this amulet is different from any I've done before. It's not your average find, and that's where you come in."

She almost hated to ask. "How?"

"I need your voice to unlock the amulet from its chamber. You are the key."

"My voice?" Tess looked around her. For crying out loud, she was in a spaceship with sliding doors and talking robots. "Can't you just simulate a voice?"

Cohl shook his head. "Not in this case. The voice must be human, very specific range, pitch, and quality. You are a perfect match."

A new fear gripped her. She whispered, "How do you know what I sound like?"

Cohl answered, "Radio waves. We picked you up across the galaxy."

She stared at him. The local radio show she'd sung on last month . . . ? "That signal would have taken years to get to you."

He laughed. "You think all those satellites floating over your planet are yours?"

Her head was spinning. "You're spying on us?"

"Not me. You're on the Galactic Net. *We* are spying on you." His grin was wide and smug.

All she could do was stare. The entire galaxy was watching Earth. She should have paid more attention during all those sci-fi movies.

Suddenly Cohl was crouched in front of her, holding both her hands in his. So close, his eyes were hypnotic, beautiful. "I need your help, Tess."

Her mind was awhirl. He was alien. He was planning to commandeer her for an indefinite amount of time. And then what? Drop her back on Earth and leave her to what was left of her life? By then, her cat would be emaciated, her car towed to God knows where, her career in shambles. To say nothing of the therapy bills. She couldn't be the only person on Earth with the voice he needed. Let him find someone else. Someone who didn't have so much to lose.

She spoke firmly. "You found me. I'm sure you would have no trouble finding another voice to help you."

His grip on her hands tightened. "I don't have time, Tess. The Traka-Nor are not known for their patience."

"Damn it, this isn't fair!" Tess pulled her hands from his. "I'm not doing it."

He stood up and loomed over her, his face drawn tight.

Suddenly the floor beneath her rocked and a loud boom shook the ship. She reached out to steady herself just as a

19

second jolt hit. The whole room shook. Cohl balanced on his feet with uncanny grace and pressed a button on his shirt. "Pitz, what's going on?"

"Traka-Sou, sir. They found us."

Bewildered, Tess listened to the robot talk. He wasn't speaking English anymore, more like a foreign language, but for some reason she understood every word.

"Man the guns. Evasive action." Cohl raced for the door. "I'm on my way."

"Wait." Tess tried to stand, but another blast knocked her back and left her ears ringing.

When she looked again, he was gone. Tess dropped to the floor on her hands and knees, shaking. What was happening? How dare he leave her here alone? She crawled to the door. It didn't open. She felt all around it. The thing had opened for him. Why not her?

Another blast rocked the ship. Tess curled up on the floor and covered her ears. *Damn him.*

Cohl careened into the doorway under another impact and glanced around *Speculator*'s semicircular bridge. A tight formation of Traka-Sou ships zipped by the front viewport.

Sahto and Figalee were on opposite ends at the gunner stations. The large frame of Beckye, the systems and communications specialist, sat hunched over her console, her fingers pounding away. At the center helm station, Pitz was calmly giving orders to the crew above the pandemonium of blaring alarms and flashing lights. "Four incoming, bearing 185, Mark 030. Sahto, load and lock on target. Fire at will."

Sahto worked the controls frantically, mumbled, "Those little bastards are fast."

Cohl dropped into an empty station next to Pitz and started checking *Speculator*'s systems status. "How are we doing?"

Pitz was plugged into the console, every light on his metal

body blinking furiously. He spun his head to Cohl. "We are outnumbered thirty-two to one. Shields are down to twenty-one percent. We have sustained undetermined damage to the upper deck. Shuttle Bay Number Two is on fire. Life support is running on auxiliary backup. How are you?"

Another blast rocked the ship. Cohl grabbed on to the console and swore. His crew had been in a few scuffles before, but they weren't trained for heavy space combat. "Can we get out of here?"

"The Traka-Sou fighters are effectively blocking our window to hyperspace by attacking in consecutive waves. The timing varies enough to preclude any discernible pattern. However, regardless of the low chance of success, a jump to hyperspace is our only viable option. If we continue to sustain damage at this rate, we will not survive," Pitz reported with typical composure.

Sahto yelled out, "I can't hit these things. Either they're too fast or we're too slow."

Cohl frowned. It wasn't Sahto's fault. Neither *Speculator* nor its crew was designed for battle. But that wasn't the worst of it. These were small, short-range fighters. That meant the mother ship was somewhere close by.

Above the pandemonium, Beckye yelled to Cohl, "Incoming communication for you, sir."

He shot her a hasty glance over his displays. "We're kind of busy. Take a message."

Beckye shrugged her hefty shoulders. "I could, but you might answer this one. Man say he Zain Masters."

Cohl blew out a breath of relief. Leave it to Zain to be punctual and, even more importantly, well armed.

"Put him on."

The comm crackled overhead. A deep voice came across. "So this is the kind of fun you have when I'm not around."

Speculator rocked under another heavy barrage. Smoke wafted up from the consoles around Cohl.

"Zain, you can't believe how happy I am to hear your voice. I don't suppose Rayce is with you. I know how much he enjoys a good party."

"Sorry, I'm solo. Need a little help?"

Cohl held on to the console as another series of blasts rocked his ship. "Just tell me you're close."

"Right behind you. They haven't seen me yet. Watch this."

A Traka-Sou ship was spinning into view. A laser flashed from somewhere behind *Speculator* and the tiny fighter burst into a ball of flame. Instantly, several fighters turned on Zain's ship. The remaining Traka-Sou seemed undaunted, continuing to pursue *Speculator* through its every evasive maneuver.

A long minute later, Zain's voice came over the comm. "What did you do to piss these guys off? Got some hot cargo aboard?"

"*Hot* doesn't begin to cover it," Cohl muttered under his breath. Then, "Let's just say that not everyone is happy about my new venture," he answered.

Smoke filled the bridge and stung his eyes as more systems failed. Even with Zain helping to pick off the smaller, quicker Traka-Sou, it was slow going.

"Battle analysis, Pitz," Cohl asked.

"I estimate we have five minutes and twenty-two seconds before hull breach, sir. At our present rate, it will take twelve minutes and sixteen seconds to destroy the enemy. Concurrently, I am picking up a large battleship approaching. I highly recommend immediate withdrawal."

Cohl nodded. "Can't argue with that logic." He addressed Zain. "I hate to bow out early, but we need to get out of here. Can you cover us?"

"No problem," Zain responded. "Send me your coordinates and launch window. I'll clear a path in front of you."

While Pitz transmitted the coordinates, Cohl asked Zain, "What about you?"

Zain answered, "Don't worry. I think the party will die right after you leave. Contact me later for a new rendezvous point. I'm ready here. Good luck."

"Thanks, Zain." Cohl cut communications. Within seconds, a series of laser blasts from Zain's ship lit up the sky, decimating another Traka-Sou ship in the process. *Speculator*'s hyperdrive kicked in and the viewport brightened with starlines. They were away.

Cohl leaned back in his chair and rubbed his face. That was too close. Too close for comfort. Too close to failure.

"Where are we heading, Pitz?"

The robot continued to monitor the ship systems while he responded. "Yre Gault. We have sustained substantial damage. It will take several days to repair. Do you wish another destination?"

Cohl shook his head. "No, Yre Gault is fine. At least we'll have some protection there."

"How is our guest?"

Cohl groaned at the reminder. "I locked her in her quarters. She's not going to be too happy with me."

"You explained the situation," Pitz stated. "What was her response?"

"No. She said no. I don't think she believes me. I can understand that. I can't believe it sometimes either." Cohl shook his head. How could her career mean more than the life of his father?

"Perhaps your mother can help," Pitz offered smoothly.

Cohl slanted him a glance. Pitz knew damn well that Cohl never discussed his mother. "The point being?"

Pitz cocked his head to the right. "She could validate your story. And she is a woman. I've found that women respond more civilly to their own gender."

Cohl shook his head at Pitz's male chauvinistic viewpoint, but the robot's insight was impeccable. His mother was a born diplomat, both persuasive and sincere. It was worth a shot. Lord knew he wasn't getting anywhere with Tess.

He did know one thing: She had to help him willingly or she'd never survive long enough to get her hands on the amulet.

The door to Tess's quarters slid open and Cohl stepped inside. The first boot bounced off his shoulder. He saw the second one coming and ducked out of the way. Thank God for his quick reflexes; she had one hell of an arm.

"Damn you. How dare you lock me up like a dog?"

Her voice was shaking. She stood near the bed with fists clenched tightly at her sides and fury oozing from every pore. He'd never seen anyone full-blown pissed look so beautiful.

He realized then he'd made a tactical error: leaving her alone with too much time to think.

But at least she was out of ammunition.

"It was an emergency. I didn't want you getting hurt." He tossed a flight suit on the bed. "I brought a change of clothes. Thought you'd like to get cleaned up before dinner."

Her expression changed instantly. "Dinner? You're letting me out?"

The hopeful look in her eyes made him feel like a real bastard. "With an escort. Me or Pitz."

She crossed her arms. "Do I get to choose?"

"No. Dinner's with me," he snapped. What was the matter with him that she could infuriate him in five words or less?

She thrust her chin at him. "First, I've got a few goddamn questions."

Cohl sighed and rubbed his neck. "Yeah, I figured you might."

She motioned to the bed. "Sit down."

He raised an eyebrow at the direct order, but did as he was told. He sat and leaned back on an elbow as she began pacing before him. The view was excellent. He liked her clothes. He hoped the flight suit he loaned her was temporary until they could be cleaned. The faded, heavy pants did justice to a fabulous rear. The black shirt scooped nicely across her breasts. As she paced, her hair came alive, shining and flowing. He wondered what it would feel like between his fingers.

She stopped in front of him with her hands on her hips. His gaze traveled up her body to her face. Those green eyes were on fire.

"First question. How is it that you look like a human male? I mean, is this your real shape, or are you going to morph into something hideous?"

Cohl flashed a smile. "What you see is what you get."

She regarded him skeptically, clearly unimpressed. "Then explain the physical resemblance. And don't try to tell me that you were all alien babies from abducted Earth women."

He stifled a grin. So, that's what she'd been talking about earlier. "What makes you think you're the only humans in the galaxy?"

She stepped back, stunned. "There's more?"

Cohl nodded. "Billions upon billions, everywhere."

"But how?"

He shrugged. "I don't know. Maybe the seeds of humanity were scattered across the universe. Some took, some didn't. I'd like to think we were all created by the same hand."

"So we all look exactly alike?" she asked, obviously fascinated by the revelation.

Cohl thought about that. "Not exactly, no. Every planet's environment has an impact on its inhabitants and their physical adaptations. Variations abound." He paused, the corner of his mouth lifting. "I see yours run a little on the short side."

Tess glared at him. "And yours run a lot on the arrogant side. Or is it just you?"

He laughed. She was so easy to set off.

She crossed her arms when he didn't answer. "So, there's

a bunch of you aliens flying around and spying on us. Why don't you just contact Earth?"

"You're unstable."

"I beg your pardon?"

"Your world is too unstable. You haven't conquered your own solar system; your political system is a disorganized tangle and your ecosystem is tenuous at best."

She put her hands on her hips. "We're galactic rejects?"

He grinned. "I guess you could say that."

"Lovely." Then she took a deep breath. "Next question. If we are from different planets, how can I understand your language? What did you do to me?"

He heard the quaver in her voice, the hint of fear. He'd been talking mostly in English since Earth—so she'd feel comfortable. She must have overheard his native tongue in the brief conversation with Pitz during the attack. He didn't know if she'd understand the technology, but he had to try. Anything to wipe the fear from her eyes that he'd put there.

"It's a neural language-translation interface. Works the same as learning a new language, only faster. Nothing harmful, I promise. I interfaced with your language as well. I wouldn't do it if it wasn't safe."

She eyed him warily, scanning his face. He held his breath. She must have believed him because she moved on to the next question.

"What happened to the ship a while ago?"

She was still dead serious. He could lie but he had the distinct feeling she'd know it. "We were attacked by the Traka-Sou."

She frowned. "The southern half of that planet? Why?"

"They are trying to stop me from securing the amulet for the Traka-Nor."

It only took a few seconds for her to fully understand what he was saying. Her face paled. "They know about me? They are after me, too?"

26

Cohl frowned. He would have preferred a less observant captive. "I'm afraid so."

"Where are we going now?" she asked bluntly.

"We're en route to my home planet, Yre Gault."

"Far from the Traka-Sou, I hope."

He eyed her. "They won't get near you."

"You can guarantee that?"

He paused. "If they do, it'll be over my dead body."

She narrowed her eyes. "Your body won't do me much good dead, will it?"

He'd answered enough questions for one day. Time for a change of topic. He pushed off the bed and walked to the smaller door. It slid open.

"You probably want to clean up. This is the lav. I'll show you how everything works."

"Get out."

He turned to her. She stared back at him with frustration and anger.

"I said, get out," she whispered and pointed to the door.

He could have refused, could have held his ground, but she was right and he knew it. He had dragged her into a life-threatening situation on top of whatever else he'd done to her personal and professional life. She had every right to despise him. Without argument, he walked to the exit.

"I'll be back in thirty minutes to get you."

As the door closed behind him, he heard a boot hit it.

Tess spent the first five minutes storming around her room and using every cuss word she knew. She wanted to scream, needed to vent in some way. The man was going to get her killed.

And to think that three days ago all she'd had to worry about was her career and her cat.

Now, Cohl was taking her to some alien planet where they probably ate Earthlings for dinner every night. She stopped and cradled her head in her hands. Either this was the worst nightmare she'd ever had or she was losing her mind. If she didn't relax, she'd be on blood pressure medication before this was all over.

Tess took a few deep breaths and peered curiously into the lav, the lure of a shower too good to pass up. It was a small cubicle, full of gadgets and lots of buttons. She groaned. She should have accepted Cohl's offer to explain them to her, but there was no way she wanted anything from him now. Besides, how difficult could it be to use a bathroom?

The lav was too small to change in, so she stripped off her clothes and tossed them on the bed. Faded-to-white jeans, her black scoop-neck T-shirt, and short black boots—her favorite ensemble. Forevermore known as her abducted-by-aliens outfit. Great.

Tess entered the lav naked and the door automatically slid shut behind her. To her right was a seat with a hole in it. She knew what that was for, although she wasn't sure how to clear it. Hopefully it knew.

To the left was a sink with a faucet. How about that? At least some things didn't change out here. Straight ahead was a cylindrical stall. That must be the shower. She stuck her head in. A series of nozzles lined the tube. She waved a hand inside but nothing happened.

"Uh, hello?"

No response. What now? Along the outer edge of the stall were touch buttons. She kept pressing buttons until a steady mist sprayed from the nozzles. She stepped in.

Ooh, nice. It was wonderful, actually; refreshing like nothing she'd ever experienced. The water was different, cleansing her without the need for soap, caressing her skin like thousands of little fingers.

Afterward, she went through the lav wall drawers and found something that resembled a towel. Victorious, she smiled and wrapped it around her. Well, that wasn't so hard. She didn't need Cohl's help after all.

She stepped up to the lav door. It didn't move. She frowned and tried again. Nothing. There were no buttons, no controls like on the shower. Oh God, she was trapped in the bathroom of a spaceship. How embarrassing.

She pounded on the door. "Open up, you stupid door."

Suddenly it slid open, and Cohl stood facing her sporting an I-tried-to-tell-you smile. She froze. The towel felt woefully inadequate.

"Next time, try this." He reached across her body, brushing his hand along her hip in the tight quarters, and pointed to a control behind her. He straightened and stared at her with an intensity that stopped her heart. His smile slipped away as his gaze dropped to the towel. Seconds ticked by and neither moved. Then he reached out and touched her wet hair where it had separated into ringlets down her shoulders. He rubbed a single ringlet between his fingers, his knuckles grazing her bare shoulder. She couldn't breathe. The undisguised desire in his eyes terrified her. No man had ever looked at her like that. Ever.

He dropped the ringlet and backed up, his expression grim. "You can dry off using the blower to your right. I'll come back in ten minutes. Be dressed." He spun on his heel and left.

Shaking, Tess put her hand to her chest and took a deep breath to temper the intense rush of desire she'd felt when he touched her. Good Lord, the man was a triple threat. Gorgeous, dangerous to her life, and devastating to her senses. If this damn mission didn't kill her, being near him would.

She hurried to put on the borrowed flight suit. It fit perfectly. She wondered how he knew what size she wore and decided it was best not to think about it.

A familiar object in the corner of the room caught her eye.

Her handbag. She rifled through it. Comb, perfume, lipstick—a small piece of her life. The wallet still held the three hundred bucks from Sonny's gig. She touched the wad of rumpled twenties that she had risked her life to keep. They were worthless pieces of paper that meant nothing here.

The door slid open behind her. Tess closed the handbag and spun around. Cohl walked in with a casual smile like an old friend. All that intensity was gone.

He stopped well short of her. "Ready for a bite?"

Tess eyed him warily. "You don't eat Earthlings, do you?"

Cohl stabbed a piece of meat amid another burst of laughter. All eyes at the dinner table were on Tess sitting next to him. And he was in serious trouble.

He wasn't sure what was making him more edgy. The fact that she had completely charmed his entire five-man crew in less than an hour, or that she could ignore him with such totality.

Maybe he was still recovering from the aftereffects of touching her hair. What a stupid idea that had been, and a good way to terrify the captive. Thank God he'd gotten out before she could see how aroused he'd been. One damn touch.

He speared another morsel and listened to Tess play his crew with the utmost skill and ease. So far she had memorized every name and position, where they were from—even if she had no clue where it was—and learned everything about their families. Hell, he hadn't even known a lot of that.

She was saying, "So, you find legendary treasures? How exciting. I'm surprised it takes so many people to run a ship. I'd love to learn about your duties aboard it, but unfortunately Mr. Travers feels I need an escort."

Cohl stopped chewing.

Across from him, Sahto piped up. "We could escort you. It would be no trouble. What do you think, Cohl?"

Cohl looked around the table at the smiling, expectant faces of his crew and growled. Tess was batting her eyelashes at him faster than a street moll drumming up business.

"I suppose so." He was going to have a little talk with her after dinner.

"Oh, thank you, Mr. Travers. I promise I won't get in the way," Tess said with an ever-so-innocent smile. "Mr. Sahto, perhaps you'd like to show me your job first?"

Cohl glanced at Sahto. The man actually blushed. *Damn it.* She already had his crew duped.

He pushed his plate back. "Some other time, Sahto. Tess needs her rest. I hear Earth humans get cranky when they don't get enough sleep." He smiled with satisfaction when she glared at him.

"That would certainly explain your disposition," she said sweetly.

He rose and none too gently helped her to her feet. "Ah, I see it's starting already. You better come with me." He gave her a predatory smile. "I'll tuck you in."

He saw the flash of panic as Tess tried to pull away, but he held fast.

"Maybe one of your crew could escort me back to my quarters," she suggested with a tight smile.

Every male crew member jumped to his feet.

Cohl narrowed his eyes at her. "It could be dangerous. This is a job for the captain. Good night, everyone."

Cohl pulled Tess toward the door and into the corridor. Although she fought him every step of the way, he didn't slow down until they were back inside her quarters.

He shoved her in. She yanked her arm free and rounded on him. "Just who do you think you are?"

Cohl put his hands on his hips and bore down on her. "If you're trying to start a mutiny, forget it. I pay my crew well. And more importantly, I treat them well."

Tess rubbed her arm where he had gripped her. *Big bully alien.* "You hate it when someone else calls the shots, don't you?"

He took a threatening step toward her. "It's my ship. I call *all* the shots here."

Tess backed up and thrust out her chin. "You can't force me to help you."

Cohl moved closer, his voice ominous. "Is that what you think?"

Her eyes widened and she backed up again. "I don't work for you." She got the words out, but they lacked the punch she'd intended.

He took another step closer, looming over her. She bumped into the wall with nowhere else to go. *God, he's tall. And big. And hot.* She could feel his body heat as he planted his hands against the wall on either side of her head and moved his face inches from hers, blocking out everything else.

He was so close, she could hear him breathe. His lips were inches away. Beautiful lips, she wondered if he knew that. Then her gaze met his eyes. They were molten gold, mesmerizing and holding her mind hostage.

She pulled in a shuddering breath, felt her face flush. Damn, it was getting hot inside this flight suit.

"You're right," he murmured, his voice a mere rasp. "I can't force you to help me."

She licked her dry lips. "So, you'll take me home?"

His eyes narrowed and his heat intensified. Oh, she didn't need that. She was already broiling.

"I'll think about it."

What had he said? She was a little distracted at the moment, what with sweat trickling down between her breasts and blood pounding in her ears. This flight suit had to come off.

She must have moaned or something because his eyes

dropped to her mouth and her heart stopped.

Her lips parted with a will of their own and his eyes darkened. *Oh damn. Oh damn, damn, damn.* Her heart was pounding out a frantic beat, the trickle had turned to a river, and she wanted out of her clothes.

Kiss me, you alien. Her eyes widened. What was she thinking? Panic moved in like a black wedge, clearing her mind, dousing the heat.

She had heard of this happening. About women falling in love with their captors, finding compassion for their causes despite the danger to themselves. Well, this was one woman who wasn't falling for that old trick.

Her hands went to his chest and shoved him hard. Cohl backed away, taking his entrancing heat with him.

"What are you doing?" she snapped.

He scanned her face and frowned. "Nothing."

Tess glared at him. "Don't give me that. You were trying to seduce me so I'll help you."

He crossed his arms. "Actually, that never occurred to me." Cohl paused and raised a quizzical eyebrow. "Would it work?"

Tess growled. "Out."

"I think you enjoy kicking me out of your quarters."

She raised her chin. "Hey, it's the only thing I have control of here."

Cohl glanced down at her boots and then at the door. "Can I have your boots first?"

"What?" Tess asked.

"Never mind." He turned and walked out. "Sweet dreams, dear."

She watched the door close behind him and yanked the flight suit open, baring her steamy skin to the cool air. Oh, she was in deep trouble. He was arrogant and controlling and too damn gorgeous for Tess's good, but worse than all that, the man could turn her mind to mush. It was like a Vulcan mind-meld or something.

She pushed her damp hair back. If he had kissed her, would she have stopped him? Where would they be right now? A shiver ran through her. What would it be like to make love with an alien? She blinked. Were they even physically compatible? He *felt* compatible, but who knew what was lurking down there? What "variances" the humans on his planet had experienced.

She stomped her foot. *No, damn it.* She wouldn't give in. There was no way, no matter how tempting Cohl was. He thought he could just manipulate her with the promise of wild, unbridled passion.

The ruthless bastard. He just might be right.

She groaned and leaned back against the wall, rolling her head from side to side. What was he doing to her? This is what happened when you hadn't had a decent date in a year. Between cleaning up the financial mess after her parents' accident and trying to jump-start her singing career, there was just no time.

Tess closed her eyes, fighting back tears. Everything she'd worked for was zipping further away at a bazillion miles an hour. *Why now?* Just when the doors had begun to open. Just when she was on the brink of her dream, a dream she'd watched slip by, day after day for eight years while she helped her parents struggle with their business.

Now this—dragged against her will into someone else's problems, unearthed, and alone with a man who could burn her from the inside out.

Chapter Four

"Tell me what you have seen, Nish."

Beneath his deep hood, the old man smiled at Rommol's impatient command and continued his painfully slow limp across the dark inner chamber in silence. He finally collapsed into a chair while the restless Rommol tapped his fingers on his stone desk in a pool of light.

Rommol, the leader of Traka-Nor. The impatient one. The dangerous one. The child. From under his guise, Nish eyed the slew of detestable advisors lined up behind him. Rommol seemed immune to their stench, the combined smell of lies and betrayals and death.

"Well?"

"The Finder has acquired the key to the amulet."

Rommol snapped, "None of your crazy riddles, old man. Speak Basic."

Nish sighed. "Travers has found the woman, the key to acquiring the amulet. Now he needs only the location."

Rommol's face turned red. He sputtered, "What? Travers

35

doesn't know where it is yet? You told me he was the best."

His face hidden by fabric, Nish frowned at the outburst. "He is."

Rommol pushed himself to his feet, a black cape swirling around him, his face twisted and enraged. "He had better be. And if he isn't, I will kill his father and send the man's body back to Yre Gault—piece by piece." He pointed a finger at Nish. "Along with yours. This plan was your idea. I will not be made a fool of."

Nish grinned. Rommol's threats meant little to him. "The Finder will not fail us."

Rommol straightened and a cruel smile creased his face. "Then Trakas will be mine."

"There is a complication," Nish continued, his voice gentle. He was dealing with a child; he had to remember that. "Your brother, Gothyk, has discovered your plan. Twice, he has attacked the Finder. The mission could be in jeopardy."

Rommol exploded in a loud roar. "Who told him? The plan went no further than this room."

Nish answered, "Someone you trust." He wasn't about to reveal the traitor. The man had saved him the trouble of building a leak himself.

Rommol spun around to his vile collection of advisors. Each wore a stunned look on his face.

Pointing to one, Rommol snarled, "You. You are the one." The others took a step back from the accused.

The accused blinked at his leader, panic spreading over his face. "No, lord. Not I. I would never betray you."

"Liar!" Rommol motioned to his guards. "Take him away."

"I did nothing, I swear." The man shook his head vehemently, repeating the words over and over in desperation as guards hauled him from the room.

Rommol sat back in his seat and wrapped his cape around him. "Krahel."

As Krahel stepped forward, Nish growled silently. Uncontrollable, reckless, this one was. Nish had seen his work, cruel and barbaric. Krahel had helped capture the Finder's father. *Krahel, the false puppet.*

Rommol ordered his henchman, "Take your ship and track Travers down. Kill any Traka-Sou in your path. Protect the woman at all costs. I will not tolerate failure."

Krahel bowed low and answered, "As you wish." As he departed on his appointed mission, Rommol leaned back with a satisfied smile.

Nish nodded. For now, the child was happy and the plan was secure.

Tess stifled a yawn as she trailed behind the sprightly and much too chipper Sahto. It was too early in the morning for a ship tour, *if* this was really morning. She had no idea, nothing to measure time against. Her wristwatch was useless since it showed no A.M. or P.M. Her body was equally confused and the brain fog of sleep had yet to burn off.

"And this is the captain's office," Sahto said as he swept Tess through a doorway to the crammed, round room. She followed him to where racks of equipment purred with life. Tabletops were littered with stacks of old documents and food containers.

Tess stopped dead in her tracks, her mind suddenly clearing. A four-foot-tall cylindrical grid hummed atop a round table that occupied the center of the room. Within the luminous grid's three-foot center, a solar system that looked exactly like her own hung in miniature.

"Is that *my* Earth?" she asked, pointing to a blue-and-white-marbled planet.

Sahto walked past and punched something into a box near the grid, and it focused on the little jewel of her planet with startling speed.

"Sure is. A real-time projection." He smiled up at her

cheerfully. "Would you like me to zoom down to the surface?"

Tess's head snapped around to look at him. "You can do that?"

"You bet. Where to?"

Tess approached the table in awe. "Can we see Marley Corners?"

Sahto nodded and entered more commands. The image zoomed in on the planet in dizzying surges until the telltale crossroads of her little hometown emerged. There was the corner grocery store, the post office, even her house. Scattered street lamps lit empty streets. It was dusk at Marley Corners. A red car waited at the one stoplight in town. She had the sudden urge to wave or yell for help, it seemed so close. Her chest tightened.

Home. And everything that meant anything to her.

Sahto stepped to her side. "The holodeck is a useful tool in our operations. We can look at any site—either real time if we have a visual link, or from computer memory using a multitude of projection techniques."

Tess gave him a wry smile. "Can you see where they towed my car to?"

Sahto laughed. "Of course. I can see anything and everything. How do you think we found you?"

Tess stared at Sahto, then back into the grid, and swallowed. They had tracked her down from right here at this table. That's how Cohl had known where she was. She rubbed her arms at a sudden chill.

All those bizarre lunatics walking the airports were right: *Aliens really are watching us.*

"Can you see if my cat is okay?" she asked quietly.

Sahto shook his head. "Sorry. I don't know where he is at the moment."

She nodded. Hopefully, her landlady had taken pity on Griz by now. She hadn't named him Griz for nothing. He could probably take on a grizzly bear—but even a plump cat needed food.

Sahto gestured toward the door. "Ready for the rest of the tour?"

Tess nodded and preceded him out, walked into the center corridor that ran the full length of Cohl's ship. From here she could look down the hall and out through the massive bridge viewport into space. It still seemed unreal.

A small robot with more than a passing similarity to a canister vacuum cleaner zipped along the edge of the corridor. Another was attached to the wall like a bloodsucker. Neither robot acknowledged her or Sahto's presence as Sahto ushered her through the med center.

An explosion of red hair that hadn't seen a brush in a very long time greeted her as Witley gazed up from his work just long enough to give her a curt nod of acknowledgment.

Sahto led her down the corridor again and gestured toward the open doorway of the next room. "You've already seen the crew lounge."

Tess smiled at the few crew members seated at the table where she had dined last night. They waved back.

She looked up to find Pitz approaching, hovering off the floor.

"Hi," she said uncertainly. How else did one greet a robot who talked?

"Good day, Tess. Sahto," Pitz replied efficiently and slipped past to the front of the ship.

Tess leaned toward Sahto. "He's not like other robots, is he?"

Sahto gave a light laugh. "Hardly. Most of our robots are machines designed for specific duties like cleaning and repairs. Pitz is a super-intelligent hybrid. He learns, adapts, reasons—and gives orders like Cohl, unfortunately."

"Huh," Tess replied. "Has he been here long?"

"At least ten years. He came with Cohl," Sahto answered.

He stopped in front of a doorway. "You're really going to like this next room."

He punched in a code on a wall panel and the door slid open. Tess stepped into a silent, circular room bathed in blue light. The room was empty except for a podium. Satiny smooth walls surrounded her. Three-foot wide, flat circles on the floor mirrored an identical set above them on the ceiling.

Tess turned to Sahto. "What is this?"

Sahto's eyes twinkled. "We call it the Fantasy Maker."

Tess lifted an eyebrow.

He chuckled. "It's a VirtuWav, a virtual simulator. Stand in the center of the circles and you can put yourself in any real or fabricated program. Any situation, event, place. It's absolutely realistic right down to all five senses."

Her gaze was drawn back to the circles that shimmered with virtual life. "How does it work?"

Sahto touched a panel on the podium. A translucent, aqua-blue tube rose up from the bottom of one circle until it reached its mate on the ceiling. Within the tube's interior, what looked like liquid undulated. Then jagged fingers of electrical charges snapped across the interior.

"Incredible," Tess whispered.

"Mmm." Sahto nodded and watched the tube with great reverence. "When you are inside the tube, VirtuWav takes control of your brain synapses and redirects the processing through the system. You can load in an image or story and be dropped right in the middle of it."

Tess frowned at him. "Is that safe?"

"Oh yes. You get the sensation of pain as well as pleasure, but you can't get hurt and that's part of the fun. You can put yourself through all kinds of trauma and the simulator will tell you every statistic you want to know about your virtual well-being." He started counting on his fingers. "Heart rate. Blood loss. Dismemberment. Percent of body function available. Percent of body intact. Mortality score. Things like that."

He smiled wide. Tess felt suddenly ill. "So what happens if you die?"

Sahto shrugged and turned around to shut down the system "You get bounced out of the program. No big deal. Just start it up again."

She followed him out of the room. "What would you use that VirtuWav for?"

The little man stopped and grinned at her. "Entertainment mostly. It can simulate any experience you can imagine—and a few you'd never think of in a millennium. Spending weeks on end in a ship this size gets real boring. A few fantasies never hurt anyone." He winked, then swept a hand down the corridor. "Crew quarters, engineering, and shuttle bays await."

Hell of a way to start the morning, Cohl thought as he slithered on his stomach under a large conduit. The shuttle bay floor was cold and hard beneath him. *Wonder what Tess is doing right about now?* She was probably lying in bed, that soft, warm body curled up under the blanket. He'd bet anything she slept naked. The thought provoked a silent groan. Why was he doing this to himself?

Blame it on her scent that had haunted him all night. He'd grown up around fragrances his entire life. Exotic perfume was Yre Gault's acclaimed distinction and primary export. His nose was experienced, but the scent she had was different, like none he'd ever smelled. Primal. Simple. Sexual. Whatever it was gave him itchy hands and an instant hard-on when he should be thinking about how to convince her to help him. He pursed his lips. Getting attacked by the Trakas wasn't helping his cause.

A laser reflected off the floor and singed his ear. He swore, rolled to the right, and dashed for the cover of an empty cylinder. Returning fire at Pitz, he threw himself behind the upright cylinder. *Damn it.* His ear burned. That's what he got for thinking about Tess when he should be concentrating on whipping Pitz's metal butt in their daily simulated tactical exercise.

Lucky for him, it was only a burn agent in the laser guns they were using. Otherwise, he'd be missing an ear.

He leaned back against the container and listened, tuning his senses up to high, searching for his enemy. The calm of battle settled over him. There. To his left. He lowered himself on his haunches and watched Pitz's shadow slide across the floor.

Cohl leaped to the left across Pitz's incoming path, firing all the way. He hit the floor, rolled over on his shoulder, and dove behind another container. He'd given away his position, but delivered a valid hit. One point for him. He glanced around the corner to find Pitz charging with all guns firing. So much for finesse.

Cohl toppled the container in Pitz's path to slow him down and headed along the wall of the shuttle bay at a run. Laser fire surrounded him. He was almost to his intended cover when Tess's scream rang out.

He turned toward her and a laser caught him in the shoulder, knocking him off his feet. He hit the floor with a grunt and blacked out.

"You killed him!" Tess screamed at Pitz as she ran to Cohl with Sahto right behind her.

Pitz got there first and hovered like a mother hen. "The ammunition is not lethal."

"To you," she hissed. Tess knelt next to Cohl and frantically checked his pulse. It was there. Strong and warm.

"He's alive," she said.

Sahto nodded. "I'll get Witley." He disappeared out the shuttle bay door.

Tess gently felt Cohl's still body for injuries. No broken bones. The back of his shirt was singed and the skin beneath it burnt and red.

She glared at Pitz. "Why were you shooting at him?"

Pitz answered, "We were engaging in a tactical exercise. Cohl utilizes them to keep his skills honed. He was fine until you screamed and broke his concentration."

Tess's mouth dropped open. "What was I supposed to do when I saw you shooting ten guns at him? Do you really think that's a fair fight? He's only got one."

Pitz sounded indignant. "His weaponry is his choice."

"And," Tess continued, "you've got all that armor. He has nothing. Look at his shoulder." Then she gasped and pointed to his head. "And his ear."

"Will you two shut up? You could wake the dead."

.Tess looked down at Cohl, who was rolling over on his back with a long groan.

"Oh, thank God." She wasn't sure where to put her hands and settled on his forearm. "Don't move. Mr. Sahto is getting help."

Pitz clicked softly. "I gather the exercise is over for the day, sir?"

Tess glared at him. Cohl sat up with great effort and casually waved the robot off. "Yes, thanks, Pitz. We'll try it again tomorrow."

Pitz whirred away.

"What?" Tess choked out. "You can't be serious. That shoulder is going to take a long time to heal."

He looked at her, his face serious and somber. "In another situation, you could have gotten me killed."

Tess backed up in surprise as he pushed himself to his feet and added, "You need to trust and not distract me, Tess. Your life may depend on it someday."

"Oh, right. I'm going to trust a man who kidnapped me." She stood up, brushing off her flight suit and berating herself for having cared. Maybe if he got shot, she could go home.

His eyes narrowed. "I did what I had to. We all have to make tough decisions sometimes."

She glared at him. "Well, I for one don't like your decision."

In his eyes, she caught something flash. Sadness? Regret? For her?

After a few moments, he answered steadily, "Believe me, no one is more unhappy about this mess than I am."

Cohl took the chair next to Pitz on *Speculator*'s bridge and rolled his shoulder. After twenty-four hours, it was almost back to normal thanks to the healing-accelerator injection from Witley.

The hyperspace engines hummed, bringing him closer to Yre Gault and a past he'd tried to forget for ten years. With any luck, he wouldn't be staying long enough to dig up many unpleasant memories. Repair the ship, convince Tess to cooperate, and get out. Sounded simple enough. Then again, nothing was simple with Tess.

"How long do you estimate the repairs to the ship will take, Pitz?"

Pitz spun his head to Cohl. "Two days, six hours, and twelve minutes."

Cohl dragged a hand down his face in frustration. "Longer than I'd anticipated. Rommol is not going to be happy."

Pitz said, "It is hardly your fault that the Traka-Sou discovered his plan."

Cohl gave him a hard look. "I doubt Rommol gives a damn about that."

"We could take one of Yre Gault's military ships," Pitz suggested.

Cohl considered, then shook his head. "No. It would take a while just to train my crew on a new ship's operations.

Besides, I know what *Speculator* is capable of, even if it lacks the firepower I'd like."

He looked at Pitz. "We need to fix that."

Pitz's eyes flashed. "Yes, sir. I will add ancillary armaments to the maintenance list."

Cohl nodded, "Once we get to Yre Gault, I want a status report every four hours. I need to arrange another rendezvous with Zain when the repairs are nearly completed. Is the protection I ordered in place for our arrival over Yre Gault?"

"It is."

The added military presence was welcome but Cohl knew it was largely for show. After all, Military Operations had done nothing to prevent his father from being kidnapped. Even now, they had no idea how such an act had been carried out right under their noses. Yre Gault's Mil-Ops was wholly ineffective, and Tess's safety would ultimately be his responsibility.

"You've notified my mother?"

Pitz answered, "Of course. She is looking forward to meeting Tess."

Cohl nodded. "Did you explain the situation to her?"

"Yes. She will help in any way she can." Pitz paused. "She said she is very eager to see you."

He took a deep breath. Guilt, thick and suffocating, descended over him. This was the first time he'd be home in a decade, and he knew his parents had missed him. But going home meant giving them hope that he'd stay—and that was the last thing he'd want to do.

"How long before we reach Yre Gault?"

Pitz made a humming noise. "We will drop out of hyperspace in thirty-two minutes."

He had only a few days to find a way to get Tess to trust him. Both their lives would depend on it. The legend and rumors of the horrors surrounding the hiding place of the Demisian Amulet worried him. He'd been through worse acquisitions, but not with someone else tagging along—particularly someone who didn't take orders well. But first, he needed to get back on speaking terms with her.

For some reason he couldn't fathom, she was angry at him for the incident in the shuttle bay. *He* was the one who should be mad. Instead, she had successfully avoided him for the past day by spending every minute with one crew member after another—no small feat on a ship this size.

He glanced around the empty bridge. "Where is everyone?"

"In the crew lounge," Pitz responded.

Cohl frowned. "What are they doing there?"

"Unknown. Tess gathered them."

"Hell. She's probably planning the takeover of my ship. I should have known better than to leave her alone this long."

Cohl shot from his seat and stormed down the corridor to the crew lounge. As he drew near, he could hear a steady beat, music and laughing. What was that?

Nothing could have prepared him for the spectacle that greeted him when the crew lounge doors parted. A funky, lively tune blared at high volume from the room's speakers. In the center of the chamber his crew was dancing around in a circle with their hands linked. He watched dumbfounded as his entire adult crew stopped and started tapping their fingers together at each other, flapping their arms, wiggling their butts, and pecking and strutting like a bunch of crazed birds.

Tess was yelling over the music and laughter, "A little bit of this and a little bit of that, now clap your hands." *Clap, clap, clap, clap.*

Everyone doubled over, laughing. Another circle went by, the strange chant and bizarre dance, before Tess noticed him standing at the door.

She smiled and waved to him. "Cohl, come and join us."

Every member of the crew stopped and turned to him in unison. Their faces dropped one by one.

He stared at Tess as a steady roar filled his ears. "I don't think so. Computer, music off. Don't some of you people work for me?"

Within seconds everyone had cleared out except Tess. She planted her hands on her hips. "Well, I hope you're happy."

He walked toward her, anger burning him up. "Happy isn't even close to what I feel right now. Who do you think you are commandeering my crew for your idiot dance?"

She gaped back at him indignantly. "Idiot? The only idiot here is you. For your information, the chicken dance is an enormously popular number at weddings. We were just having a little harmless fun. In case you hadn't noticed, you run a very boring ship."

He kept advancing on her, the fire building with every step. "Fine. We'll all be enjoying ourselves when the Traka-Sou blow us to bits."

She didn't back down, even when he was nearly on top of her. The clear challenge in her green eyes only fueled his own fire.

"You might be able to scare off your crew, but you don't frighten me." She narrowed her eyes. "You hate that, don't you? That you can't control me."

"I'm in no mood for this, Tess," Cohl growled, fully aware that she was pushing him, testing him, and he couldn't do a thing to stop her.

She grinned. "That's it, isn't it? You can control your crew and your ship and your life, but not me." She bobbed her head up and down. "That makes you crazy."

"That's enough."

She poked him in the chest. "When was the last time you danced or sang or did something just for the hell of it? For a hotshot space cowboy, you sure lead a dull life."

He could smell her now, that scent she wore. "Stop it, Tess."

She thrust her chin at him. "Make me."

He reached out and grabbed her by the arms, slamming his mouth over hers with all the frustration he'd built up over the past few days. The fire exploded within him in a surge so hard it nearly brought him to his knees. He couldn't get enough, couldn't stop. His hunger took over, devouring her, delivering her into his fire. She'd started this; damned if she wasn't going to burn along with him.

But she wasn't burning. She trembled under his hands like a captured animal. Reality snuffed the fire. He broke off the kiss and thrust her away. Her eyes were huge, her breathing rapid, her expression stunned. And for once she was speechless.

"We will be arriving at Yre Gault shortly. Get ready to leave." He turned and walked out, cursing himself silently. She'd pushed him to the edge and over, broken his control. How could one small woman do that?

Somewhere along the way to the bridge, he broke into a reluctant smile. He'd finally found a way to shut her up. Coincidentally, it also turned out to be an effective cure for his itchy hands.

Chapter Five

Tess walked around the spacecraft sitting in the center of the shuttle bay. It looked like a giant flying beetle with its flat body and fins for wings. "What is it?"

Cohl glanced up at her from some sort of electronic pad he was reviewing with Sahto. "It's a transport shuttle. Short-range. *Speculator* needs to stay space-docked in order to be repaired properly. That's our ride to the planet."

Tess looked it over again. It looked awfully small and flimsy. "Can't we just beam down to the planet?"

Cohl frowned. "Beam?"

She took in his confused expression and waved him off. "Oh, never mind. Obviously, you aren't that advanced yet."

Tess looked away quickly from the deep scowl on his face, careful not to provoke him. She was still recovering from that kiss and wasn't about to push him again just yet. A shudder ran through her. He had shocked her with his raw power and animal hunger, his total possession of her. She had been right. He didn't scream or yell or throw things when he got mad. He simply kissed her within an inch of her life.

Cohl handed the device to Sahto and murmured a few last-minute instructions. Then he led her toward the open door of the shuttle with Pitz tagging along behind.

"Why does Pitz have to come along?" Tess whispered.

"He's my protector," Cohl answered as he helped her through the shuttle door.

"Your what?"

He showed her to a front seat and strapped her in. Tess noticed he was careful not to get too close or touch her. *Interesting.* Maybe she wasn't the only one being careful.

"My protector. He was assigned to me when I was a child. I've known him my entire life."

He slid into the seat next to her.

"Your best friend is a robot?"

"You have something against robots?"

She shrugged. "No, but is that normal for your people?"

He punched at a console in front of him. "No."

"So why do you have him?" she asked, exasperated. Getting information out of the man was impossible.

He cast her a glance with those golden eyes. Hunger flashed there, taking her breath. "I'm special—or hadn't you noticed?"

Before she could reply, the shuttle lifted off. It shot out the gaping shuttle bay door into endless space, and Tess clutched the arms of her chair, a soundless scream stuck in her throat. There was nothing above or below them, just a million stars dotting the black canvas of endless space. Her breath came in short, hard bursts but utter fear quickly gave way to awe. The experience was incredible. Impossible yet real, its beauty humbled her before greater powers. Here was a startling reminder of how very small and insignificant she really was in a universe too vast to fathom. How could one person make any difference at all?

In the front window, Yre Gault hung before her like a colossal Christmas ornament with swirls of blue, green, and white.

"Oh, it's beautiful," she whispered in reverence.

Cohl glanced at her, then went back to his console. "How are we doing, Pitz?"

From behind them, Pitz replied, "Clear. No unusual activity. Military Operations has secured the area."

"A miracle," Cohl muttered.

As the planet drew near, Tess was able to pick out the green land masses and vast blue water. Mountain ranges appeared in long ridges that sliced across the land like deep furrows. Narrow ridges ran in parallel lines and crossed the seas where only the tops peeked above water. Yre Gault was a striped world of endless mountain ranges, some surrounded by land, more by water. The topography transformed from an impressionistic painting to reality as they made their way deeper into the planet's atmosphere. She could see white etchings along the tops of the protruding land like intricate carvings in relief. Closer yet, and the carvings came to life as cities stretched from edge to edge atop even the smallest mountain peaks. Domed objects became buildings, intersecting lines turned to streets, dots into people.

They glided toward a particularly large city, a diamond-shaped island between two deep crevices. From the very edges of the sheer cliffs, streets converged into a starburst center circle where five massive statues of giant men stood proudly in the nucleus, looming and watching over the land. Trees, tall and massive, lined the streets. Canals of blue water crisscrossed and pooled into square lagoons. Every structure gleamed white, as if carved from the same block of pure, virgin stone.

Between the buildings, bold, bright fabrics worn by pedestrians flowed like a rainbow river of brilliant color, lively and alive. A kaleidoscope of flags waved from every rooftop in welcome.

"What is this place?" she asked Cohl.

"Caldara. The capital city of Yre Gault."

She cast him a quick glance. He was watching the controls with utter concentration.

"Pitz told me that your mother will be greeting us?"

Cohl didn't look up from his panel. "Yes."

Tess crossed her arms. "Your conversation skills leave much to be desired."

"I know."

She glared at his profile and turned back to the planet. They were descending at an ungodly speed toward a sprawling ivory compound with a series of interconnecting buildings and lush courtyards.

Suddenly they were below the level of the compound, in the shady chasm surrounding Caldara. Balconies lined the white stone cliffs but other than that, there was nothing below them for what looked like a mile. Tess couldn't figure out where they were going to land until a giant sheet of metal slid out from the cliff just beneath them.

Cohl and Pitz exchanged landing procedures, and the shuttle thumped to a stop in the middle of the metal landing pad. Tess looked out. All she could see was air.

She licked her lips. "I hate heights. Did you know that?"

Cohl unstrapped himself. "No, I didn't. The landing area is bigger than you think. Ready?"

She looked at him, trying desperately not to panic. "Don't let go of me."

He hesitated a fraction of a second before he smiled and reached over to unstrap her harness. "I won't. You are safe here. I promise."

She took the hand he offered and stepped out through the rear hatchway into an alien world—and came to an abrupt halt.

It didn't matter that she was miles above the bottom of a chasm. It didn't matter that there were no railings around the small landing pad. She gazed down the length of the canyon and forgot everything else. *Massive. Breathtaking. Unreal.* The words came to her in the face of endless cliffs of stone. Vines as thick as redwood trees hung down the steep slopes like garland, covered with great clusters of flowers. Long, flat spacecraft resembling open-bowed racing boats hovered in thin air. Standing atop them, workers were harvesting the giant petals and piling them high in the ships.

Then the breeze hit her with a fragrance so strong and exquisite she rocked on her feet. Cohl slipped an arm around her waist, anchoring her. Tess breathed in the intoxicating smell and nearly moaned with pleasure.

"Smells good, huh," Cohl was saying in her ear.

"I think you could get drunk on it," she said with a lazy smile. "Is it the flowers? I've never seen any that huge."

Cohl chuckled. "I did notice the ones at your home were pretty puny."

Tess whirled on him. "Hey, I worked hard on those marigolds. It's not my fault there was a drought this summer."

His laugh echoed across the canyon as he led her off the landing pad and through a doorway into the side of sheer rock face. Just inside, a single guard nodded once and admitted them down a long corridor.

Cohl explained as they walked. "Yre Gault's chief export is rare perfume and dyes from those flowers, as well as various other plants and some insects. The planet is largely agricultural. Technology is the chief import."

Tess shivered. "Insects?"

"You don't like insects?" He shot her a side glance, then nodded at another guard stationed at the entrance to a wider corridor.

"Does anyone?" Tess grumbled.

They emerged into direct sunlight, and Tess raised her

face to an alien sun. It had been days since she'd seen or felt the familiar heat of a sun, even if it wasn't hers.

She found herself in the center of a magnificent courtyard, lush and crowded with bizarre plants. The surrounding white stone walls of a three-story residence glistened in the sun like a blank canvas. Terraces of flora meandered around statues of posed men and women amid fountains and carefully manicured foliage. Someone had one hell of a gardener.

A woman approached in azure-hued flowing gowns that fluttered in the breeze, iridescent in the daylight. As she drew near, Tess recognized the golden eyes, the tawny hair streaked with white, and the walk of a panther. Cohl's mother moved with effortless grace, a tall, willowy line of poise and elegance. The tilt of her oval face and her slender chin gave her a regal appearance.

Cohl stepped forward to greet her. The woman wrapped her arms around him gently, but there was a quiet desperation to her embrace. She kissed Cohl lightly on both cheeks and looked at him as a mother regards her most precious possession.

"Cohlman, I've missed you so."

"Mother."

Tess frowned. His voice was strangely cool after such a warm greeting from his mother. He stepped to the side and pulled Tess forward.

"This is Tess MacKenzie. Tess, Adehla Trae Salle. My mother."

His mother took both of Tess's hands in hers. They were welcoming and strong. "Thank you so much for coming to help us. You are a brave woman to undertake such a difficult and daunting task and so far from home." She smiled the kind of smile that warms one's soul.

Tess just looked at her. Now, what was she supposed to say? What had Cohl told her? Before she could formulate a reply, Cohl interjected, "She hasn't agreed to help us yet."

Tess glared at him. How dare he put her in this position?

Adehla raised a single eyebrow. "Then why is she here?"

Cohl crossed his arms and looked at the ground. "Her voice matched."

His mother's mouth dropped open. "Cohlman Trae Salle, you didn't bring her here against her will, did you?"

Cohl raised his eyes to meet hers. "I had no choice, Mother. They won't wait much longer for the amulet."

His mother laid a hand to her forehead. "Oh, have I taught you nothing? Pitz, how could you allow this to happen?"

Pitz spoke from behind Tess. "He is correct, my queen. And Tess has not endured any hardship."

Tess blinked. Had the robot said *queen?*

Adehla gave him a reproving look. "How can you say that? You have abducted her against her will, dragged her across the galaxy, put her through a language interface, and coerced her into helping you. That, my dear Pitz, is hardship."

Tess looked at her. A queen? She gazed around at the stately and immaculate gardens, the prestigious location, remembered the guards at the entrance. This was no ordinary home.

"Do you govern this place?" she asked Adehla.

Adehla smiled gently. "My mate and I govern the entire planet."

Tess's gaze swung to Cohl, who was watching her intently. That would mean that he was . . . he was . . . "A prince." Her own crisp words cut through the still air.

Adehla looked at Tess in surprise. "Of course he is a prince. He stands next in line to rule this planet. Didn't he tell you?"

Cohl didn't say a word, just watched her. Tess felt the heat of humiliation burn her cheeks. He was a prince. Royalty. A minor detail that everyone else in the world knew except her.

"No, he didn't tell me. An oversight, I'm sure."

Adehla sighed. "I'm sure. Come. You must be exhausted after your ordeal."

Without a word or a look back, Tess fell into step beside the woman, leaving Cohl and Pitz behind. A prince, he was a prince. Why hadn't he told her? If for nothing else than to save her the embarrassment. She hadn't even dressed for the occasion.

Adehla swept her hand toward a bench overlooking a fountain lined with silent statues. "Why don't we sit for a while? You look tired."

"Thank you." Tess dropped to the bench, more exhausted than she'd realized. Sunlight soothed her like an old friend. She turned to Adehla. "I'm not sure how I should address you."

"My close friends call me Ad."

Tess's eyes widened. "I can't call you that."

Adehla laughed as she settled next to Tess. "Of course you can. I'm just a woman."

"A queen is hardly just a woman," Tess said, her eyes taking in the breathtaking landscape. What a beautiful place to wake up to every day.

"And Cohl is just a man." Adehla raised an eyebrow to Tess. "Has he mistreated you?"

Tess sighed. This wasn't going to be easy, talking to a mother about her son. "No, he hasn't."

"Unsettled you, then?"

Tess eyed Adehla. "How do you know?"

She shrugged gracefully and folded her hands on her gown. "He can be intimidating and stubborn when he wants to be. A trait from his father, I'm afraid."

Tess gazed out over the richness and beauty of the alien world. *World.* With a king and queen and a son who was prince, who would be next in line to govern the entire planet . . . The logic floored her. It wasn't just his father's life he was saving.

"How many people live on this planet?" Tess whispered.

"About three million," Ad replied. "Why do you ask?"

Tess squeezed her eyes shut. *Millions.*

She licked her lips. "Is it true about his father being abducted? About an amulet that can win wars? About my voice being the key?"

Next to her, Adehla twisted her hands on her lap. "It is all true. I fear for my husband's life—and the future of this planet and my people. I do not know if I could rule the planet by myself. It is difficult enough for two."

Tess blinked at her. "You still have Cohl. He's next in line."

A sad smile touched Adehla's lips. "Cohl has forsaken his birthright." The queen's eyes met Tess's, somber and full of regret. "It is our fault, of course. Neither his father nor I delegate well. Our life is our work and our people. I'm afraid that Cohl's upbringing was lonely without us. He grew up too quickly, angry and bitter. We just were never around to see what was happening to him until he was gone." Her gaze fell to her lap. "I blame myself."

"So he just left?" Tess asked, stunned.

Adehla nodded and looked away to a distant past. "The arguments with his father grew worse with each passing day. I don't know who was right and who was wrong. It doesn't matter now. Cohl secured a ship and he was gone. This is the first time he's been back. It is the only good to come out of this tragedy." She took a deep breath and said wistfully, "I was hoping that coming back here . . ."

Adehla stopped and smiled at Tess weakly. "Well, he is here to save his father from the Traka-Nor and that is all that matters."

Tess asked, "But why did they choose Cohl? Can't anyone get this amulet?"

The queen shook her head. "Cohl is quite successful at what he does—even I have heard the stories. And although he's decided on a different life than one we would have favored, he is still his father's son. He would never trust anyone else to do his work for him."

Adehla's eyes met Tess's, brimming with tears that she blinked back. "I realize the sacrifice is great and it is beyond my right to ask, but I would be forever in your debt if you would help us in this dire situation."

Tess looked at the woman who carried the burden of millions on her slender shoulders. It was the same expression she had seen every day on the faces of her parents in their struggle to make their business work. There was nowhere in her heart to refuse, even as her own dream clamored for attention. How could she be so selfish as to turn her back on such desperation?

Tess nodded. "I will do what I can."

Cohl was not happy as he marched through the high arches of the royal house toward his old room. "Damn it, Pitz. I thought you explained the situation to my mother."

Pitz whirred along behind. "I explained that we were bringing Tess to meet her."

Cohl growled, "But you didn't tell her that Tess hadn't agreed to help us."

"I have no doubt that your mother will secure Tess's cooperation, sir," the robot answered.

Cohl certainly hoped so. "My mother looks exhausted," he muttered. *And older,* although he didn't say it. "What's the official statement on my father's absence?"

"He is on a peacekeeping mission in the Kansari Region. The situation is complicated and is taking longer than anticipated to resolve."

"Good. That will buy us a little more time." The next question he didn't want to ask but he needed to know was, "Who are the candidates for succession?"

"There are no candidates," Pitz reported.

Cohl stopped dead and turned slowly to face the robot. "No candidates? Why not?"

Pitz hovered before him. "Your parents have not requested any."

"My parents must know they can't rule forever. They are taking a huge risk."

"I agree. Perhaps there are no qualified candidates on the planet," Pitz offered.

Cohl gave a short laugh. "It shouldn't be very difficult to find someone more qualified than me to rule.

Pitz's head tilted to the side. "Then perhaps it is an issue you should discuss with your mother."

Cohl resumed his walk. "I plan to. Have any security changes been implemented recently?"

"Yes, several months ago."

"Who authorized them?"

"Your father."

Cohl frowned. His father hated security of any kind. It was one of the issues they had frequently argued about.

Pitz added, "Apparently, your father used Logen Du Vaul's security consultant services. I believe you know him."

"I know him," Cohl muttered. "He made my life on Caldara's streets miserable."

"Yes," Pitz replied. "I do recall several unpleasant exchanges, most of which resulted in bodily injury to you."

"Thanks for reminding me, Pitz. I'd almost managed to forget. What were the security changes?"

Pitz's lights flickered. "Additional security measures around the compound, as well as an increased personnel presence."

"Well, it didn't work very well, did it?"

"No, sir."

Cohl didn't like this at all. The timing was too coincidental. Besides, how had his father hooked up with Logen, of all people? It had been a long time since he'd tangled with him, but people didn't change much. The thought of Logen inside this residence was not comforting.

"I won't need you the rest of the day, but do me a favor and check up on Du Vaul. I'd like to know what else he's been up to lately."

"Yes, sir," Pitz replied. Then the robot disappeared down a side corridor.

Cohl walked on alone under the arches and massive columns that lined the primary hallway through the royal residence. He shook off the chill that twisted and knotted his gut like a relentless jeer. Tess was furious with him. He should have filled her in more, let her know who he really was. But how was he supposed to know it mattered? It certainly didn't to him.

Pitz was right, though. His mother would secure Tess's cooperation. Tess would not turn down a face-to-face appeal. He would never forget the concern in her eyes when he'd been shot by Pitz and heard her passionate defense of him. Regardless of what she'd said, she had more compassion than he would ever understand. For everyone except for him. He'd seen to that.

The first step into his former room jarred him from the present into the past. His throat constricted to the point of pain as he surveyed the room in which he'd grown up. It hadn't changed a bit since the day he walked out.

The bed sat at its center, massive and low, covered with fine, handmade covers, glorious in color. Paintings and holographic images of space and beyond lined the walls: his youthful vision into his future. He circled the room, touching this, holding that, as memories tumbled and collided between the child and the man.

At last, he sat down at the desk and released its top drawer. The picture was there, its impact on him as strong as ever. It could still rip his heart out. A young prince and his parents at an official function, looking like the perfect, happy royal family.

He slammed the drawer shut. *What a farce that had been.* He could still recall how the holographer had told them how to smile, how to stand, how to touch each other. As usual, everything had been decided for him.

Cohl pushed himself to his feet, crossed the room, and collapsed on the bed. An arm over his eyes did nothing to block out the memory of Tess's final look of betrayal. It was his own fault. He should have told her, but somehow the words "I'm a prince" hadn't formed on his lips. And they never would.

Why did she care?

He was already dreading the next time they talked, but it was just as well. It was best that he find no joy in their interaction. After they retrieved the amulet, she would be back on Earth, pursuing her own dreams.

He had to give her credit. Tess knew what she wanted. She'd fight for it with the same energy that she had when she went toe-to-toe with him. Fearless and headstrong—that was who she was. Nothing he did could change that.

Chapter Six

Standing alone in the grand courtyard below her guest room, Tess rubbed her arms against the chill of the night. Yre Gault's two moons divided her attention—one small, delicate, pale yellow and the other larger, a striking red. Sitting side by side in the evening sky, they were a bizarre reminder that she was a long way from home.

Soft halos ringed them, lightly touching like the tentative kiss of cosmic lovers.

She gave a short laugh. The red one would be the male—stronger, bigger, more aggressive. He probably lied and told the sweet little yellow moon that he was different from any other moon she'd ever met. So typical. Or he didn't tell her he was different.

Tess looked at the yellow moon in sympathy. *Don't believe him, whatever he says. He'll drive you crazy.*

She shook her head to clear it. This had been a long day, and she was well beyond exhausted, with an internal clock that was clinging stubbornly to Earth time.

She cast a glance at the royal residence surrounding her: an incredible place with its endless corridors and countless rooms, all decorated with rich colors and fabrics. Queen Adehla had sacrificed the entire day to escort Tess around, waving off haggard assistants who tagged along behind trying to get her approval on various items.

After that, Tess and Adehla had laughed and chatted throughout dinner. They'd talked about Yre Gault's history and people, from architecture to wildlife—everything except for one topic: Cohl.

There had been no sign of him all day. Just as well. She wasn't ready to face him yet. Self-control had never been one of her strengths, and the reckless way she felt right now, she'd regret whatever she said to him.

She sighed and looked to the sky again. The courtyard perimeter framed an alien night where nothing looked familiar, not a Big Dipper anywhere. She was on a different world. The realization had just begun to set in. It was frightening and undeniably exciting.

She shivered, but it wasn't from the cold. Energy pumped through her, pushing her beyond what her body could tolerate, yet leaving her wonderfully alive. The only other time she could capture this feeling was onstage, pouring her heart out in song.

What she wouldn't give to be back at Sonny's with her band behind her and the music thumping through her chest. The smell of smoke and beer. The faces watching her behind a cigarette haze. Not the most romantic of places but, as always, she'd tolerated it for the opportunity, the privilege to sing.

For some, singing was an ordinary event. Not for Tess. At the moment of creation, the instant her voice became song, there was heaven on earth. Words rolled and slipped off her tongue, winding together like sinuous lovers. There were times when the pure joy of singing would threaten to choke her, the perfect note bring her to tears. She'd use her voice like a finely tuned instrument. The twist of a phrase, the vibrato held just so, until . . . perfection. There just was no better feeling—not chocolate, not even sex. Absolute freedom. Divine release.

The gift had been there for as long as she could remember and longer than any friend she'd ever known. Her music always comforted her when the dream moved yet again beyond reach.

Like now.

She hung her head. As close as she could figure, today was Friday. The day she and her manager, Bill, were supposed to meet with destiny in the form of a producer, Mr. Roger E. Blackman. It would have been her first real break into the elusive music world. It was a shot she'd been working toward for the past two years, singing in bars and nightclubs and any place that Bill would send her. Now that chance was gone. Bill would be very upset but worse than that, Mr. Blackman wouldn't appreciate being stood up by a no-name, wanna-be, struggling singer who didn't have the decency to call and postpone a once-in-a-lifetime meeting.

Maybe if she begged and pleaded, he'd give her another chance. She laughed to herself. Oh, right. *Mr. Blackman, you'll never believe what happened to me on the way to your interview. I was abducted by aliens who dragged me across the universe and forced me to do their bidding. But I'm fine now. Really.*

Tears fell hot and silent to the ground. The dream was crushed beyond any hope of recovery thanks to one man.

"What are you doing out here alone?"

Tess jumped and spun around to find Cohl standing in the shadows of an overhanging balcony. He moved toward her with the terrifying silence of a ghost. How could anyone so big make no noise?

"Waiting for a handsome prince to come and rescue me.

64

Unfortunately, it's just you," she muttered as she hastily wiped the tears from her eyes. No sense in giving the enemy a smell of her blood.

He kept coming, finally stopping a short distance from her. The moons lit up his big frame. She could see now that he was wasn't wearing a shirt. Talk about perfection. Hard muscle, smooth skin, shoulders you could spend days exploring.

But it was his eyes that stole the breath from her lungs. Yellow and menacing in the moonlight, they were like glimpsing the soul of a panther. There was no question: she was his prey.

"Do you ever think before you speak?" There wasn't an ounce of humor in his voice.

Tess licked her lips nervously. Mental note: the man had excellent hearing. Now was not the time to push him no matter how sweet the temptation. "Occasionally, but I find it dulls my rapier wit."

She watched as he folded his arms across his chest. *Muscled* arms across *massive* chest, she corrected herself.

"Is that what you call it?"

Rudely torn from admiring his chest, she batted her eyelashes at him. "We all have our gifts. I think yours is not wearing a shirt."

Feeling more than a little punchy, she crossed her arms like his and asked, "So what do I call you? Cohl Travers or Cohlman Trae Salle?" She raised one bold eyebrow. "Or simply Your Royal Highness?"

His yellow eyes caught in the moonlight, narrowed but shining. "Cohl Travers is the name I go by. Trae Salle is too well known. I've found that people tend to treat me differently when they find out I'm royalty."

She smiled. "Really? I hadn't noticed. So, when were you going to let me in on the fact that your parents are the rulers of a planet? It's not just your father's life on the line here, is it?"

There was a beat of silence. "No. If he dies, it will affect Yre Gault."

"Why did you leave them?" she asked.

The air around her took on a chill, and an eerie silence followed as Cohl took a step toward her. She stepped back, her instincts sensing trouble. His voice was dangerously soft when he said, "I had my reasons. It's time to go to bed, Tess."

She stepped back again. "I'm not sleepy."

He moved forward with her. "Yes, you are. My mother said you were exhausted at dinner."

"When did you talk to her? You weren't even there."

"I had business to take care of. It didn't go well, and I'm in no mood to argue with a stubborn woman who hasn't slept in twenty hours."

Tess glared at him and dug in. "Well, I'm not moving, but you can go inside. Don't worry about me. I've already hit my mugging quota for the year."

The next instant she was dangling upside down over Cohl's shoulder, the air knocked from her lungs. Her fists made useless contact with his hard, muscled back as he carried her back into the residence.

"Damn you, Cohl. Are all aliens this bossy?"

She looked down, dizzy and suddenly too tired to fight. Exterior stones gave way to interior floor tiles, then the familiar pattern of her guest room. Abruptly her world was upright again, then horizontal. When her head settled, she was lying on her back, her feet dangling over the edge of her bed with Cohl looming over her. His body cut a menacing shape against the faint moonlight through the window. She suddenly felt small and defenseless.

He whispered, "Now, are you going to behave, or do I have to wrestle you into submission?"

Tess's heart pounded. "You can't treat me like this. You have no right—"

He interrupted, his voice sharp. "I don't want you outside the residence without an escort. It's too dangerous."

Tess blinked at him. "You said I was safe here."

"You are, as long as you stay with me." He looked down at her, his face shadowed and serious. "Make no mistake, Tess. I will do *whatever* it takes to keep you safe." Then he turned and disappeared into the shadows.

She lay still in the darkness as her heartbeat returned to normal. His parting words echoed in her mind and the unspoken message stunned her. He'd keep her safe so she could complete his mission, save his people and his father. He'd protect her from the Traka-Sou and the other dangers they would face in getting the amulet. As long as he needed her, she would be safe from physical danger.

But the big question was, who was going to keep her safe from him?

Cohl strode back to his dark room next door. Pitz illuminated a far corner by the open balcony doorway.

"Did you return Tess to her room, sir?"

Cohl stalked past him out to the balcony and into the cool, clear night air. "Yes. She's back inside." He slammed his hand against the railing. "Damn it, I can't believe Mil-Ops hasn't figured out how the Traka-Nor took my father out of here without anyone seeing or hearing a thing!"

Pitz hummed softly from behind him. "Perhaps you should remain with Tess at night."

Cohl nearly choked. "No, I don't think that's a good idea." She asked too many questions; she made his hands itch and he would *never* get any sleep.

"Perhaps I could guard her," Pitz offered.

Cohl cast the robot a glance and shook his head. "I doubt

Tess would like that. No offense, but she hasn't exactly warmed up to you."

Pitz sighed dramatically. "And I have tried so hard."

Cohl gave a short laugh. "Don't feel bad. I'm not doing so well myself. Station yourself in the corridor near her door and monitor her room. Wake me if you hear anything suspicious."

"Yes, sir. Good night." Pitz whirred out.

Cohl contemplated the moons of Yre Gault, the small yellow and the giant red. He'd seen them in every formation and partnership during his life on the planet. Tonight they were side by side and although the yellow one was farther away, they appeared to be a mere kiss apart. He looked at the red moon. *Don't do it. She'll drive you crazy.*

He braced his hands on the railing and hung his head. He couldn't even begin to describe the panic he'd felt when he spotted Tess standing in the courtyard alone and unguarded. He should have treated her with more consideration, but as usual, she'd pushed him. So he'd dumped her unceremoniously into her bed. Her hair had fanned out, soft in the moonlight. He'd wanted to touch it, gather its heavy weight in his hands, feel its coolness against his face. He'd wanted her and in a most unrefined way. It had taken all the willpower he possessed to walk out of her room.

He rubbed the back of his neck. With the lack of sleep, the pressure of this mission, and pure sexual frustration, he'd become one miserable man. And unfortunately for him, she would not leave his sight starting tomorrow. Especially after the exasperating day he'd spent with Mil-Ops.

They still had no idea how his father could have been abducted from his office right under their noses. No one entered the premises. No one exited. No clues. How could someone have gotten close to his father without an alarm going off? The hair on the back of Cohl's neck stood up. He knew his father would never succumb to a kidnapper without a fight. Yet his office had appeared undisturbed.

The only thing Mil-Ops knew for sure was that his father was last seen working late into the night.

Cohl shook his head. For as long as he could remember, Montral Trae Salle lived on four hours of sleep a night. The other twenty-six belonged to Yre Gault.

Cohl could only imagine the conditions his father was enduring in the hands of the Traka-Nor. With the repair delay, the situation was becoming even more serious for him and Yre Gault. There was a very good chance he would never speak to his father again. The prospect chilled him to the bone. Yre Gault would lose their leader. He would lose a man he never even said good-bye to.

He gripped the railing. The last argument had been a repeat, over duty and responsibility and birthright. But all Cohl ever saw was the endless hours, sleepless nights, and thankless tasks. There had to be more to life than that and he hadn't been ready to fulfill his destiny until he'd tried everything else first. Once Yre Gault was his, the opportunity would never come again.

Leaving had been easy, easier than he could ever have imagined. Just find a ship and fly off with a head full of legends to pursue and conquer. The successes had come quickly along with a few memorable failures. He grew to love his life with *Speculator* as his only home. He could control everything in his little world without losing himself in the process. After a few years, the idea of returning to Yre Gault had faded.

Then the call had come from his mother, alarmed and shaken like he'd never heard her before. *Please come home, Cohl. Something terrible has happened. We need you.*

The words tore through him, dragging him back into the past with terrifying speed. Duty had finally caught up with him.

He gazed out over the darkened courtyard. No matter how

many times he took in this view, it never felt like home. The picture of him as king never solidified in his mind. The crown was just too big, too heavy. Suffocating.

Frankly, he couldn't wait to leave.

"Wake up, Tess."

The annoying words broke through her dream. Tess swatted at the pest and rolled over, dragging the covers with her. "Go away."

Cohl's low chuckle rumbled beside her and the bed dipped under his weight. Tess opened one eye to find him sitting on its edge with Pitz hovering behind him.

"What are you doing here?"

He sat bathed in sunlight with an arrogant smile on his lips. "Getting your beautiful butt out of bed."

Tess regarded him warily, but there was no sign of the sullen man she'd dealt with last night. Then she smiled back. "You think it's beautiful?"

He laughed and shook his head. "Do you always wake up in a good mood?"

Tess rolled onto her back and stretched under the covers. "Not before coffee, I don't. God, I really need a cup this morning."

"It's almost midday, and what's coffee?"

She froze and looked at him, horrified. "Don't tell me you don't have coffee?"

Cohl shook his head from side to side. "Nope."

Tess sat straight up clutching the blanket to her chest as another more urgent, unconscionable thought invaded. "What about chocolate? Do you have that?"

Cohl's gaze lingered on her bare shoulders. When he spoke, his voice was husky. "No chocolate either."

She flopped back on the bed and pulled the covers over her head. "Shoot me now. It's not worth living."

Cohl swatted her leg. "No, you don't. We're leaving as soon as you dress."

She yanked the covers back down to her neck. "We are? Where?"

He stood up and his expression darkened. "I figure the only way to keep you from escaping at night is to give you a tour of Yre Gault."

Tess eyed him, unsure how to take that comment. "Is this a truce of some sort?"

Cohl gazed down at her and paused just long enough to make her fully aware of her nudity. "Let's just say it's my way of thanking you for deciding to help us."

Then he turned to leave. "Be ready in thirty minutes, Tess. I hate to wait."

Her mouth dropped open in disbelief at his casual audacity. "You know, just because you look like Mel Gibson doesn't mean you can order me around."

Cohl stopped and turned to face her with a speculative look. "Pitz?"

Beside him, Pitz clicked and purred. "Mel Gibson. Famous male actor and entertainer. Considered handsome and desirable by millions of women on Earth."

Cohl smiled.

Tess groaned and buried her head under the covers. "Heaven help me."

Distraction number one: She slept naked. The thought kept returning at the most inconvenient times—like right now while he was weaving through Caldara's inner city traffic in a ground shuttle. Cohl had guessed that, but still, the actual confirmation of it this morning was more intrusive than he had expected.

Staring him in the face was distraction number two: Her nicely curved rear. Tess was hanging half out of the open shuttle window on the passenger side, captivated and enchanted by the city of Caldara. Every few seconds, she'd pop back inside and ask another question.

Cohl shook his head and returned his attention to the traffic in front of him before he ran over some poor, unsuspecting pedestrian who couldn't possibly understand his predicament.

Distraction number three would be Caldara itself, although not much had changed here since he'd left what seemed like a lifetime ago. Not that much could. Caldara occupied every square meter of space it could squeeze from the top of the mountain from which it was carved. Like all the island cities on Yre Gault, it had been painstakingly cultivated from the solid rock. Every structure, road, and causeway had been preplanned before a single stone was cut. Then, from the flawless white stone of the mountaintop, the city was born. A perfect metropolis emerged like a flower from the earth.

He guided the ground shuttle around a stack of crates being unloaded on the side of the street. The workers waved as the shuttle skirted them, their tapestry uniforms brilliant in the sunshine. Tess waved back.

She turned to him and nearly caught him staring at distraction number two. "When are we going to get out and look around?"

"We aren't. It's too dangerous."

She gave him a look that he recognized all too well. That I-don't-like-your-answer look. He shrugged. *Too bad.* It was dangerous, that much was true, but there was another reason that he didn't want to discuss with her. The last thing he needed was an angry mob recognizing him, converging on him and Tess with accusations of abandonment and questions he'd rather not answer. That's why he'd chosen this shuttle with its one-way view. Except for Tess's open window, no one could see inside.

He glanced at her again. She was hanging out the window,

but he could tell by her stiff posture that he hadn't heard the last of that issue. He resigned himself to the inevitable and concentrated on driving. The traffic was a little worse than he remembered, the streets a bit more crowded. But it was still spotless, still incredibly stunning in its simple architecture and style. He hadn't found another more beautiful place in all his travels.

Rings of connected buildings around the central plaza glistened in the sun, their stone facades unblemished and timeless. In the center, watching over all of Caldara, were the giant statues of the Great Kings of Yre Gault. As long as he could remember, they had stood here as reminders of great men of a great world.

Tess craned her head to gaze up at them as the shuttle circled. "They must be fifty feet high. Who are they?"

"Yre Gault's kings," he said.

"Is your father here?"

He turned the shuttle away from the shadows of statues and onto a side street. "They stopped adding kings a long time ago. Now the plaza is used for ceremonial functions."

She twisted around. "They are certainly impressive. Your people must have loved them."

Cohl nodded absently. They had been loved and with good reason. He'd studied them all, from the first to his father's current reign, and been overwhelmed by their greatness. Powerful, fearless men who ruled Yre Gault through good times and bad with absolute confidence and courage. Men who'd taken responsibility for millions of lives, men who cared. Men who had been willing to sacrifice their lives and their dreams.

Unselfish, wise, and ensnared by duty.

"Stop!" Tess screamed suddenly.

He slammed the shuttle to a dead stop and looked around for the problem. There wasn't any.

"Damn it, Tess. Don't do that."

She was already out the door and running down an alley they had just passed. Cohl swore and jumped out to follow her, leaving the shuttle behind.

For a small woman, she could sure move. He didn't catch her until she had cleared the other end of the alley. Then he glimpsed her destination: a quartet of street musicians on the corner. They were playing a lively instrumental with a strong beat—typical Yre Gault music. How the hell had she heard their music from an entire street over?

"A band!" she exclaimed as she pointed to them, her cheeks flushed from the run and her green eyes brighter than he'd ever seen before. The smile on her face could send a proud man to his knees. It was the music that did this to her. Her dream, her calling. He doubted there was another thing that could bring that much life to her soul. For some reason, the thought made him jealous. Would she look like that for a man she loved?

She turned and ran across the street. He walked along after her and watched her jump right into the midst of the band. She picked up the beat, clapping her hands and dancing to the music, her body becoming a channel for the rhythm. The musicians seemed to sense one of their own because they accepted her intrusion with delight. She moved with such utter ease, swaying and swinging her hips as if the song emanated from inside her instead of from the musicians' instruments.

After a few minutes, she broke into song, making up her own lyrics as she went. Cohl nearly stopped breathing. Her voice was ten times more amazing live than it had been on the transmission he'd heard across the galaxy. So pure and clear, untainted and unspoiled. The song for the song's sake. In her face, the joy of the act was too beautiful for words.

The musicians reveled in her voice, playing the song on and on. From nowhere a crowd closed around them, all smiling and clapping and moving. Before long, Tess's lyrics were being echoed down the street by a chorus of voices.

Cohl found himself lost in the moment, captivated by her. She was a performer, through and through, drawing them into the show, freeing their inhibitions. Beautiful. Perfect.

A sadness stole over him. This was what she was born to do and she knew it, allowing herself to be lost to it. He doubted anyone or anything could draw that much light from her soul.

"Aren't you the prince?"

The small voice came from his left side. He looked into the face of a young woman who was smiling brightly.

Cohl frowned. The last thing he'd needed was for someone to recognize him, but it was too late. Face after face in the crowd turned his way. Their eyes lit up as they realized who he was. *Shoot.* Here it came. They would hate him for abandoning them. They'd probably drive him out of the city. He'd better find an escape route and fast.

"You *are* the prince. Welcome home," the young woman said, her smile growing in radiance.

Cohl blinked at her. Then one by one, the others welcomed him by nodding or shaking his hand or by verbal greeting. The crowd seemed to squeeze around him as they peered over each other to get a glimpse. Questions popped up. Where was he staying? Had he found a mate? Could he do something about the export problems?

He smiled numbly at them, completely confused. Something must be wrong. How could they not hate him? They acted as if he'd never left. They acted as if he were here to stay.

He didn't notice that the band had changed songs and that Tess was no longer singing until she was standing next to him. She looked at the crowd that was huddled around Cohl and squeezed his arm. "Is everything okay?"

The young woman pointed to her. "The princess."

Cohl groaned inwardly. This was getting completely out of hand.

Tess's eyes widened; then she smiled. "Gee, I've never been a princess before."

"Very funny," he mumbled.

He took her by the elbow and bowed slightly to his people. "We must be leaving. Thank you for the warm welcome."

With that, he pulled Tess back down the street with the band playing behind them. He didn't look back, couldn't look into the faces and pretend that he was here to stay. Couldn't admit that he cared. Couldn't face the music.

Tess knew Cohl was running. "What's wrong with you? They just wanted to talk. Didn't you see their faces? They were so happy to see you."

"I don't have anything to say to them."

Tess struggled to keep up with his long strides. "I don't believe that. You have plenty to say. I think you're afraid that once you start, you won't be able to stop."

He stared straight ahead. "It's really none of your business."

She glared at him. How could he be the only one who didn't see it? There had been as much longing in his eyes as there had been in the eyes of his people. He loved this planet.

They were about to cross the street when a loud voice rang out. "Well, well. If it isn't the wayward prince come home."

Tess twisted toward the source of the comment. Her first reaction was repulsion, although she wasn't exactly sure why. The man walking toward them was anything but repulsive: Dark, handsome features, a massive, muscled body that moved powerfully, blue eyes the color of cobalt. Her gut churned as he stopped a few feet from Cohl, effectively blocking her out.

She didn't like him. There was an arrogant, lopsided sneer of a smile on his goateed face, too much cockiness in his stance and too little warmth.

He spoke again, his eyes trained on Cohl. "Get bored with the high-life or did you just run out of credits?"

Tess's eyes widened at the callous challenge and glanced at Cohl. Apparently they knew each other.

Cohl gave him a killer's smile. "I see you haven't changed a bit, Logen. Still the star hole you've always been. I'd have bet that someone would have killed you by now."

Logen smirked. "You know I'm too good to let that happen. Even you couldn't do it, although I gave you plenty of chances."

Logen turned his cold gaze to Tess. Somewhere deep inside her, every feminine instinct screamed *run*. She had the strangest urge to hide behind Cohl.

"Since Cohl has no manners, I'll introduce myself. Logen Du Vaul. And you are?"

"Taken," Cohl interjected, moving close enough to stake his claim.

"Interesting name," Logen said with a grin. "However, I see your taste in women has improved."

Tess moved closer to Cohl.

"So, how's the security business these days?" Cohl asked coolly.

"Busy. Your father has been a most engaging client," Logen said, crossing his arms over his barrel chest. "In fact, I think he kind of fancied me the son he never had." He smiled and spread his arms. "Can't you just picture me as ruler?"

Tess shuddered involuntarily. She felt Cohl's entire body tense. When he spoke, his voice was steel.

"You will never rule Yre Gault."

Logen laughed. "Who is going to stop me? You?"

"My parents would never allow it," Cohl said. "And it would be over *my* dead body."

"Now," Logen replied, crossing his arms, "there's an interesting thought. Tell you what, if you can finally beat me on the grid, I'll reconsider my position." The air around him chilled as he leaned forward. "But if I win, I never want to see your face on Yre Gault again."

Tess sucked in a breath. Cohl's hand curled around her arm.

"Go to hell, Logen—*if* they'll take you."

He pulled her toward the alley. Tess nearly ran ahead of him as she fought back impending dread. She wanted to escape from Logen before something terrible happened. Fate had other ideas. They were almost there when she heard it.

"Run away as always, Trae Salle. Go back to Earth with your woman. Don't worry, I'll take good care of Yre Gault."

Cohl stopped, nearly toppling Tess in the process. She pulled on his arm. He simply stared straight ahead. Panic rose within her.

"Ignore him, Cohl. He's just trying to start a fight." She'd seen enough barroom brawls started simply because one person couldn't walk away.

Cohl looked down at her with determination. "Not this time."

She put her palms on his chest and whispered desperately, "He won't do what he promises. He's lying."

"I know. This is important, though, Tess. Trust me."

Tess gazed up into his beautiful face and realized she did trust him. "What's the grid? Is it dangerous?"

"No more dangerous than a tactical exercise with Pitz." He turned to face Logen. "You're on."

Logen smiled crookedly. "My place in an hour."

Cohl shook his head. "Neutral setting. The grid at Zagar or nothing. Unless, of course, you can't win anywhere else but your own private club."

Logen's cheek twitched. "In an hour then."

Chapter Seven

The Grid at Zagar was little more than an airless, windowless domed arena covering a giant hole in the ground about thirty feet in diameter surrounded by seats. A large metal grid stretched from edge to edge. Tess moved forward and took a closer look at the grid itself. The bars were only four inches wide, and there was a two-foot empty space between each diagonal grid block. Under the grid, the pit was black and endless. She swallowed and wondered how deep it went into the solid rock. No net, nothing to stop a fall. It looked positively medieval.

"Pitz, what kind of game is this?"

The robot blinked beside her. "Grid BaStun dates back several thousand years, when most of the population dwelled along the shores. The combatants would stand on logs in the water and try to knock each other off with sticks. It has evolved with technology into arenas where spectators can cheer on their champions in relative comfort. The planet now has over one hundred arenas."

She eyed him. "And it's safe?"

Pitz's lights flickered. "Safety depends on many factors."

"What the hell is going on, Pitz? I told you to take her back." Cohl strode toward them from the changing area. Tess turned toward him and her breath caught. He was wearing only loose pants, his chest and feet bare. In the glaring lights, fine scars emerged on his broad chest and steely arms. The chin-length hair was pulled back into a short tail. But his eyes, his eyes were hard and cold. The eyes of a warrior going to battle.

Pitz whirred and buzzed uncharacteristically. Tess almost felt sorry for him, but frankly she was more worried about herself.

"She refused, sir."

Cohl's fierce gaze swung from Pitz to Tess. She took a step back. He took a step forward.

She smiled sweetly and shrugged.

Cohl took another step toward her and leaned forward, inches from her face. "There are reasons why I don't want you here, Tess. You need to learn to follow orders."

"I'm not going to sit back at the palace in the dark like a mushroom. I want to be here, Cohl."

"You may not like what you see," he said as he strapped on his heavy-duty gloves. Nasty-looking metal spikes protruded from them. Maybe she didn't want to be here.

She whispered, "Is this really necessary, Cohl? I mean, you don't have to impress me. There's no shame in walking away from a fight."

He lifted his golden gaze to hers. "I'm not doing it to impress you. He knows you are from Earth."

Tess blinked up at him. "So?"

Cohl's expression hardened. "No one knows that except me and my crew. And maybe the Traka-Sou."

Her mouth dropped open. "Then how—"

"I don't know," Cohl interrupted. "But I'm going to find

out." He nodded toward the grid field. "Out there, if possible."

"Can't you just arrest him and interrogate him or something?"

Cohl shook his head. "I know Logen. If I dragged him into custody, he'd engineer a tremendous amount of sympathy for himself. And in my father's absence, that could be good for him and risky for us. Besides, his entire life has been based around his success here on the grid. Humiliation in front of his fans will devastate him—enough to leave the crown alone until I can bring my father back."

"For Yre Gault," she said softly. He glanced at her sharply and then looked away. She knew it. He wasn't just fighting for her or his father but for all of Yre Gault. He couldn't lie to her about that.

Pitz appeared from behind Tess, carrying two stubby, black clubs. "Your weapons check out, sir."

Cohl took them, clipped each to a short tether on his combat gloves, and flipped them easily in his hands. They were just over two feet long, indented in the middle for handgrips.

"What are they?" Tess asked with growing dread.

"Stun pikes," Cohl answered. "One end fires a single-shot laser burst. You're given one shot per pike; then it's empty. The other end houses a contact stunner."

Tess gaped at him. "Can they kill?"

Cohl grimaced slightly. "No. Just deliver a nasty jolt and temporary paralysis."

"Good Lord," she muttered. "Can't you just play a nice game of baseball?"

The doors to the building opened and a boisterous mob of people poured in, rushing for the spectator seating that circled the pit. Foul language echoed within the dome.

"Who are *they?*" Tess asked as the people bickered over the choice seats on his opponent's side of the grid.

"I'm hoping they're Logen's staunchest supporters."

A collective cheer resonated from the crowd as Logen strutted in, bare-chested and fully armed with a stun pike in each hand. Tess stared at the mountain of a man. He had to outweigh Cohl by thirty pounds—all of it pure, pumped-up muscle.

Logen stopped at the far edge of the grid and grinned like a wolf. He hefted twin pikes and twirled them around him, faster and faster until they were nothing but a blur. He lunged and parried, spinning the clubs in perfect timing. The crowd went crazy behind him.

She licked her lips and gripped Cohl's rock-hard biceps. "Are you sure there's no other way?"

His muscle flexed and rolled under her hands as he gripped the stun pike harder.

"He's a threat to you, my planet, and the mission. I have no choice."

Logen stopped his flashy display and shouted across the grid, "Hiding behind your woman, Trae Salle? Maybe we should make her part of the deal."

A deep growl rumbled through Cohl's chest. Then he stepped forward, balancing his body on the first narrow grid bar.

"Pitz," he commanded softly. Pitz scooted beside him. Cohl kept his eyes on Logen and his voice low enough so that Tess couldn't hear him. "If anything happens to me, get Tess out of here."

"Understood," Pitz replied. "Do you expect a problem?"

Cohl spared him a quick glance, then turned his sights back to Logen. Logen who wanted his planet and his people. Logen who knew too much about Tess.

"I won't lose," he said with conviction.

"Yes, sir." Pitz slid back beside Tess.

Cohl took a deep breath and called forth his inner warrior. Behind him, the protective plasma screen rose up, protecting

Tess and Pitz as well as Logen's vocal supporters from the battle about to be waged. The people cheered, but he barely heard them. He was too busy focusing on his enemy. He owed Logen for a lifetime of humiliation.

Both men crossed the grid until they were within six meters of each other.

"She's mine after I beat you, Trae Salle, and you won't be able to stop me," his enemy said with a cocky grin. "Just wanted you to know that."

Cohl opened his mouth as if to reply, then lunged forward and struck Logen's shoulder with the contact stun on his right club. Unprepared for the ruse, Logen yelped as the stun pike sustained a direct hit and paralyzed his right shoulder and arm. Cohl took advantage of the hesitation and smacked the left side of Logen's head with the end of the other club. Logen recovered and stepped back just as Cohl's second swing split open Logen's lip. The crowd was on their feet, screaming as the first drops of blood were drawn.

Cohl leaped backward, mindful of his footing atop the narrow grids. Logen's face twisted in rage as he bared his teeth, blood running down his chin. One arm hung lifelessly where Cohl's contact stunner had done its job.

They circled each other slowly atop the perilous gridwork, each looking for an opening or a weakness. Time and time again, stun pikes lashed out in a flurry of blows. Cohl ignored the hits that grazed his arms, shoulders, chest, knowing that he was doing more damage to his opponent. Logen's frustration was mounting, his moves becoming more bullish with less finesse, rage undermining his control.

Suddenly Logen lifted his stun pike and released its single laser burst at Cohl's head. Cohl kept his feet planted on the grid bars as he twisted his upper body. The laser blast passed over his right shoulder and harmlessly into the air.

That was one shot away, Cohl thought. Only one left, and that pike was on Logen's paralyzed side.

Suddenly a second blast flashed and struck him in the left arm. He grunted and stumbled back as it burned deep into his flesh. The crowd thumped and cheered wildly. Cohl grimaced in pain and looked down at the wound, smoking and bleeding profusely. *What the hell?* That was no burn agent in the laser. He glanced up at Logen, who was smiling back insanely with his first pike still pointed at Cohl.

Cohl leaped sideways, almost missing the grid as another burst came from Logen's pike. He knew immediately that, contrary to one of the few sport rules, there were probably six full rounds of live ammo in each of his opponent's weapons. This was no game. Logen was here to kill him. That meant all rules were off.

Before Logen could get off another shot, Cohl fired one of his own shots directly at Logen's outstretched pike. The weapon exploded in the man's hands, metal shards lashing his face and arm. As Logen roared with pain, his useless pike clattered to the rocks below.

Cohl tossed his own discharged pike to the side and switched the other to his good hand. Just as Logen did the same, Cohl fired. The shot hit Logen's firing hand. Logen screamed in pain and rage as his second pike dropped and swung from its tether. The crowd hushed.

Logen snarled like a madman, blood streaming from numerous gashes on his face and body. One arm and his opposite hand were numbed, but that didn't stop him. He charged Cohl with his head down, thumping wildly across the grid field.

Cohl tried to evade, but he slipped in his own blood on the grid beneath his feet. Logen's head caught him square in the stomach, and they landed side by side across the grids.

The crowd were on their feet, screaming for their hero to get up. Logen lay on his back shaking his head.

Cohl braced his pike across a grid square to support himself, then slipped his body through the opening to the underside of the grid surface right beneath Logen, dangling from his pike with one hand. He swung up and anchored his legs on a bar, reached through the grid, and locked his good arm across Logen's neck.

He squeezed. His weight alone was enough to make Logen gasp for air. The man flailed his muscle-bound body helplessly.

Cohl, who was out of reach, brought his face to Logen's ear. "Now tell me, you bastard, how you know so much about Tess."

Above him, Logen coughed. "Don't. Don't know."

Cohl let his body relax, creating more pressure on Logen's neck. "How, Logen? Or all these nice people are going to watch you die on the grid. How'd you like that as your epitaph?"

That worked. Logen spat it out in gasps. "Mil-Ops. Leak."

"Who?" Cohl hissed.

Logen wheezed. "Don't know . . . was trying to find out . . ."

Cohl hung on, deciding whether or not to believe him. Logen's struggling was slowing. He had to let go soon or Logen would die. Not today. Humiliation was far better than death.

He slipped his arm from Logen's throat, swinging under the grid and pulling himself up on the upper grid field once again. Logen didn't move, just stared blankly up at Cohl. His lips were a nice shade of blue.

Cohl addressed him quietly. "Sorry to hear that your plans to rule Yre Gault are history. Your security services are no longer needed. And if you come *anywhere* near Tess, I will kill you." The words cut a clean swath through the stagnant air. Logen's eyes bulged.

Cohl turned to face the silent crowd. They gaped at him in shock and awe as if he were a god.

He turned and hobbled across the grid field back toward

Tess, hoping to reach the other side before he collapsed from exhaustion. The screen lowered just as he approached the edge where Tess waited. He couldn't bring himself to look her in the eye, not with the battle still roaring in his blood. What would she think of the beast within him?

She was there when he stepped off the grid, her arms around his neck in a desperate embrace. Not what he expected, but he'd take it. A wave of relief rolled over him, more soothing than any drug.

He tried to hold her away with his good arm. "You're going to be covered in blood, Tess."

She pulled back. The fire in her eyes took him by surprise. "You think I'm worried about that after what I've seen? Do you know how lucky you are to be alive? Logen was trying to kill you."

He smiled at her anger on his behalf. "I figured that one out myself when he shot me with live ammo."

She looked down at his bloody arm and her face paled. "Oh God, Cohl. You need a doctor." She turned to Pitz. "Can we get out of here?"

Pitz answered, "Transportation is waiting outside."

Tess nodded and slipped her arm around Cohl's waist. He leaned into her, spent.

She said softly, "Come on. You can tell me what you and Logen were chatting about out there."

"Lie down with me, Tess."

So quiet was his request, she almost thought it was her imagination. Sitting next to him on his bed, she could sense the thin thread of consciousness he held on to. She wiped his forehead again with a wet cloth and he closed his eyes at the ministration. That was about all he could do. The drug the medic administered had turned him into a pussycat and there wasn't an ounce of fight left in him. It was a miracle that he'd made it back to his room at all in his condition.

She sighed, setting the cloth aside. She should let him sleep but she couldn't deny him after what he'd been through. She slid in along his side, carefully laying her arm gently across his chest. He wrapped his good arm around her and pulled her tight to him.

Then his fingers grazed her jaw, stroked her face, down her throat with the caress of a feather. Who would have thought that a warrior could be so tender?

She rested her head on his chest and whispered, "I would consider it a huge personal favor if you didn't do Grid BaStun again."

"Okay." He slipped his fingers through her tresses. "Did I ever tell you that I love your hair?"

Tess raised her head and looked into his half-mast eyes. "Okay? That's it? No argument?"

He smiled weakly at her. "No argument."

"Humph," she said in amazement. "I want a supply of that drug the medic gave you for future use."

He let out a lazy chuckle. "See? I can be a reasonable man. Ask anyone."

Tess lowered her head again and listened to the strong beating of his heart, the steady breath, a man alive. Thank God. She couldn't bear it if he'd died trying to protect her. This was bad enough.

"Do you miss performing?"

Cohl's question surprised her. "Yes. Why do you ask?"

"You looked so happy today with the street band." His words came slowly now and with tremendous effort. "I'm sorry, Tess," he said, beginning to slur. "I didn't mean to ruin your dream."

She swallowed hard at the unexpected apology. "I can understand why you did it. I think your people are lucky to have you."

He rolled his head from side to side. "No excuse. No right to take you. Dangerous."

His eyes closed as a drugged sleep claimed him.

Slowly, she slipped out from under his arm and sat on the edge of the bed. He looked so battered. Her chest squeezed tight with all the emotion she'd been holding back. Watching him battle Logen was worse than anything she'd ever been through. She felt every grunt, every shock, every meaty collision he endured as if it were her own.

Cohl was stronger than he looked though and faster, both of which shouldn't have been a surprise. He certainly moved fast enough with her. But she hadn't expected the warrior that emerged on the grid, the way he focused on the battle and the violence he could unleash. Cohl was a dangerous man. He could have killed Logen if he wanted. Yet even with all the times she'd pushed him, he had kept all that savagery in control. She would never have guessed it ran so close to the surface. It was an intoxicating revelation.

But when he had dropped out of sight under the grid, she'd held her breath—afraid to scream, afraid not to. It had only been seconds but her world had frozen in time. Only when he reappeared did her heart begin pumping again.

She looked at him, asleep and helpless, and tried to hate him for screwing up her life. It was impossible. She'd heard the pride in his voice when he answered her hundred questions about his home planet. She'd seen now why he'd taken her, to save the planet he loved. She'd seen his guilt today when he spoke to his people and witnessed his courage when he battled Logen for Yre Gault.

The truth was crystal clear to her. He needed his people as much as they needed him. She knew how they felt. She was beginning to need him, too. How could she ever have thought him unfeeling?

A familiar whirring sound advanced on her as Pitz approached.

"Is he asleep?" Pitz inquired quietly.

Tess nodded and whispered back, "Just now. Is he going to be all right?"

The robot replied, "Affirmative. The medication will heal him quickly. This outcome is not atypical."

Tess stroked his arm. "I can see that. So many scars. Where are they all from?"

Pitz clicked softly. "It is an inherent risk in adventuring."

She frowned at the dimly lit robot. The decision made, she stood up and walked toward the door. "Come with me, Pitz. I have a feeling you are the perfect one to fill me in on the fine art of adventuring."

Nish gave a deep groan, grateful for the support of his bed. His old bones quickly registered the cold and dankness of his room through the fog that always followed his journey out of a vision. Despite the tremendous effort it took to transport beyond this plane, the result was well worth the discomfort of returning to his ancient body.

This time Nish had seen the Finder, the man they called Travers. There had been a struggle within him and the battle with Logen, a man who had a larger part in the game. With Travers was the woman with great strength and courage—the key to the amulet. The bonds were already building that would sustain them for the journey ahead to the lost planet of Demisie.

He stared up at the ceiling of a small, shabby room he was lucky to call home. An old man who could not lift a weapon was of little use on Trakas since the reign of the brothers had begun, carving up the planet between themselves after their ruling father had died. If only he could see the future as well as the present. Perhaps then he could have foreseen the death and destruction the brothers were to unleash to feed their private greed. But he didn't need to see the future to predict that Trakas would be destroyed much as Demisie had been. After all, the same Demisie blood ran through his veins and much of the Trakas population. If only they knew who their ancestors were and the tragedy that had cost them their planet a thousand years ago.

No, the final hope for Trakas lay in his gift, his knowledge, his wisdom of age. They were the tools he would use to manipulate Rommol, the brother of the north. But all deceptions had their peril and Nish had experienced his first.

Travers, a man of great integrity, had refused to help. Rommol's anger had roared and now Traver's father was a hostage. A most unfortunate development.

Nish caressed the bridge of his nose where a steady pain throbbed. More players, more complications, but he could only see so much.

He needed the lure of the amulet to save what was left of Trakas. One last chance to use a gift he could not pass on to another generation, the end of his Demisian blood.

His old hand formed into a hard fist with all the strength of his forebears. He had grown to love this world with its fertile land and peaceful people. They would not be forsaken for the mistakes of fools. He would control what he could and pray for the rest.

But he would not fail.

Chapter Eight

"Cohl? How do you feel?" Tess's voice was close.

The fog cleared slowly, painfully, and without mercy, dumping him into his own private hell.

"Cohl. Please." She was more insistent this time, worried.

He wouldn't have opened his eyes at that moment for anyone else. She was leaning over him, her mass of dark curls hanging over his face. Green eyes watched his every move with deep concern. Her scent filled his senses, quelling the fire in his brain and starting another in his groin. He had the strongest urge to gather her up in his arms and nuzzle her close. Too bad his arms weren't listening.

Tess gave him a sad smile. "You slept all night and most of the day. The wound looks much better. How do you feel?"

"I'll tell you in a minute." He rolled onto his side and gave a heartfelt groan. *Damn.* That was the last Grid BaStun match of his life. He vaguely remembered making that particular vow the last time, too. Proof that age didn't necessarily bring wisdom.

He gritted his teeth and sat up with Tess's help. The familiar swill of the drug, Aritrox, swam through his system, bringing a pleasant numbing effect with it. The accelerator speeded up the healing while the painkiller told you everything was fine. He knew better.

"Hell. I feel like hell."

There was a lengthy silence and then, "That's too bad."

The flat response brought his head up quickly. Furious green eyes looked back at him. So much for sympathy.

She stood up and paced his room in a tight, angry circle. He could see the eruption building, the calm before the storm. He frowned. At least when she was throwing things at him, he could tell how she felt. Even the explosion wasn't what he expected. It was more like an implosion and more dangerous than any hurled boot. The calm, crisp tone of her voice cut through the air.

"When were you going to tell me about the amulet, Cohl? About the maze it's housed in? About how dangerous adventuring is?"

Every muscle in his body tensed. "What do you know about adventuring?"

She stopped pacing and stared him straight in the eye. "Pitz is a wealth of knowledge. He spent most of last night listing all the adventures you've done—the good and the bad." She pointed to the fine scars on his chest. "Including how you got each of those."

"Damn it. I'm going to deactivate him," he muttered low.

"Why? For telling me the truth? When were you going to enlighten me? Once we got inside the maze? 'Oh, Tess, by the way, there are four death traps to master before we reach the amulet.' " She started counting on her fingers. " 'There's the Wind of Death, the Tunnel of Death, the Army of Death, the Beasts of Death.' " She waved her hand in the air. " 'But don't worry, they're nothing really. Piece of cake.' "

He watched in fascination as she carried out her animated, mock conversation without him.

" 'But the real fun begins when we actually get through all those and reach the amulet. Then I shove you into a small room where you need to sing a very specific song with very specific words in a very specific voice or you'll be shredded into a million pieces by your own sound waves.' "

She finished with a flourish, standing before him shaking with anger.

He rested on his elbows and considered his options: beg forgiveness or throw out a diversion.

He squinted at her. "You didn't get any sleep last night, did you?"

Her green eyes nearly burned a hole in him. He winced. Wrong choice. Beg forgiveness, it was.

"I'm sorry, Tess. I should have told you all the risks in the beginning. The right moment just never presented itself." He glanced at her. She hadn't moved a muscle, didn't budge from her position. He gave a sigh. "Look. It's bad enough that I dragged you into this mess. You shouldn't have to worry about the details, too."

"I want the details, Cohl," she said firmly. "It's not your place to make that choice for me."

She was right and he knew it, even if he didn't like it. How was he going to earn her trust if he kept leaving out little facts that could kill her?

"Would you have agreed to help us if you knew the risks?" he asked.

She didn't reply right away and then said softly, "I'd be pretty selfish if I put myself and my career before your father and a few million people who needed my help."

Her answer didn't surprise him. Tess would always do what she had to. It was all he'd hoped for, but now he wasn't so sure. Tess had become more than just his key to the amulet.

"No matter what happens, I'll make sure you are safe, Tess. I swear." He put his heart in every word and hoped for the best. It was all he had left.

She stared back at him with eyes full of hurt. "Do you have any more secrets for me, Cohl?"

He could almost hear the words "last chance" ringing in his head. "Not that I'm aware of."

"Don't lie to me again," she whispered and turned to walk out the door.

Cohl fell back on the bed with a grunt. He'd been reluctant to tell her about the amulet dangers but he hadn't counted on the alternative being even worse.

There was a faint noise at the door and he looked up to find his mother standing there, a single, quizzical eyebrow raised. He groaned. This day was going to hell in a hurry.

"My dear, you really need to work on your courtship skills."

Cohl sat up in bed and swung his legs over the side. The sudden move brought a blast of yellow stars that lit up his vision. He shook it off.

His mother sat down on the bed beside him, folding her gown carefully in a familiar regal pose.

"She cares a great deal for you."

Cohl glanced at her. "You wouldn't say that if you had seen her a few minutes ago."

Adehla chuckled. "I'm sure you'll resolve it." She took in his bandaged arm and the bruises across his body that shorts didn't cover. "Well, maybe not today. I see you haven't outgrown Grid BaStun yet. You lost?"

He frowned. "I won."

Both of her eyebrows rose daintily. "I can only imagine what your opponent looks like."

That prompted the first smile of the day.

"Do you plan on having any more matches while you are here?" The concern in her voice caught his attention.

"No. Once every ten years is plenty."

She patted his hand and looked at him with the eyes of a mother. "Good. I don't want to lose you."

For a few long seconds their eyes locked and the past vanished. Guilt lashed out at him. As a rebellious younger man, he'd taken up Grid BaStun because his parents hated it. But hurting his mother was the last thing on his mind today. He fought back the urge to embrace her, his strict grooming overriding the action as always. He had been trained well.

Adehla dropped her gaze, a flash of disappointment quickly turning to cool composure. She resumed her proper position and cleared her throat. "I have a problem. Several months ago, your father and I planned a large celebration for the top officials of our governing board. For tonight." She looked at him apologetically. "I was hoping your father would be back by now."

Cohl clenched his teeth. She wasn't blaming him but that didn't make him feel any better.

"So what's the problem?"

Adehla sighed deeply. "It seems you were spotted in the city. No doubt during your Grid BaStun match."

Cohl grimaced. "No doubt."

"As you know, word travels fast on Caldara." She hesitated. "They think you are back to stay."

He looked at her elegant profile. "I'm here to save my father."

She nodded. "I know that and I'll deal with the repercussions after you leave. But unless you want speculation as to your true reason for being here, you will need to make an appearance at the festivities."

She was right. If he didn't show up, rumors would abound. Someone might even put it all together. Someone like Logen.

"I'll be there."

She didn't rise. "With Tess."

He looked at her sharply. "No."

Adehla turned to him. "They don't know her real reason for being here either."

Cohl eyed her. "Who did you say she is?"

She smiled at him with mild amusement. "*They* think she is your mate. I did not deny it. The people were quite taken with her. They think she'll make a fine queen someday."

His jaw dropped. Oh, Tess was going to love this.

Adehla patted his hand once more before standing.

"She will have to attend, too. I'll tell her. I assume you will see to the necessary security precautions?"

Cohl nodded. "Yes." He couldn't trust Mil-Ops until he'd had a chance to check out Logen's allegation.

Adehla got to the door before turning to face him. "I suggest you work on your courtship skills before this evening." She gave him a knowing look and disappeared into the corridor.

Cohl stared at his empty doorway, waiting for the next disaster to strike. It came in the form of Pitz. The robot glided into the room and stopped in front of him.

"We have a problem, sir."

Cohl hung his aching head. His arm had begun throbbing also. A duo of pain. "So what's new?"

"There's been a death threat against your mother."

The hair on the back of Cohl's neck stood up. He swung his gaze up to Pitz.

"My mother? Any explanation? Anyone claiming responsibility?"

Pitz answered, "Your mother, yes. Explanation, no. Responsibility, no."

Cohl shook his head. "I can't see anyone on the planet wanting her dead except . . ." *Logen.* God, how Cohl hated that name. "Does she know?"

"No, sir. I received notification and proceeded directly here."

"I want you to guard her tonight, Pitz. Keep a low profile." Pitz clicked acknowledgment. "And Tess?"

"I'll take care of Tess. She won't be out of my sight this evening." He hoped. Who knew what kind of reception she'd give him now?

"One more thing, Pitz. Logen said his information on Tess came from Mil-Ops. I want you to check out every guard who has access to this residence. Look for some connection to the Traka-Nor. I have a distinct feeling that this leak about Tess has something to do with my father's abduction."

Cohl sighed. "And I suppose it would be too much to ask for *Speculator* to be ready any time soon."

"Repairs will be completed by tomorrow morning," Pitz responded.

"First good news I've had all day," Cohl mumbled. "Be ready to leave early."

"Yes, sir." Pitz spun and whirred toward the door.

Cohl called after him with some trepidation, "Is anyone else waiting outside my door?"

Pitz checked the corridor. "No, sir."

Cohl muttered, "Good. I've had about all the company I can handle today."

The moons were linked tonight, big red riding pale yellow like shameless lovers before an audience of millions. Tess gazed up at them from her wide bedroom balcony over-looking the courtyard, feeling like an intruder, an outsider. Alone.

The breeze kicked up, bringing with it the sweet caress of fragrance. She couldn't deny that Yre Gault was beautiful. She breathed it in deep and strong, building a memory. As long as she lived, whenever she smelled perfume she would remember this place.

But she missed her own moon and fireflies that danced on hot summer nights. She missed her cat snuggled at her feet in a bed where she was safe and understood her world.

And today she had missed yet another gig. A few more of them and the jobs would stop coming. The damage to her career would be irreparable. Poor Bill was probably sucking down Maalox by the gallon by now. Even if she survived this crazy mission and got back to Earth, how could he ever trust her again?

She should be furious with Cohl for doing this to her but it was hard to hate a man who apologized so well, who meant so much to her. Too much.

"Cosmic coupling."

The deep voice came from behind her. She turned to him and inhaled sharply. Cohl walked toward her with military precision, looking every inch a prince.

The black boots rose to his knees where ivory fitted pants took over, hugging his slim hips. A shimmering, midnight-blue cape was slung over one shoulder of a deep gold jacket. The cape swirled around his legs as he strode across the balcony from the ballroom. His face was dark in the moonlight, unreadable and distant.

He stopped at the railing next to her, locked his hands behind his back, and gazed up at the moons. "Cosmic coupling is what the locals call the moon position. It only happens once every eighty-eight days. Some people take it as a decree to follow suit. Probably why our population continues to grow at such a balanced rate."

She blinked at him. Was that a joke or a social commentary? He sounded so serious, she couldn't tell. Was it the clothes that gave him that untouchable quality? Gone was the man with the warm eyes, killer smile, and dry humor. In his place stood someone reserved, unreachable, guarded. A stranger.

When she didn't respond, he looked at her with tired eyes that lacked their golden luster. Eyes that hid everything—all emotion, all joy, all that she wanted to see. Then he dropped his gaze to her dress and she saw the light flash for a split second. He was in there, after all.

"You look beautiful, Tess," he said softly.

She had to look away, somewhere else other than the growing intensity of his gaze. She glanced down at the dress and ran her fingers through the long, flowing ribbons of green iridescent fabric that wrapped around her waist and fanned out to her ankles. It made her feel like a Greek goddess.

"Your mother was kind enough to let me borrow it. I've never worn anything like this before. My wardrobe consists mostly of denim."

She gazed back up at him, hoping the intensity had waned. It hadn't. He looked at her as if she were the only woman on Yre Gault.

"You are my mate tonight." The way he said it made her tremble. His *mate*. *Wife*. Adehla had told her the scenario for the evening, the story to be told to the guests.

She realized for the first time since she'd started this little adventure that she was truly nervous. Tonight she would be more than his mate. She was impersonating royalty. No matter how hard she tried, she doubted she'd fool a single soul there.

"Yes. I'm not sure what that entails," she said, unable to take her eyes off his. Her eyes widened when she realized the implications of what she'd said. "I mean, from a hostess standpoint."

An amused smile crossed his face. "We greet guests. We mingle. We smile. We dance."

Tess blew out a breath in relief. "I can do that." Then she did a double take. "Dancing? I didn't think you approved of that nonsense." She batted her eyelashes.

"I don't. It's just another part of the job." He hesitated, his eyes darkening as he smiled. "On the other hand, it does have its moments."

He reached out and pulled her easily into his arms without asking. The dress swept around her as he locked his fingers in hers.

"I'll teach you how we do it here. Follow me," he murmured in her ear. Then he lowered his head to hers and moved to a silent beat. She closed her eyes and let her body hear his song. It was there, slow and sensual, for her alone. In big, sweeping circles he guided her around the balcony—a spin, a turn, a dip. This was heaven, locked in Cohl's arms, dancing to his private rhythm. As they glided, his cape entwined with her dress, a sensual ebb and flow.

He smiled down at her as they continued a simple waltz. "You're a natural. Where did you learn to dance?"

Tess shook her head as the spell broke and old memories flooded back. "Aunt Germaine's living room with all my cousins." Then she chuckled. "We'd play the music horribly loud and dance our hearts out, stepping on each other's toes and laughing until we cried."

Cohl led her through a wide turn. "Sounds like a fun way to learn."

"Fun but destructive. Poor Aunt Germaine. Her house was always full of kids with runny noses and wet mittens. It was perfect chaos."

She looked at Cohl, who was grinning along with her. "Where did you learn?"

His smile slipped into oblivion. "I had professional instruction every fourth day until I was sixteen. All part of the training."

The statement was so cool, she could almost see his breath. Dancing was *training*? No wonder he didn't like it.

"No cousins?"

He shook his head. "No family besides my parents. Apparently my parents didn't do much moon-gazing."

She frowned. "Are one-child families common on Yre Gault?"

"No."

There was resignation and careful control in that one word. She'd heard that tone before, every time she got too close.

"So." She cleared her throat. "Greet, mingle, dance. Anything else?"

He halted in the middle of the balcony and looked down at her. She nearly tumbled over him. When she looked up, all she could see were his golden eyes, deep and rich with desire and promise.

"There is one other thing," he said as he lifted her chin and brushed his lips against hers. "And this part is very important."

His kiss deepened and Tess leaned into him. He pulled her close, her dress fluttering around both of them, bodies pressed. She felt his hand slide up and bury itself into her hair as he rolled the strands between his fingers. His mouth caressed hers, firm but gentle. It was a real kiss, not frantic like the first one. Sweet and smooth, just the way she'd imagined it would be.

She let him seep into her senses, making her strong, leaving her weak. He had the power to make her want to forget so much with one kiss. A kiss destined to be nothing but a memory in time. This wasn't real, wasn't meant to last. She already had a home, a perfectly good home. His tongue ran tenderly across her lips and she gave a little moan. If only she could remember what her home looked like.

He lifted his head and looked at her with such steamy intensity, her knees nearly buckled.

"I think we have that down," she whispered as she clutched at his arms, trying to find her land legs again. He was drowning her.

He chuckled. "It's important to give a convincing performance."

Cohl lowered his head again and felt her small hand on

his chest, but she wasn't fighting him. He just needed one more kiss to satisfy the hunger. When her kiss answered his, he took it, pulling her into his wondrous banquet. There was no urgency, no hurry to finish the meal. He wanted to savor her taste, her scent.

An ache started in the center of his chest that had nothing to do with his injuries. He didn't want to scare her off. The need to touch her was too great to risk it. She tasted sweet, spicy, hot. A feast for a starving man.

This time he wasn't feasting alone.

This time she was with him—right up until he felt the half sob that shook her body. He held her away and stared at the raw fear in her green eyes.

He frowned. "Tess?"

She stepped back, shaking her head. "I can't stay," she said in a hushed voice and then ran inside, her gown flowing wildly out around her.

He exhaled hard. Well, that was a mistake. She had him hot and hard inside his royal uniform, a first for him and the suit, but that was still no excuse. His mother was right. His courtship skills *were* lousy.

His hands flexed absently. Itchy hands. He couldn't help it. He wanted her, wanted her out of that dress and into his bed. He shook his head. No, more than his bed. Into his life with all that energy and heart and courage she carried around with her. But he had nothing to offer, no right to take her, no right to even tempt her. About a thousand light years-away, she had a whole life waiting for her that didn't include him.

He straightened his shoulders and made a firm, if not painful pact: after this evening, he wouldn't touch her again for the rest of the mission. Even if it killed him. For tonight, she was his and that would have to be enough.

He glanced up at the moons, locked in an intimate embrace. At least someone was enjoying the evening. *What's your secret, pal?*

From the other side of the palace, he heard the band begin a slow, subdued tune. They were waiting for him. He exited the balcony and proceeded toward his duty, ignoring the throb in his injured arm, the headache that came from Aritrox, the fatigue that gnawed at him. They would disappear in time.

That throb in his chest was another matter.

Tess was living a dream. It had to be a dream because reality could never come close to this.

Music filled the enchanted circular ballroom with its towering cathedral ceilings and lavish decor. The walls gleamed with ivory and stone, carved and cut and engraved with reliefs so numerous that no amount of contemplation could do them justice. Animals, scenes, and figures from the far corners of the creator's imagination stretched and spanned the walls from floor to ceiling. Frozen eyes gazed down on an equally unusual menagerie of guests—a living, moving collage of faces and laughter, music and costume.

But it was the ceiling high above that kept her eyes skyward. Like a great fresco, a kaleidoscope chandelier of crystal rods hung down until they culminated toward the center in a fantastic crescendo of brilliant gemlike colors.

Her dance partner, Limpert Val Dees, swept her around in a tight circle. A tall, portly man squeezed into a too-small red and yellow jacket, he reminded her of her uncle Frank: loud, jovial, and a practiced winker. Tess could only smile.

Adehla's event was a whirlwind carnival for the senses, a fairy tale complete with a prince. Tess glanced around. From across the room, Cohl's eyes met hers instantly as she knew they would. Her heart took a powerful lurch. Must be his formal uniform that strung her tight every time she locked eyes with him, leaving her breathless and restless.

She could still taste him on her lips. His kiss on the balcony had surprised her with its honesty and beauty. She wouldn't have believed it possible that a kiss could hurt. Even more of a surprise was how deeply she could be pulled into it, how much she wanted it . . . and more. And all she could do was run away—probably a first in her life, a pure survival reaction. She'd had no choice. Those kisses were striking dangerously close to her heart.

"Where are you from, my dear?" Limpert asked, his face flushed and red from the exertion of the last three dances.

Tess answered smoothly, "Abroad. How about you?"

His brown, large eyes twinkled. "A divine little province here on Yre Gault called Muro Cardenas." He winked for the tenth time. "You should really visit us. A wonderful place to kick off a new union."

She nearly lost a step. "Thank you. I'll be sure to mention it to Cohl." The song finally ended and she prayed for some relief from the overly kind, dance-deprived Limpert.

Before she could fumble through an awkward exit, Cohl was at her elbow. He nodded to Limpert as if dismissing him from duty. The elder man gave Tess one last wink before lumbering off into the crowd.

"You looked like you needed rescuing." His voice was low and amused as he led her easily into the next dance.

Tess narrowed her eyes. "I think you enjoy watching me squirm."

He grinned. "I don't get many chances."

She wrinkled her nose and made a face.

He laughed and then raised an eyebrow. The other dancers had cleared a circle around them and all eyes were upon the prince and his new mate dancing. His mood sank. Duty called once again. He wanted to apologize to Tess for dragging her into his commitment. But she was gazing up at him with a look that could keep him dancing forever, all smiles, as if she was actually enjoying this charade.

Around the small area, they spun, eyes locked. He'd always hated these events, but she'd made tonight more bearable. Somehow she'd changed obligation into a pleasure. Even dancing.

As the song wound down, Cohl drew her to a halt. Her lips parted as he bent down and kissed her lightly. Outside their intimate little world, the crowd clapped approval. When he pulled back, Tess was smiling at him like a glowing light, drawing out all the colors in the room. He held on to her tightly, obligation forgotten, not wanting the spell she'd cast over him to break. She'd turned the night all around. For the first time ever in his life, he knew this evening would end too quickly.

All eyes turned as the bandleader raised a hand and waved Tess forward. Cohl caught her arm before she could head for the stage.

"What are you doing?" he whispered.

She looked at his hand on her arm and then up at him. "I'm going to sing. I practiced a few numbers with the band while you were sleeping."

He frowned. "You're an easy target alone onstage."

Tess waved him off. "Don't be silly. What can possibly happen here?"

She freed her arm and made her way toward the stage while the bandleader introduced her to the crowd. Cohl watched her ascend the stage and greet her clapping audience with the composure of a born performer. Poised, alive, and happy.

The song opened. Tess closed her eyes and moved to the slow, seductive beat, her green and gold dress flowing out and back in rhythm. Clear and pure as a starry night, her voice carried across the room. The audience drew a collective, silent gasp at a voice so true.

He watched with singular concentration as if trying to burn her into his memory forever. Who was he kidding? He *was* trying to burn her into his memory. In a short time, it would be all he had left of her. Nothing he had to offer could replace her dream. She would never want the solitary life he'd chosen for himself. It would kill her spirit.

Out of the corner of his eye, Cohl noticed Pitz entering the ballroom. A bad sign since Pitz normally steered well clear of celebrations. Cohl walked through the crowd and met him just inside the entrance.

"What's wrong, Pitz?"

The robot used a low voice reserved for confidentiality. "Sir, we have received another threat against your mother."

Cohl glanced across the room to where his mother was watching Tess's performance.

"Follow me," Cohl said as he led Pitz out to the corridor away from the celebration.

Once they were alone, Pitz held out an object in his mechanical hand. "We found this on her bed."

Cohl took one look at it and swore. "A blast device. On her bed. How the hell did someone get in her room?"

"Unknown," Pitz responded. "All guards have been accounted for and every guest was cleared for weapons. The device failed detection at all checkpoints around the palace. I have no explanation at this time."

Cohl stared at the device. "Pitz, I want you to stay close to my mother for the rest of the evening. Keep all your weapon detection sensors on wide-band scan. Remain outside her door and monitor her room all night. Notify me if anything happens."

"Yes, sir."

Cohl watched him slide silently into the ballroom toward his mother's position. He rubbed his forehead where that Aritrox headache wouldn't give up. Just what he needed. Some lunatic on the inside. Someone who knew his father was missing and was coming after the throne. The logical target would be his mother.

Although he hated to leave Pitz behind on Yre Gault, someone had to protect her. There was a systematic order of succession if the queen left for any reason, but the questions and concerns would rock the planet. Cohl didn't want to think how easy it would be for some latent power to step in. Logen's face flashed in his mind. No, Pitz must stay here with his mother.

Tess's voice sliced sweetly through his thoughts, seducing him back into the ballroom. He made his way through the crowd to the platform stairs. Alone on the stage, she sang a slow, haunting song about love and hope and dreams. Her words flowed and leaped, finely crafted like a priceless work of art. A man could lose himself in that voice, gladly and forever.

After her set, Cohl met her at the bottom of the stairs and drew her out to a side balcony before she could be overwhelmed by her newly won fans.

She looked up at him with that brilliant light in her green eyes, the light that only singing could turn on.

He stood before her, unsure where to put his hands, uncertain what to say. The pact: no touching, no kissing, no tempting. And for God's sake, don't look at those damn moons.

"I don't think I've ever told you how beautiful your voice is, Tess. You've captivated my people."

She gave him a brilliant smile that matched her eyes. "They're an easy crowd."

Cohl nodded and laughed. "Just don't teach them that stupid chicken dance."

There was silence. He glanced at her enlightened expression and knew he'd made a major blunder.

"What a great idea," she said with reverence.

He frowned. "It was a joke. Forget it. You aren't doing it."

She put her hands on her hips. "Why not? I think they'd enjoy cutting loose a little." She leaned toward him and whispered, "You must admit they are a rather stuffy bunch."

"I won't have you making fools of *my people*."

She folded her arms. He recognized it as a battle stance. "They aren't *your people*. You don't want them, remember?"

He narrowed his eyes in warning.

She didn't take a hint well. "I'm getting tired of you ignoring me whenever you feel so inclined, Cohl. So for once, answer the question. Are they your people or not?"

He couldn't help wondering when exactly he'd lost control of the conversation. "My obligation to Yre Gault is none of your business, Tess. Stay out of it."

Her green eyes flared. "I can't. You are the only one who doesn't see it. The reality of the situation is that they need you."

He took a step toward her. "Do you want to know what reality is? It's working twenty-six-hour days, every day, for Yre Gault. You need a break? Too bad. Your schedule is booked months and years in advance. That's reality, Tess."

"Your parents need you," she shot back.

"It's their life and their choice, not mine. I didn't ask to be born into this."

She didn't back down. "No one can choose their life, Cohl. We all have to play the hand we are dealt."

"Just because I was born into the job, Tess, does not make me the best choice. Based on your own ancient history, you should know that. How many dynasties on Earth were wiped out by a poor ruler?"

She blinked at him, clearly stunned. "You would never do that."

He ran a hand through his hair. "Not on purpose, but all it would take is one or two bad decisions." He pointed toward the ballroom. "Every single one of their lives would be my responsibility. Think you could sleep at night with that?"

She stepped forward. "How do you think I feel? If I screw up that song, I die and I take your father and your planet with me." She waved a hand toward the crowd. "And I don't even know those people."

Cohl froze as her words echoed against the outer walls like the guilt that bounced around inside him. She was scared but she still was willing to help him. His heart started to ache again.

"You won't be alone, Tess. I'll be right beside you."

She shook her head hard. "Don't do that. Don't change the subject. Fight with me, fight for Yre Gault. This is your home. No one will care about it the way you do. No one would fight for it like you would. Whether or not you believe it, you belong here."

Her expression was so beautiful, caring. The next sentence slipped out before he could stop it. "And where do you belong, Tess?"

Long seconds ticked by as they stared at each other. He could see the uncertainty in her eyes, the battle waging that he wasn't a part of, a personal hell much like his own.

"Onstage," she finally said. "I belong onstage. I promised them another set." She walked away, leaving him standing under the moons.

Tess pounded the pillow and flopped back on it again. The dual moons gave her bedroom a ghostly glow. But that wasn't the reason for the restlessness she felt. The exhilaration of singing again had awakened her. The performance had gone smoothly, the crowd loved her, and she had never felt better on stage. Just a little taste of her long-delayed dream had brought back all the thrill she remembered, along with the frustrations of the past eight years. Time was slipping away from her, day by relentless, merciless day.

She stared at the ceiling, trying to sort it all through—her dream, Cohl's father, Yre Gault. Earth was so far away and the dream with it. Last week everything seemed so clear but Cohl's last question haunted her. Where did she belong? No answer came to mind—a very bad sign.

They had made a great team tonight, greeting, mingling, and dancing. He'd been a true prince and made her feel like a princess, like she could almost pull it off. She remembered the way he kept her by his side, whispered little bits of gossip in her ear as she tried not to giggle, looked at her as if she were the only woman alive. Special.

Little, sweet words sang in the back of her mind. *You're falling.*

Tess swallowed hard. Good Lord. What kind of fool falls in love with an alien? *For Pete's sake, he's from another planet.*

She gave a little laugh at the idea of a man like him on Earth. No, he wouldn't be playing horseshoes with Uncle Frank or hiking in the Adirondacks or bouncing their children on his knee. Earth wasn't big enough for him.

Besides, he only wanted her for her voice. She sobered. When his mission was over, she'd be nothing more than a blurb in Yre Gault's history books, if at all. Meanwhile, her *real* life, the one she was supposed to be in right now, was falling apart on an hourly basis. All this because she didn't know how to say no. *No, I can't help you. No, I have to go home now. No, stop killing me with kisses.*

Falling in love with an alien. It wouldn't be the stupidest thing she'd ever done, but it would be close.

"I'm so confused," she whispered in the dark.

A faint click next to her bed startled her to a sitting position, clutching the sheets to her chest. She exhaled in relief when she saw who it was.

"Pitz, you scared the life out of me. Is something wrong?"

There was no reply. Tess peered at the robot positioned at the foot of her bed. "Pitz?"

A short arm emerged sporting a laser light that she had seen only once before—back on Earth. Her breath froze in terror. She raised her hand toward him. "Pitz, no!"

There was a burst of light; then everything faded to black.

Chapter Nine

"Sir, wake up."

Pitz's voice interrupted what was promising to be a prize dream with a beautiful woman who looked suspiciously like Tess in a big bed. The dream burst like a bubble as *trouble* screamed in Cohl's head.

He shot up in bed and squinted at Pitz in the dark. "What's wrong? Did something happen to my mother?"

Pitz illuminated the room with a soft light. "Not your mother, sir. Tess. You need to come with me immediately."

Cohl was already tossing the covers aside and pulling on a pair of pants. "What is it?"

"She is mobile."

He shrugged on a shirt and slipped the laser gun holster over it. "What do you mean? In the courtyard again?"

"No, sir. She is flying." Pitz disappeared out the door.

Cohl yanked on his boots and took off after Pitz's shadow down the corridor. The robot was already well ahead of him

Cohl caught up with him as they cleared the first checkpoint, where a surprised guard waved them on.

"Explain, Pitz," Cohl barked. He took the steps two at a time as they descended to the palace's ground level.

Pitz complied. "Four minutes ago, she left her room out through the balcony, rose straight up two levels, skimmed over the roof, descended the outer wall of the palace, and is making her way through the city."

Cohl waved off the next checkpoint guard. "Tess can't fly, Pitz."

"I realize flying is outside her physical abilities. Obviously she is with someone who can." Pitz activated the outside gates and fresh night air filled Cohl's lungs.

"A shuttle is waiting," Pitz said as he sped toward the parked ground transportation. Cohl followed and jumped into the passenger side beside him. Seconds later, Pitz was guiding the shuttle out of the palace, across the wide avenue, into the city. The moons lit up the symmetrical streets in a stark, ashen glow.

"How do you know her course?" Cohl asked, watching for any sign of Tess ahead of them. Occasional lights shone from a late-night shuttle but otherwise the streets were empty and eerie.

"I mapped her molecular pattern into my scanners but my detection range is only two hundred and forty meters."

"Then move."

Pitz executed a hairpin turn down a pitch-black alley, the sides of the shuttle sparking off the walls with a hair-raising screech. They turned down another street and Cohl peered into the alleys they crossed. Where was she? And who had her? Tess would never leave on her own like this. She knew better. Someone had taken her. Fear built in his belly, the kind he always felt when a situation was out of his control.

"How about some theories, Pitz? A ship would have been too big to maneuver that close to the palace, so that's out.

She couldn't fly out unless she was wearing a flight suit. Even if she did, she wouldn't know how to use it. And I personally modified the palace's scanners to pick up any unauthorized intruders on the grounds anywhere, including her room."

They drove past the corner where Tess had sung with the street band.

"Human intruders."

Cohl frowned and turned back to Pitz. "Of course, human intruders."

"But not mechanical devices." Pitz slowed as they approached an intersection.

"Are you suggesting that Tess was abducted by a machine?"

Pitz stopped the shuttle at the corner.

"Yes, sir. That is precisely what I am suggesting. It is also a strong probability that this is the manner in which your father was successfully abducted."

Pitz projected an arm toward the house in front of them. "She is inside the residence of Logen Du Vaul."

Breath hissed through Cohl's teeth. *Logen has Tess.*

Cohl surveyed the three levels of the darkened structure. "Where exactly?"

"On the second level and moving up."

Cohl's gaze was drawn up. "Damn it. Tell me that's not a landing pad on that roof."

"Affirmative. I am also picking up the engine noise of a transport jet in the vicinity."

Cohl hopped out of the shuttle, crossed the intersection, and stopped directly in front of Logen's house. He examined the three stories of smooth, polished exterior. No way could he scale those walls. Going through the house would take too long and who knows how many people he'd run into? Only one option left.

"I know it's pushing your limits, Pitz, but can you get me up there?"

Pitz answered from behind him. "There is a forty percent chance that I will lose the necessary velocity to take you safely to the top. There is a one hundred percent chance that you will suffer serious injury if I do not."

"I've survived worse odds."

Cohl swung around and stepped onto Pitz's back, hooking one arm around the robot's head. He drew his laser gun from its holster with his free hand. "Let's go."

Pitz shuddered slightly as he lifted off the ground. Cohl kept his eyes on the goal of the roofline and off the walkway sliding away below him. He was more worried about Tess's odds than his own.

Cool night air rushed through his hair as Pitz gained momentum. Twenty meters, ten, five—the roofline was nearly within reach when Pitz's thrusters strained and whined. With a lunge, Cohl shoved off the robot and gripped the roof edge just as Pitz lost all momentum. He transferred his weight to the lip of the roof and pulled himself over, rolling flat with his pistol out.

The back end of a large transport jet sat about fifty meters away in the center of the roof area, a square shadow blocking out the starry sky. Cohl could feel the vibration of the engines through his belly. It was primed for takeoff.

Without Cohl's extra weight, Pitz stabilized and hovered easily just below the roofline behind Cohl.

"Craft analysis, Pitz," Cohl asked with a voiceless whisper.

Pitz hummed for a few seconds. "Model M22, short-range transport. Maximum crew capacity of eight. Four laser guns, burster torpedoes—"

"That's enough. I get the picture," Cohl interrupted. "Can you scan for crew members from here?"

"Four life readings. Tess is not one of them."

"Then where is she?" he whispered toward Pitz.

Suddenly the door to the roof slid open, revealing the

silhouette of a robot—a robot that looked exactly like Pitz. Cohl sucked in a breath.

No wonder no one had stopped him. It was the perfect cover: a nonhuman that could evade traditional sensors, inconspicuous in a house full of robots, capable of flight, programmable to carry out any task solo and under Logen's control. Why hadn't he thought of that before?

The Pitz-clone hovered toward the landing pad, carrying a small, limp body wrapped in a blanket across his metal arms. *Tess.*

The robot disappeared into the side hatch of the waiting transport. Cohl's teeth clenched against the urge to run after her. He couldn't very well attack while the robot had her in its arms.

"Is she alive?" Cohl asked in Pitz's direction.

Pitz answered, "Yes, but I cannot determine her exact state of health. However, I have found her to be exceptionally sturdy for a human."

Cohl nodded. He was counting on that. Desperately. "Can you incapacitate the transport?"

Pitz clicked softly, processing the variables. "Not without posing an unacceptable risk to Tess."

Cohl swore. It was to be a night of limited options. The transport's thrusters kicked up to high speed. Time was up.

"Get me inside."

"Sir?"

"A ship that size must have a cargo hold. Get me in it."

"Cargo holds are not meant for humans. The temperature is not regulated—"

Cohl cut him off with a hiss. "Just do it. Let me worry about freezing to death."

Pitz shut down his lights and ascended fully above the roofline. His black shadow slid in front of Cohl.

"Follow me," the robot ordered on low volume.

Cohl crouched behind him and they made their way silently toward the rear of the ship where the cargo hold was located. Pitz was disabling the hold's external locking mechanism when a lone figure appeared through the entrance to the roof. Cohl froze against the transport as did Pitz. Unaware of company, the shadow limped across the roof and disappeared inside the transport.

Cohl ground his teeth. Even with the limp, he'd recognize that cocky walk anywhere.

"Now, Pitz. Get me in now."

Cohl heard the pop of the rear cargo door latch. A second later, he was wedged between a stack of canisters and Pitz's hard metal body. The door slid shut and locked.

"What are you doing in here? I need you to stay on Yre Gault," Cohl snapped.

Pitz's lights came back on, illuminating the cramped quarters. "Cargo holds do not replenish oxygen. I carry oxygen."

Cohl opened his mouth to object, then closed it. As always, Pitz was right. A minor detail he had forgotten about.

"Thanks," he muttered. So much for Pitz protecting his mother. Nothing was going right tonight.

The transport lifted off, and then everything in the cargo hold shifted as the craft lurched forward into Yre Gault's atmosphere. Cohl dropped his head back against the wall. They were on their way. He only wished he knew where the hell that was.

He ran a hand through his hair. He'd failed Tess miserably, should have watched her more closely, stayed with her. How could he have allowed this to happen to the only woman he could think about?

Somewhere along the line, she'd become more than just the key to his father's safe return. Somewhere along the line, she'd become *his*. And he needed her back.

Now Logen had her. Cohl clenched his fists, wanting more than anything to pound on the thin wall that separated them.

He wanted to shout that he was here, that he'd do whatever it took to save her.

As for Logen, he was a dead man.

"Is it clear yet?" Cohl shivered in the cargo hold while Pitz's lights activated at full capacity, scanning the area around the transport.

He was cold, worried, and stiff and he wanted out. They had touched down somewhere over fifteen minutes ago. What was taking so long?

"All transport occupants have departed. The immediate area is clear of any life signs. I do not detect any artificial intelligence devices more sophisticated than a hover pallet."

Cohl repositioned his legs in the cramped quarters to reach his laser pistol and groaned. "Good. Let's get out of here before I get stuck in this position forever."

Pitz opened the cargo hold hatch and exited first, scanning the vicinity, weapons ready. Cohl climbed out behind him into a warm shuttle bay and crouched behind Pitz. The heat felt good after two hours warmed only by Pitz's circuitry but the first breath in almost gagged him.

"What the hell is that stench?" he spat out.

Pitz held his position in front of Cohl. "I register no dangerous emissions. As you know, I have no olfactory sensors."

Cohl shook off the wave of nausea that rolled through him. "Consider yourself lucky."

He surveyed the shuttle bay. It was a big one, a bad sign. Big shuttle bays were generally reserved for even bigger places and lots of people. He glanced around and found the massive shuttle bay doors, the decompression controls, the containers of environment suits. They had landed on a starship.

The dirt-mottled floors were littered with refuse. He heard a shuffling sound and drew his weapon around in time to catch the furry tail of a ship scurgie diving into the debris.

Cohl shuddered involuntarily. He hated those disgusting things.

Storage containers were stacked haphazardly around the perimeter. Drawers and cabinets lay half opened, their contents stuffed hastily inside. The entire ship appeared to be in general disrepair and neglect.

Cohl scanned the signs on the walls and whispered to Pitz, "What's the language?"

"Either Traka-Sou or Traka-Nor," Pitz responded. "They speak the same language."

Cohl swore at length. Logen and the Trakas. It was starting to make sense. He spotted a system terminal across the bay on the wall and pointed to it. "I'll cover you, Pitz. Plug in and see who owns this lovely vessel."

Pitz hovered to the terminal and hooked up while Cohl kept watch. After a few seconds, the robot began reciting vital statistics. "Traka-Nor ship. Skeleton crew of sixty-six men aboard at present."

Cohl frowned. What the hell? Why would the Traka-Nor want Tess? She was supposed to be getting them the amulet.

Pitz continued. "The ship is scheduled to jump to hyperspace in thirty-nine minutes and ten seconds. Heading: Trakas."

He stared at Pitz in disbelief. This was getting stranger by the minute. He shook his head. He'd deal with all that later. First things first. Thirty-nine minutes and counting. Not much time. Interrupting a hyperspace jump was a tricky and dangerous proposition he'd rather avoid. That meant they had to move fast.

"Can you locate Tess?"

Pitz clicked for several seconds, then answered, "Level two, confinement cell."

Cohl blew out a breath. A confinement cell, not the med center, not the morgue. She was alive. And knowing her, she was probably tossing the room by now.

"Give me a quick rundown of the ship's layout," Cohl told Pitz.

Pitz activated the wall monitor and brought up the ship diagram. It was triangle-shaped with the bridge at the point and the rest of the ship filling the triangle back to the other two corners. They were currently situated at the rear of the vessel in the shuttle bay section.

Pitz narrated as the monitor flashed several different perspectives. "The ship is angular in shape and three levels deep. Each level contains a main open walkway running along the entire right side of the ship. Lifts between levels are spaced every fifty meters."

Cohl pointed at the empty space to the immediate right of the main walkway. "Is this an open atrium?"

"Yes." Pitz brought up a cross section of the ship that showed the three levels clearly. "The three walkways are step-tiered, one above the other, so it is possible to see all occupants on each level."

Cohl put his hands on his hips. "Good for visibility. Lousy for sneaking around."

"Precisely." Pitz isolated a floor section on level two. "All secondary corridors extend in the same direction off the main walkway on each level, running the full width of the ship."

He elongated a metal arm and pointed to one cell at the very end of the center corridor, midway between the bridge and their current position. "Tess is here."

Cohl memorized the schematic, building a matrix in his mind for future use, complete with exits, entry points, and lift positions. This ability was a gift that had kept him alive many times. He locked in the most direct route to Tess's cell as well as any alternates. There weren't any. Every secondary corridor had one way in and one way out. A long, exposed gauntlet. And he thought adventuring was dangerous.

He glanced down at his lone laser pistol. Next priority:

weapons. Can't have a rescue without some protection, especially when you are outnumbered sixty-six to two.

"I'm going to need more firepower, Pitz. Can you locate a weapons cache?"

The screen flashed a blur of floor plans until Pitz settled on one. "Twenty meters from here. Off the main walkway."

Cohl shook his head. "*Everything* in this ship is off that main walkway. Lead the way. Let's see if we can make it twenty meters on this death trap without getting killed."

With a nauseous lunge, Tess came to in a strange place knowing she was naked and not alone. Instinctively she curled back up into a fetal position on the hard bed and nearly vomited from the suffocating, putrid odor. Pain seared across her brain in all directions at once, suffocating and paralyzing her. Thoughts flipped by like pages in a book, refusing to mesh and hold together. But fear outweighed pain as she forced her eyes open and blinked at a giant man standing alone on the other side of the small cell.

He sported a lecherous smirk while his bloodshot eyes traveled over her body. She trembled and curled up tighter into herself, trying desperately to hide her nudity from this monster in front of her.

The giant said something in a voice that was thick with domination and cruelty. She recoiled as the booming voice ricocheted in her head like thunder. The language was unrecognizable so she tried to interpret what he was saying from his mannerisms. The exercise proved revolting.

Dark hair of indistinct color clumped and stuck to his filthy, unshaven face. A massive forehead hung over dark-circled eyes and a broad, flat nose. Around his neck was a necklace of small dark objects that looked vaguely like body parts. His clothes were a mass of dingy rags wrapped and tucked around his massive body. A stained cape of layered animal furs swept forward as he took a terrifying step toward her.

She realized that the repulsive smell was emanating from him and closed her eyes at the overwhelming stench when he stopped just short of her. Bile crept up in her throat.

He barked something else at her, obviously dissatisfied with her lack of response. Pain rammed through her head again. Even if she had the strength to tell him to go to hell, it would only piss him off and she couldn't lift a finger to protect herself.

A low, insistent beep interrupted another verbal barrage. He slapped at a pin on his cape. A male voice jabbered on the other end. Tess heard the filthy giant snarl and felt the breeze of his cape as he swirled around and left the room through the only door.

She swallowed another surge of bile, buried her face in the cold bed pad and let out a sob.

Cohl. Where are you?

"What is your plan, sir?" Pitz asked from his lookout position at the closed doorway to the weapons room.

Cohl clipped another flash-concussion charge to his weapons belt. "Plan? We find Tess and get her out of this hellhole."

Pitz clicked softly. "Interesting plan, sir. I assume you have a more precise breakdown?"

Cohl surveyed the dimly lit shelves of the weapons cache. "Nope." He grabbed a high-power laser rifle, slung it around his neck, and let it hang down his back. "You got one?"

Pitz answered as Cohl knew he would.

"I have been evaluating a list of possibilities and strategies based on the relative locations of crew personnel and the ship's capabilities, allowing for variables and ancillary obstacles."

Cohl stuffed a spare laser pistol down the back waistband of his pants. "Uh-huh."

"The odds of us escaping this ship in a transport without getting fired upon are extremely poor."

"You're right about that," Cohl agreed as he rifled through a box of detonators.

"Therefore, we will need to disable either the crew or the ship in order to make the two-hour journey back to Yre Gault safely."

Cohl nodded, distracted by a case of small, round metal balls he'd never seen before. He shrugged and shoved two of them into a shirt pocket.

Pitz continued. "It will be difficult to disable the entire ship. We would have to disarm the weapons system, the ship's onboard fighter jets, the propulsion system, the communications systems—"

Cohl interrupted. "Got it. So we take out the crew. Any ideas?"

"There are several ways to incapacitate the entire crew without destroying the ship or fighting each crew member one by one," Pitz offered.

"I'm all ears."

"Sir?"

"Just give me options, Pitz."

"Yes, sir. The ship has a gas-saturation capability. However, it is limited to certain sections of the ship and not all species are susceptible to the effects."

Cohl spotted a laser knife and slipped it into his boot. "Can't have that. Go on."

Pitz continued. "There is an armed distresser aboard. I could detonate it within the confines of the ship."

Cohl cast the robot an are-you-nuts? look. "Only one problem. Everyone aboard the ship would be dead including us. I don't think I like that option, Pitz."

Pitz ignored Cohl's obvious sarcasm. "The other possibility is an audio burst through the ship's main communication system. A scatter burst with a wide enough band could temporarily incapacitate every living being on board."

Cohl stopped in the process of attaching three full clips of prisoner restraints to his weapons belt and looked at Pitz. "Can you pull that off?"

"Of course but I can only execute the commands from the main board on the bridge."

Cohl swore. The bridge. All the way at the other end of the ship.

"Any other options?"

"No, sir."

Cohl nodded. "Then I'll take the third one. You'll have to go alone. I need to find Tess. We'll meet you back at the shuttle bay."

Pitz responded, "Understood. Sir?"

"Hmm?"

"You might want to procure two sets of ear protectors. It would be most helpful if you and Tess did not succumb to the audio bursts."

"Good thinking." Cohl searched around the room until he located the ear inserts and stuffed them in his top pocket.

Pitz stilled, his sensors scanning steadily. "I detect two crew members approaching."

"Shit." Cohl pulled out his weapon and crouched behind a canister where he could get a clear shot at the door. Pitz moved off to the side and dimmed his lights.

Belligerent voices drew closer until the door slid open. Two massive men entered and the door slid shut behind them. Their wrangling continued until they spied Pitz and reached for their weapons. Too late. Pitz shot the closest man at the same second that Cohl picked off the other. Both men crumpled to the floor. Two down. Sixty-four to go.

Cohl jumped out and dropped to his knees next to the first body. Immediately, he recoiled and grimaced. "God, not only do these guys stink, they're damn ugly too."

Fighting off repulsion, he searched the bodies and found weapons and their communications/security units. He sat back on his heels and looked at their ragged clothing. The animal skin capes were huge, hanging almost to the floor. He smiled.

First rule of sneaking around: use whatever is handy.

He rolled the first man out of his cape, tossed it over Pitz's shoulders, and yanked the hood over his robot head.

Pitz blinked furiously. "Sir?"

Cohl chuckled. "Just be grateful you can't smell. This is our cover, Pitz. Complete with comm-sec units. Let's hope they open some doors for us." Cohl stepped back and admired his handiwork. Except for the fact that there were no legs holding up the cape, Pitz looked passable.

Cohl heaved the second crewman out of his cape and put it on. The thing was bulky and heavy on his shoulders. It would slow him down. Hopefully, he wouldn't have to run much.

After they dragged the bodies behind some containers, Cohl pulled the hood over his head and headed for the door.

"Let's go, Pitz."

"What do you want, you idiot!" boomed Krahel as he strode onto the bridge.

Logen looked up from a systems station and growled at Rommol's ex-advisor. "I'm not one of your imbecilic giants, so back off."

Krahel approached him, his face gnarled and red. "I was about to interrogate the woman."

"I told you not to touch her," Logen snapped. "We need her alive and unharmed if we want that amulet."

Krahel grinned and fingered his necklace of human digits. "We only need part of her."

"Your sadistic hobbies are going to have to wait. We have

a problem." Logen turned back to the ship's system display. "We detected some movement in shuttle bay number six after we departed the transport."

Krahel stepped up to the display and grunted. "Scurgies."

"Must be damn big scurgies. I think we should check it out," Logen countered.

"Everything on this ship is big, Logen. You've been living with the gentry for too long. I'm the captain and I say it's scurgies," Krahel barked.

Logen narrowed his eyes at his partner and hissed low, "Don't tell me what to do. We are in this collusion *together*. That was the deal."

"I never agreed to let you run my ship," Krahel snarled. "Your job was to hand over old man Trae Salle to Rommol."

Logen drew himself up to his full height, bearing down on Krahel with no fear. "You know damn well what I mean. I'm the one who risked grabbing the woman. She will lead us to the amulet and the power it wields. Don't forget who is making it possible for you to take down Rommol."

A growl rolled through Krahel's throat. "More than Rommol. I want Gothyk, too. I want *all* of Trakas."

"And I want Yre Gault. *No one* is going to destroy my plan," Logen added pointedly.

Krahel snorted and dismissed him with a careless wave. "If you don't believe me, go check it out for yourself." Then he turned away and began laughing. "And make sure you bring your laser weapon. You might discover a whole band of fat, mutant, man-eating scurgies ready to take over the ship." He slapped his leg and roared with laughter at his own joke. The Traka-Nor bridge crew nodded and grunted at their captain's pleasure.

Logen glared at Krahel's back, then turned to his robot hovering behind him. "Come. Let's check out shuttle bay number six."

Chapter Ten

A small crew on a ship this size was a lucky break. Probably the only one he was going to get, Cohl thought wryly. He and Pitz had passed just two other crewmen on their journey down the main walkway. The ugly-twins were too busy arguing with each other to give him much more than a cursory grunt of acknowledgment. But just in case they noticed his clean face or Pitz's metal one, Cohl had his weapon drawn under his cloak.

The atrium was certainly impressive but no doubt unappreciated by the current crew. It ran from one end of the ship to the other for at least one hundred fifty meters and forty meters across from the inside walls to the outer hull with three stepped walkways extending out over the open space. At equal intervals along the outer hull side, massive round viewports displayed spectacular stars and planets. Cohl noted the ship was still stationary, not in hyperspace. Yet.

126

"How much time until the jump?" he barely whispered to Pitz.

Pitz's enhanced hearing picked it up. "Twelve minutes and forty-four seconds."

Cohl nodded. Time was going to be a problem.

From their position on level two, he cast a glance at the levels above and below them and frowned. The walkways lacked railings, so anyone below them could see that Pitz had no legs or feet.

"Pitz, stay between me and the inside wall. We don't want anyone looking up your cape," he whispered.

Pitz complied, moving a step behind Cohl as they continued their trek down the exposed walkway. Cohl checked each side corridor when they passed by. The ship was quiet. Quiet meant no alarms. Quiet meant no one knew they were aboard the ship. Another lucky break. He hoped they didn't use up all their luck too soon.

Tess's corridor was next. Cohl turned down it casually, then slowed to take in any activity. A stingy line of lights cast a dim path. Cohl knew the corridor dead-ended but he couldn't see it.

"Scanners, Pitz."

Pitz's scanners hummed. "There is one guard at the end of the corridor guarding Tess's cell. I also detect several life signs inside the other cells."

Cohl came to a halt. "How many and where?"

"Six crew. Stationary. They appear to be sleeping or resting. Two on the right side, four on the left."

Cohl nodded. "I'll take it from here. Proceed to the bridge. If you can't get to the main bridge console, then head back to the shuttle bay. We'll take our chances and blast out of here."

Pitz blinked. "It is more important that you escape with Tess. It does not matter if I am left behind. I am replaceable."

Cohl looked at his Protector, astonished at the robot's statement. Pitz was more than a crew member, more than a machine. He was family.

Cohl clapped the robot's metal shoulder. "Forget it, pal. We're a team. Get moving before someone spots us."

"Yes, sir." Pitz turned around and disappeared down the main walkway.

Cohl checked the charge on his pistol once more, then made his way down the long, dark corridor. The only movement was one small, flat servo-unit that whizzed along the floors in a futile attempt to clean the piles of filth and rubbish littering the halls.

The stench increased as Cohl ventured farther across the heart of the ship. He adopted the same sloppy gait as the Traka-Nor they'd met on the walkway, keeping a sharp ear out for any action.

As he drew near the dead end, he could make out the large mass of the guard propped against the corridor wall between him and Tess's door. He was a big bastard, but weren't they all? He pulled his hood down farther.

The guard looked up as Cohl lurched toward him. He called out a greeting, apparently mistaking Cohl for the former owner of the cape.

When Cohl didn't answer, the guard growled and abruptly raised his laser pistol. A split second later, Cohl pulled the trigger from under the cape. The laser blast burned a perfect hole through his cape and then through the guard's cape. As the man fell forward, Cohl caught him, grunting under the dead weight.

He cast a quick glance back down the length of the corridor. Confident that all was clear, he approached the door's activation field. It opened automatically for the guard's comm-sec unit and Cohl stepped inside, dragging the guard with him. He dumped the body on the floor.

Then he looked up and saw Tess. She was sitting naked

on a bunk, curled into a tight ball. She raised her head slowly at the sound of the door closing.

Cohl inhaled sharply and froze. In the feeble light, he could see her hair snarled around her face, bruises on her arms. *No!* The word screamed in his head.

She stared at the dead man on the floor for a long time, then at Cohl, scanning the massive cape until her gaze met his. She had the eyes of a wounded animal—dull and beaten. Gone was the fire, the strong-willed spirit, the essence of the woman. She didn't even blink.

"Tess?"

She rocked slowly and squeezed her arms tight around her legs like a small, defenseless child. "They wouldn't give me anything to wear."

Oh God. He reeled under the fist to his gut. He had expected her to be up and fighting, not stripped of everything.

Hands shaking, Cohl walked toward her, toward his worst fear. His fault. This was all his fault. The guilt beat at him relentlessly. He crouched next to her—afraid to touch her, afraid not to.

"Did they . . ." he started, swallowed, continued. "Are you hurt?"

"No," she whispered back, her voice weak and trembling. "I don't know."

He clenched his teeth at the rage that ripped through him. Bastards. For the first time in his life, he wanted to kill in cold blood. He had tried not to think about what was happening to her during the abduction, too worried that it would undermine his concentration. Seeing the cruelty firsthand dragged unchecked savagery from his very core. *His woman.* They had hurt his woman. Nothing was going to save them now.

Tess whimpered softly and the red veil of rage subsided. He took a deep breath and blew it out while rationality returned. She didn't need him losing control and he needed to get her out of here. But after that . . .

Moving quickly, he shrugged off the heavy cape and liberated his weapons, dumping them in a pile on the floor. Tess watched him in detached oblivion.

He yanked off his gray shirt and showed it to her. "You can wear this," he said softly.

She stared blankly at the shirt, then up at him. He rocked under another fist to his gut.

"Please, Tess. I'm getting you out of here."

"Pitz shot me . . ." she started with a sob.

One look into those vacant eyes told him that she was suffering from the shocky aftereffects of a potent stun blast and those bastards had just left her like this. He fought to control his fury so he could give her the care she needed. Later he'd unleash that venom on the ones who had shattered her.

Gently, he took her cold hand and wrapped it in his. "Not Pitz. A clone, a look-alike. Pitz would never do anything to hurt you."

Cohl held up the shirt in front of her eyes. "We don't have much time."

Tess nodded in her lethargic daze. On his knees, he helped her into the shirt, fastening the front when she swung her legs off the bed. She started to tremble, then shake violently beneath his generous shirt.

Cohl scooped her into his arms, holding her tight, trying to help her control the terror of helplessness.

When the shaking had subsided, he cupped her fragile face in his hands. Tears were running down her cheeks. Carefully, he brushed them aside. He laid his forehead against hers and spoke in a voice filled with the absolute conviction of a man who had much to lose. "I'm so sorry, Tess. I swear, they won't touch you again. I swear it."

He felt her head nod once.

"Not sleeping naked anymore," she murmured.

Cohl closed his eyes as he bore the brunt of another blow. Time. They were running out of time. "We have to go now."

He stood up and restrapped his weapons and belt around his torso. Then he tossed the detestable cloak over his shoulders. By the time he finished, Tess was standing next to him staring numbly down at her bare feet.

She looked small and fragile. There was no way she could wear the dead guard's heavy cape.

He retrieved the ear inserts and fitted them in her ears, as well as his own.

"They'll give you protection from the audio bursts. Don't take them out. They block out certain frequencies, but you will still be able to hear me fine," he told her, even though she never asked.

She didn't respond. He frowned. What if she never came back to him? What if he'd destroyed her forever? The thought was too painful.

First, he'd get her out of here. Then, he'd find a way to heal her, no matter what it took.

He raised his laser pistol with one hand and took Tess's hand with the other. The door opened when they approached it. He waited just inside, listening for activity. With all quiet, he leaned out farther and checked the corridor. Blessedly empty.

He squeezed Tess's hand gently. "Stay behind me."

She followed him as they made their way down the corridor, stepping around the lone servo-unit on its mindless mission.

They were nearly to the main walkway when the alarms blared out. Tess froze in place, sheer terror registering on her face.

"Come on, Tess." Cohl pulled her with him as fast as he thought she could handle, down the rest of the corridor. He saw the barrage of laser blasts crisscross at the end of the corridor over the main walkway. He immediately recognized Pitz's green laser fire amid the red return fire of the other robot. When they reached the end of the corridor, he stopped, tucked Tess behind him, and took in the sight.

Pitz and the clone were battling down the open atrium, using every weapon in their inner arsenal against each other. Laser blasts bounced off the ship's interior as the two robots flew up and down the three levels of the walkway in tight formation.

The clash had drawn a crowd. Cohl could hear the grunts and cheers of the Traka-Nor from their hiding spots around the walkway. Even they were smart enough to stay out of the way of the two metal warriors.

"Damn," he muttered.

"There's two of them?" he heard Tess ask behind him.

"One of them is Pitz. The one with the red laser fire abducted you."

"Bastard," she whispered. The anger in her voice made him feel slightly better. She was coming back to him.

Cohl scanned the level two walkway. It was at least seventy meters to the cover of the shuttle bay entrance. Run-and-gun time. He shrugged off the cape and swung the laser rifle around under his arm.

Tess watched him curiously. *A good sign,* he told himself. Now he just needed to get her to say more than one sentence at a time.

He handed the laser pistol to Tess. "Ever shoot a gun before?"

She took the pistol with both hands and frowned at it. "Soup cans in the backyard."

"Good enough. Just pull the trigger. It does a lot of damage so be careful what you aim for," Cohl said. "Can you run?"

She gazed up at him, focused, and a faint light flashed in her eyes. "I'll do whatever it takes to get out of here."

He nodded. *Almost there.*

"I'm going to shadow you. Shoot at anything with a weapon except me and Pitz. Don't look back and keep running no matter what."

She blinked. "Shoot them?"

He touched her cheek lightly. "If you don't, they will shoot you."

She stared at the pistol for a moment and nodded. Cohl hefted the rifle in one hand and activated a timed flash charge with the other. Pitz and the clone zoomed past them toward the front of the ship.

Cohl heaved the flash charge into the air toward Pitz and the clone. "Now!"

She darted out of the corridor and hit the main walkway on a dead run, her bare feet barely hitting the floor. Cohl grinned as he took off after her. Damn, she was fast.

The subsequent explosion and flash lit up the entire atrium, effectively blinding anyone looking in the general direction of Pitz and the clone. A chorus of Traka-Nor roars followed.

They had made it only twenty meters when the first laser shot sizzled by his head. He twisted the rifle around and fired behind him at the attacker on the lower level. The Traka-Nor screamed as Cohl's shot caught him in the chest. He tumbled off the walkway and into the atrium.

Forty meters.

More shots from the level above and ahead. Tess fired her pistol at the Traka-Nor, hitting him in the leg and bringing him down. As they approached the next side corridor, Cohl sped up and ran in front of her. He blew a steady stream of ammo directly into the corridor to take care of any would-be shooters and heard a servo-unit explode.

Thirty meters.

Ahead of them, a trio of half-asleep Traka-Nors stumbled onto the walkway from the next side corridor. Cohl got one. Tess got another. The third was faster, weapon ready and pointed at Tess when he was struck by a staggering laser shot. Cohl looked up as Pitz scooted by, his metal body spinning and spitting gunfire. Immediately, Pitz reversed course and reengaged the fast-approaching clone, drawing him away from Cohl and Tess. They hurdled the three dead Traka-Nors and kept going.

Ten meters.

Amid a new spray of gunfire, they raced through the entrance to the ship's shuttle bay section. Cohl caught up with Tess and stopped her just behind the doorway. He flattened against the wall and fired a volley of bursts back down the length of the walkway. Two more Traka-Nors reeled and collapsed.

Then he turned to check on Tess. She was resting against the wall breathing hard, her face grimaced in pain. But at least she had some color in her cheeks now.

He gripped his rifle hard to stop from taking her into his arms and holding her forever. "Are you all right?"

She nodded. "My head is killing me but it beats getting shot at."

Cohl smiled. She was back. His little fighter.

He cast one last look behind him at the battle raging. He couldn't help Pitz. He didn't have that level of firepower or mobility. Decision time. The shuttle bay was in the other direction. There were times when being the one in charge really sucked.

He slipped his hand around Tess's waist and turned toward the bay. "Come on. We're leaving."

Tess gripped his arm, stopping him. "Aren't you going to wait for Pitz?"

He gazed down into her concerned face. "We can't wait, Tess. The whole place knows we're here. Hopefully, Pitz can hold them off until we're clear of the ship."

She shook her head, her voice impassioned. "No. You can't leave him here. He saved us back there."

Cohl took her firmly by the elbow and dragged her toward the shuttle bay. "I have no choice."

They rounded the bay doors and came to an abrupt halt, face-to-face with Logen and five of his closest and ugliest friends. And everyone had a gun.

Logen pointed his at Cohl. "Well, well. What a nice surprise. Drop the weapon, Trae Salle."

Cohl didn't budge.

Logen smirked and swung his pistol toward Tess. "Or I'll kill her."

Cohl's rifle clattered to the floor, followed by the weapon's belt and the plasma knife.

Logen looked at Tess. "Yours, too. Or I'll shoot him."

"You coward," she said as she tossed the pistol to the floor. Logen motioned to a guard, who lumbered over and retrieved the weapons.

"Now, that's not nice," Logen said smoothly and gave her body a long, thorough skim. "I liked you better naked." His smile turned wolfish and smug.

Tess heard the explosion of rage as Cohl launched himself at Logen, catching him by surprise. They tumbled to the floor in a heap, fists flying as Logen's gun skidded across the bay. They rolled several times before Logen shoved Cohl off him using his feet. Cohl fell back, latching on to Logen's collar and dragging him face-first into the wall with a bone-crunching thump. Blood spattered across the floor courtesy of Logen's nose.

Tess watched in familiar horror as they fought, kicked, and beat their way around the shuttle bay with the five Traka-Nor thugs cheering them on in delight.

Damn it, she wasn't going to stand by and do nothing. No one was paying attention to her. This might be her only chance. As she searched frantically for something to use against Logen, she felt a lump in Cohl's pocket. Reaching in, she pulled out two smooth, metal balls. They didn't look like

135

much but she'd bet they packed a wallop if you nailed some-one hard enough with them.

Cohl and Logen were standing again and locked together by the shoulders, each trying to push the other over. Tess wound up and hurled the ball at Logen. He twisted at the last second and it missed narrowly, bouncing harmlessly across the shuttle bay floor. No one even noticed.

She exhaled in disgust. Only one ball left. Hefting the final ball, she whipped it at Logen's exposed back. It made the strangest sound when it struck with a thwack and stuck fast to the back of his uniform. It didn't move even when Logen tried to swat at it. Then he froze. Cohl's fist connected with his stomach but Logen didn't seem to feel it.

Horrified, Tess watched as the ball started to glow and burrow through the fabric of the uniform. A guttural, primal scream emanated from Logen. Cohl backed off in confusion.

Tess covered her mouth with one hand, muffling her own cry as the ball disappeared completely into Logen's back. The five Traka-Nors stood by like a bunch of rocks as Logen began screaming in earnest, his body twitching and jerking. Abruptly, his screaming stopped as a violent shudder tore through him, blood gushed from his mouth, and he fell to the floor.

For a moment, no one moved. Then the Traka-Nor all turned and looked at Tess.

"I didn't know," she whispered. She took a step back, shaking her head, her hands up in self-defense.

Suddenly, all five giants screamed and grabbed at their ears. She watched them drop one at a time to their knees, then to the floor—unconscious or worse. Only she and Cohl were left standing.

"Are they dead?" she asked in absolute bewilderment, looking from one man to another.

She watched Cohl step over the guards and bend down to retrieve his confiscated weapons belt on the floor.

"No, just knocked unconscious for a while," he answered as he strapped the weapons belt back on.

She blinked at him. How could he be so calm? "What happened?"

"I think Pitz won."

"What?" Tess asked, even more confused.

"He initiated a ship-wide audio burst. Renders most beings unconscious." Cohl tapped one of his ear inserts and grinned. "We were protected from the audio burst frequency."

Tess felt the plugs in her ears. "How did these get here?"

Cohl gave her a long, concerned look.

She put a shaky hand to her head. Her gaze dropped to Logen, his bloody face frozen in abject torture. She had killed him and in a most horrible way, an image that would be in her mind for all time. Seconds later, Cohl's big arms were wrapped around her, blocking out Logen.

"You didn't know, Tess. It's not your fault," he said into her hair.

Her voice shook. "I just wanted to distract him. What were those things?"

"I found them in the weapons cache on board but I've never seen them before. Apparently, they only activate on contact with a heat source."

She pressed her cheek to his bare chest, his heartbeat, so soothing and strong. His bare skin, warm and smooth. He had come back for her. She knew he would. For the first time since she'd been brought here, she felt safe. She clung to him like a lifeline to sanity.

He tightened his embrace and whispered, "I'm sorry, Tess."

She clung to him. "I know. It's not your fault."

His body tensed and he abruptly kissed the top of her head. "I need to restrain these guys before they wake up."

She let him go, baffled by his sudden withdrawal. He

moved silently from man to man, securing their hands with thin rings that looked like handcuffs. He had just finished when Pitz zipped in.

Cohl eyed him with amusement. "Hey, what took you so long?"

Pitz halted abruptly with a puff of smoke. Scorch marks scarred his body and his engines were whining dreadfully. "I encountered some minor trouble."

Cohl smiled wide. "I hope there's nothing left of that clone."

Pitz snorted. "An inferior imposter." He turned to Tess. "So nice to see you safe."

Tess gave him an affectionate smile. How did you hug a robot? "You, too."

Cohl cleared his throat loudly. "Well, now that we are one big, happy family again, I suggest we finish restraining the rest of the crew." He tossed Pitz the second clip of restraints. "We have about an hour before they revive?"

"Yes, sir. And *Speculator* is on the way."

Cohl nodded. "Good job, Pitz."

The robot's lights flashed an uneven pattern. "Thank you, sir. I will secure the crew on the bridge." Pitz puffed away in a cloud of smoke.

Tess stepped up to Cohl and extended a hand toward the third clip. "I'll help, too."

Cohl's eyebrows lifted. "Are you sure you are up to it?"

She took the clip from him and turned toward the exit as he fell in step beside her. "I can handle it. Of course, they may wake up with a few new bruises."

She glanced over and caught him grinning at her.

Cohl paced in his office on *Speculator* on an incensed rampage with Pitz watching every step. Just knowing that Rommol was on the other end of the communications link was enough to do it.

"Listen, you son of a bitch. If you want that amulet, you better make damn sure you stay the hell out of my way," Cohl snapped with barely controlled fury.

Rommol barked back, "I didn't authorize Krahel to—"

"You can't control your own people," Cohl interrupted. "I've got enough to handle without worrying about them, too."

Rommol roared over the comm link, "I don't want excuses. I want the amulet or your father will die."

Cohl stopped pacing and stared at the comm unit. "Maybe he has already. How do I know he's still alive?"

The comm unit was silent, then clicked sharply. Rommol snapped, "Speak to him yourself."

"Cohlman?"

Cohl's breath caught. He'd recognize that voice anywhere. The years rushed back. "Are you all right?"

His father snorted on the other end. "As well as can be expected. These barbarians stink to high heaven. My nose will never be the same."

Cohl smiled. "Glad to hear you still have all your faculties."

There was a short pause. "How is your mother?"

"She's holding up well."

Another pause. "Protect her and Yre Gault at all costs—"

Rommol's voice interrupted. "Enough. I want the amulet in seven days, Trae Salle."

Cohl grumbled. "Seven days? Like hell. Ten days or you'll never see your crewmen from the ship again."

Rommol laughed, then came back. "Do you think I care? Kill the traitors. It will save me the effort. Where is my ship?"

"I destroyed it," Cohl answered and silenced Pitz with a hand. "It was a piece of junk."

"Damn you! I needed that ship!" Rommol swore viciously.

Cohl smirked. "Consider it fair retribution. Keep your ugly bastards out of my way."

"Seven days, Trae Salle, or your father dies." The communications broke off.

Cohl let out a long breath and dropped into a chair. "Damn. That didn't go well."

Pitz whirred over to him. "Why did you lie about the ship?"

Cohl looked at the robot. "I have plans for that ship. We are going to take a little ride."

"Sir?"

"To Trakas," Cohl added and began punching up the coordinates on his console. "To rescue my father."

Pitz clicked furiously. "Please explain, sir."

Cohl leaned back in his chair and stared straight ahead. "Rommol can't be trusted. His own people are not loyal to him. My father's life is precarious at best."

"But Rommol promised—"

He held up a hand. "Rommol will do whatever is necessary to take control of Trakas. Including lying through his teeth."

Pitz blinked. "Yes, sir. A rescue attempt is highly possible with the Traka-Nor ship and *Speculator*—"

Cohl interrupted. "Not *Speculator*. Just the Traka-Nor ship."

The robot's lights flashed furiously. "The use of the Traka-Nor ship to covertly infiltrate Trakas airspace and provide access to their planet will increase our rescue odds by sixty-three percent. But I do not understand why *Speculator* will not be in the equation."

Cohl tapped in the coordinates. "Because Sahto will be taking Tess back to Earth in it, that's why."

Chapter Eleven

Nish frowned at the child as he ranted and raved across the inner chamber. The lesson was his to learn, but Nish knew that would not happen. The child blamed the world, never himself.

"That bastard Krahel! The traitor this entire time." Rommol kicked a heavy chair over and his dwindling line of unholy advisors backed up in unison.

He spat at the floor on Krahel's customary spot. "Right here in my inner chamber."

Then he pointed an accusing finger at Nish. "You are the Seer. You should have warned me."

Nish spoke to the child with tired patience. "I did. You chose the wrong man."

Rommol's eyes widened in rage, but that rage abated quickly. Nish smiled beneath his cowl. The child knew he had made a mistake but no apology would come. That would require manners

Rommol stormed back to his chair and dropped into it,

pouting. "At least he was stopped before he could harm the woman." He glared at Nish in his seat across the chamber. "Right?"

"The woman is safe with the Finder."

"So now what do we do?" Rommol leaned back in his chair and crossed his arms over his chest.

Nish spoke softly. "Time will cut the path for us."

Rommol gazed up at him with clear disapproval and slammed a fist on his desk. "We should be following them. How do we know Trae Salle won't keep the amulet for himself and turn it against us?"

Nish sighed. Impatience would destroy everything. The Gothyk piece was not yet in place. He rubbed his gnarled hands together. "It would be better to wait until the amulet is within reach. If we follow now, the Finder may abandon the mission."

Rommol threw his head back and laughed a fool's laugh, thoughtless and full of complacency. "Not if he wants his father back alive."

The old man didn't bother to explain that the Finder had many options. The Finder would simply find another way to save his father.

Tess shivered under Cohl's big shirt. Even though their medic, Witley, had treated her gently, the med center gave her the creeps with all its high-tech equipment. Witley rattled around the imposing equipment with blissful familiarity, explaining each procedure he was performing on her in passionate detail.

"Your clothing is being transferred from Yre Gault," Witley told her as he inspected her eyes with yet another gadget. "Would you like a clean flight suit for now?"

Tess hugged Cohl's shirt around her. "No. Maybe later." She wasn't ready to give up the comfort of the ample garment or his scent that clung so sweetly to it. When she had lost everything, the shirt had become more than just a covering. It was a shield, a barrier against fear and evil. And, she realized, Cohl's atonement to her.

In the hours since they'd returned to *Speculator*, he'd said little and every time he looked at her, there was guilt and worry in his eyes.

Why? she wondered. It wasn't his fault that Logen betrayed Yre Gault. It wasn't his fault that a Pitz clone fooled everyone. It wasn't his fault that the Traka-Nor were a bunch of smelly, disgusting, no-good, butt-ugly lummoxes. After all, he'd risked his life to save her. For that, she would be forever grateful.

"Lie back on the table, Tess," Witley ordered. She stretched out on the examination table for the tenth time and closed her eyes. For a man who didn't want to get involved, Cohl certainly took his responsibilities seriously. His heart spoke louder than his words. Whether it was his duty to Yre Gault or her safety, no one could carry that much guilt for something he cared nothing about.

"Do you want Aritrox for those bruises?" Witley questioned as a blue laser strip scanned her from toe to head.

Tess remembered how the Aritrox had affected Cohl, and shuddered. She finally had her brain cells running on all cylinders. No way did she want to go through that disorientation again.

"No, thanks." She smiled weakly. "They don't hurt."

Witley gave her a skeptical look and shrugged. "Let me know if you change your mind. You can sit up now but don't go anywhere yet. I want to check one more thing." He disappeared behind a counter, only that explosion of red hair sticking out.

Tess sat and caught Cohl's intoxicating scent on the shirt. It triggered a chain reaction in her body that started low in her belly and moved lower. Her nipples hardened in response, her breath deepened.

She wanted to rub her cheek against his bare chest again, inhale his scent, feel warm skin, iron muscles beneath her hands, take his weight with her body. She groaned quietly. All this from a shirt, it was downright pathetic.

Maybe it was residual adrenaline from their escape. Maybe it was the fact that he had come to her rescue like a real hero. Maybe it was because she had lived as a nun for almost two years. Whatever the reason, she wanted him desperately. She stilled. And why not? She was a grown woman, adult enough to choose, old enough to know when it was right. Suddenly the med center was a very warm place to be.

Her body was already singing with anticipation. She had never seduced a man before. How hard could it be? She gnawed on her lower lip. First she needed to erase his worries and burden. She had the distinct feeling that he would refuse her if he didn't let go of all that guilt.

Then there was the question that had nagged her since the beginning. She glanced at the flash of red hair as Witley popped up from behind the counter, scrutinizing an electronic pad.

"Well, it looks like your chemical levels are all normal. There's no internal damage. Nothing permanent. You can go." He flashed a requisite smile and turned his attention back to the pad.

Tess stayed on the bench, twisting Cohl's shirt in her hands. "Witley, can I ask you a question?"

"Huh? Oh, sure."

Damn, this wasn't going to be easy. "Would you say that I'm physically compatible with the male species . . . uh, out here? On this ship?"

Witley froze. Only his eyes moved, fixing on her with the intensity he'd previously given the pad. Then he made a humming noise and began pacing the med center, rubbing his chin. Tess watched him with growing dread. What would she do if he said no?

He stopped and turned to her. "It's the technologically superior status, isn't it?"

Tess blinked at him. "Excuse me?"

He nodded. "Most women find that intriguing. This happens quite a bit."

Tess shook her head to clear it. He'd lost her.

Witley put his hands on his hips and gave her a sympathetic look. "I have to tell you that I'm already mated."

Oh good Lord. Tess had to work to keep her mouth from dropping. "Well, actually—"

He held a hand up. "I know this is devastating now, but I'm sure you will get over me soon enough."

"Uh, right. Right." Tess nodded emphatically. This was beyond humiliating. Forget it, just forget it. She'd find out the old-fashioned way. She vaulted off the table and cleared her throat. "Do you know where Cohl is?"

Witley consulted a display amid his plethora of screens and panels. "Looks like the bridge."

Tess nearly ran out of the med center. "Thank you. Thanks for everything."

It felt incredibly good to be back on his own bridge. Cohl slanted a glance at Tess, who was curled up at one of the bridge stations with his shirt wrapped tight around her. When her eyes met his, he gave her a small smile but he was worried. She wasn't right. Too quiet.

Witley had cleaned her up and declared her healthy except for a few bumps and bruises. But there were wounds that even a good medic could not treat. She was probably mentally and emotionally scarred for life from the whole experience.

He should never have taken her. How could he ever have thought this would be simple? How could he ever have thought he could protect her against everything they were up against? He'd promised to keep her safe and he had failed.

Overwhelming guilt had him turning back to the data pad he was reviewing. Prisoner list. Mil-Ops had already taken the groggy Traka-Nors into custody and back to Yre Gault. Cohl put a strict order of silence in place. No one on Yre Gault was to know what had happened out here until he had his father back.

Several of the prisoners had been very cooperative if it meant their freedom, particularly Rommol's double-crossing advisor, Krahel. Cohl growled low, remembering the way Tess had started shaking when they found his unconscious body on the walkway. Krahel could talk all he wanted but he would never walk free.

According to Krahel, he and Logen had worked together to abduct Cohl's father using the Pitz clone robot. After that, they had gotten greedy and double-crossed Rommol, abducting Tess to secure the amulet for themselves. The good news was that the death threat against his mother had been nothing more than a diversion so Logen could get to Tess more easily.

Cohl exhaled hard. The amulet could stay hidden for another thousand years for all he cared. There was no way he was going to take anything more from Tess. She'd stay here tonight for medical observation; then tomorrow he would let her go, back home where she belonged.

He nodded absently. That was the best way. No one said he had to like it. Cohl cast Tess another glance. She was still watching him, the expression on her face thoughtful yet unreadable. He'd ask the medic to look at her again.

He turned away, unable to reconcile his failure and unwilling to imagine what his life was going to be like without her.

"Cohl?" He didn't realize she'd moved until she was standing beside him. Her pale face looked up at his. "I never thanked you for coming after me."

He squeezed his eyes shut, remembering her wounded

expression, the bruises. "Tess, don't. Don't thank me for doing this to you. For putting you through hell."

Her palm slid warm against his cheek, guiding him to her. Her mouth fell soft against his lips. A kiss, gentle with forgiveness, absolved his soul. He took the absolution, imparting his remorse into her, seeking haven from his pain. Her boundless compassion humbled and healed him. It was more than he deserved and all that he desired.

Then her kiss grew bolder, more urgent, wicked, and promising. It spoke directly to the man in him, an unmistakable calling. She pulled away, her eyes hooded. Without another word, Tess walked slowly off the bridge. Just before she disappeared around the corner, she cast him one long, lusty look that dropped him a full notch lower on the evolutionary scale.

It was all he could do not to howl.

A control bleeped on a nearby console, a reminder that he was standing in the middle of the bridge with Sahto staring at him.

He cleared his throat and followed casually after Tess. "Sahto, you have the bridge."

From behind him, Sahto huffed. "Yeah, no kidding."

Cohl strode down the corridor and caught sight of her entering his quarters. He slowed to a stop in front of the door. Now what? He ran an unsteady and itchy-as-hell hand through his hair.

She was waiting for him and he knew what she was going to offer him, something he could not accept. Not after all she'd been through. As much as he wanted her, he didn't deserve her. He couldn't touch her. He owed her that much.

And he needed to tell her that she was going home. That should make her happy. Any man could stay in control that long, and hell, he was a master at self-control.

Feeling confident he stepped up, activated the door, and walked in ready to tell her everything. The words stuck in his throat as the door slid shut behind him. She had removed his shirt and was clutching it to her breasts. His heart rate went from eighty to eight hundred in 2.4 seconds.

The shirt hung down, and beneath was supple skin, legs long and lean, the gentle curve of a hip. A goddess couldn't have looked more beautiful or more tempting.

Slowly he approached and stopped an arm's length from her, afraid to break the spell she'd cast over him with those bewitching green eyes.

Her voice was steady and clear. "I wanted to return your shirt."

No matter how tempting, he kept telling himself, he had no right. She was going home. He would stay in control. "Are you sure you are ready for that?"

She nodded. Cohl took a deep breath and prepared to throw away the perfect dream. "Maybe you should keep it for a while."

Her eyes made a remarkably fast metamorphosis from sultry to angry. "You are refusing it?"

Cohl exhaled. This wasn't going to be as easy as he'd hoped.

"God no, Tess. It's just that you've had a tough day. Stunned, abducted, shot at." He ran a hand through his hair in frustration. *Lies, lies. Tell her the truth. Tell her she's leaving tomorrow. Tell her it can't mean anything.* "I don't know if you are thinking clearly."

Her mouth gaped open. "How dare you presume to think for me?" She shoved the shirt at his chest hard. "Here. Take your stupid shirt. I don't need it."

She tossed back her hair and headed for the door.

"Uh, Tess."

She spun around and glared at him. "What?"

He was staring down at her body. Oh God, she was naked now, just like she'd been on the Traka-Nor ship. Only this time, she didn't feel helpless or threatened. From the expression on his face, she felt incredibly beautiful—strong and safe.

Still, he'd refused her, humiliated her. And damn it, she'd just given him the shirt. She wasn't going to ask for it back again. But she couldn't very well walk out into the corridor stark naked. But if he kept looking at her like that, it wouldn't matter. She'd simply melt right here on the spot.

"Do you want the shirt?" His words were spoken in a barely civilized baritone.

She took a deep breath. *Decision time, Tess. Make it one you can live with.*

"No," she breathed. "Just you."

He shuddered visibly. Then those golden eyes blazed and flashed incandescent. He tossed the shirt to the side and moved toward her like a raging wildfire. She trembled as he backed her to the wall and lowered his mouth over hers.

Instantly, the sheer power and essence of him swept over her. So much, so real. All she could do was hold on as blazing passion shattered her control, unleashing emotions raw and powerful, unbridled and reckless.

She nipped at his lips. His tongue ran over her mouth as she opened to him. Mouths ravaged and took. A lone whimper escaped her. His hands were everywhere, leaving a sizzling trail across her skin. A woman could burn alive in this heat.

She skimmed his broad shoulders and chest, pressed satin over steel. With a groan of need, she shoved her hands through his hair and pulled him closer.

His thigh slid between her legs, the fabric rough against tender skin—both erotic and frustrating. She reached down and tugged at his pants.

"Off," she gasped. *Now, now.*

"Bed," he mumbled. He lifted her easily and crossed his quarters to the bed. She fell back on it as he kicked his boots off and stripped his pants with one tug. Then all she could do was stare.

From head to heel, he had a warrior's body—strong, powerful, solid, yet sleek and beautiful like a Michelangelo statue. And he was all hers. Tess licked her lips where his kisses still burned. Then her gaze dropped lower. Her eyes widened appreciably.

Compatible. They were definitely compatible.

She looked back at his face, wondering what was taking him so long to come to her. He was just standing there with his eyes closed, flexing those big hands. Head thrown back, every muscle tensed, he looked primed to spring. In a flash, it hit her. He was ready to bolt.

She'd kill him.

"I don't know how this works where you come from but I think we need to be a lot closer," she whispered, trying to downplay her panic. Maybe she wasn't what he wanted after all. Maybe the bruises had turned him away. Maybe . . .

His golden eyes opened to hers, alive with trapped fire. "I'm trying to move slow. I don't want to scare you."

Tess smiled with relief and stretched slowly on the bed. "Maybe I'll scare you."

A wide grin crossed his face. "God, I hope so."

He climbed on the bed and flowed over her, hot and unstoppable like molten lava. Tess sighed. No wonder those lunatics loved standing next to a live volcano. The power, the danger, the heat. His mouth was on hers, gentle but thorough. Slow-moving lava. It swept through her until she was burning to the core. Enveloped in living fire, her body sang with delight.

Patience had never been her forte and her hands dragged across his body, smooth skin and iron muscle. She wanted him to move faster. He was too slow, had too much control. Breath hissed through his teeth when her hands dropped lower and found him, hard and ready.

"Tess, you're going to be very disappointed in your first alien encounter if you keep that up," he growled into her ear.

He guided her hands to his chest where she quickly found his small nipples. She nipped at his throat, reveling in his burgeoning urgency. He rumbled powerfully and lowered his head to her breast. She offered it up like a virgin sacrifice to the volcano god as he breathed fire across her body. The first touch of his tongue tore a broken moan from her.

He worshipped one breast, then the other. She rolled her head. A tongue like that should be insured. She buried her hands in his hair, couldn't tell when one breath ended and the next began. So many sensations. Every single nerve ending was screaming on the edge of overload.

He came back to her mouth and murmured, "Beautiful."

"Please," was all she could say, arching against him. His hand took a maddeningly slow, leisurely slide down her belly. *Oh, please. Oh, please.*

And he touched.

Ignited.

His name was dragged from her lips.

He retreated. She arched. *Please.*

He hummed with pure male satisfaction and found her again. This time, he didn't stop that wonderful, wicked caress. The one that had the pressure within building tighter and tighter into a screaming ball of fire. Then ecstasy exploded in wave after wave. She sobbed at the sheer brilliance of it.

When she opened her eyes, Cohl was smiling down at her. She loved him. It struck her like a bolt of chain lightning. Loved him. Wanted him. Needed him.

She knew the second he saw it. The precise moment when this became more. More than just sex. More than just the act.

His smile faded, replaced by startling intensity and possession. He found her hands, laced his fingers through hers, binding them together. Their eyes remained locked as he found his place and eased into her slowly, inch by inch, until he filled and stretched her to just beyond comfort. He stopped, his big body taut, his breathing strained. And waited.

"Big," she gasped, trying to control the sudden panic of such an unaccustomed invasion.

He bent down to nuzzle her neck. "Perfect."

His tongue skimmed along the outer edge of her ear and she trembled. His teeth tugged delicately on her earlobe and she moaned. How could he know every one of her sensitive spots? Her deep sigh spread across her entire body, relaxing each muscle.

Then he moved, flexing and driving with long, steady thrusts. She followed, fascinated and captivated by all that power, just like the volcano watchers.

So this is what it felt like to make love to the man you wanted with all your heart. She vaguely heard her name, his sweet whispered words in her ear as an ancient rhythm reigned. The volcano was rumbling, building to drown out everything except the man and the passion.

His ironhanded control shattered in a thundering roar. All that shackled force unleashed as he lifted her bottom off the bed with one hand and buried himself one last time. Her name echoed across the room and the volcano erupted, glorious and spectacular. Liquid heat broke over her in a pleasure so intense there was nothing left but the tears.

He might have slept, he wasn't sure, didn't care. Nothing mattered except the warmth and wonder of pure peace. God, he felt good.

Beneath him, he felt Tess's gentle shove on his chest.

"You know, you weigh a ton," she murmured.

With a supremely contented grunt he rolled the rest of

NAME:_____

ADDRESS:_____

_____

_____

TELEPHONE:_____

E-MAIL:_____

_____ I want to pay by credit card.

__ Visa   __ MasterCard   __ Discover

Account Number:_____

Expiration date:_____

SIGNATURE:_____

Send this form, along with $2.00 shipping and handling for your FREE books, to:

Love Spell Romance Book Club
20 Academy Street
Norwalk, CT 06850-4032

Or fax (must include credit card information!) to: 610.995.9274.
You can also sign up on the Web at <u>www.dorchesterpub.com</u>.

Offer open to residents of the U.S. and Canada only. Canadian residents, please call 1.800.481.9191 for pricing information.

If under 18, a parent or guardian must sign. Terms, prices and conditions subject to change. Subscription subject to acceptance. Dorchester Publishing reserves the right to reject any order or cancel any subscription.

the way off her, tucking her under his arm. She snuggled against him, her fingers tracing a lazy path across his chest.

He needed to ask her if he'd hurt her when he lost control, if he'd frightened her.

She was humming softly.

He smiled. *Guess not.*

He ruthlessly pushed back the guilt, determined not to let it ruin the only blissful night he was bound to have for the next fifty years or so. He'd face hell tomorrow when he had to let her go. Tonight, she was his.

He had never realized until she entered his quiet little world how very lonely he had been. He wasn't looking forward to going back to it without her. For a secret moment, he imagined what it would be like if she stayed. A reluctant smile tugged at his lips. She would drive him crazy every day, bring total chaos to his ship and anarchy to his orderly world.

The smile faded. She would also bring laughter and spirit, light and passion—all the colors of life. He was going to miss her when his world went back to black and white and gray.

"You were right," she whispered in the dark, interrupting his increasingly depressing thoughts.

He squeezed her shoulder. "About what?"

She let out a sigh that would feed his ego for years to come. "It *was* perfect."

Tess woke up alone and stretched out under the covers. God, she felt good. Sore and stiff, but good. She turned over and slid her hand across his side of the bed, recalling a morning kiss that had turned into much more.

Sometime after that, he'd mumbled something about work and disappeared. Maybe she did scare him after all. She giggled. Good. Why should she be the only one scared to death?

She loved him. Couldn't deny it, control it, or fight it, and didn't want to. So where did that leave her? Did he love her? Last night was more than sex and she knew it. He must know it too.

She checked the time and realized it was late morning. Time to see where in the wide, wide universe they were heading today. As she sat up, she spotted her jeans and black T-shirt at the foot of the bed. Cohl. Her eyes closed at the memories of last night. Perfect seemed such an inadequate word. It had been beyond perfect, as sweet and clean as a newly drawn breath. He'd worshipped her body, caressing the ugly bruises, burying the horrible memories forever. Whether urgent and hot, or leisurely and thorough, he had loved her as if there were no tomorrow.

She hopped out of bed, snatched up the clothes, and headed into the lav, singing all the while. The shower felt more erotic than it should, the air lighter, the world wonderful.

Showered, changed, and still humming one of her own songs, she stepped out of Cohl's quarters and made her way through the ship toward the bridge.

Beckye looked up and smiled crookedly as Tess waltzed in.

"Morn," Beckye greeted her.

Tess smiled brightly. "Morn, yourself."

Beckye was an Amazon of a woman with big hair, teased and rolled to a staggering height, making her even larger and more intimidating than her six-foot-plus frame. She had the coarse, tough drawl of a seasoned waitress at a truck stop diner. Tess had liked her instantly.

Tess glanced around the empty bridge. "Where is everyone?"

The big woman turned back to her console and began tapping the flat panel.

"Shuttle bay number one." Beckye shrugged. "Guess they say their g'byes."

Tess frowned. "What good-byes? Who's leaving?"

Beckye cast her a speculative look. "Cohl not tell you?"

Tess swallowed. For some reason, the world began a creepy, slow slide away from her. "Tell me what?"

The big woman leaned far back in her chair and crossed enormous arms across an equally impressive chest. "He leave for Trakas in that ship he took. Gone to fight for his father. Probably get himself kill but he not listen to me." Beckye shook her head, then looked up at Tess. "And you go home."

"Home?" The word stuck in her throat. "To Earth?"

"Yah," Beckye replied, more interested now. "He not tell you?"

Tess gripped the back of the nearest chair. "No. He not."

Beckye broke into a husky laugh. "Men. You can't live with them and you can't run them through with a laser knife."

Tess seethed. Oh, she wouldn't need a laser knife. She shoved off the chair back and paced the bridge area, trying to get her temper under control.

He had lied to her again. Well, technically it wasn't a lie, just another little something he forgot to mention that affected her directly. Did he think she didn't need to know? Did he think she wouldn't care?

She clenched her fists. So last night didn't mean anything to him. How blind could one girl be? Tears threatened and she bitterly willed them away. Damn him. He had needed her for the amulet and that was all. Now he had no use for her and that was why he was sending her home.

Home. She closed her eyes at the pang that accompanied that word. Home, where it was comfortable and safe and where her entire life was waiting for her. Yes, she wanted to go home, more than anything. She could just walk away now and be free of this mess. Leave Cohl and his father and Yre Gault to their own devices. That's what he wanted. Fine.

She opened her eyes and stared out of the viewport into the heart of her galaxy. As if it were that easy.

"Beckye, what are the chances of Cohl rescuing his father from Trakas alive?"

The woman frowned deeply. "I see Cohl do some amazing things but . . ." She didn't finish.

Tess sighed. If only she hadn't seen beautiful Yre Gault and talked to Ad. If only her heart didn't beat just a little faster when Cohl was near. If only she could forget how wonderful he felt lying next to her.

We all have to play the hand we are dealt. Those were her own words, words she lived by. They might very well be the words she died by but there really was no other choice. Cohl's best chances were with her, whether or not he agreed and whether or not he loved her. She would finish what she started and do what she promised. She was his best chance. And beyond that?

Beyond that, she didn't want to think about right now.

"Shuttle bay number one, right?" Tess asked.

"Yah." Beckye nodded and grinned. "You need help to find?"

Tess gave her a smile. "If you don't mind."

Beckye shoved her big body out of the chair. "Mind? Hell, I pay to see this show."

Chapter Twelve

Cohl saw her coming, followed by the big mass of Beckye grinning a "you in big trouble, boy" smile. He swore softly and threw the box of supplies into the back of the Traka-Nor transport before Tess could use it against him as a lethal weapon. He didn't need a mind-gazer to tell him that she was not pleased. *Too bad.* He wasn't backing down. No one was more unhappy about this than he but the only thing worse than losing the woman of your dreams was doing it face-to-face.

He should have left quietly this morning, slipped out without a sound. Instead, he couldn't resist one last kiss, just one more to live on. Then she'd pulled him down into that sweet, warm, beautiful body of hers and there was no way he could escape. Not that he wanted to. One final moment of ecstasy before returning to a life that until now he'd thought was perfect.

He drew himself up for a battle he didn't want to wage and turned to face her. Her green eyes flashed against that fiery auburn hair, a startling combination. God, she was amazing when she was mad. It was almost worth the argument.

She stopped about two meters from him and calmly crossed her arms. "Going somewhere?" She could freeze air with that tone.

He pursed his lips and gave her a cursory glance. No weapons. Good. He could still take her.

"I didn't want to wake you." There. *Chivalry lives*.

Tess stared a hole through him. "Coward."

Hmm. Apparently, her idea of chivalry differed from his. He ran a hand through his hair and glanced around the shuttle bay at the crew members watching the proceedings with morbid fascination.

"We should probably clear the deck for this one, huh?" he asked Tess.

She shifted her weight to her other hip. "Only if you want to keep your dignity."

Cohl eyed her determined stance, her blazing green eyes. Never boring. Life with her was never boring.

"Everyone out," he ordered aloud.

A collective groan passed through the crew as they shuffled out, muttering among themselves. Cohl could have sworn he spotted Beckye and Sahto making some sort of wager.

Then there was nothing but silence and simmering rage.

"I want you out of this, Tess," he said, taking the offensive. "I can't protect you and I won't put you through any more. It's as simple as that. You are going home where you belong." He casually picked up another container and tossed it into the cargo hold.

She never flinched as the container landed with a hard thump. "You weren't going to tell me. You were prepared to leave without even a good-bye."

"I said good-bye this morning." He winced as soon as the

words came out. It was as if he had a latent death wish or something.

"That's right," she said coolly. "After you made love to me. How could I forget?"

He exhaled. "I'm sorry. I should have told you yesterday."

"Yesterday? You knew this yesterday and you didn't say anything?" she snapped.

Cohl rubbed his neck. How was he going to tell her that he couldn't say good-bye to the only woman he would ever need or want? For a long time he stared at the floor, trying to put it into words. Finally, he gazed up at her.

"I couldn't watch you leave, Tess."

She appeared surprised but then her jaw set. "Well, I'm not leaving, so you don't have to worry about it."

What the hell? He thought she'd jump at the chance to go home. Why would she want to stay? There was nothing here for her. No music career, no family, no part of her happy life on Earth. Only a perilous dance with death.

A thought tickled in his head. Maybe she wanted to stay for him. His heart took a joyful leap but he shook it off and grabbed another container. It didn't matter how much he wanted her or what her reasons were, it was simply too dangerous for her to stay. "Oh, you're leaving all right. As soon as I finish this last supply run to the Traka-Nor ship."

Her hands were on her hips in a flash. "Did you hear what I said?"

He pitched the container into the hold. "There is no reason for you to stay, Tess." *Liar.* There were a million reasons, all of them selfish.

"No reason," she repeated with reverence. "What about the amulet? What about your father?"

"I'm going after him."

Her green eyes lit in frustration. "You think you can defeat all the Traka-Nor by yourself? Are you insane? That's suicide."

He rounded on her. "So is trying to get the amulet, or haven't you been paying attention?"

Her chin came up. "Whatever it takes, I can handle it."

"Maybe you can, but I don't think I could." He reached out and stroked her cheek. So soft. "I've never had a partner on an acquisition before. It's dangerous enough for me alone. I'd rather not try to guide someone else through it."

He dropped his hand. "Besides, the last part I can't help you with. The song." He shook his head of the horrible visions he'd been conjuring up for the past few days. "That worries me more than anything. If you miss a word or hit the wrong note—"

"And you don't believe I can do it?" Tess interrupted, clearly offended.

He smiled grimly at her. "I think you can do anything you want to but adventuring isn't a game, Tess. Screw up once and you are going to die alone and in some horrible fashion that you can't even begin to imagine. You have to be very careful, very patient, and follow directions perfectly. In case you don't know, those aren't exactly your strengths."

That one bounced right off her without a fight. "You were willing enough before. What happened?"

He one-handed another small box into the hold with the others. "I have a Traka-Nor ship now. I've got a good chance of getting close enough to Trakas to launch a full rescue."

She huffed loudly and began to pace in a tight circle, her head down. "You won't survive, Cohl. And neither will your father. I can't believe you'd take such a risk."

"I won't risk you either."

She stopped in front of him and gazed up into his eyes. "I'll assume full responsibility."

His heart wrenched in his chest. Was she doing this to protect him? A little voice in his head chimed in, *It makes no difference.*

"No."

She raised her voice in challenge. "I think we should try. If we fail, *then* you can go after your father."

He shook his head. "If we fail, it'll be too late for all of us. You are going home, Tess. You've done your duty."

She stared at him silently, knowing she was powerless and defeated. Then she looked away, across the shuttle bay, and nodded slowly. "Throwing me to the wolves then?"

Cohl frowned. "What?"

She walked away slowly, then turned to face him. "The Traka-Nor were a real fun bunch. I can't wait to see how the Traka-Sou will treat me when they have their turn."

Oh hell. Cohl closed his eyes for a second and exhaled hard. He'd forgotten about them.

She walked back, her eyes brimming with tears. "You got me into this and now you are just going to walk away? How long do you think it will take them to track me down on Earth? A week? And what happens to me when you get killed playing Rambo? Who's going to come to my rescue then?"

She rubbed her arms, looking suddenly very fragile. The ghosts in her eyes were real and close enough for him to touch. Ghosts that haunted them both. "I can't survive another encounter with the Trakas, Cohl. I can't. Don't do that to me." A tear escaped down her cheek. Then her voice dropped to a whisper, her lower lip trembled. "And tell me that last night meant nothing to you."

The depth and swiftness of his reaction rocked him. He heard the snap in his head, felt the painful squeeze of his heart. A flash of heat stole the breath from his lungs as he reached for her, pulling her into a reassuring embrace. Her scent seeped into him like a healing balm. How could he think it would be so easy to just walk away?

She clutched his shirt. He felt the burn of hot tears through the thin fabric.

"Tell me it meant nothing to you, Cohl, and I'll leave," she sobbed,

He held her closer. "I can't." It had meant everything. His mouth found hers, eager and frantic, as his fingers caressed her face and dove into that mass of wild hair.

Last night flooded back. He would never be free of her, could never replace her. Tess molded her body against him and just like that, they were one again. As if they were made to be that way.

His comm unit beeped softly, breaking the moment.

He nuzzled her neck, activating the unit with the one hand.

"Cohl here."

From the Traka-Nor ship, Pitz answered crisply. "Sir, we are ready to leave. What is your ETA?"

Cohl felt Tess stiffen in his arms. He peered into her anxious eyes.

"I'm not departing," he replied, never dropping his gaze. "New plan. Hang tight and I'll contact you later."

There was a pause. "This is highly unusual, sir."

Cohl smiled. "Don't worry, Pitz. The new plan is nothing you can't handle with a little luck."

Pitz gave a snort. "I *never* worry and luck is hardly a valid component. There are other tangible factors that—"

Cohl cut the communication and smiled down at Tess. "He could go on forever if you let him."

She asked dubiously, "Keeping me around for a while?"

His heart sang. Fate had bought him a little more time. And more danger to Tess. He wouldn't let her out of his sight from now on. "I won't feed you to wolves but I can't promise you won't be facing something even worse. Are you prepared to become the student?"

In a slow but beautiful transformation, her expression brightened. "I've been told I'm a fast learner."

Pitz's mechanical voice came over the *Speculator*'s bridge comm. "What is the plan, sir?"

Cohl double-checked the main console. "Tess and I are taking *Speculator* to Demisie. I want you to take a direct route to Trakas, infiltrate Traka-Nor airspace, and lie low. Wait there for orders from me. If necessary, I want you to move in and rescue my father."

"If you are indeed acquiring the amulet, why do you need me over Trakas? I would be more useful on Demisie."

Cohl stared blindly at the display. "Because Rommol or someone else may kill my father and I'll be too far away to prevent it. I'd like to have you close by." *In case we fail,* he added silently.

Pitz's voice came back. "I do not understand your concern. Rommol promised—"

Cohl interrupted. "Let's just say that Rommol's ratio of truths to lies is quite low. I also don't believe his own people can be trusted."

"Yes, sir. I understand."

Cohl asked, "Any sign of the Traka-Sou?"

Over the comm, Cohl heard Pitz whir, chug noisily, then whir again. "Mil-Ops has been scanning the region continuously since we arrived. There is no sign of them."

Cohl frowned. That made him nervous. No sighting of them for days. He'd much rather know exactly where they were.

He told Pitz, "You are all clear to go. And, Pitz, get some maintenance on your thrusters. You sound like you have the Xu virus."

"Yes, sir." Pitz signed off.

Cohl watched the Traka-Nor ship disappear into hyperspace through *Speculator*'s bridge viewport. "Beckye?"

Beckye swiveled her chair at her station. "What?"

"Have you heard anything from Zain?"

"Sure have. He send new coordinates. And he ask about you." She leaned back and crossed her big arms across her big chest. Her grin was wide and smug.

Cohl played along. "And what did you tell him?"

Becky shrugged. "I tell him we bored as hell."

Cohl laughed and shook his head. "Bored. I'd give just about anything for bored. So where are we heading?"

Beckye glanced at her console. "Just off the planet Velgarta. We be there tomorrow."

Cohl nodded approval. "Lock in the new coordinates. Sahto, we can leave at your convenience."

"Yes, sir," Sahto replied and started entering the hyperspace launch sequence.

Cohl stood up, rolling his tight shoulders and back. He needed to loosen up. Tess was waiting for him.

"If you need me, I'll be in shuttle bay number two."

Sahto cast him a curious glance. "Maintenance?"

As he walked off the bridge, Cohl smiled over his shoulder. "Combat training."

Cohl leaned over a shipping container and scanned the shuttle bay area, his laser pistol held high. Tess was in here somewhere. Damned if she wasn't being quiet as hell.

He slid forward to get a better angle of vision in the cavernous bay. He'd never tried the tactical exercise with anyone except Pitz. In deference to Tess and his own good health, Cohl had replaced the traditional burn agent in their two laser weapons with a harmless dye. Other than that, normal combat rules applied—all direct hits counted and the one with the most hits would win.

He'd walked in ten minutes before as originally agreed. She received the initial advantage of knowing his position, but so far she hadn't made a move, and although he was halfway across the bay, he had not located her. No sound, no activity. Maybe she fell asleep. He stifled a chuckle. Doubtful. This whole thing was her idea. He just hadn't expected her to be so good at it.

He slid forward another meter. Instinctively, he whipped

the laser pistol sights toward a small black object that sailed silently through the air and landed in a heap ten meters from his feet. He squinted under the dimmed lights. It didn't move. Looked like cloth.

Then another dark object dropped a few meters from it. Was that a sock? He lowered his weapon. What the hell?

The sock's mate landed next to the first one. Cohl stepped out from his cover and stared at them. He looked up just in time to snag a pair of pants out of midair aimed at his head.

Tess emerged from behind a nearby container, smiling triumphantly and sporting nothing but a black lace bra and matching panties. It took a while for him to notice her weapon pointed at his chest. His was hanging limp from his hand, much like his jaw.

"Gotcha," she said smugly.

Her breasts peeked luridly from behind the lace. His gaze skimmed down the slender waist and firm legs in direct proportion to his rising body temperature.

He tossed his laser pistol to the floor. "I surrender."

Tess gaped at him, then huffed and rested her laser pistol against her hip. "I thought you were good at this."

He suppressed a grin. She had no idea how good he was but she was about to find out. He sighed dramatically and raised his hands over his head. "You win. I'm your prisoner now."

Tess's eyebrows rose in unison. A devilish little smile crossed her face. She licked her lips. "Really?"

He tried to look beaten and woeful. "Really. Now that you have a prisoner, what are you going to do?"

She sauntered toward him with a certain impudence, her gun pointed vaguely in his direction. He was already hard but as she circled him several times, it became downright uncomfortable.

"Tess?"

"I'm thinking."

He blew out a silent breath. *Oh boy*. He might be in trouble after all.

She stopped in front of him with a shrewd smile. "Do the chicken dance."

Cohl narrowed his eyes. "You may as well shoot me now."

Tess laughed aloud. "It was worth a try."

Then her gaze traveled over his body and something gleamed in her green eyes. She waved her laser pistol at his chest.

"Then take off your shirt," she ordered, clearly enjoying her newfound power.

He did so . . . slowly, watching her obvious approval. He balled up the shirt and it joined the other clothing on the floor.

The amount of time she devoted to visually scrutinizing his chest and arms nearly ended his little gambit. Thankfully, she moved on. And lower, to where his pants strained.

Her eyes widened. She met his gaze through her long lashes. "Impressive, prisoner."

He raised his hands again, maintaining a straight face. Hell, he should have earned a commendation for that alone.

She gave him a downright sinful smile and stepped in close, close enough that he could feel her heat. With one finger, she traced a line from his lips to his navel and below. A fine sweat broke out all over his body. Maybe there was something to this prisoner thing after all.

"Kiss me."

His lips curved at her overconfident tone. Time to spring the trap. Like a good little prisoner, he leaned down and skimmed her lips at the exact moment that he snatched her pistol and turned it on her.

Tess stepped back and blinked at the weapon, then up at him in fury. "That's not fair."

Cohl laughed at her naïveté. "You didn't shoot me and

you didn't restrain me. First rule of combat: never underestimate your opponent."

She pouted and crossed her arms. "I want a rematch."

"Uh-uh. This lesson isn't over yet. There are a few other rules you need to learn." He pitched the pistol across the shuttle bay.

She watched the weapon until it slid to a stop, then eyed him warily. "Such as?"

"Initial speed."

He lashed a hand around her waist and yanked her body to his, then went down on one knee taking her with him. A split second later, she was on her back with him sprawled on top. The maneuver left her wide-eyed and out of breath, her hair fanned around her like a red flame.

He covered her body with his and traced the edge of the black lace across her breasts with his fingertips. He buried the other hand in her hair and murmured against her soft throat, "Rapid initial speed guarantees maximum penetration on an opening move."

"I see," she gasped beneath him. "Works surprisingly well."

"Mmm. Now your opponent has you off-balance. What do you do?" He smiled down at her.

Tess licked her lower lip. "Well, I could use try *this*." She reached down with both hands and cupped him firmly.

He hissed loud as the action jolted his lower body, shattering his ability to think straight—a ruthless and highly effective tactic.

"Sorry, Tess. Illegal target."

"What? How can there be illegal targets in combat?" she snapped and tightened her grip.

Without another word, he clutched her to him and rolled them both over once. Tess cried out and instinctively spread her hands to stabilize herself as she came to rest on her back again. He snagged her flailing wrists, anchoring each one to either side of her head.

She gave him a glare that would have mortally wounded a lesser man. Luckily, he was well up to the challenge.

He grinned wide. "Rule number two: Don't ever believe anything your opponent tells you. There *are* no illegal targets in combat. Followed closely by rule number three: If you are going to attack, do not fail, because your opponent will emerge stronger and very pissed."

"I want to see this rule book of yours," she muttered.

In one hand, he held both her wrists over her head and shook his head with regret. "The only way to learn something is to experience it. Ready for the next lesson?"

Tess blew a hair off her face in disgust. "Do I have a choice?"

Cohl slid a knee high between her thighs and watched her eyes register the sensual move. "The next lesson relates to positioning."

An intrigued smile spread across her face. Green eyes narrowed to slits. Cohl could almost feel the steam rise.

"I take it positioning is important?" she breathed, her words seducing him even as he seduced her.

"Positional superiority is crucial."

"And why is that?"

He held her gaze as he reached down and slipped off her black panties. "Absolutely essential for unimpeded mobility and tight maneuvers."

As he loosened his own pants, she slid a smooth calf along his thigh with masterful technique. He nipped her lower lip in warning. "Pay attention, Tess. You don't want to miss anything."

"Believe me, you have my undivided attention," she murmured.

Cohl cleared his throat with grave authority. "Next comes Line of Attack."

She arched an inquisitive eyebrow.

He obliged her. "Look for an undefended opening."

Tess giggled beneath him. "That's not a real rule."

Her giggling stopped abruptly when he pressed himself against her most vulnerable spot.

"Identifying your opponent's unprotected zone is the fastest way to ultimate conquest." Then he released her wrists and rested on his elbows, gazing down into her glittering, hooded eyes. "Seems I've found yours."

"Now what?" Her rapid, hot breath caressed his face as he lowered his head and nibbled along her jaw.

"Constant forward pressure."

She inhaled sharply when he surged into her. He moaned right down to his heels. So good, warm, and tight, buried alive in the woman of his dreams.

She wrapped her legs around him and pulled him closer. His next line came out as a low growl. "Constant pressure keeps the opponent off-balance and at your mercy."

"A definite advantage," she sighed in his ear. Her palms skimmed across his shoulders, down his back, and over his buttocks. Nothing felt as good as her soft hands on his hard body.

She burrowed her face in his chest. "Next?"

He started to rock in slow, torrid thrusts. The final instructions were strained snippets. "Timing. Tempo. Vary your body motion. Alternate speeds. A mix of tension and relaxation, forward and backward motion."

Tess's nails dug into his back. "Timing. Tempo. Got it."

Cohl struggled for air, feeling his control slip away as it always did with Tess. She definitely had it.

"Then victory is yours," he said roughly, barely hanging on to coherent thought.

"Mine," Tess repeated. A low growl slipped from her lips, primitive in abandon, as her head arched back in fierce release.

Cohl forgot the lesson, who was the instructor, who the student. Forgot the rules, that this fantasy was only temporary. Everything else faded into the background except the woman beneath him, surrounding him.

As he hovered on the bittersweet edge of ecstasy, one single question held together: How would he ever let her go?

Nish stood before Gothyk the Glutton and watched him lick his filthy fingers. Alone in a pool of light with his odious meal sprawled across the table, the leader of the Traka-Sou belched loudly. Nish wrinkled his nose beneath the deep cowl.

"So you are saying that I should get the amulet for myself?" Gothyk spat at him. The broad, flat face bore a permanent snarl, and bits of food stuck to his unkempt hair and beard.

Nish nodded. "If you do not, Rommol will use the weapon against you. You would do well to secure the amulet for yourself and defeat Rommol once and for all."

Gothyk pushed back from the table and crossed his arms across the enormous girth of his food-stained shirt. "Why should I believe you, Nish? You are an old man who says he can see everything." Gothyk snorted. "Can you prove it?"

"Your ships have failed twice to kill Travers and the woman. They were decimated badly in the last attempt. They are now far off Yre Gault awaiting further instructions from you."

Gothyk's face dropped and he leaned far forward. "How do you know this?" he hissed.

Nish answered quietly, "I see all. I also see that your people placed a tracking device aboard Travers's ship while it was being repaired over Yre Gault. When Travers leaves the safety of his planet, you can follow him with ease. A most impressive maneuver on your part. You will make a good leader for Trakas."

Gothyk stared at Nish for a very long time. Nish waited

patiently. Imbeciles took longer than most to process simple information.

Finally, Gothyk leaned back in his chair. "Why are you telling me all this? What do you want?"

Nish smiled under his cover. "I only want what is best for Trakas. That is why I am here."

"So what do you suggest I do?"

"Do not attack Travers again. He is very close to finding the amulet. His orders are to return it to Rommol in exchange for his father. *You* will need to seize the amulet from Travers soon after it is freed," Nish replied. "Follow him to Demisie."

"Why should I go? I have plenty of warriors who can take an amulet from one man," Gothyk huffed.

Nish leaned forward. "Which one of your men can you trust with the power of the amulet?"

There was a long silence before Gothyk rose to his feet and lumbered over to where Nish stood. Gothyk's stench followed in his wake and filled the air when he came to stop in Nish's face. He pointed a pudgy finger at Nish and said, "If you are lying to me, old man, I will enjoy watching you die."

Nish folded his hands under his cloak. "You will discover that I never lie. I will contact you when the time is right."

"Very well," Gothyk snarled, turning back toward the food-laden table. "Now leave. You've interrupted my evening meal."

Nish bowed low and exited through the passageway and past the guards from Gothyk's inner chambers to the outer courtyard.

He stopped to rest on a bench and cast a look up into the breathtaking night sky over Trakas. Another key piece was in place. Gothyk would follow Travers.

Nish brushed away the twinge of guilt. Travers and the woman were now bound. It was more than he could have foreseen. He shrugged. The pieces remained the same and were all in place.

Now he just had to make sure that Rommol followed Gothyk.

Chapter Thirteen

The sleek transport slid into the gaping door of shuttle bay number one. A low hum reverberated through *Speculator*'s metal walls.

Tess leaned close to Cohl. "Couldn't Mr. Masters have just *sent* you the location of the planet we are looking for?"

Cohl grinned as the transport set down in the center of the bay. "Zain Masters doesn't trust encryption technology."

He took Tess by the hand and led her to the exit hatch of the transport just as it opened. Zain Masters filled the hatchway, large and powerfully built. He sported a beige shirt, tan pants, brown boots, and one hell of a body to fill them with.

Cohl greeted him by gripping his wrist. "About time you showed up, Zain. You're late. Did the cosmos freeze over?"

Zain regarded Tess with acute curiosity and nodded a silent acknowledgment. Then he gave Cohl a halfhearted glare. "Talk to Beckye. She wanted a date before she'd give me clearance."

Cohl shrugged. "No accounting for taste, I guess."

A slow smile crossed Zain's face as he hitched his head back toward the transport. "So in retribution, I brought trouble."

Right behind Zain stood another big man with silky, black hair and stunning blue-green eyes. Good Lord, Tess thought. Maybe Earthlings *did* run a little on the short side. Both were lean, hard, and broad-shouldered like Cohl. Tess could only imagine the number of women who had fallen at their collective feet.

"Got any ravishing, available women aboard this piece of junk?" he asked smoothly, pinning Tess with a riveting gaze and a smile that could make a girl forget her own name.

Cohl laughed and wrenched Rayce out of the transport by his wrist. "Rayce. What the hell are you doing here? I thought you were heading to the Kansari Region?"

Rayce's blue-green eyes flashed with genuine zeal. "Following a hot business proposition. And looking for a few good backers."

Cohl groaned audibly. "It figures. How come I only see you when the credits are flowing your way?"

Rayce crossed his arms and made a poor attempt to look offended. "Trust me a little. This one is guaranteed."

"You said that last time and now I can't show my face in the Berillian Sector again," Cohl muttered.

Rayce replied, "Hey, who knew those masks were highly flammable? And you have to admit, the Berillians look much better without all that facial hair."

Then Rayce set his sights on Tess. When he walked past Cohl toward her, she heard Cohl's soft warning, "Down, boy. She's mine."

Rayce ignored him and expertly lifted her hand to his lips. His eyes met hers, full of mischief and the devil himself. She couldn't help laughing when he winked.

"The name's Rayce Coburne. Proprietor of the fastest ship this side of Yre Gault. Need a ride anywhere?"

Behind him, Cohl crossed his arms over his chest, looking less than happy. For a nanosecond, she considered playing the quiet, demure Earth girl. But what the hell. Life was too short as it was.

Tess batted her eyelashes playfully. "Tess MacKenzie. Finest voice this side of Earth. And there's no way your ship can be faster than you."

The only one who didn't bust a gut laughing was Cohl. He brushed by Rayce and slipped a possessive arm around her waist. He advised Rayce, "You might as well save what few good lines you have. Tess is here to help me pick up the amulet."

Cohl motioned to Zain, who stepped forward. "Tess, meet Zain Masters, captain of *Careen*, and obviously the only man I can trust today."

She eyed Zain's panther moves—all intensity and strength with those piercing, jet-black eyes and dark brown hair pulled into a long, braided tail. There was a definite sensual hum buried beneath Zain's cool, imposing exterior.

With introductions out of the way, Cohl ushered them out of the shuttle bay and toward his office, keeping Tess close to his side. Rayce and Zain fell into step behind them.

Rayce cleared his throat loudly. "So, Tess. Are you enjoying your travels across the galaxy? I hope Cohl hasn't bored you to death."

She glimpsed Cohl's surly expression and stifled a smile. She just couldn't resist. "It's been an adventure. Why, just yesterday, Cohl instructed me on combat rules."

Cohl's head snapped around, his eyes narrowed to warning slits. Tess bit back a laugh.

"So how do you all know each other?" Tess asked as they entered the main corridor toward Cohl's office.

Cohl said, "Through business. Each of us has a specialty. Zain's is mapping star systems. Mine is difficult acquisitions.

Rayce does a good job of linking me to buyers when he's not busy picking up women."

"Sounds like you would make a good team," Tess observed. Around her, the three men chuckled in unison.

"What's so funny?"

Cohl shook his head. "It would never work. Too many captains and too little space between them."

They entered Cohl's office and settled around the darkened holodeck table. Seated next to her, Cohl quickly turned serious.

"The timetable has moved up. I only have six days to find the amulet. Or Rommol kills my father. And believe me, he's more than happy to do it."

Rayce nodded. "Zain told me the whole story. Damn shame. From what I hear, Rommol and Gothyk are having one hell of a time ripping Trakas apart."

Cohl asked Zain, "You said you found Demisie? I hope we are relatively close."

Zain nodded and slipped a slender cartridge out of his jacket and into the panel next to the holodeck. "From our current position, it's only about two days at hyperspeed."

The mesh cylindrical grid sprang up from the table base. Tess's eyes widened at the explosion of stars inside the grid, alone and in groups, between fuzzy clumps and swirls of clouds. Incredible.

Zain began. "According to every star map I could find, Demisie doesn't exist. However, I uncovered a single incident where a ship actually landed there about one thousand years ago."

Cohl frowned. "If a ship found it, then how can there be no record of its location?"

"Apparently the ship landed under distress conditions. The planet literally appeared out of nowhere according to crew accounts. On departure, they lost the coordinates and were never able to locate the planet again. The details are scarce and for good reason." Zain tapped the controls. The holo image zoomed into a small patch of clouds and stardust.

"I believe Demisie is located in this area," he noted. The image zoomed closer to the region in surging stages until one small star appeared, surrounded by a thick red layer of gaseous, billowing clouds.

Tess squinted at the image. "So where's the planet?"

"Hiding in the clouds," Zain answered with conviction. "The area surrounding the star has an unstable magnetic field. Watch closely."

He entered more commands. Immense magnetic arcs cut across the image, crisscrossing and overlapping each other until it looked like a giant donut surrounding the single star.

Zain continued. "The lines simulate magnetic fields. In the center is the star, the nucleus of the solar system and the only clearly visible part. Around it, an entire area hidden within an intense magnetic field. Demisie would show up as a ghost shadow at best."

"Damn," Rayce muttered. "An invisible planet could do some serious damage if you tried to fly through it."

Zain grinned. "When you get close to the planet, Demisie's own magnetic field would take over and you'd have time to divert. However, the way you fly, Rayce, there'd be no hope."

Rayce snorted. "And you fly like my mother."

Zain chuckled and turned back to the holodeck.

"Cohl, I can't give you the planet's precise orbit inside the shielded area but you should be able to locate it within a day. You will have to use some rudimentary tools for your search. That much magnetic concentration is going to wreak havoc with *Speculator*'s systems, specifically navigation and communications. That's one reason this planet hasn't been detected. Spacecraft avoid the entire system. Too much static. And just to make things interesting, the magnetic bands can shift without warning."

"Wait a minute," Tess cut in. She turned to Zain. "No

offense, but how do you know there's a planet in there? And how do you know it's the planet we are looking for?"

Zain eyed her. "Simple. I've eliminated all the places that it could be. All that's left are the places it shouldn't be."

When she gave him a skeptical look, Zain broke into a blinding smile. "Let's just say that I have a talent for finding lost planets. And an occasional lost treasure. The legend surrounding Demisie speaks of lavish architecture and art. An adventurer's dream."

Tess blinked at him. "Won't they be a little upset if we just waltz in and steal their amulet?"

Zain shook his head. "I doubt it. The ship that landed on Demisie rescued the last group of survivors. They told stories of war and famine, decimating the planet's population below maintainable levels. Those who weren't killed in the civil war died later of disease and starvation. I'd be surprised if there's a single living soul on Demisie right now."

"I see," Tess said sadly. "How many people?"

Zain replied, "At peak, probably about a million. We're talking an entire planet here."

Tess nodded. A whole civilization, self-destructed. She thought about Earth and its one hundred plus current wars. It could happen there, too. She would never get used to looking at life and death from a planetary level.

Cohl's hand squeezed her thigh and she looked into his smiling face. Golden eyes narrowed, the sign of banked desire. It was enough to take her mind off Demisie's plight.

"What else do you have, Zain?" Cohl asked.

"Not much. Nothing solid in my archives. I have a few individual reports but they are sketchy at best."

Cohl studied the image in the holodeck. "What about the last group of survivors? Any idea where they ended up?"

Zain shook his head. "They were dropped at a central space station and dispersed from there. Even if you could track the descendents, you probably wouldn't get much useful information from them. Specifics tend to get lost after a few generations."

Quietly, Tess asked him, "Do civilizations die like this all the time?"

"Unfortunately, yes. But then again, new ones are always starting," Zain said with an encouraging smile.

She closed her eyes. "Of course." But the people Demisie were gone. And now she was going to steal one of their precious artifacts, a link to the past and a world lost forever. Robbing their graves. Would others follow? Would they strip and scatter Demisie's civilization across the galaxy? She thought about the pyramids, Stonehenge, the odd wonders on Earth that seemed so un-Earthly. Were they the historical crumbs from another world?

"Tess?" Cohl's voice was close and tender.

She opened her eyes to find all three men looking at her. With a weak smile, she replied, "Sorry." She pushed up from the table. "You'll have to excuse me. I promised Beckye that I'd help her with the meal."

Tess shot Cohl a look before heading for the door. "Don't be long. I'm looking forward to hearing a few war stories."

Rayce whistled long and low after the door closed behind her. He leaned back in his chair and propped a boot up on a nearby chair. "Cohl looks a little tired, don't you think, Zain?"

Beside him, Zain examined Cohl intently. "Sure does. Something must be keeping him awake nights."

Cohl crossed his arms and endured the friendly grilling he knew he would get sooner or later.

Rayce leaned his head toward Zain conspiratorially. "Maybe he found a night job. Those are hell on your body."

Zain nodded. "Or an undercover operation. Brutal hours."

"Are you two just about done?" Cohl asked in a bored tone.

Zain and Rayce both shook their heads in unison.

Cohl laughed. "She's a good woman."

Zain's eyebrows raised. "Planning on keeping her around for a while?"

Cohl's expression sobered. "Only until the mission is completed. Then I have to take her back."

"Now why would you want to do that?" Rayce said in a slow drawl.

Cohl stared at the table for a moment before answering. "I abducted her off Earth for this mission. It's not something I'm particularly proud of but I had no choice."

He stood up and paced the room. "At first, it was so clear. Just find her, secure the amulet, and get my father back. Simple plan."

He stopped and ran a hand through his hair. "But something happened. Something I didn't expect."

He looked up in time to catch the amused look exchanged between Zain and Rayce. "It's not what you think. This entire mission has gone right to hell. I don't want her to get hurt or worse. I've already tried to send her back but there's a problem."

Rayce muttered low, "Does it involve a cold bed?"

Cohl ignored him. "The minute I identified her as the key to freeing the amulet, I placed a price on her head. Now she's not safe anywhere. She has already been abducted by the Traka-Nor. There's no way I'll let the Traka-Sou or anyone else get their hands on her again."

He didn't realize how threatening he looked with his eyes fierce, his fists clenched, and his entire body taut, until he glanced at the two other men in the room. They both regarded him with raised eyebrows.

"And there's another problem." He stalked over, retrieved a data pad from the table, and handed it to Rayce. "I received this file shortly after Rommol contacted me about my father."

Rayce took the data pad, scanned it, and then glanced up at Cohl. "What is it?"

"A song, *the* song," Cohl replied simply. "The song that unlocks the amulet. Complete with voice match analysis and music."

Rayce swore low. "How convenient."

Cohl nodded. "Isn't it though? You think it's legit?"

Rayce shook his head. "No way of telling. There's more," he murmured. Then his head came up. "Cohl, this is a description of the find, traps and all. Who sent this?"

"Good question. It came in a one-way, untraceable transmission shortly after my father was captured. I had Beckye working on it for days. Nothing."

"It could be a setup," Rayce offered.

Cohl rubbed the back of his neck. "Pretty elaborate setup. Frankly, I don't think the Trakas are that smart."

Rayce tossed the data pad on the table. "Either way, it smells bad, Cohl. What does Tess think?"

Silence hung while Cohl sat down and leaned back in his chair.

Rayce asked, "You *did* tell her, right?"

Cohl blew out a long breath. "Not exactly."

There was a collective groan from Rayce and Zain.

Cohl raised a hand in self-defense. "I explained about the traps and the danger in screwing up the song. She just doesn't know that the information we are going on is less than credible."

"Not everyone appreciates your warped sense of adventure like we do. I suggest you talk to her soon," Zain pressed. "I'd hate to hear of your untimely death."

Rayce looked around. "Speaking of untimely deaths, did that overbearing robot of yours finally become obsolete? Shouldn't he be butting in on this conversation?"

Jumping at the change of subject, Cohl replied, "Pitz is keeping an eye on Trakas for me. I want him close in case we fail or Rommol turns out to be more of an idiot than I already think he is."

"So let me get this straight," Rayce said, tapping a finger on the table. "You've got both sides after you now? How'd you manage that?"

Cohl shook his head. "Damned if I know. First, Rommol kidnapped my father for the amulet. Then Gothyk, leader of the Traka-Sou, discovered that I was looking for the key to the amulet, so he's been on my ass almost since I started. After that, I had to deal with some of Rommol's renegades. What can I say? I'm popular these days."

Zain frowned. "I didn't detect anyone following you but if I were you, I wouldn't stay in one place too long."

"We won't. As soon as we finish eating, *Speculator* will be in hyperspace."

Rayce stood and stretched. "Then let's move." He grinned wide at Cohl. "Over dinner, I'll fill you in on my new venture."

Cohl groaned. "If I just say yes now, will you go away?"

"Forget it," Zain said as he got to his feet. "If I have to suffer through the pitch, so do you." He shot Cohl a long look. "Unless you can find a way to keep Beckye at bay. Can't you send her to the VirtuWav a few times a day?"

Cohl laughed hard and slapped Zain on the back. "Tried that. She keeps burning out the power supply."

Alone in his office, Cohl listened to the gentle hum of *Speculator* in hyperspace en route to Demisie. He studied the statistics from Zain's holodeck image. He owed Zain for this one and mentally added it to the collective pool of favors Zain, Cohl, and Rayce had established over the past ten years. It was nice to be able to count on someone to cover your back on a regular basis.

Cohl stared at the red haze where Demisie was hidden and felt the rush he always got with the thrill of the hunt.

Normally that rush would be a welcomed part of the adventuring process. However, this wasn't going to be a regular acquisition. This time was different. This time his father's life was on the line. And so was Tess's.

Uneasiness invaded. His hand clenched into a tight fist. He would protect her at all costs. With his last breath, he would make sure she got safely back to Earth where she belonged. Back to her dreams and her life—without him in it.

The comm unit buzzed in Cohl's ear. He activated the unit. "What is it, Beckye?"

"Pitz for you," she snapped.

Cohl grimaced. Apparently, Zain had dodged her. There'd be hell to pay for weeks.

"Put him through."

The comm crackled. "Sir?"

"Pitz. How is it going?" Cohl leaned back in his chair and folded his hands behind his head.

"We are in position, sir."

"Anyone bothered you yet?"

Pitz replied, "No. I do not believe they will either. The Traka-Nor intership operations appear disjointed and sporadic. The military structure is not well organized and there does not appear to be a coherent ranking system among them."

Good, Cohl thought. The last thing he needed was a well-coordinated military force. On the other hand, that left a lot of room for rebels and traitors.

"What about communications traffic?"

Pitz replied, "We currently possess all the Traka-Nor encryption codes. Therefore, I can intercept intership and planetary transmissions. Several recent communications place both Rommol and Gothyk on-planet in their respective residences."

"Have you uncovered any information on my father?"

The line buzzed. "Nothing helpful except that he is currently detained somewhere close to Rommol's position."

Cohl nodded. "I figured that. Let me know if you detect any unusual activity. And, Pitz, somehow you *must* get a definite fix on my father. If you don't hear from me within four days after we reach Demisie, you will have to initiate a rescue."

"I do not understand," Pitz came back after a brief pause.

Cohl sighed. "We will be in total communications blackout once we get close to Demisie. At that point, you are on your own. It should not take us more than four days to find the amulet and contact you. If you don't hear from me after that time, then get my father out of Trakas any way you can."

Static filled the line. "Are you sure, sir?"

"Positive. I will send you one last message outside Demisie's solar system. Start counting from then."

"Understood."

"Out."

Cohl cut communications and rubbed his forehead. He already knew that the odds of a successful rescue attempt were slim. Pitz's formidable firepower was no match for the sheer number of Rommol's loyal guards. Even if Pitz managed to find Montral Trae Salle, getting him out alive would be practically impossible.

The door to the office slid open. Tess walked in with a warm smile.

"Hey, handsome. Anything new to report?"

He watched her graceful walk, caught her scent as she stopped in front of him and looked him over with those bewitching green eyes.

"Come closer and I'll tell you all about it," Cohl said in a lazy voice.

She shifted her weight to one hip and cocked her head. "You know, you're easily distracted."

"On the contrary, I have very linear, very focused thought processes." He flexed his hands.

With that, Tess took a small step back to what she probably thought was a safe distance. Her chin went up. "Stop changing the subject, Cohl, and tell me what you were so worried about when I walked in here."

He took a deep breath. "Nothing is wrong. Pitz arrived at Trakas and is attempting to locate my father's exact position."

Tess frowned. "Why?"

"In case Pitz needs to launch a rescue."

She watched him for a long time. "You don't think we are going to make it, do you?"

Cohl scanned her troubled face. "I don't know. Every acquisition is different and this one sounds more difficult than most. Alone, I'd be all right. Having you along increases the risk considerably. I warned you that this would be dangerous."

Tess stared at the floor in thought and then fixed her gaze on him. "Would more training help? Sahto said you used that Virtu-whatever to practice. Maybe you could take me through a real acquisition?"

Cohl's eyebrows raised in surprise. "We can do that. Are you sure you are up to it?"

Challenge flashed in her eyes. "You have to ask? I'm ready for anything."

He grinned slow and wide. "I'm glad to hear it. Come to think of it, we haven't finished combat training yet either."

Tess's eyes widened. "There's more? Like what?"

"Did I mention reach?" Cohl lunged forward and pulled her down on the chair to straddle his thighs. Her hair tumbled around her face. He glimpsed the fight in her eyes. *Damn, who knew combat training could be so stimulating?*

"The power of reach is deceptive," he said smugly.

Her hands spread warm against his chest. Her sensual gaze

heated the rest of him. She asked, "Did you actually study all these rules or are you just making them up as you go along?"

He chuckled low and deep. His hands began a long slow slide down her back and around her buttocks. "I learned from Zain. He's military trained. For obvious reasons, his training technique differs considerably from mine."

Her gaze sharpened. "So how many women have you trained?"

Cohl's hands stopped and he looked directly into her eyes. "Just you."

She scanned his face as if searching for the truth. Finally she slid her arms around his neck and began nipping at his jaw. Her soft voice set him ablaze. "Since you are obviously well trained, I really have only one choice. I surrender."

Cohl's hands skimmed over the front of her black shirt, across her breasts, and down the rib cage, one rib at a time. He murmured thickly, "Not that I'm complaining but that was pretty easy. I expected more of a fight from my best student."

Slowly, she wriggled the length of her body against him until he hissed through his teeth. Her hands slid down his stomach, her fingers slipping beneath the waistband of his pants.

"Who said I was going to go easy on you?" she whispered.

Chapter Fourteen

Tess stared down at her feet planted dead center in the blue, shimmering circle of the VirtuWav. Her gaze traveled straight up to the matching circle above her head.

"Are you sure this is safe?"

Cohl glanced up from the VirtuWav control panel, the insidious blue light giving his smiling face a ghostly cast. "I do it all the time. It is safe. Trust me."

She gave a short laugh. "Do you have any idea how many women have gotten in trouble believing that line?"

"Would I lie to you, Tess?" There was an amused undertone in his statement.

"No. You would just leave out the part where my brain explodes." She smiled sweetly at him.

Cohl tapped the controls. "Only if I thought it would scare you."

"Not funny, Cohl. I told you I want to know everything. That includes any minor details that may affect my ability to walk with the living."

She heard his soft chuckle. "How could I forget? You nearly carved it across my forehead. Believe me, you are perfectly safe."

The door to the VirtuWav room slid open and Sahto walked in. He greeted Tess, then took over the control of the VirtuWav panel from Cohl. Tess swallowed hard.

"So explain to me exactly what happens here," she said. "And don't leave anything out."

Cohl stepped into the circle next to her. "The tubes will rise and fill with a buoyant gas. You will still be able to breathe. Then the computer interface will engage. Feels like fingers touching you. It doesn't hurt. Just relax. And don't fight the interface."

He grinned at her, his gold eyes gleaming. "I know that goes against your natural instinct."

Tess glared at him.

Cohl laughed aloud and nodded to Sahto, who tapped the panel.

An instant later, everything changed. The blue tube rose up around her and locked on to the circle above. Warm, heavy air filled her little world and lifted her off her feet. Weightless and lighter than air, she floated like a cloud; her hair flowed around her much as it would underwater.

When she steadied herself with a hand on each side of the tube, Cohl's voice came to her as if he were inside her mind. "Don't fight it, Tess. Relax."

She turned to look at him, but his floating image was fading away into a sleepy dream despite her fervent effort to control it. Electrical charges surged around her, tickling at her skin. Tess stiffened as they probed and attached to her, gently holding her flailing body in place. Once she was immobile, Tess felt the delicate invasion into her brain as her real world succumbed. After a few long terrifying seconds, her mind relinquished its struggle and the image sharpened.

She found herself standing in a strange world with Cohl nearby, frowning at her.

"I told you not to fight it. You're going to have one hell of a headache when we get back."

She knew he was talking but whatever he said was lost on her. The dirt beneath her feet, the distant mountains, the smell of foliage, the warm sun beating down—all so real. Cohl had told her what the VirtuWav was capable of but this was unbelievable.

They were standing in a clearing between a sheer rock face and an odd-looking forest of column-shaped trees in various hues of green. Mossy tendrils hung in large clumps from rocks and crept along the ground. Humid air with its heavy, pungent smell was so real that her nose itched. She glanced up as a flock of birds screeched their way across a blue, cloudless sky.

"I can't believe this is only in my mind," she whispered.

"It *is* amazing," Cohl agreed. "Sometimes I take it for granted." He reached out and squeezed her hand. It felt just like it should, warm and strong.

Tess stared at her hand in his, then down at herself—all there, same body, same clothes. She took a tentative step forward. The ground felt solid and real beneath her. She turned to examine Cohl from head to toe. He looked magnificent as usual.

"You want anything changed?" He crossed his arms over his chest.

Tess met his gaze, confused. "What?"

A wide smile crossed his face. "The program can change my appearance. I can be taller, broader, bigger if you want."

Tess blinked at him. "Bigger?"

Both his eyebrows rose. It was then she realized exactly what he was talking about.

She shook her head emphatically. "Oh, heavens no. No, thanks. Don't change a thing."

Cohl chuckled softly. "You had me worried for a minute."

"What about me?" she asked, half joking, half serious, mostly curious. "Anything you would alter?"

His golden eyes shimmered as he regarded her intently, lightly stroking his chin. "I'd prefer you naked." Then he smiled wide. "But that would put an end to this little expedition pretty quick."

She laughed and surveyed the strange new world inside her head. "So where are we?"

"Fa Lipele," Cohl replied from behind her. She turned to find him running his hand along a rectangle depression in the rock face.

Tess frowned. "You've been here before?"

"You wanted to see what a real acquisition is like. I tackled this one about a year ago."

She licked her lips. "So you know what to expect, right?"

He gazed up at her sincerely. "Whatever happens, I'll be with you, Tess. You won't be alone."

His hands roamed over the rock, finally settled into an almost invisible line. "Besides, I want to see how well you take orders."

"Wasn't I a good student in combat training?" Tess folded her arms across her chest and raised a single eyebrow in quiet challenge.

Cohl's fingers froze on the stone. His eyes slowly met hers. "The best student I've ever had."

Tess's heart took a powerful leap. "I have an excellent teacher," she said in a husky voice.

"However perfect it was, we don't need any distractions along the way," Cohl replied. "You can get hurt here just like you would in reality." He returned to the rock, his fingertips following a fine crack.

"You said it was safe."

He nodded, not looking up. "I did. You can't die in here

but pain is pain. Unless you specifically cancel it out, it's going to hurt just like the real thing."

His fingers slipped inside a narrow fissure. "Got it."

A deep rumble emanated from the towering stone cliff and an entry door opened before them.

Tess peered inside. "It looks awfully dark."

Cohl reached into the backpack at his feet, produced two baseball-sized balls, and tossed them in the air. Tess watched in fascination as they floated to midair and started glowing. One shimmied to Cohl; the other one flew to Tess. Hers stopped about two feet away and blinked at her.

"What are they?" Tess asked.

"Lightballs," he answered. "They are programmed to stick close to you and provide no-hands lighting."

"They are so cute. Can I name mine?"

Cohl shook his head and chuckled. "Whatever makes you happy."

Tess reached out and gently touched her lightball. "Hello, Tink."

Cohl swung the pack over his shoulder. "Follow me. And do exactly what I tell you."

She wrinkled her nose. "I know, I know. Horrible death, dismemberment, and all that. Don't worry, I'll be a good girl."

He gave her a skeptical look to which she batted her eyelashes. Then he entered the cavern with his lightball zipping along ahead of him. Tess stayed close behind as the brilliant day outside disappeared around the first turn. The lightballs shone a path through the terminal darkness.

The walls were giant slabs of rock, wedged together in a crude fashion. Cohl stooped slightly under the low ceilings but she could still see the bounce in his step. He was in his element.

Tess could feel the humidity, smell the fungi that grew along the rough, stone walls. A low, steady roar emanated from the darkness in front of them, increasing to a deafening level as they moved forward. Cohl led her into an open cave filled with spectacular stalagmites and jagged walls ringed with color.

A five-story waterfall plummeted into a deep pool to their right, swirled and churned into a forty-foot-wide river that cut through the center of the massive cave, and disappeared under a stone wall on the other side. Tess covered her ears. The view might be magnificent but the damn noise could kill you.

Thick, sweet mist hung over the entire cave. Through the mist, Tess could just make out the opposite shore and outlines of hundreds of stalagmite formations. It looked like something out of Dungeons and Dragons.

Cohl walked to the edge of the raging river. Tess followed, feeling the kinetic energy of the falls vibrate the ground beneath her feet. She watched Cohl studying the far shore and wondered if he even realized he was smiling. She imagined she looked much the same way when she sang.

"How do we cross it?" she shouted to Cohl, who was already stooping to retrieve another goodie from the bag. He stood up, holding a cannonlike device sporting a grapple hook on each end.

"Watch out," he ordered. Tess stepped out of the way as he held the device out horizontally in front of him and pulled the trigger. Two grapple hooks shot out simultaneously. The first wedged tightly in the rock face behind them with a puff of dust. The other smacked into a giant stalagmite on the other side of the river.

It all happened in a split second and suddenly they had a bridge across the river. The cable snapped taut and Cohl slid the barrel slider back and forth along it.

Then he reached into the bag and pulled out two harnesses. The first one, he secured around his own torso and legs. The second, he helped Tess into and tightened the harness webbing snuggly.

He hitched his head toward the far side. "I'll go first, then send the unit back to you. Just do what I do."

She frowned at the setup. "I'm not a star athlete here."

Cohl attached his harness to the slider. Gripping it, he swung underneath and wrapped his legs around the slider. "All you have to do is hold on."

He showed her the control trigger and immediately shot across the pounding river, dropping safely on the other side. His lightball followed, blinking through the mist. He detached and shoved the slider back toward her. It glided across the cable and into her hands. She caught it. Looked like such a flimsy little thing to trust your virtual life to.

Tess gritted her teeth. She was the one who had offered to do this. She wasn't going to chicken out now.

She clipped her harness to the unit just as Cohl had and let her weight drop beneath the cable.

Her lightball hovered around her head. Tess whispered, "Okay, Tink. Here goes nothing."

With her legs wrapped tight around the slider, she activated the motor. It launched her, screaming like a banshee, over the water at breakneck speed.

About halfway across, she realized that she didn't know how to stop the damn thing. Luckily Cohl did. He grabbed her just before she smacked into the stalagmite on the other side. Tink zipped to her side.

Tess laughed a bit hysterically as Cohl set her on her feet. "Wow, that was almost fun."

Cohl chuckled as he disconnected her from the slider and helped her out of the harness. "Want to do it again?"

"No. I'll pass." She waved him off. "Oh, and by the way, thanks for telling me how to stop."

He grinned. "I realized that little omission when you hit the halfway point."

"I knew it. I knew you'd leave out something. Trap number one down, right?"

He was already slinging the pack over his back. "Right."

She trailed behind him, climbing between the massive stalagmites, fresh adrenaline pumping through her veins. She was beginning to see why Cohl was so hooked on this.

"What's next?"

He cast a glance over his shoulder. "I don't think you are going to like the next one as well."

Tess skirted a particularly large pillar. "Spill it, Cohl."

A cool breeze hit her in the face as they turned a tight corner. He abruptly caught her arm and pulled her tight against his chest. Face-to-face, with their shoulders wedged against a stone wall, she looked up at him in confusion.

He grinned. "Whatever you do . . . don't look down."

All the blood drained from her face and only her eyes moved as she cast a worried look around. They were standing on a narrow ledge over a bottomless chasm. At least twenty feet of thin air separated them from the opposite sheer rock face.

"Oh God," she gasped and squeezed her eyes shut. "I'm going to kill you when we get out of here."

She pressed herself back against the rock, trying desperately to become one with the wall.

"Breathe, Tess."

"I can't. You breathe for me."

She felt his warm lips against hers and she moaned softly.

"Trust me," he whispered in her ear.

"I do. I don't trust myself."

His lips skimmed hers again. His fingers caressed the nape of her neck. "Believe in yourself. You are far stronger than you know."

She let out an uneven breath. "It's just a simulation, right?"

"Right."

"What happens if I fall?"

He gave her a reassuring smile. "Program," he said aloud, "terminate exercise if Tess falls."

She looked at him sadly. "Will we have that option on Demisie?"

"No," he answered simply. Then he glanced down the length of the narrow ledge. "And if we don't get moving, we'll be here all day."

He slid over and flattened against the wall next to her. "Go first, Tess. It's only twenty meters. Just keep moving. You can choose your next step, but try not to look directly down at your feet."

She nodded. *It's only an illusion.*

As her foot slid a few inches over, her stomach clenched hard. Another few inches and she wondered if vomit would be real or an illusion in here.

"Cohl?"

He paused. "Sing, Tess."

She turned her head to look at him. "What?"

"I said, sing. Do you write your own songs?"

She blinked. "Yes, but—"

Cohl linked his fingers in hers. "Then sing me one of your songs."

"Right now? Why?" she asked in disbelief.

"Because I've noticed how singing relaxes you. It gives you strength."

"I love to sing," she told him, as if he didn't already know that.

His eyes met hers, and in them there was a strange sadness. "I know. You miss it. So sing. Anything but the chicken dance."

She closed her eyes. A song. A song. She knew a thousand of them. Why couldn't she think of one now? Probably because she was hanging by her fingernails off the edge of a cliff with a madman who actually was enjoying himself.

One song came to mind in a flash.

"Holding on under the deluge . . . Strolling where only fools would tread . . ."

The words echoed sweetly across the chasm as her voice grew stronger and she slid into the familiar warmth of her music.

"An uncharted place you call your heart . . ."

Wonderful acoustics in a bottomless chasm. She'd have to remember that. She felt Cohl nudge her gently along, her back pressed to the wall, her feet moving inches at a time.

"Fools have nothing on me . . . Fools have nothing on me . . ."

One line led to another until Cohl's strong arms pulled her off the ledge and into another open cave.

"You did it, Tess."

When she locked on to him with a semideath grip, his golden eyes narrowed into a sensual gaze. His loaded kiss caught her off guard and Tess's breath caught at the immediate sexual pull.

Noting her stunned look, Cohl answered her next question before she could ask it. "Yes, you can make love in the VirtuWav. It's hell keeping my crew from practically living in here."

Grinning, he took her hand and guided her through a maze of rectangle rock formations stuck haphazardly into the sand floor. Tess studied their curious shape. Not stalagmites like in the other cave. In fact, these didn't look natural. They looked man-made. A chill ran through her.

"I've got a bad feeling about this," she whispered. "Cohl?"

"Yeah?" he answered, drawing her around the chaotic arrangement of monoliths.

She slowed down, eyeing each one warily as she passed it. "What are these?"

"The rocks? The legend of this find says that they turn into warriors who protect the treasure." He shrugged. "I didn't have any trouble the first time. I think it's just a myth."

A large fist came out of nowhere and struck Cohl in the side of the head with a sickening crack. He grunted and staggered, then collapsed on the ground almost landing on his lightball.

Tess screamed and scrambled out of the way as the massive hand then swatted at her. She fell down on her butt and gaped up at a man made of stone. He had to be seven feet tall and weigh a couple of tons. Crudely cut facial features gave him a comical look and his movements were jerky and slow but highly effective.

She rolled to her feet, dodging another clumsy swing. Stumbling her way through the monoliths, she flattened behind one, saying a silent prayer that it, too, didn't decide to come to life. Her lightball flitted to her side. Tess waved it away.

"Shoo, shoo, Tink. You're giving me away," she hissed.

Then her full attention was on the ground-shaking steps of the stoneman walking. She peered around her cover. He was heading right for her like a man on a deadly mission.

She heard Cohl's low groan. Stoneman stopped and swayed from side to side; then he turned slowly toward Cohl.

No. Stoneman must respond to sound.

Without thinking, Tess stepped from behind her cover and waved her arms. "Hey, over here, you big lummox."

Stoneman reeled to a stop and fixed his sightless gaze on her. Tess swallowed. *Damn.* Now what?

She watched Stoneman lumber toward her in a straight line of attack. Combat training came to mind. After all, this was combat. What had Cohl said was first? Oh, yes. *Initial speed.*

She turned and took off in the opposite direction of Cohl's position, the thump-thump of Stoneman's footsteps following. Her heart pounded in her head, making mush of coherent thought. Sure he was slow. Sure he was stupid. But how did you stop him?

Timing, tempo, alternating speeds. She ran a random pattern through the formations with Stoneman following her relentlessly. He was one persistent virtual illusion. Occasionally shouting at him to keep him interested, she led him in a wide circle around the perimeter of the cave. Even Tink was having trouble keeping up with her but no matter how many twists and turns she took, Stoneman showed no signs of tiring. The steady, rhythmic *ca-thump, ca-thump* of his footsteps rang in her ears, unmerciful and incessant.

Out of ideas and out of space, Tess found herself back at the edge of the chasm where they had entered. She stared down at the endless drop and then turned to watch in sheer terror as Stoneman bore down on her. His arms and legs pumped at what she figured to be top speed for a stoneman.

Positioning for mobility and tight maneuvers. That's what Cohl had said. Hopefully he was right.

Closer Stoneman drew. She held her ground. Tiny pebbles on the ground jumped around her with each jarring step. She moved back, as close to the edge as she could stomach.

His arms stretched forward for her. Ten feet, five feet, two.

Tess sidestepped left onto the narrow ledge and out of his path as Stoneman took his last step into thin air. There was a great suck of air as he dropped over the edge and out of sight like the proverbial brick.

Tess clutched the rock wall and fought to control the shaking that had taken over her body. Forcing herself around the edge of the doorway, she slid back into the relative safety of the cave onto her hands and knees. The fine sand felt real and solid between her fingers. However comforting, the numerous monoliths surrounding her were an unpleasant reminder that Stoneman might have friends.

She got to her feet and ran as fast as she could on legs that continued to tremble. Illusion or not, scared was scared.

She rounded the corner to find Cohl just regaining consciousness. Tess dropped next to him and he immediately grabbed her arm.

"Are you okay?"

She nodded. Hell no, she wasn't okay. She pointed back at the chasm. "But I'll tell you one thing right now, Cohl. There is no way I am going back out on that ledge. Never, never again, and if there's one on Demisie, you are on your own."

He regarded her babbling with a dazed and baffled expression, and then rubbed his head. "What hit me?"

"Stoneman," Tess muttered, then grabbed at his fingers covered with blood. "Oh God, you're bleeding."

Cohl ignored her as he scanned the area in concern. He reached out and gripped her wrists, pulling her close. "What happened, Tess? Where is he now?"

"Probably a pile of gravel at the bottom of the chasm."

He squeezed her wrists harder and enunciated every word. "Tess. What happened?"

She blew out a long breath. "I led him over the chasm back there courtesy of Combat Training 101."

Cohl stared at her in disbelief for a full minute, then shook his head. "I'm glad you're a good student. Next time I screw up, do me a favor and cancel the program."

She glared at him. "Well, I would have if I'd known I could."

He pushed himself to sitting and leaned back against a rock. "Sorry. I'm not used to a partner. Program: report body status."

The computerized voice replied crisply, "Participant Travers is eighty-nine percent functional. Minor loss of blood. Not considered life-threatening. First-degree concussion."

Tess froze. "Cohl?"

"I'm all right. Nothing serious." He dragged the pack over

and reached in to get a square bandage that he slapped over the wound on his head.

"Damn careless of me," he muttered. "I should have been paying attention. I keep forgetting that you are a major distraction."

He rose to his feet and swung the pack over his shoulder. Motionless, Tess stared after him as he walked away. The lightball danced behind him.

After a few seconds, he realized she wasn't following and turned. "We need to keep moving, Tess. It's not safe here."

"How can you continue?" Her voice was a whisper.

He shrugged. "Head wounds always look worse than they are and I've had concussions before. Besides, this is only illusion, remember? I'll be fine once we leave the program."

Cohl rolled his neck. "I'm just lucky Stoneman didn't knock my head right off my shoulders." He smiled. "For a minute there, I thought you had one hell of a left."

She struggled to her feet. "I don't understand this, Cohl. You told me that you didn't have any trouble the first time."

"I didn't but the VirtuWav program takes certain liberties based on the information I load into the system. Using my specifications, it generates an exact recreation of the acquisition site."

Tess stopped in front of him, feeling thoroughly and realistically drained. "Liberties. Is that what you call that thing that tried to make roadkill out of us?"

Cohl's expression softened as he drew her into his arms. He lifted her chin with a finger and kissed her—a touch of reality in an insane, unreal place. She clung to it like a life raft.

"Had enough for today?" he murmured into her hair.

Tess rolled her head back and forth against his chest. "I'm fine. But I'm warning you, if I see one bug in this little exercise, I'm out of here."

"No bugs. Not that I'm aware of anyway."

He released her and headed toward a low doorway that Tess had somehow missed in her game of keep-away with Stoneman. Through a low corridor, Tess tagged along behind him, silent and worried. He acted as if nothing had happened, as if this were normal. She wondered how many narrow escapes he'd had. How many times he had dragged himself out of a trap, bloody and injured.

Then her head shot up. She smelled fire. Not fire. Something else. Cohl stopped abruptly and handed her a small face mask.

"What's this for?"

He pushed the mask onto her face, covering her nose and mouth. Then did the same for himself. "Gas ahead."

"Gas? As in blow-us-to-smithereens gas?" Tess asked nervously through the mask.

Cohl eyed her. "I don't think so. More like I'm-losing-my-mind gas. It dissolves brain tissue. Drives you insane."

She put her hands on her hips and gaped. "How did you figure that one out?"

He pulled out a small, palm-sized device and handed it to her. "It's a SAMA unit. Detects all types of interesting elements that can eat you, melt you, blind you, paralyze you, maim you." He waved his hand vaguely. "You get the basic idea."

Tess regarded the unit, then his grinning face, and decided that he was having entirely too much fun. She handed back the unit. "What's SAMA stand for?"

"SAve My Ass," Cohl answered as he pocketed the slim unit.

Tess laughed. "That figures. Do I get one?"

Cohl glanced over his shoulder as he headed down the final length of the corridor. "Protecting your rear is my job."

Tess followed him into a small round room containing nothing but a graceful, stone pedestal table in the center.

Atop the pedestal sat a small, finely detailed figurine carved from a single, flawless pink crystal.

"Stunning," she murmured through the mask, moving closer.

Cohl nodded. "Exactly what I said when I first saw it. No matter how good your sources are, the real artifact is much more striking."

She took another step toward the pedestal and felt Cohl's hand on her shoulder.

"That's close enough, Tess."

She glanced at him in confusion. "It's right there. We just take it and we're done, right?"

"Not quite. Anything that looks easy will probably kill you. It took me a while to figure out this one's defenses."

He retrieved a small white packet from the pack and tossed it at the figurine. The packet stopped in midair and dropped. When it hit the ground, it shattered into small pieces.

"What happened?" Tess asked, gazing at the little shards that were once the packet.

Cohl answered, "An ice shield. Freezes instantly. You could imagine what would happen if you stuck your hand in there."

Tess cringed. Unfortunately, she had an excellent imagination.

"So how do you retrieve it?" she whispered.

"The ice shield only exists above the table to the ceiling."

He withdrew a small club from the pack and activated it. A long blade shot out the end in a tube about one inch in diameter and three feet in length.

"Oh, a light saber!" Tess said.

Cohl cast her a puzzled look. "It's a plasma cutter. What's a light saber?"

Tess shook her head and laughed. "Never mind. It was

long, long ago in a galaxy far, far away and you wouldn't believe it if I told you."

He raised an eyebrow. Then shrugged. "Better stand back."

Cohl swung the plasma cutter through the pedestal base. The stone snapped, then toppled over. The figure fell to the soft ground below. Cohl deactivated the cutter. He picked up the figurine and handed it to Tess.

She held the figurine up into Tink's light field. Thousands of facets lit and flashed under the light. Even with her inexperienced eye, she could tell it was exquisitely made.

"Was it valuable?" she said in a hushed voice.

"Very. Enough to fund my next few expeditions. Rayce found an excellent buyer," Cohl answered.

She turned it over in her hands, finally settling on the front. Up close, the woman's expression was profoundly tragic.

"It's so beautiful. So sad," she whispered. Tess gazed up into Cohl's grinning, victorious face. Her eyes were drawn to the right side of his face covered with blood from Stoneman's attack.

At that moment, she realized just how high the price was.

Chapter Fifteen

"I really, *really* hate this," Sahto muttered as he worked the helm controls. He cast an annoyed look over his shoulder at Cohl standing behind him. "You do realize that I can't see a damn thing in there."

Cohl looked out *Speculator*'s main viewpoint at the dust clouds that had cloaked Demisie for millions of years. The solitary red dwarf star gave a soft, pink tinge to the dark billows of galactic gas and fine particles. It almost looked too heavenly to be threatening. Cohl knew better.

"Where's your sense of adventuring, Sahto? I thought you enjoyed a challenge."

Sahto snorted and turned back to the controls and the numerous lights that flashed warnings.

"Challenges, yes. Suicide, no. There's a reason why ships avoid this godforsaken system. Half the instruments haven't been working right since we dropped out of hyperspace. I can't depend on any of them because I can't tell the difference between false readings and good ones."

Cohl slapped him on the shoulder. "Do your best. Once we breech Demisie's magnetic field, it should be easier to see."

"Don't count on it," Sahto shot back. "It could get worse. We might be completely blind."

Blind. *Damn,* Cohl thought. He hated this too but he sure wasn't about to say that aloud. Ruthlessly, he shoved aside the persistent fear that they might not even be close to the amulet, that Zain's instincts might be wrong just this once.

Too many times in the last two days those doubts had reared up to bite him when he least expected it, subverting his best intentions.

And then there was Tess. The closer he got to the amulet, the less time he had left with her. When it was all done, Yre Gault would get his father back. Cohl would find the next treasure to be unearthed. Tess would return to her singing. Rommol would have his damn amulet. Everyone would be happy. So why did he feel so lousy?

"Beckye, hail Pitz for me," Cohl ordered.

Within seconds, Pitz's mechanical voice answered the hail. "Any activity, Pitz?"

"None, sir."

Cohl nodded. "Good. We are heading into the Demisie system now. Start your countdown. By my direct order, your primary command is to protect my father at all costs."

"Yes, sir. Primary command accepted."

"Good luck, Pitz."

There was a pause. "Good luck to you too, sir."

Cohl stared out the viewport into the unknown.

"Sahto, take us in."

Perhaps another man would have buckled under Rommol's rancor, but Nish was beyond that. Old men didn't quake for anyone. Besides, he simply didn't have the energy. He could

205

only hope that his aged body would survive long enough to finish the game he had started.

The low light of Rommol's chambers cast dark shadows into the far corners. They were alone. No advisors to interfere or deflect the next move. The timing was perfect.

"You better have a good reason for waking me," Rommol snarled. He looked uglier than usual at this hour.

Hidden beneath his guise, Nish nodded. "The Finder has located the lost planet of Demisie but your brother moves against him as we speak. The time to proceed is now."

Rommol's eyes bulged. "My brother?" He jumped to his feet. "Why didn't you tell me?"

He slammed the communications console and barked a series of orders into it. A brief exchange confirmed that Gothyk had already boarded his personal starship. Rommol burst into a string of sharp instructions and obscenities.

After the communications were cut, Rommol spread his hands atop the desk and leaned toward Nish.

"You are coming with me, old man," he commanded. "I want your head close by in case this entire scheme falls apart in front of my men."

Nish spoke gently. "Of course. I would have it no other way. May I suggest that the Finder's father also accompany us?"

There was silence. Nish waited. Rommol's reluctance was expected. From the beginning, Nish had no doubt that Montral Trae Salle was never to see his planet Yre Gault again. Once Rommol possessed the amulet, he would not bother with prior agreements or deals. The least Nish could do was attempt to save the pawn's life.

Nish added smoothly, "He could provide additional enticement for the amulet if the Finder changes his mind."

Rommol frowned. "Very well. Now move. I don't want to lose Gothyk."

* * *

Tess walked onto *Speculator*'s bridge. Equipment hummed low around her, all quiet except for Sahto's endless tapping and Beckye's occasional chatter. Cohl sat at the center station, staring in the incessant red haze that filled the viewport.

She drew a slow breath. For nearly two days, it had been like this in the search for Demisie within the madly fluctuating magnetic field. The tight crisscrossing search pattern had been further hindered by a tortuous slow pace and the limited range of *Speculator*'s scanners. With every passing hour, Cohl had grown quieter and more withdrawn. He'd slept little, spending most of his time right here.

She placed her hands on his broad shoulders and began rubbing out his tight neck muscles. He moaned softly beneath her touch.

"You'll find it," she said quietly. "Don't give up."

He grunted. "I'm beginning to wonder. How is the song coming?"

Tess kneaded her way across his broad shoulders. "Fine. The lyrics are a bit unusual, cryptic. Strange phrasing. It's almost a chant. Beautiful music though. Haunting. I don't think I'll have any trouble with it."

"I seriously hope not." He placed one of his hands over hers and caressed it gently, not taking his eyes off the view.

Tess frowned. His voice sounded as tight as his shoulders. And tired. He had to sleep and she only knew one way to get him into bed.

Tess leaned down and whispered in his ear, "How about some more combat training?"

His hand stilled. His head turned until his golden eyes made a blindingly fast transformation from somber to sizzle.

"You think you can distract me with sex?" His voice was low, quiet, and loaded.

She smiled sweetly. "Actually, I *know* I can distract you with sex."

Cohl shook his head. "Hell. I'm predictable."

Beckye snorted loudly at her station on the bridge. Cohl glanced at her. "Is there a problem?"

She swiveled around and frowned. "Something keep on come through the comm. Can't make sense of. Listen."

A shrill tone filled *Speculator*'s bridge, then cut out, then came back. Intermittently, voices interrupted the gibberish of squeals and screeches.

Beckye shut it down. "Been doing that for hours."

Tess felt Cohl's shoulders tense up as he asked, "Can you cut out the noise any?"

She harrumphed again. "Do I look dim? I try. No good. Too much noise from out there." She waggled a long finger toward the viewport. "But I bet it be Pitz," she went on, turning back to her station.

Tess asked, "Pitz? Why do you think that?"

"Too persistent to be anyone else, that why," Beckye shot back. "You know him. Got to report ever little thing."

Cohl swung out of his chair and came up behind Beckye's station. "He knows damn well he can't reach us in here. What the hell could he want?"

Beckye waved a dismissive hand over her head. "I sure it nothing that can't wait."

Watching Cohl's deep scowl as he scanned Beckye's bank of displays, Tess doubted that very much.

"I've got something, Cohl!" Sahto's shout cut through the conversation.

Cohl sprinted back to his station and tapped the console. "Where?"

Bouncing in his chair, Sahto replied, "Dead ahead. It's big. Definitely planetoid-size."

"How long before it's in visual range?"

"Very soon. In fact . . ." Sahto stopped and looked up. "There it is."

Abruptly the red haze cleared and a dazzling planet filled

the viewport. Tess jumped back. It was already so close that she couldn't see the whole planet at once.

"Pull up, Sahto," Cohl ordered sharply. "Damn, that was fast. I'm glad we were moving at a crawl. I owe Zain a drink."

Tess stepped up to the viewport, unable to take her eyes off the planet. It was different even from Earth or Yre Gault, all rust-red landmasses and emerald oceans. Pink clouds swirled and hugged the planet. Such strange colors, like a child's rendering.

"Demisie," she breathed.

Cohl slapped his palm on the console. "Yes!"

He jumped to his feet, grabbed her, and spun them around, his eyes alive and awake. He kissed her soundly on the lips, then glanced at Sahto. "Head to the quadrant we discussed earlier. I want to get a detailed aerial map of the entire region before Tess and I take the transport down."

Tess blinked. "When?"

Cohl grinned down at her. "As soon as possible. You're going to love this."

"They went in there?" Rommol pointed an accusing finger toward the viewport. Every officer on the bridge of Rommol's flagship fidgeted nervously.

A massive, rosy nebulous cloud shimmering with magnetic energy filled the viewport. Entranced, Nish stood still as if frozen in a distant moment of time. Somewhere deep in his mind's eye the vision was familiar—warm and perfect. Delicate swirls and wispy arms reached out from the clouds, welcoming him home to a place he'd never been.

He had felt nothing during the two-day journey here until the moment they had dropped out of hyperspace to the spot where Gothyk had led them. Suddenly, he'd heard the summons, felt the lure of something so ingrained that it was as natural as taking a breath.

An ancient strength began seeping into his bones, his

muscles, his heart; surprising in its power and frightening in its speed. A steady stream of energy pumped into him, countering the pain and discomfort of old age. Instinctively he knew the source far within the clouds. Demisie.

His mind screamed, *Closer! Take me closer!*

Under his cloak, Nish clenched his fists and bit back the impulse to push the game forward before the time was right.

Rommol rounded on his navigation officer. "Are you positive they are in there?"

The officer cowered over his station. "Gothyk's signal was tracked to here just before it vanished. Th-there is nowhere else he could have gone."

Rommol snarled, "How long ago?"

The badgered officer checked his displays. "Six hours."

Rommol's long cape swung around him as he paced a rigid path across the bridge. With growing impatience, Nish watched the Traka-Nor leader although there was no doubt of the outcome. Rommol could never allow his brother to beat him to the amulet, regardless of the danger to himself or his crew. Nish took a deep breath and waited for Rommol to say the inevitable.

"Well, what are you waiting for?" Rommol snapped at the officer and waved a hand toward the nebula. "Follow him!"

The navigation officer jumped as if he had been shot and carried out the order. The other crew members cast nervous glances around, then turned back to their stations. Standing cocky and sure, Rommol looked profoundly proud of himself.

Nish smiled and turned to exit the bridge area. Even as he walked through the long corridors, his body grew stronger. He finally reached his quarters and entered.

Alone at last, he shrugged off the cape and stood tall. The room seemed abruptly too small, too confining. His old back stretched sound and straight. He looked at his hands. The gnarled joints were less swollen, the constant pain gone. Something wonderful was happening.

And the transformation went deeper than just his body. His mind was suddenly quicker, more intense, restless. He stilled. The restlessness was a danger. He had come too far to make any mistakes now. He needed to keep this metamorphosis to himself, at least until the game had played itself out.

Besides, another task was at hand. Nish stretched out on his bunk and closed his eyes. He cleared his mind and the vision sharpened almost immediately, far more easily than ever before. Nish took his place and settled into it.

He could see Gothyk standing aboard his own ship's bridge, looking as arrogant as his brother. The obese boor labored from one end of the bridge to the other, ranting at his officers, his arms flailing wildly.

In the background, a red haze filled the viewport. Rommol's communications officer had been right. Gothyk was indeed inside the dust cloud searching for Travers and Demisie. From the look on Gothyk's grisly face, they were not having much luck.

Nish carefully extracted himself from the scene. He searched for and settled into another. This one came to him in a jolt of cognizance. The bridge of *Speculator*, and in the viewport, Nish saw Demisie.

He would recognize the planet even if he did not know how it should look, even if the stories he had heard as a child were not detailed. It was almost as if it spoke to him. *I am here. I am real. Welcome home.*

Nish watched Travers the Finder kiss the woman. He saw the invisible strings that bound them together and the blinding light of love, deep and strong and brilliant in its clarity. Unforeseen, this development. Would it be enough, he wondered, to help them survive the game?

* * *

211

Tess scanned the planet of Demisie scarcely miles below them as Cohl's transport skimmed low over jagged, red mountains skirted by a thick blue mat of foliage and grass. Emerald lakes and rivers peeked up through the crowded canopy in the valleys between.

Cohl indicated they were looking for a city, but other than an occasional breeze that ruffled the treetops, little moved. No fires, no smoke, no buildings. The only sign of life was an occasional birdlike creature that glided below.

Zain had warned her it would be like this but deep down she had hoped he was wrong. Any sign of civilization had long since been swallowed up by the dense forest and the building materials returned back to the soil from which they came.

After nearly five hours, the steady hum of the transport engines had almost put her to sleep despite the fact that she'd sung aloud every song she knew. It was kind of like a five-hundred-mile-an-hour road trip.

She glanced at Cohl piloting the transport beside her. He'd been silent for a long time and she already knew that when he was quiet, he was concerned. She wished he trusted her enough to share those burdens. Time was running out and beneath that cool, calm exterior of his, there was a world of worry.

She sighed loudly, determined to draw him out. "Are you sure we're looking in the right area?"

"Nope," he said with a forced smirk. "Just thought we'd fly around in circles all day."

She groaned. "Just when I thought you knew what you were doing."

He grinned at that. A good sign.

"*Speculator* is too far out to get the kind of topographical detail we need. That's why we are flying low. Unfortunately, we can't cover as much territory this way." He glanced up from the controls and out the front viewport. "I didn't expect the terrain to be so difficult. We should have spotted the City of Eyes by now."

She wrinkled her nose. "Eyes? What does that mean?"

Cohl shrugged. "I suppose we'll know it when we see it."

Eyes, thought Tess. Why didn't that sound good? She pressed her face back to the viewport window. Another hour passed without incident before Cohl spoke up.

"It's getting late." He pointed to the forest below. "We'll land in that clearing over there, get some sleep, and save our fuel for tomorrow. Can't see a thing at night anyway."

She nodded and looked down at the tiny clearing nestled amid the tangled forest below. It was open, flat, and large enough for the transport. Odd considering the dense vegetation. Very odd and remarkably convenient.

The setting sun cast long fingers of shadows across the land as night clawed its way around the planet. Just before they made their descent, she glanced up one more time at the spectacular sunset. She might never get another chance to view the startling combination of purple skies, streaks of pink-tinged clouds, and a sun red as blood.

Then they dropped below the mountain ridge and plunged into the heart of an alien forest. Darkness seemed to reach up and drag them into its domain. Tess watched the treetops approach at a startling speed, then soar above her as the transport dropped into the clearing and landed with a light thump. The engines whined loudly.

She noticed Cohl staring out the front viewport. "What's wrong?" She followed his grim gaze and froze. All the air in her lungs came out in a whoosh.

The exterior lights revealed that they had settled into a stand of smooth-barked trees, long and leggy below the canopy.

And eyes were staring back at them. Thousands of them, almond-shaped and embedded in the tree trunks, peeking

213

out with an eerie, golden vigilance. A lightning-quick shiver scampered up Tess's spine.

"Oh, I'm going to have nightmares about this," she groaned aloud.

Cohl shut down the engines and scanned his plethora of equipment. "Air mix and temps look adequate and stable. A bit on the tropical side but at least we won't need survival suits." He glanced out the viewport. "I'm getting some hot readings close by. Something's alive out there."

"Is that good or bad?" Tess asked warily.

"Depends on where you stand in the food chain," he answered with a smirk. He pulled out a laser pistol and checked the charge.

She frowned. "What's that for?"

He glanced up at her. "Just in case we are on the bottom."

She watched in disbelief as he climbed out of the seat and put on his weapons belt, looking all the world like he was going somewhere. Nervously, she followed him to the back of the transport.

"Are we leaving?" she asked, casting a worried glance at the deep, dark, and uninviting woods.

"*You* are staying here," he replied firmly. "I want to take a look at those trees."

Cohl retrieved another weapon and handed it to her. She grimaced. "Why do I need a gun?"

"Animals. I need you to guard the transport while I'm gone. Be prepared to kill anything that moves." He smiled. "Except me, of course."

"Kill?" Tess gasped. "Why?"

His eyes met hers with a sharpness she knew meant business. "I don't have a Demisie field guide handy, Tess. By the time we figure out if an animal is dangerous, you could be a late-night snack."

She sighed defeat and ran a finger down the cold metal

barrel of her laser pistol. "It just seems a shame to destroy what's left of a ruined planet."

Cohl's warm fingers lifted her chin. Golden eyes warmed her heart.

"You're too soft," he said in a voice somewhere between amazement and envy.

She smiled. "And you're too hard."

He brushed his lips against hers. "That's your fault."

Tess giggled against his mouth. The moment was broken by a scratch-scratching on the exterior of the transport. The kiss froze between them. Cohl backed off slowly and put a finger to his lips.

She nodded at his silence gesture and watched him ease a long, lethal-looking rifle from a side panel. He leaned against the transport hatch and listened. She watched the change in him from lover to warrior. After a few quiet minutes, he reached over and retrieved a lightball from a backpack. It illuminated and scooted to his side.

Cohl whispered to Tess, "I won't be gone long, but I want the hatch open in case I need to get back in a hurry. Can you cover me?"

In reply, she trained her weapon on the hatch door while a rousing rendition of "lions and tigers and bears" singsonged through her head.

He touched the control panel and the door slid open.

Tess reeled under the first blast of warm, spicy air. She'd thought the planet dead, but the exotic sounds of a healthy wildlife population emanating from the forest around them said differently. The beasts had made Demisie their own.

There was a full range of high screeches, low rumbles, flittering songs. The good news was, she didn't hear a single lion or tiger or bear.

"Oh my," she whispered.

Cohl leaned out, making a quick sweep of the immediate area around the hatch with his laser rifle. She held her weapon on the open doorway as he exited and disappeared from sight, his lightball in hot pursuit.

Then she was alone. It suddenly occurred to her that if anything happened to Cohl, she wouldn't have a clue how to get them out of here in the transport. And with all the magnetic interference, they couldn't even communicate with *Speculator*. Her finger tightened nervously on the trigger of the laser pistol. She hated not having options.

Of course, there was one obvious solution. She could learn his world. The idea intrigued her immediately. Why hadn't she thought of it sooner?

How hard could it be to learn how to fly one of these things or to work all those gizmos and screens on *Speculator*? Although advanced, the technology looked simple enough to use. Any fool with half a brain could push a button. Sitting in the center of an alien forest full of wild beasts with nothing more than a little laser pistol, she definitely qualified as a fool with half a brain.

Of course, the entire concept assumed that she *had* a future. Who knew what tomorrow would bring?

A second later, she heard Cohl whistle softly before he reappeared in her line of fire. The lightball flitted into the transport and deactivated itself.

"There are some teeth marks around the starboard engines," Cohl told her as he vaulted back inside and closed the door behind him. "Apparently they didn't like the way the transport tasted."

Tess lowered her weapon and gaped. "Is that supposed to be funny? Exactly how big were these teeth marks?"

He cast her a quick glance, then tapped away at the control panel. "Do you really want to know?"

She thought for about half a second and waved him off. "No. No, I don't. The only difference between big teeth and small teeth are the number of bites."

The panel lights flashed and he said, "We'll be safe tonight.

I set up a proximity alarm. Hopefully it'll scare off any more hungry visitors."

"So, did you check out the eyes?" she asked, stowing her laser pistol.

Cohl propped his rifle against the transport wall and slipped off the weapons belt. "I did. They actually belong to stone faces embedded in the tree trunks. Yellow incandescent eyes and a small red mouth. Sight and speech. Interesting choices."

Tess shook her head. "I don't understand."

He put his hands on his hips and stared at the floor. "No ears for listening. No hands for touch. No nose for smell. You can tell a lot about a civilization by their art. Fascinating."

Tess rubbed her arms. "Creepy, you mean. Maybe all these people had were eyes and mouths."

Cohl chuckled. "Maybe. What's really amazing is that after over a thousand years, the colors are still brilliant."

He pulled a blanket from a side panel and spread it in the tiny bit of floor space in the back of the transport. "But at least now we know we have a bearing. The eyes are there to watch all who enter. If we take a heading facing them, we should hit the city."

Tess frowned at the familiar self-preservation alarm that clanged loudly in her brain. "How do you know that?" She crossed her arms over her chest. "In fact, how did you even know where to begin looking? This planet is huge."

He glanced up at her and Tess saw *guilty* written all over his face. Her eyes turned to warning slits.

He raised a single eyebrow and started talking. "I received a file from an anonymous source shortly after Rommol contacted me. It contained a great deal of detail on Demisie."

She said softly, "You had information about the planet and you didn't tell me?"

Cohl sighed. "I couldn't verify the source, Tess. I had no

idea if the data were credible. It could have been a trap."

"And now?"

He nodded once. "It's been completely accurate."

Tess planted her hands on her hips. "I want to see the file, Cohl. I mean it. I want to know everything."

A slow smile crossed his face. His hands slid around her waist and pulled her against his chest. "I'll show you how to use the data pad first thing in the morning."

By way of diversion, his kisses burned a line of fire down her throat. Helpless against such a sneaky detour, she wound her arms around his neck. "And what about tonight?"

"I think we better sleep in the transport." He glanced at the blanket on the floor and gave her a sinful grin. "It'll be a bit tight."

Tess shook her head in wonder. "I swear you lie awake at night planning these things."

Chapter Sixteen

The faces on the trees had indeed pointed the way. Deep within a furrowed valley—a hint of civilization peeked out. As Cohl piloted the transport closer, he knew the verdict was irrefutable. Man had made this.

Poking its pointed hat above the tree line, a building in the shape of a head sat with giant eyes staring blindly ahead. Around it, other smaller heads shared the same blank expression, positioned in tight formation atop a flat building. In silent solidarity, they stared across a long, wide courtyard crowded by the surrounding forest. Behind them, a multitude of smaller structures lay tangled among the encroaching vegetation.

Again, the information in the anonymous file was correct. Again, Cohl wondered who the sender was.

"Eyes and mouths. The same as the trees," Tess observed in awe, her body stretched forward to gaze out the viewport. "My God, they're huge. Must be three or four stories high,"

Then she sat back down and concentrated fiercely on the

information in the data pad. Cohl shook his head. It was the first thing she reminded him of this morning when they awoke. Before they took to the air again, he had shown her how the unit worked. As usual, she'd proven to be an excellent student.

She reported, "According to the file, this building is part of the entrance to the City of Eyes. The open courtyard in front of it was used as a marketplace, a gathering place for all people . . ." Her voice drifted off.

Cohl reminded her, "It's going to get harder, you know. Brace yourself now."

She nodded and set the data pad on her lap. "I realize that. It's just so tragic. What a terrible loss." She glanced over at him. "If word gets out about this planet, what will happen to it?"

Cohl eyed her uneasily. She was probably worried about artifact thieves. Guys like him.

"There is a preservation consortium I know of. I'll contact them as soon as I get back to Yre Gault. Hopefully, the consortium will be able to get an order of protection over the entire planet right away. Then it can be documented accurately and preserved."

"Except for the amulet," Tess amended softly.

Cohl frowned. "Except for that. Yes."

He pointed to the open courtyard looming well below them. "Looks like a good place to land."

She didn't say another word during their descent, simply stared sadly out the viewport. Why did he suddenly feel so guilty about taking the amulet or any other artifact, for that matter? He wasn't hurting a single living soul. In fact, he was unearthing magnificent treasures for the rest of mankind to see. How else would anyone know about the beauty buried in catacombs and tombs? Besides, more than half the artifacts he uncovered ended up in public exhibits. So much had been discovered about lost civilizations from their art. He was instrumental in that pursuit.

The more he thought about it, the more irritated he became. He guided the transport to the center of the courtyard, facing the forest, and cut the engines. After one quick scanner sweep of the area, he pushed out of his seat and headed directly to the rear of the transport. Tess looked surprised as he wordlessly began shoving some last-minute supplies into the two packs he'd prepared earlier.

She came up next to him quietly. "Cohl?"

"No one owns what's left of this civilization, Tess."

There was a short pause. "I know that."

"Then what did you expect?" he snapped and pinned her with a determined look.

Stunned, she raised her hands and dropped them in defeat. "I don't know. Maybe just a little respect."

"I've never destroyed a find, Tess. I take what I need and leave the rest untouched." Cohl shoved another food ration into a pack. "I'm not doing anything illegal."

She let out a little gasp. "I never thought that, Cohl."

"And I'm not leaving here without that amulet," he stated, turning his back to her to reach up for a water container. "Whether or not you approve."

He halted in place as her warm hands slid under his shirt and up his bare back. One touch. That's all it took to snuff out all of his anger.

She whispered softly, "Easy, big guy. I never meant that I don't approve of what you do." Her hands moved around the front and over his torso like a healing salve. Her soft breasts pressed against his back. "I'm only thinking of Demisie. Nothing more."

A wave of relief flowed through him. What the woman he loved thought of his chosen occupation definitely mattered, regardless of what his pride said.

The woman he loved. *Damn. When did that happen?*

He turned to her, filling his hands with Tess and pulling her close. She melted against him like a gentle breeze, her cheek pressed to his chest. As long as he lived, he'd never find another more perfect fit.

"I promise I'll try to protect Demisie," he said.

She nodded. "That's all I ask."

Cohl glanced out the front viewport at the thick forest. "There may not be much to save. It's been over a thousand years. Few man-made structures and even fewer works of art survive the passing of time well."

She pulled away and smiled up at him. There was love in those green eyes. Part of him rejoiced, part of him died. At this rate, there would be nothing left by the time she was gone.

He released her gently and pulled on his pack. "I'd like to find the entrance to the amulet today, but even then, we will probably sleep at least one night in the open. It's not a good idea to walk into a series of traps exhausted. You'll have to carry a pack too," he told her. "Are you up to it?"

She smiled and pulled on her pack. "I've done a little hiking. I'll manage."

He held a laser pistol up for her to see. Their eyes met in silent understanding. Tess nodded and he slipped it into the weapons holster in her pack where she could get to it easily. He knew she hated it, hated the thought of killing, even if it was in self-defense. *Too soft. Everywhere.*

When he looked up next, she was checking the data pad again. He had to smile. He'd probably never get his hands on the thing again. Somewhere along the line, she had become the navigator and his partner. Somehow in the last few days, he'd become accustomed to her sweet song nearby. And sometime in the near future, she would become a memory.

He realized that time was quickly becoming his worst enemy in more ways than one.

* * *

Tess heard it the minute Cohl popped the hatch door open—the low hum of a chorus of voices, human voices carried on the wind. Her trained ears told her so. She clutched the data pad in her hands as if trying to keep a grip on reality.

She watched uneasily as Cohl checked the area around the hatchway with his rifle, then jumped out. The next thing she knew, he was waving her out as if everything were fine.

She walked to the door and peered out, expecting to be confronted with a full choir of aliens. Instead, a patio of red stone slabs gave way to the brilliant blue-green forest around them. Tendrils of vegetation crisscrossed the dew-covered courtyard. The crimson sun hung low, early in its journey across the sky. A gust of wind carried the now familiar spicy fragrance and the choir strengthened.

Cohl helped her out of the transport, frowning in concern. "Are you okay?"

She snapped her head around at him in disbelief. "Don't you hear that?"

He shrugged. "Nothing unusual."

Tess shook her head vehemently. "I hear voices."

Cohl raised an eyebrow and cast a glance around. "Can you tell where they are coming from?"

Closing her eyes, Tess concentrated as the wind kicked up again, swirling in a dizzying pattern around them. She walked blindly toward the source, letting her ears guide her. Finally she stopped, pointed straight out, and said, "There."

When she opened her eyes, she nearly fell over. At the end of the long avenue of barren courtyard were the collection of faces they had seen from the air. The flat diamond-shaped eyes of gold and mouths—red and pouty—decorated the pale, white faces. Little aqua and purple triangle caps with long stone veils around the sides sat on each giant head.

Cohl came up behind her. "Ever get the feeling you were being watched?"

Tess muttered. "This is spooky *now*. I can't wait for nightfall."

Cohl pointed his rifle toward the perimeter of the courtyard. "Just so you don't tell me I didn't warn you, there's more."

It took her a minute to see what he meant. Dozens of stone statues shaped like monks lined the entire courtyard, their hands locked beneath their cloaks, golden eyes peeking out from under stone hoods. Most of them had been swallowed whole by the foliage with only an occasional eye peering out.

"They watch all who enter," Cohl recited from the file.

Tess shook off a chill. "Do you think that's what the race looked like?"

"Maybe. Or it could just be an art style they developed." He hefted the rifle over his shoulder and started walking toward the building of faces. "The transport is locked up. Let's go."

Tess ran to catch up with his long, determined strides. He was all business now, wielding that rifle with familiar ease.

"So tell me you see stuff like this all the time."

Cohl's sharp eyes continued to sweep the area around them as he walked. "Never."

She muttered, "Great. Why did it have to be on *my* acquisition?"

Cohl grinned. "Just lucky, I guess."

The wind launched another chorus of hums and Tess locked her wide-eyed gaze on the stoic heads looming before them. The only other sound was the clicking of their boots along the stone slabs. Even the beasts in the forest were silent.

It didn't take them long to reach the stone archway at the end of the long avenue. The building with the strange heads stood beyond the city entrance in a large common lined with more statues. As they approached the building of faces, the humming grew much louder and Tess could virtually hear the inflection of words. It sounded terrifyingly familiar.

"The Demisians were accomplished stonecutters," Cohl said, pointing to the stone pavers at their feet. "Look how tight these joints are." He walked a few paces ahead of her and examined the base of the large building. "These appear to be stone blocks as well. Very smooth. Polished. Although the basic design is simple, the engineering behind a structure this size is pretty complicated. I didn't—"

"They are singing something," she whispered. Cohl stopped his inspection of the architecture and turned to her. "Who?"

"The faces." She stared at them as they stared back. "The song is coming from them. Look at their mouths."

Cohl glanced up and nodded. "You're right. I can see the wind holes. They used the wind shifts to generate tones. Brilliant. But I still don't hear any words."

"You haven't been practicing that song," Tess whispered, her voice barely audible. "It's the first line, Cohl."

With the next gust of wind, she started singing the words while the giant pipes offered backup vocals. The wind picked up around her and she was sucked into the vortex of song, stronger than anything she'd ever felt before. A chorus joined her with their strong and soulful chanting. She was sinking into the incantation, deeper and deeper.

They were so close, standing right beside her in long-flowing vivid dresses. She could hear the inflection, the vibrato, the power and energy of many. They undulated and blended into a perfect stream. Her voice became theirs, theirs hers, and together they tightened the chord until the song was one strong voice. And she became the conduit as the song poured from her in a rush.

Abruptly, they faded and the chant lost its grip on her. When Cohl shook her, she blinked back to reality. His face was lined with deep concern. "Stop it, Tess. Stop singing."

"What happened?" she gasped, shaking loose the cobwebs in her head. The connection had been cut. It was almost painful.

Cohl checked her eyes closely before letting go of her arms. "I don't know. You went into some sort of a trance. I almost couldn't get you out of it. Has that ever happened before?"

She shook her head. Never. She definitely would have remembered.

He frowned. "Then do me a favor and save the song for the amulet."

Tess nodded in quick agreement. She could have sworn there were live beings singing with her a minute ago but now the courtyard was quiet. The wind had died down. Stoic peace from the faces. Unnatural silence from the forest.

Cohl took the data pad from her and checked it. "There's supposed to be a series of stone markers leading to the location of the amulet." He pocketed the unit and readied his rifle. "This way."

She watched him slip back into his serious, all-business demeanor as they moved forward. Although she knew it was important for him to maintain a sharp watch, she missed his easy smile and wandering hands. He carried none of the excitement she'd seen in the VirtuWav exercise. Perhaps he was just worried about his father and the nearing deadline but intuitively she felt it went even deeper than that. It was almost as if he'd retreated from her at some fundamental, subconscious level. Whatever the reason, it worried her.

They rounded the central building and Tess stopped in her tracks. Ahead of them lay a wasteland of broken and crumpled buildings. Red stone remnants of connected walls and homes stuck out of the rubble. The wind wound a mournful path through what had once been wide avenues, now littered with toppled pillars and an occasional brave plant.

And the silence. Like a tomb, Tess imagined.

The destruction stretched as far as she could see within the confines of the encroaching forest.

"Oh my," she said in a hushed voice. "What happened?"

Cohl had stopped next to her and replied simply, "War."

Tess frowned and looked back over her shoulder at the neat and orderly courtyard. "Why doesn't the entrance look like this?"

He scanned the ruins. "Maybe they cleaned it up."

"It's almost like they were expecting company," Tess murmured.

Cohl eyed her. She shrugged. "Hey, it's the only time I clean my house."

"Take a look at this," he said as he walked over to a massive toppled stone pillar. Tess could make out some kind of designs carved into one side of the four-sided block.

Cohl squatted and rubbed a hand along the carvings. "Sculptural reliefs."

Then he leaned back and studied one end of the stone. "Here's the base the stone used to stand on. I think this is the first marker. There are supposed to be four of them leading to the entrance where the amulet is hidden. Together, they tell the story of the civilization's final years."

Tess kneeled down beside him and just stared. She couldn't believe her eyes. In the stone was carved a series of Demisian celebrations. Dancers with hands linked, smiling and laughing in the courtyard she and Cohl had just walked through.

"It appears that we've discovered the origins of the chicken dance," Cohl said with grave seriousness.

Tess turned slowly and glared at him. "See?" she quipped. "Everyone does it."

Cohl broke into a husky laugh.

She took in each happy scene on the marker. The depictions were joyous and spectacular, a snapshot in time. Carefully, afraid to break the spell, she ran her fingers along a glimpse of a lost past, a lost people.

Then her gaze settled on one. It showed a man wearing a pointed cap and side veils, holding a small girl in his arms. She was beautiful and delicate. In her little hands, she held up a round object that hung around the man's neck. Five sunburst spokes extruded through a circular ring with the bottom spoke substantially longer than the others.

Tess's mouth dropped open. "Cohl?"

"Hmm?" He leaned toward her.

"Is this the amulet?"

"Damn." Cohl bent down and blew the dirt off the carving to get a better look. "That's it. And I'll bet that's one of Demisie's rulers."

"And his daughter," Tess finished.

Cohl nodded. "Yes. Strong resemblance."

"I don't get it. Look at these pictures. They all appear so happy. What could have happened?" she mused, glancing at the ruins.

"It must have been something catastrophic." Cohl pulled out the data pad and waved it over the reliefs one by one. "I'm going to scan the images into the data pad and analyze them later."

While he scanned, she squinted at the carving of the dancers. Something was wrong with the building behind them.

"Cohl. The giant faces aren't here. They are missing," she gasped.

He paused in the process of stowing the data pad. She watched his mouth set into a grim line as he examined the picture. "They must have been built later."

Tess turned her palms up. "Why? You said they watch all who enter. So who were they suddenly watching for?"

Cohl rose to his feet and resettled his pack. "Let's keep

moving. Maybe the next marker will give us some answers."

She followed as he led the way through the piles of rubble, down what Tess assumed was once a main street. Small rodents scattered as she and Cohl climbed over stones through the maze that had been homes. Every once in a while, she had to stop. The tragedy was too great. Within these walls had once been children and laughter, arguments and loving. Now all that was left were the dust of bones.

The breeze had returned to its fickle ways, blowing debris around in circles. The air grew spicier and more humid with every passing minute. It wasn't long before she had swept up her hair and tied it into a ponytail. Perspiration was already soaking her clothes. Tess was grateful for Cohl's foresight in the lightweight shorts and tops they wore.

As the red sun climbed into the sky, the ruins gave way to a forest of tall, leggy trees.

Cohl moved ahead of her with powerful ease despite the pack that she suspected weighed much more than hers. He reminded her of the surefooted grace of a big cat, well equipped with its package of thick, smooth muscles and effortless strength. She watched his appealing tush beneath the heavy pack and cocked her head to the side. A wicked smile bloomed.

"You have great legs, you know that? In fact, it's a darn nice view from back here."

He cast a lingering look over his shoulder, zeroing in on where her straps cut around her breasts, but continued his hard, steady pace. "Keep that up and you'll be on your back in the dirt."

Tess laughed and shook her head. "I forget how little encouragement you need."

He shot her a promising smile but that was all. Back to business. A small wave of disappointment swept through her.

The road ahead narrowed and entire sections disappeared beneath an avalanche of ground cover. They hiked in silence as the street became a path and the path became a broken trail. The sunlight filtered through the thick canopy and speckled the ground below. A warm breeze pumped around them.

Tess looked up and saw a familiar face staring back at her from a tree trunk.

"Cohl."

Without breaking a step, he replied, "I see them. We must be heading in the right direction."

"Trail markers," she said with sudden understanding. "Spooky but effective." She shrugged off the uncomfortable feeling of their hard, dead stare.

The forest was considerably quieter during the day then it had been at dusk last evening. Under the crowded canopy, nothing moved except for an occasional creepy-crawly thing that scuttled across their path. She hated those little critters that could sneak up on you without warning. At least you knew when the big creatures were nearby.

Something rustled overhead to their right. Cohl swung his rifle up toward the sound with startling speed and waited. Tess froze behind him, only her eyes following the direction of his weapon. High above them hung some kind of nest, attached in four places to the tall trees. It swayed gently in the breeze, dark against the blue-green leaves.

Cohl lowered his weapon and scanned the rest of the canopy in complete concentration.

"A nest?" Tess whispered.

He nodded but his tone was grave. "Probably. I didn't notice it before."

Tess didn't like the sound of that. She doubted Cohl missed much now that he was in adventuring mode. "What do you think is in there?"

Cohl started back down the path, more slowly this time,

his rifle ready. "Do you really want to guess?"

She gave a shudder as she fell into step behind him once again. "No. This place gives me the creeps. I always feel like I'm being watched or followed or—"

A high shrill scream over her head cut through her sentence. She looked up as the nest swooped directly toward her with terrifying speed. A single glassy eye at its heart hypnotized her.

Suddenly, Cohl yanked her by the arm and out of the way. She stumbled past him to the forest floor, rolled once, and looked up just in time to watch him pump laserfire into the nest that had come alive. It hit the ground with a savage snarl and rose to four legs, swaying and screaming. Tess grimaced as the primal, wrenching sound of a dying animal echoed through the forest. The beast managed to walk a few feet toward Cohl, absorbing hit after hit from the rifle before it finally succumbed into a heap of charred, thatchlike fur. The smell of burnt flesh wafted her way.

Cohl fired a few more rounds to make sure it was down, then waltzed over and hauled her to her feet.

"Sorry that took so long. I had a hell of a time hitting a vital organ. Are you okay?" he asked as he casually brushed some dirt off her shirt.

She realized her mouth had probably been open for some time now. "You know, nests never attack us back on Earth. What was that thing?"

His attention was already elsewhere, scanning the upper canopy. "I can tell you with absolute certainty that it wasn't a nest."

"Thank you for that breaking news flash," she snapped and rubbed her forehead where a nasty little headache had just formed directly over the scared-shitless part of her brain.

"We better keep moving," he said dryly. "Watch for any more nests. I'll bet those things can move pretty fast along the tree line. We'll take them out before they jump us."

231

Much as she hated to, Tess pulled out the laser pistol that Cohl had stowed in her pack. "How did the Demisians live with those things? I mean, look how long it took you to kill it. I don't think they had laser guns."

Walking ahead, he answered over his shoulder, "Every planet has its predators and prey. A food chain."

Tess shot a glance up at the red sun peeking though the leaves directly overhead. "What happens when it gets dark and we can't see them dropping?"

He hesitated just long enough so she realized he didn't have a good answer for her.

"Hopefully, we'll be out of the forest before nightfall. We can't sleep under these trees, that's for sure."

"Who would sleep?" she whispered, looking around.

Far ahead in a small clearing, a single ray of sunlight lit a tall, dark column that stood just off the path.

"The second marker?" she asked as they drew near.

Cohl pulled out the data pad and handed it to her. "Looks like it. Use the data pad to scan the images while I keep a watch above us. We'll take a closer look at the reliefs later."

Tess accepted the data pad and approached the stone pillar with respectful awe. It rose out of the forest floor like an old gravestone. Identical to the first one, it was cut from a single slab of red stone, around twenty feet high with a series of reliefs on the front. She pulled back some climbing vines to get a look at the finely etched pictures.

"What can you see?" Cohl urged, his back to her as he stood guard.

Tess frowned, trying to make sense of the weathered depictions. "The king appears upset, anguished, his head in his hands. All the people are crying around him. The only good news is that he's still wearing the amulet." She moved onto the next one. "This one shows an army. I think they are searching for something." She quickly scanned the others as something unholy gripped her. "Cohl, I don't see the little girl in any of these pictures. I think something happened to her."

Cohl asked, "Does it show a funeral? A burial?"

Tess cleared some more vines. "No. She's just not there. I think they are searching for her. Maybe she got lost."

"Or kidnapped," Cohl added grimly.

Tess stood back from the pillar. "How awful. Her father and the people look devastated. The pictures are so desperate and solemn. Not like the first ones. There's no dancing in these." She glanced at Cohl's serious profile. "Do you think it had something to do with the collapse of the civilization?"

"I have a distinct feeling we'll find the answer to that on the next marker," he answered. "Scan the images, Tess. We need to keep moving."

She worked quickly, now anxious to find the third marker to see if the father ever found his beloved daughter. Although deep down she already knew the answer, she just didn't want to admit it.

Cohl took the lead again when she had finished. They trudged along the path while the red sun began its slow slide down the sky.

"Tell me about your family," Cohl asked, breaking the silence.

Tess was momentarily taken aback by his casual request.

"I thought you and Pitz already dug up everything there was to know about me," she said, unable to resist a little dig herself.

"I want to hear it from you."

She shrugged. Her life was boring as hell compared to his. It wouldn't be her fault if he fell asleep listening to it. She stepped over a big root in her path and began with her brother who lived in New Jersey and worked ungodly hours as a V.P. at a major marketing firm. Then she moved on to her sister who had the smarts to leave snow country and settle south in North Carolina with her husband and two kids.

Then Tess proceeded to tell him about their childhood and her parents, Christmases with more love than presents, warm summer nights spent catching fireflies. One memory ran into another until she realized she'd been talking non-stop for a very long time. And Cohl hadn't said a word, not shared a single family memory of his own. It struck her sadly that perhaps he didn't have any to share.

"Do you miss them?" he finally asked after she'd halted her life story.

She shrugged and answered honestly, "We only speak on the phone every few months and I haven't seen them in years. They have families now, it's harder for them to travel. And I'm always too busy working to take time off to visit."

She smirked. "However, they *were* on the same planet. There's something oddly comforting about that."

Cohl nodded. "I imagine you'll be happy to get back home then."

She nearly lost a step at his cool response. It was the first time since they had argued in the shuttle bay that he talked about her leaving. A cold sense of dread descended over her.

She would help him. He would return her to Earth. That was the original agreement but now she wasn't so sure that's what she really wanted.

She shook her head hard. Of course, that's what she wanted. She had a life back on Earth, a promising singing future, a slew of friends and family. Everything she knew and loved was there on that little planet. Well. Almost everything she loved.

It took all her willpower to focus on the path as she navigated through the threat of tears. Even if she wanted to stay with Cohl, he hadn't asked. And she knew he wouldn't. He was more than ready to send her back. She couldn't very well stay with a man who didn't want her around on a permanent basis. If this was all she could get from him in the short time they had left, then she'd take it and stow away the memories of his passion and power.

How could she have let this happen? Get in this deep? So deep that getting out unscathed would be impossible? What kind of idiot falls for a man who lives on the other side of the galaxy—worlds away?

She blinked quickly. Looked like she was the only one foolish enough to fall in love.

Abruptly, the canopy thinned and the ground cover deepened in the open patches of sunlight.

And where the forest gave way to an open meadow, stood the third marker.

Chapter Seventeen

Cohl hadn't needed to see the last series of reliefs to tell him the tragic turn the Demisian civilization had taken. He'd known the minute Tess noticed the young daughter missing on the last marker. He shielded his eyes from the sun's direct glare as he stepped out of the forest.

The marker stood in silent vigil on the edge of a flat, grassy field. Pink-tinged mountains in the far distance set a stunning backdrop to a single, lonely mark of Man.

Running past him, Tess reached the marker first. She scanned the pictures frantically. Then her shoulders slumped. Her hand was flat against the red stone when he came up behind her.

"She's not here. They didn't find her," Tess whispered. She pointed to a burial scene, a portrait of mourners and death. "And look. The king died." Her voice cracked. "Oh, he never found her, Cohl. His heart must have broken. I wonder if his death was related to her disappearance. Maybe he couldn't bear to live without her."

"Possibly. We'll never know for certain. I doubt there will be many more clues left besides these markers."

Cohl studied the funeral scene; the king laid out before the multitude of mourners. The amulet was nowhere to be seen. The next scene depicted the war and destruction that apparently followed the king's death.

"Power struggle," he murmured.

Tess's voice sounded fragile as she stared at the past. "Do you think that's what triggered the war?"

"I'm sure that was part of it. Wars have been waged for less than that," Cohl replied. His eyes followed Demisie's tragic history, forever captured in stone. The next scene displayed a line of robed figures walking out of the forest. The same robed figures that guarded the entrance. Cohl moved in for a closer look. The leader held the amulet in his hands while the city burned behind him.

"Guardians," he said quietly. "They watch all who enter."

He cast a quick glance back into the forest. "They came right through here, probably on this very path, with the amulet."

"To hide it?" Tess offered.

"Must be. Maybe they felt its power was too dangerous or that no other leader should wear it," Cohl surmised.

"Or perhaps they were waiting for someone to save them," Tess said gently. "That's when they built the faces and these markers. But no one came." She gazed over the silent fields. "And they died waiting."

Cohl took a deep breath. *What a mess.* He turned to Tess and watched two giant tears roll down her cheeks. He drew her into the circle of his arms. She sobbed quietly against him as he stroked her hair.

"It's all right," he soothed her. "It is history now. No more suffering."

Even as he said it, he couldn't pull his gaze away from the marker. Rarely in his career of adventuring had he given much thought to the events leading up to how the treasure came to be "protected" by its own people. He had never contemplated why a civilization had disappeared or what had transpired to bring a people to such desperation that they would go to great lengths to preserve part of themselves from oblivion.

Demisie's civilization had crumbled in a ruler transition. There had indeed been massive suffering as each and every person on this world died and disappeared without memory. Nothing but a rock to mark their passing. He held Tess closer. Her softness must be rubbing off on him.

She regained her composure and brushed the tears from her face. "You warned me. I just wasn't ready for anything like this."

Almost reluctantly, Cohl released her and cleared his throat. "Me neither."

Tess wiped her hands on her shorts and looked at him expectantly. "Now what?"

Cohl retrieved the data pad and calculated their trek thus far from marker to marker. Despite the twists and turns of the path, they were traveling in a relatively straight line across the countryside.

He surveyed the terrain and pointed toward a far mountain. "That way."

One day had passed and, Nish hoped, one step closer to the final moves of the game.

Before him, Rommol paced the bridge in long, angry strides, venting the lack of progress on the nearest sacrifice. His mood had been brutal since entering the red mist cloaking both Demisie and his bitter blood enemy, Gothyk. Every officer scoured the disoriented scanners for a glimpse of Gothyk's ship.

Nish alone stood behind Rommol and endured the wrath of the child while the bridge crew busied themselves in an obvious effort to avoid becoming the target of the next outburst.

But as Rommol's mood blackened, Nish's became lighter, more powerful, and less tolerant of the childish behavior. Although his body still bore the badges of age, Nish trembled beneath his guise with the energy of youth and its surly audacity. The visions were now attainable on command at any time, in any place aboard the ship. All he needed to do was wish it. Even in his prime of youth, the gift had never been so blessedly easy.

Rommol made another glowering pass. Nish gave a silent sigh and closed his eyes. Then he let the vision come. It sharpened obediently on the bridge aboard Gothyk's ship.

In the viewport, Demisie glowed brilliantly. Nish inhaled sharply, nearly severing his vision. So breathtaking. He could barely contain his growing excitement and the itch of energy with no outlet. Gothyk had found Demisie and very soon, Nish would set foot upon his ancestors' soil. All the players would finally be together.

The game was nearly at hand.

"We'll camp here," she finally heard Cohl announce after ten minutes of studying the site. With a heartfelt groan, Tess slid her backpack off where she stood. Hiking in the Adirondack Mountains of New York State had never been this exhausting.

Cohl turned at her groan and smiled. "That bad?"

If she'd had the energy to spare, she would have come up with something really witty, but all she could muster was a bite-me glare that made him chuckle.

She slumped down on her pack and took one boot off, rubbing the soreness from her foot as she gazed around. Behind them lay the rolling hills they'd spent half the day crossing. In front of them rose the sheer face of a thirty-foot-high cliff that solidly blocked their path. She squinted at the red rock that stretched across the land as far as her eyes could see, deep gouges and long rifts scarring its face. It didn't look, well, natural. But then again, she huffed, nothing on this planet had been exactly normal so far.

She dropped her gaze in absolute reverence at the beautiful, inviting pool of water they would be camping next to. Emerald-green water turned fluorescent as it slipped from a shallow, crescent basin into the deep hole where it hugged the cliff. Powdery red sand edged the large pond, radiating outward until it met the grassy field. The soothing water promised nirvana.

Now, if she could only find the energy to move.

Several feet away, Cohl squatted to unpack pouches of all sizes from his pack. Her eyebrows rose higher as he pulled object after object out. That pack must have weighed a ton but he didn't even look one bit tired. In fact, he looked as fresh as when they'd set off this morning.

She blew a stray hair off her face. *Show-off.*

The setting crimson sun was behind them now, adding a rosy tinge to the gently swirling water. A light breeze rippled the fields into gentle waves and carried a sweet, yeasty smell. Shadows lengthened, changing the alien landscape yet again. The pinks turned red, the reds to a sinister black.

In the center of the camp, Cohl pushed a stubby post into the soft sand. The device came to life with a low hum, and a ghostly circle of blue light surrounded them and their immediate camping area.

"Proximity alarm?" she asked.

"Right. It'll set off a warning if anything enters the perimeter of our camp."

Tess looked toward the water, out of the circle's reach. "Do I have time to take a swim before it gets dark?"

"No swimming," Cohl stated firmly. He knelt down next to the pack and efficiently peeled back the cover of a flat container.

Tess gaped at him, then at the glorious, refreshing, utterly heavenly water, and then back at him.

"Why on earth not?"

"Because you don't know what kind of nasty creatures live in deep pools," he said casually, stirring the contents of the can he was holding.

She wrinkled her nose. Recalling those nests, she decided he was right. But damn it, she needed to wash off the grime of the day. Maybe she could at least dip her feet in the few inches of water at the shallow end.

"Hungry?" he asked, holding out the small tray to her.

Cleanliness took a rapid plunge on the priority list. Having not eaten since morning, Tess ignored a chorus of stiff muscles as she nearly fell over her own feet getting to him. She grabbed the food and eyed the thick, spicy stew. It smelled wonderful. She realized that none of the ingredients looked even vaguely identifiable but it didn't last long enough to matter.

They ate in silence as the bloodred sun disappeared below the horizon and darkness slipped over them like a warm, steamy blanket. All was quiet, a sharp contrast to the active forest and blissfully welcome, as far as Tess was concerned.

Fed and feeling decidedly more civilized, Tess sat on her pack and watched Cohl set up the campsite with simple ease. She loved to watch him move. There was something so elementally male and sure about everything he did, comfortable in his own skin and capable of anything. She felt safe with him, a trust so deep and absolute that it startled her. She could trust him with her very life. Right up until the moment he sent her home.

He spread out a sleeping pad big enough for both of them that looked wonderfully inviting. Despite protesting muscles, Tess moved over to the pad and stretched out with a groan, coming up on an elbow so she could watch what Cohl was doing.

"Do you always carry so much gear?" she asked.

Cohl withdrew a fat pouch from the pack. "Usually Pitz hauls everything I need. At least, to the site. He can't fit into tight spaces so I usually do the traps alone."

"So, how do I rate as a partner?" she asked.

"Well, you don't complain as much as Pitz. You smell better." Cohl flashed her a smile. "And you're a hell of a lot more fun when you're fully charged."

Tess laughed. This felt good, just the two of them alone in the night, camping, talking. It was almost like home except for the fact that they were the only people on an alien planet under an alien sky and there wasn't a marshmallow within a bazillion miles.

"How close are we to the amulet?" she asked.

"Very. We'll find it tomorrow, I'm sure," Cohl said as he sorted through the contents of the pouch. "We have to. Time is nearly up."

She watched him work. She waited politely. Curiosity won. "What's in the bag?" she asked.

"Medical supplies." He held up an injection of Aritrox to show her.

Tess frowned as harsh reality burst her happy little camping-under-the-stars fantasy. She recalled Pitz's detailed recital of Cohl's prior exploits—successes and failures. It was the failures that filled her tired head.

With a fingernail, she drew little circles on the sleeping pad. "What happens if you get hurt and Pitz isn't there to help you?"

Cohl shrugged. "I treat myself. Hole up in the trap a few days until I'm healed enough to continue."

Tess gaped at the horror of it. "Does that happen often?"

He looked up at her through his long lashes. "Once in a while."

"How?" She shook her head. "I mean, I thought you were the best?"

His golden gaze turned dark. "I am but even I miscalculate occasionally. A slip of concentration, a split second late. It happens."

Horrible visions popped into her head. "So how long do you think can you keep doing this?"

There was a long pause and she realized that last question was a mistake. His voice dropped in warning. "I'm not too old for adventuring, Tess."

She quickly shook her head. "Not now, no." She paused, not wanting to ask but unable to ignore the obvious. "But what about in ten or fifteen years?"

Cohl resealed the pouch abruptly and shoved the kit back into his pack. "Don't worry about it."

Tess winced. In other words, *none of your damn business, Tess*. She debated the wisdom of pushing him more as Cohl snatched up his pistol.

"We need sleep," he said crisply and turned to check the alarm.

Realizing the subject was closed, Tess flopped back on the pad. Damn him for being so stubborn. And arrogant. And blind. He ignored the danger just like he ignored the fact that he belonged on Yre Gault. He only saw what he wanted.

Then something else riveted her. She blinked in disbelief at the night sky as ribbons of red light spiraled across the blackness. Northern lights, but more magnificent, stretching the length and width of the open sky. Long whiplike snakes slashed and curled, undulating like heavenly lovers.

Cohl dropped onto the pad next to her and threw his arm over his eyes, completely ignoring the show. Tension radiated from his body. Tess pretended not to notice. She swallowed the hard lump in her throat. If he was hell-bent on killing himself, then fine. As if she'd even know when it happened.

And with that single thought, her heart seized up. It was true. She would never know when or where. In fact, she would never know anything else of his life. If he was happy or if he found another woman or had children. Never even see him again. Ever.

The display above her strengthened as sheets of light danced and shimmered. Then disappeared before another took over. Just like their brief time together, Tess acknowledged sadly. Brilliant and blazing while it lasted. Then ended without a trace.

She closed her eyes at the lights. She had no right to question what he did, wouldn't be here long enough for it to count. At some point, she would have to let him go and live the rest of her life never knowing. Get used to it, she warned her heart. Or it will eat you alive.

"Why did you stay, Tess?"

She startled at his rough voice and turned to him. He hadn't moved.

"What do you mean?"

He rolled on his side, his eyes dark, his face illuminated by the now fever pitch of the Demisie auroras.

"Why didn't you want to go home when I gave you the chance?"

She could feel his warm breath against her face, he was that close. There he was, handsome and real, framed by the glorious show in the sky. The man she loved. Oh, this was going to hurt, losing him. And she knew she would. She was no competition for Yre Gault or for his love of adventuring. The realization settled over her so clearly, it nearly crushed her under its surge.

Even if she told him she loved him, he belonged to Yre Gault and eventually he would realize that. He would never fit in on Earth. It was too small and confining. Cohl was meant for bigger things than to live some mundane and uneventful life with her. Yre Gault needed him and he it. Her loss, their gain. Her eternal happiness versus the welfare of millions. Hardly seemed worth a debate.

He waited. Why indeed was she still here? In a small voice, she lied, "The Traka-Sou, remember?"

"And that's the only reason?" he pushed.

She swallowed and nodded, willing back the tears as she let him go. He didn't belong to her and she would not tempt him.

Cohl's eyes narrowed, darkened. She held her breath. Was that doubt that flashed? Disappointment? She couldn't tell. In the shadows, they looked the same. He didn't move, just stared at her intently as if waiting for more. Maybe he'd say something now, admit that he cared and wanted her to stay. . . .

Then he rolled onto his back and laid the pistol across his chest.

"Go to sleep, Tess. Tomorrow is going to be one hell of a day."

Lying on his stomach, Cohl opened one eye just enough to see that it was morning and that the perimeter alarm was quiet. Tess was tucked under his arm with her back against his side and her hair strewn between them. He inhaled the smell of it, capturing a moment of heaven. He loved her. And he couldn't keep her.

He had tried last night. He had given her the perfect opportunity to tell him exactly how she felt.

She'd lied. And she was a lousy liar. There was more and he'd wanted to hear it. He had waited for her to admit that she loved him, wanted to stay. Something remotely offering hope.

Nothing, although her profound sadness surprised him. He shrugged it off. If she did love him, it was not enough to give up her life back on Earth.

Hell, he was just as bad. He could not even consider living on her world, so far from Yre Gault. Sure, he had left Yre Gault years ago but he always kept track of its state of health.

Something kept him bound to his world, some invisible tie that he couldn't even define and didn't particularly want.

Now all he could think of was Demisie's tragedy. A tragedy that should have, could have been avoided. But there it was, carved in stone—his worse nightmare for Yre Gault.

He clenched his fists. He would not allow that to happen on his world, to his people. No matter what it took, he would personally ensure that Yre Gault didn't fade into oblivion, forever lost and forgotten.

Cool air replaced the heat where Tess had been as Cohl felt her slip out from under his arm.

With his head propped in her direction, he watched covertly and with lazy appreciation as Tess stood and walked across the sand toward the shallow pond, stretching the length of her body in the late morning sun. For a few long moments, she just stared at the water. He could almost see the brain cells working feverishly.

When she shot him a quick look, he froze behind the cover of his arm, unwilling to give up his private show.

Then to his utter surprise, she tugged off her shirt, and her shorts and panties dropped around her feet. Unaware of her stunned audience, she picked up a bowl and a cloth.

Cohl was suddenly, painfully alive as her nude form sauntered straight into the shallows. In the sunlight, that mass of hair shone red and her skin glowed like a polished statue. His gaze swept down her straight back to a perfectly shaped bottom and long, slim legs. He loved everything about her body. It was as if she were custom-made just for him, curved and cupped in all the right places.

Gingerly, Cohl adjusted his position for more comfort, aware of how hard the ground beneath him had become. It flitted, however briefly, through his mind that he should be angry that she deliberately disobeyed his orders to stay clear of the water. But his pride was firmly trounced, outvoted, and silenced beneath a stampede of raging hormones.

With her toes, Tess skimmed the water, drawing ripples in the calm much as she had in his own life. She'd sure as hell screwed it up good, too. He would never be happy with another woman, never look at life the same way. He was doomed to misery. Every male cell in his body agreed.

Standing in water to midcalf, Tess turned to face the sun that had just crested over the low cliff face. Her ivory profile silhouetted against the shadows of the cliff, she stretched again, warming her bare skin in the sun's heat.

His eyes narrowed to slits when she dropped to her knees in the shallows. With a deft sweep, she scooped water into the bowl. Cohl held his breath as she lifted the bowl high above her head and turned it over. A steady stream of water poured out, down and over her. Water fell like crystals over hair and skin, rolling down her body in sheets and rivulets. Bowl after bowl followed until her hair and body glistened and droplets flashed and fell from her hardened nipples.

Cohl's breath came in hard, shallow bursts as she began washing every part of her body with the cloth. Long strokes up and down her legs, circular caresses over her breasts, erotic glides across her neck. Moving in slow motion, she was a goddess rising out of the water alone in the wilderness around them.

A great surge of heat took him. Blood pounded in his ears. Blind desire gripped and shook him. He growled softly in the back of his throat. She was his. No matter how much damn space or how many light-years separated them. No matter who else touched her. He bared his teeth at the thought. Another man's hands on her, an Earth man. He hated them all.

That's when the beast within emerged, fearless, restless, ruthless. He rolled over and bolted to his feet. Tess's gaze swung around and her eyes widened as he descended upon her. On the way to the water, he unfastened his shorts and

• kicked them off, letting her know in no uncertain terms what he intended.

He heard her sharp intake of breath as he sloshed into the water. She knelt frozen, her wide eyes riveted to his. With one smooth motion, he swung around, crouched behind her in the water, and tucked her back against his chest. He wedged her bottom between his splayed thighs, his heavy erection pinned against her back. He took the cloth that hung limply from her hand and slipped it into the warm water.

With absolute precision and tenuous self-control, he proceeded to bathe her from the hollow of her throat to the swell of her thigh. She moaned low and relaxed into him, her skin wet and warm against his. Leaning over her shoulder, he discovered a glorious new angle to view her from.

Intrigued, he tossed the cloth aside and used both hands to stroke her from knees to shoulders. Like a spectator, he watched his hands minister long, slow slides up her smooth thighs. His fingers spread wide across hipbones, spanning a flat stomach, dipping into her belly button. Up and over her elegant rib cage before molding and cupping each breast as she arched against his hands. Thumbs circled hard nipples and strummed gently. She made a throaty, guttural sound that was his reward.

With a feral growl, he nuzzled her hair, ear, and throat until her breath gasped and fluttered and every muscle trembled against him. Ravenous, he licked droplets from her earlobes and jaw. He wanted to devour her, drink her into his soul where he would never have to let her go. Where reality didn't apply to lovers and good-byes were forbidden.

Her arms slid up around his neck as she turned her lips to his and pulled him down. Bordering on madness, mouths nipped and taunted, bodies pressing and surging instinctively.

His fingers slid back down her smooth belly, searched and

248

found her, hot and slick with need. He tormented her with fingertips and water, reveling in the frenzied little sounds she made. Then she stiffened and cried out his name. It echoed along the cliff wall, the sweetest sound ever to his ears.

Awakened now, she wriggled in his arms, slippery and wanton, wanting more, begging. The savage within him broke loose in an answering call as he lifted her bottom and drove into her in a single stroke. He threw his head back and roared like the wild beast he was, staking his claim. Pure male instinct dominated in a primitive and fierce rhythm. Tess braced herself on all fours beneath him, accepting his absolute possession of her and her of him. Thrust for thrust, she stayed with him until she strained in the throes of another climax.

He gripped her slick hips, losing more and more control as her climax squeezed him. His body coiled into red-hot muscle—driving, giving, taking—until just the animal remained. Release started deep within and burst from his lips as salvation came in near-painful waves and echoed off the cliffs endlessly.

In the quiet aftermath, the water calmed around them. Cohl felt the sun on his shoulders as his labored breathing slowly returned to normal and the human side of him returned. He rubbed her hips where he was sure he'd left marks and chastised himself for losing control. Only with Tess was he powerless against his own hunger.

"I'm sorry if I hurt you," he rasped.

Tess didn't answer, her head lifted high. In fact, she didn't move.

Cohl frowned in concern. "Tess?"

"I think I know where the amulet is," she whispered.

Cohl's head shot up as he followed her line of sight to the cliff face. The sun had just broken the plane of the cliff edge, shining down and across the unusual slope. He saw it, too.

At any other time of the day, the rough carvings would have disappeared with the others in the rock face. The sun's angle and the viewer's vantage point had to be perfect to see the crude circle with spokes extending in all directions—an exact replica of the amulet.

Cohl squinted against the glare of the sun off the water. The bottom spoke looked darker than the others and deeper—a slender rift in the rock.

That would be the entrance.

Chapter Eighteen

Tess peered into the narrow fissure in the cliff. Dark. Very, very dark with danger written all over it.

"There's no way Pitz would be with you on this one."

Standing next to her with his hands on his hips, Cohl scanned the entrance from top to bottom.

"You're right about that," he concurred, clearly distracted. "We'll have to travel light to squeeze through."

He turned his head and his golden eyes met hers. For a steamy moment, she knew precisely what he was thinking. No more than thirty minutes ago, they had mated in the water like howling beasts. The aftershocks still skittered through her nerve endings. He'd ravished her completely, possessing her down to her very soul. God help her when this was all over. She would never feel this alive again.

Cohl broke the brief, charged connection and dropped to his knees next to his pack. Out came anything that wasn't absolutely necessary, leaving only the bare tools of his trade and a few other essentials like water. She noted the medical kit also stayed. He took her pack and did the same, handing it back considerably lighter. Then he produced the two familiar little lightballs and tossed them up into flight.

Tess smiled as hers zipped over to her. "Hi, Tink. Nice to see you again."

Cohl stood and laughed. The laugh died and he just stared at her intently with those golden eyes that she loved so much.

"Something wrong?" she asked.

He closed his eyes. For a split second, she thought he was going to say something. Instead, he shook his head as if to clear it and said, "Follow me."

Dragging the pack behind him, he slipped through the narrow fissure. Tess went next, dragging her pack. The brilliant morning light outside disappeared into a jagged sliver behind her while Tink shone a beam of light into the terminal darkness ahead.

Once through the fissure, Tess stepped out into a rudimentary tunnel hand-hewed from solid rock, the chip marks and gouges prominent. She took a deep breath. The air was fresh, clean, cool. Not what she expected. They donned their packs and Cohl went first. Moving slowly with his laser pistol leading, he stooped in deference to the low ceilings.

Tess couldn't help grinning as she walked tall. "The Demisians must have been a little on the short side."

He threw her a quick smile. "Luckily, I'm partial to short people these days."

Rounding a corner, she slowed when she heard the howl of the wind. It grew louder and more intense with every step until the tunnel ended where a narrow cavern cut across their path. On the other side of the ten-foot-wide cavern stood a massive solid stone wall rising straight up into the darkness. The space between the end of their tunnel and the sheer face of the wall raged and wailed with a horizontal wind of a terrifying magnitude.

Tess covered her ears with her hands but the vibration and roar were still unbearable.

Over the din, she yelled, "Did they build this?"

Cohl shook his head. "Probably a natural formation in the cliff."

He snagged his lightball, manually pointing the beam straight ahead and up the rock face to a roughly cut doorway five stories above them.

Tess pointed to the opening and shouted, "We have to go up there?"

Cohl nodded and from his pack pulled out a white square package that she had seen before in the VirtuWav. He tossed it out the end of their tunnel and into the wind. It disappeared out of sight so fast that Tess could only gape. They'd be pummeled to death in that wind. She turned to Cohl, who was looking up the length of the wall and frowning.

"How are we going to do this?" she yelled.

Cohl was silent for a long time, scrutinizing the wall with his lightball. Finally he reached into the pack and withdrew a stubby metal cannon, a foot in length and downright nasty looking. Then he retrieved two body harnesses from the pack, handed one to Tess, and donned his own.

While Tess snapped into her harness, Cohl picked up the short cannon, checked the settings, and hefted it onto his shoulder. A laser beam shot out the end and bore into the base of the wall on the opposite side, carving a perfect hole. He slowly raised the beam in a straight line toward the doorway high above. The laser continued to eat a two-foot-wide, two-foot-deep swath through the stone as if it were butter.

Within minutes, he was done. Tess looked over his shoulder at the vertical ditch he'd just cut into the rock, straight up to the doorway. He smiled at her and reached into the bag.

This time he retrieved a pistol with a grapple hook on the end. He aimed it into the wind and to the left of the new ditch and pulled the trigger. The grapple sang out, caught in the wind, and struck the ditch dead center directly in front of them. The cable sagged hard but Cohl held the pistol handle firmly.

"Nice shot," Tess whispered.

Cohl clipped their two harnesses together and then to the attachment on the end of the pistol. Then he snagged the two lightballs and stuffed them into his pack. In the pitch-dark, he shouted, "Hold on to me."

"May the Force be with us," she mumbled as she closed her eyes and gripped him tightly around the waist.

He activated the controls on the pistol and they were sucked at once into the torrential wind. Tess screamed as the wind hurled them against the far wall. She heard Cohl's painful grunt when his back struck the rock wall hard and her body slammed into his. The cable snapped tight. She buried her head into his chest against the pounding wind. Several moments passed before she realized they were being dragged slowly, steadily back toward the newly cut ditch.

After what seemed like eternity, Cohl drew her into the recessed ditch with him. He wrapped his arms around her and told her, "All clear."

Tess's eyes snapped open. The space around them was illuminated once again by the pair of lightballs. Enough for her to see that Cohl's head was back and his eyes were closed.

"Cohl?" she shouted over the wind roaring behind her.

His eyes opened slowly. "I'm all right. Just need a minute to get my breath back." He was already looking up. Tess followed his gaze to the ceiling above the doorway.

He grinned at her. "Now comes the easy part."

"You don't know how relieved I am to hear that," she said.

Cohl withdrew the grapple hook from the rock and aimed it at the ceiling. It hit and stuck with a solid *thwap*. He clipped their harnesses to the pistol and they shot into the air with a jolt.

Tess winced every time his shoulder struck the ditch as he shielded her. Seconds later, they were above the wind inside the safety of another tunnel.

Cohl released them from the grapple and stuffed the pistol in the pack. "Leave your harness on. We might use them again."

When he turned toward the corridor, Tess saw the bloody and battered skin on his shoulder.

"Cohl," she gasped.

He cast a quick glance over his shoulder. "It's fine. Nothing serious."

Tess squeezed her eyes shut. *Don't think about it. Don't think about the next time he does this.* When she opened her eyes, he had already disappeared into the tunnel. She tagged along behind him, silent and worried, knowing he would never give this up before it killed him.

She nearly bumped into his still body. The grinding noise got her attention next. She peered around his big frame and saw why he had halted. The corridor had turned into a round, stone tunnel at least thirty feet in length and spinning at an ungodly rate.

Cohl tossed another square packet into the tunnel. It dropped to the bottom, then was sucked against the tunnel wall, becoming no than a blur of a line.

"Good Lord," she gasped.

"Ah, this one is too easy," Cohl commented. He took from his pack the double grapple device she had seen before in the VirtuWav. Cohl extended the body and positioned the device so that one end pointed down the spinning tunnel and the other was aimed at the wall behind them. In a flash, the grapple hooks shot out. The first one stuck to the wall behind them. The other one hurtled down the tunnel. Tess heard the smack as it hit something solid on the other side.

The cable snapped tight. Cohl peered down the length of the cable to the far end. "Perfect." He grinned. "I'll go first, then send the unit back to you."

Cohl attached his harness to the grapple device and swung beneath it. "Just like in the VirtuWav, Tess."

He disappeared into the tunnel. She watched him slide through the center and emerge from the other end. He detached and shoved the club back toward her. It whirred back through the tunnel until she caught it in her hands.

"Come on, Tess. You can do it." Cohl's shout came through the grinding tunnel.

She muttered a few choice words about her present state of mind as she hooked up to the unit and let her weight drop below it. With her legs wrapped tight around the club, she activated the motor. It jerked her at breakneck speed. Her scream echoed inside the tunnel as it spun crazily around her. Tink zipped along happily behind her.

Cohl caught her in his arms. Her hair flew everywhere. She tried to make some order with it and finally gave up. Adventuring wasn't for wimps.

"Trap number two down, right?" she asked.

He nodded, looking down the tunnel. "Number three is the narrow path through the mist of beasts."

Tess grimaced. Beasts. Maybe they'd get lucky and run into Tribbles or something equally benign.

"What kind of beasts?"

Cohl shook his head. "No idea. Doesn't matter. I'm sure they aren't going to be friendly." His eyes met hers. "Just so you don't say I didn't tell you."

"So much for the Tribbles theory," she muttered as he started down the dark corridor in front of her. It seemed longer this time and Tess was beginning to think there might be a mistake when she heard them. Not the growls she expected but something else, like nails on a chalkboard.

The tunnel opened to a cavernous chamber with a

dropped floor of swirling, white mist. The mist parted in waves as some . . . thing moved beneath it. The beasts.

A single, narrow beam forged of stone spanned the forty-plus feet to a small landing on the other side. The walls were sheer, slick with condensation, and scarred with deep gouges. Tess's lightball illuminated a single, sicklelike claw as it emerged and left a new mark in the stone.

Tiny squeaks emanated from the ceiling and, with great dread, Tess looked upward at little eel-like creatures clinging and moving along it. One of them dropped into the mist below. Tess screamed as the beasts below roared and the mist boiled where the doomed creature had landed.

"Damn," Cohl muttered. "That's not good."

He retrieved a sacrificial packet and carefully tossed it on top of the foot-wide beam that ran the length of the chamber. At first, nothing happened. Then claws began rising out of the mist and the packet disappeared with them.

Tess stared at the place where the packet had been. "I certainly hope you have a plan here."

Cohl adjusted his pack, his expression grim. "Sure do. We run as fast as we can to the other side."

Tess gaped at him. "You are kidding, right? Didn't you see what happened to that poor little packet?"

"I noticed. I also noticed that it took those beasts a while to locate it. So we don't want to stand in one place too long."

Tess took a step back, shaking her head. "I can't do it, Cohl. What if they get me? What if they drag me down there?" She pointed into the mist.

Cohl's expression turned serious. "Then I'll go in and get you out."

For a long minute, they just looked at each other. She knew he meant every word. He would follow her in.

"You don't have to do that for me," she finally managed.

"I got you into this," he said firmly. "I'll make damn sure you live through it."

Tess gazed over the mist to the other side of the chamber and took a deep breath. "Let's get this over with."

Cohl withdrew a small palm-sized disk out of the pack.

Tess frowned. "What is that?"

"Low-level concussion charge." He smiled at her confused expression. "I'm going to knock down all that bait up there." He pointed to the ceiling.

"Bait?"

Cohl handed her a laser pistol and a set of earplugs. "Sorry but yes. That should keep a few of these beasts busy. You go first. Shoot anything that gets in your way but try not to take out our bridge. I'll be right behind you. Just run as fast as you can and watch your footing."

Tess turned to face the narrow beam and closed her eyes. Sharp claws scratched the stone around her.

"Ready?" Cohl whispered in her ear. She nodded.

"Start running when you hear the bang," he said.

She opened her eyes and raised her pistol. The disk flew over her head and dropped into the mist, and the entire chamber shook violently. Even with the protection of the earplugs, her ears rang. Thousands of creatures screamed and rained from the ceiling as she took off across the beam on a dead run. Tiny eels littered the beam in front of her and snagged in her hair. The mist began to boil and hideous shrieks echoed throughout the chamber.

Tess saw a claw rise above the mist ahead of her and fired. There was a shrill scream and liquid squirted from the claw as it snapped back. She could feel Cohl running behind her and see his laser shots light up grotesque shadows below them.

She reached the other side and spun around to cover Cohl. He was about ten feet away when a claw caught his ankle, nearly knocking him down. Tess raised her weapon and poured a stream of laserfire into the claw and the beast attached to it. Cohl stumbled, recovered, and leaped the remaining distance until he collapsed on the safety of the landing next to her.

He rolled onto his back with a long hiss. Tess dropped to her knees and checked his ankle. The skin was sliced neatly and bleeding profusely.

"Bastards," he growled and withdrew a palm-sized bandage from the pack. He slapped it over the wound, stopping the bleeding and starting the healing process.

Tess just stared while he stood up, adjusted his pack, and hobbled down the tunnel as if nothing happened. Realizing she wasn't following him, he turned to face her. "Coming?"

Tess nodded numbly and got to her feet. *His life, his choice.* She just could not bear it. But she knew she would relive today. Every day of every year for the rest of her life, she would think about him in these caves and caverns. Wonder when it would happen. That final miscalculation.

Cohl limped back for her as she stood, stuck in her thoughts and unable to move forward. He wrapped his arms around her and she buried her face in his shirt.

"One more to go, Earth girl."

She nodded. "I'm all right. Tell me about the last one."

"Guardians stand watch to lead astray," he recited.

She wrinkled her nose and looked up at him. "What the heck does that mean?"

Cohl shrugged and gave her a little smile. "I have no idea. We'll find out when we get there." He linked their fingers and drew her behind him.

They walked for quite a distance and then the tunnel abruptly ended at a set of stone steps that led up to a dark opening above them. Cohl slowed as they approached the steps.

"I'll go first. Come up when I whistle."

He scanned the steps over carefully and then with his weapon high, made his way slowly up into the unknown space above. Tess brushed the hair from her face and a tiny eel dropped out. She quickly checked for more. Cohl's whistle was a welcome sound and she raced up the steps. This couldn't get much worse.

That's what she thought until she looked around to find an army staring back at her. It was another chamber, this one massive and filled with thousands upon thousands of robed stone figures, lined up in close formation and facing in one direction.

"Guardians?" Tess asked in awe.

"Apparently," Cohl replied as he opened his pack.

Tess stepped to his side. "They look harmless enough."

"Yes, they do. That's what worries me."

Tess had a terrible thought. "They aren't going to come to life or anything, are they?"

Cohl replied, "I sure as hell hope not. We're outnumbered about a thousand to two."

Surveying the statues, near and far, lit only by the two lightballs, she suddenly felt trapped. The statues were so tall and the room so large that it was like standing in a cornfield on a moonless night.

She licked her dry lips. "So, where to?"

Cohl answered, "According to the file, the amulet is housed in a room somewhere off this chamber. We need to locate that room."

She looked up at the towering statues and the blackness that surrounded them.

"How?"

"With technology."

Tess blinked at the *bleep, bleep* sound of the SAMA.

Cohl began scanning the massive chamber. "I'm not picking up anything unusual."

"Relatively speaking," Tess muttered.

Cohl chuckled. "Let me be more specific. No chemical compounds that can kill us. Nothing alive. No movement. The room is roughly circular. I'm scanning for a deviation."

He stopped the SAMA in one direction. "Found it. That way. Just stick close to me."

She followed on his heels as he led her through row upon row of statues. The lightballs lit up each row, but beyond the light were hundreds more—dark shadows that seemed to follow their every move. For a thousand years, she thought, they had stood here. Waiting, watching. Now they all seemed to be watching her. In fact, she could swear they were all facing her wherever she looked. How could that be? She could have sworn that they were pointed in the same direction when she and Cohl started. She shot a terrified look around her and found them facing her, no matter where she stood.

She suddenly felt very much alone.

"Cohl?"

There was no answer.

Tess froze in her tracks in Tink's little circle of light.

"Cohl?" she said louder.

Nothing, just a million statues all staring at her.

"Cohl, answer me!" she screamed above the pounding of her heart. Her breath came in short bursts as the statues seemed to close in around her in a dizzy fog. She knew if she didn't calm down, she would hyperventilate. Clenching her fists, she forced her eyes closed and concentrated on just inhaling and exhaling. Gradually, her heartbeat slowed and her breathing with it.

She opened her eyes and blinked. The statues were all lined up in perfect order again, facing one direction.

"Cohl?" she tried one more time. Again, silence. Something had happened to him. Something awful. She had to find him. He would never leave her voluntarily.

She spun around in a complete circle but all she could see were thousands of robed figures, and by now she was totally disoriented. She looked down. Not even a footprint to follow on the stone floor. She checked her pack. Cohl had left enough water for a few days and some food. She still held her pistol and the data pad. And Tink blinked faithfully beside her. Better than nothing.

Don't panic yet, she told herself. Cohl said it was a circular room. If she followed a direct line of attack, she would run into a wall sooner or later. Tess took a deep breath, picked a direction, and started walking. As she navigated the statues, she called to Cohl. There was never an answer. Either he was no longer in the massive chamber or he was dead. With the absolute certainty of a lover, she knew he wasn't dead.

Tink zipped above her, casting giant circles of light around the statues. They didn't seem so ominous now. She tried to stay in a straight line, glancing behind her periodically. But there was no way to mark the path she was taking.

Suddenly, Tink's light flashed on something solid ahead. A wall. She'd found a wall! Tess rushed past the last few statues and flattened against the warm stone as if it were salvation.

She turned and leaned back against the wall. "Damn. What now, Tink?" Her faithful lightball hovered nearby offering no help whatsoever. Tess closed her eyes. What would Cohl do in a situation like this?

She basically had two choices: Move forward or go back through the traps. Staying put simply was not a choice; she had to find Cohl. She dismissed the going-back option as a very long and unpleasant shot. Moving forward meant finding the amulet.

Her eyes popped open. She didn't need any special tools except her voice to do that. And it held some sort of power—at least that's what the legend said. Maybe she could use that power to find Cohl. He'd said it was in a room off the chamber so if she followed the perimeter, eventually she'd find it. She pushed away from the wall, placed one hand against it, and cast a quick look at her lightball.

"Come on, Tink. We're getting that amulet."

* * *

Cohl shoved on the stone slab in the tunnel ceiling above him to no avail. Sweat drenched his body—partly from exertion, partly from the humid, hot air of the tunnel. He leaned back against the wall to catch his breath and rubbed the battered shoulder he had landed on.

"Damn it!" he yelled to no one in particular. The single word echoed in stereo down both directions of the tunnel that ran beneath the room of guardians. He looked up at the flip-over trapdoor he'd dropped through. Who would have guessed? He was so distracted by the statues that he never looked down. A major mistake and possibly his last. Most likely, Tess's last too. Now she was alone up there and he couldn't do a damn thing about it.

He wiped the sweat from his forehead. He pulled out the SAMA unit and pointed it down one direction of the tunnel. It appeared to dead-end a short distance away. He pointed in the other direction. This side was longer and it too appeared to dead-end but the SAMA picked up something else. Hope sparked. If he could find a way out, he could get back in and rescue Tess.

He pocketed the SAMA, pulled out his weapon, and ran.

The alcove was smaller than she had imagined, unobtrusive with nothing spectacular to mark its legendary treasure. Tess stepped in front of the entrance and peered inside. Cone-shaped, about fifteen feet high at its point, it reminded her of a beehive. In the center of the compact room stood a solid column of stone, atop which sat the amulet encased in a clear crystal block.

Thousands of precisely spaced tiny steps lined the interior of the room from bottom to top. She knew what those were for. If she sang her song right, they would shatter that crystal casing and release the amulet. If she sang it wrong . . . She closed her eyes. It didn't matter. She needed that amulet to save Cohl and then to save his father. Not to mention to get herself out of this place. If she failed, they would all be lost.

She turned to Tink. "Stay right here."

Carefully, soundlessly, she stepped into the tiny chamber. Tink's light backlit her own shadow on the walls where she stopped in front of the amulet.

She clenched her fists. This was it. Every adventure had brought her to this point. And for the first time in her existence, lives were literally in her hands. She suddenly understood how Cohl felt about Yre Gault and its people. Terrified. If she failed, if she stumbled, then all the danger and struggle would have been for nothing.

She licked her lips and relaxed, conjuring up the song and its cryptic wording as if she were getting ready to sing a number onstage. The melody played in her head until she was sure she had it perfect. This was a onetime performance and the audience would be merciless.

She pushed everything else from her mind and released the first note. It resonated in the room like a pure ray of sunshine, lighting up the entire space. The brilliancy nearly blinded her but she held on to her composure and let the song flow. The words swirled around her like a whirlwind, twisting and turning and feeding into itself until she could almost see the notes lengthen into ribbons of light.

From the tiny steps, a grand chorus breathed a hush as sweet as freedom. They were the same voices as she'd heard from the faces at the city entrance. Powerful and strong, the singers surged in unison and joined her. Their voices added light to the radiance, different colors to hers.

She forced the words from her lips, all the while watching in utter fascination as the dizzying tendrils wrapped the tiny room. Faster and tighter they raced, strengthened in numbers and brilliance as her final note rang out. The chorus swelled to a horrific level and spiked through her head with a violent flash and suddenly Tess was no longer alone.

She could see them all, their beautifully adorned dresses and shirts flowing around them. They swirled about her in a sea of celebration, smiling and welcoming her to their precious world. Demisie spread out before her in all its former glory. The striking buildings and splendid artwork, magnificent courtyards full of color and life—before the silent faces, before the suffering. She felt the people's hearts, their love and pride for their world.

A small girl approached through the blurring mass of color and Tess recognized her immediately. Straight black hair capped her head, framing giant brown eyes and perfect red lips. The lost daughter. In her small hands, she held the amulet out to Tess.

You have come, the girl's voice whispered in Tess's head. *We have been waiting for you.*

Tess shook her head to disagree. She was not the one they were seeking. She was merely an implement. No one special.

I can't save you, Tess thought.

The child smiled sweetly. *Do not despair. Our world is no more but you can spare others our fate. They are outside, waiting for you to show them the way. Use the amulet wisely.*

Tess looked down at the amulet in her own hands and back up at the girl who was already fading into the festive celebration wearing a smile much too old for her age. The girl spread her arms wide and the celebration faded with her.

In their place, the rise and fall of Demisie, its entire existence, played out like an old, faded movie. As the beauty was systematically destroyed and the bodies piled up, tears streamed down Tess's face. The last of the dancers faded into the wilderness and the silence of a thousand years descended. Tess sobbed at the stillness.

Then her camp outside by the entrance sharpened into sight. There she saw the dangers and the showdown about to occur in its own space in time and her place in it. The players, their faces shown to her, stood waiting, their destiny in her hands.

What do I do? Tess wondered.

They need a new leader. The little girl's voice spiraled through her head.

How do I choose? Tess asked her. *If I am wrong, millions will pay.*

Look for the light. Follow your heart and you will not fail.

The voice drifted away with the vision. The room spun back to her in a jarring jerk where she stood painfully alone and crying in the absolute silence. The stone column and floor were littered with crystalline shards. She quickly lifted her hands and stared in disbelief at the amulet glittering back at her. She clutched it to her heart in overwhelming relief. She'd done it.

Tess slipped the chain of the amulet over her head and it settled warm against her chest, alive and living in her now. She recalled the little girl's words. *You must spare others our fate. They are waiting for you to show them the way.*

Tess breathed deeply. Her mission was not yet over. She had to stop Trakas from becoming the next Demisie.

She stepped out of the amulet room and strode through the guardians toward the opening where she and Cohl had entered. She knew exactly where it was. She was no longer concerned with the traps. The amulet had been freed and she knew in her heart that the beasts would be gone, the wind dead, the spinning tunnel still. They would be quiet forevermore, their purpose fulfilled.

Chapter Nineteen

Water. He'd found water just as the SAMA had detected. In a tiny cave that dripped with moisture, Cohl knelt beside the small pool. The fluorescent green color looked very familiar. He scooped up a little in his hand. Warm. The same color and temperature as the pond by their camp. This was his lucky day. It made perfect sense. After the guardians had built the traps and placed the amulet, they would need a way out. A back door. And he had dropped right into it.

He shrugged off the pack and the harness that he still wore. They would have to stay behind. He secured the SAMA, a single dose of Aritrox, and the laser pistol in his shorts pockets.

He glanced at his lightball. "Can't remember if you are waterproof or not." Then he shook his head, unable to believe he just spoke to his lightball as if it were alive. Tess's fault. He grinned at the thought of her and the warmth it always brought and then turned serious. His fists clenched. He had to get back to her.

Cohl slipped into the pool up to his shoulders, hanging on to the stone ledge while he inhaled and exhaled deeply. The lightball hung over his head. He took one final breath of oxygen and went under.

He heard the lightball plunge into the water and caught its faint light in his peripheral vision. It propelled itself ahead of him through a long, narrow underwater tunnel. Gripping the rocks that jutted out, Cohl pulled himself along, deeper into the tunnel. No air pockets above. He could feel the burn in his lungs already.

Then up ahead, rays of sunlight filtered through the water. He pushed forward—his lungs screaming—cleared the underwater tunnel, and kicked his legs toward the surface. He breached it with a gasp, sucking clean air into his starved lungs. Just as he had expected, he was treading water in the middle of the small pool by their camp.

The big surprise was the ugly band of twenty or so Trakas surrounding him. And every one of their weapons was pointed in his direction. *Shit.* Where was Pitz when he needed him?

"Well, well." A massive, gluttonous man stepped forward. "They sure got some ugly fish on this planet."

Cohl debated over ducking back under the water and quickly dismissed the idea. Besides the fact there was nowhere to go, he was thinking of Tess. These men were here for her. Damned if he'd let them touch her again.

Stalling to catch his breath, he took his time swimming to shore. Options ran through his head as he staggered to his feet and walked through the shallows toward the leader. Since this wasn't Rommol but was equally ugly, it had to be his brother Gothyk.

Gothyk nodded to one of his men. "Take his weapons."

Cohl endured a rough body search and was relieved of his pistol and the SAMA. Meanwhile, he mentally ticked off each Trakas and all their weaponry. This was going to be a challenge.

Gothyk waddled forward and sneered. "Where is she?"

"Dead," Cohl answered stoically. "One of the traps caved in and she got caught inside. The amulet is also buried."

Gothyk's eyes narrowed. "Then you won't mind showing us exactly where it is. I'm sure we can dig it out."

Cohl stared hard at him. "I wouldn't recommend going back in there. The tunnels aren't stable."

Gothyk jabbed a laser pistol at Cohl's midsection. "Then you will go first. Move."

"Hold it right there, you fat bastard!" The command came from behind the band of Traka-Sou and they all turned in unison.

Surrounding them were Rommol and his men. Being the only one facing that direction, Cohl had seen them coming over the low hill. God, these Traka-Sou were stupid. Not one of them had the foresight to post a lookout.

Cohl contemplated the new situation and prepared his escape plan. He needed to steal a weapon and get back into the cavern with Tess. After that, things would get a little difficult.

"Drop your weapons," Rommol barked.

"Like hell," Gothyk yelled back to Rommol. He waved to his men. "Fire!"

"No!" The shout came from behind Rommol. Cohl squinted as a robed figure step forward and stood between the two sides. The flowing robe with the deep cowl reminded Cohl of a Demisian guardian.

Gothyk's face dropped and turned red with anger when he recognized the invader. "You," he hissed. "You are with them." He pointed to Rommol's men.

The robed figure pulled back his cowl. The face was that of an old man, weathered and aged. However, his eyes burned fierce and bright and he spoke with great strength.

"I am Nish, the last Guardian of the Amulet," he said. "I have seen what you have done to Trakas and it must stop."

Nish pointed a bony finger at Rommol. "You." Then he pointed to Gothyk. "And you. Come forward."

Cohl watched Rommol and Gothyk don the same expressions of rage.

"Go to hell, old man," Rommol hissed.

Nish swung around to face him. "Are you too much of a coward to face your enemy alone? Or must you hide behind your men and your people and your weapons?"

Rommol snarled and stepped forward, tossing his pistol to the ground. Gothyk hesitated, glared at Nish, and did the same. Cohl saw the precise moment when they focused on each other and forgot everyone else. He'd had no idea how deep their hatred was. Brothers. It was hard to believe.

He watched them circle each other, while their men closed around them in anticipation. As they moved forward, something caught Cohl's eye.

Alone in the back, behind the troops, stood his father, his wrists locked in restraints. Relief swept through Cohl. When their eyes met, his father smiled. Cohl glanced back over his shoulder at the cliff behind him. His father nodded understanding. The only way Cohl could save both his father and Tess was to get them all in the cavern. It was the only protection available.

Rommol and Gothyk finally lunged at each other in a meaty collision. Although Gothyk outweighed Rommol by more than half, Rommol was faster. They grunted and struck at each other, faces red, arms flailing.

Cohl took a small step back and noted that his father did the same. The Trakas on both sides were totally enthralled, cheering and roaring.

He had moved ten meters toward the entrance when he heard the nearly simultaneous laser shots. Between Trakas' legs, he saw Gothyk and Rommol collapse in a heap and knew they'd both cheated and both lost.

A silence fell and a new fear gripped him. The Trakas on both sides gaped at their dead leaders and then began looking at each other. Nor and Sou divided silently and stepped away into their respective sides with their weapons drawn.

Nish had his arms raised and was about to say something when the ground beneath them quaked hard. Great claps of thunder emanated from the cliff behind Cohl. He spun around as blasts of dust and debris burst from the narrow entrance before the entire entrance fell away, leaving a massive hole.

Cohl watched in horror. *Tess.*

Then the quake ended. For a few minutes, there was only stunned silence. Suddenly, a light filled the hole and Tess stepped out through the dust into the gaping entrance. She stood there, a luminous figure against the dark backdrop of fresh red stone. A hush descended.

The amulet glowed white against her chest, the same glow that encapsulated her body. Cohl inhaled sharply. She had completely changed. Her stance was taller, regal, all-powerful like a goddess.

The wind picked up, whirling sand around them. It wailed a mournful song as the sky darkened and the ground trembled.

She raised her arms. "Look around you." Her voice rang out in deep resonance, amplified across the courtyard, demanding respect and heedfulness. Even her voice was not her own. It was the voice of many.

She stared straight at the Trakas, her eyes glazed over. "You are surrounded by death. The silent remnants of my people lost, our life destroyed. You have wandered through our empty homes, listened to the wind whistle down barren roads, seen the destruction at hand."

Cohl frowned at the "we" references. She was speaking as if she were one of the Demisians. What had happened? Where was his Tess?

He cast a glance around. The hard, ugly faces of the Trakas had been transformed into the wide-eyed stare of a child. Gone was the hate that twisted features and minds. The power of the amulet was working, captivating and controlling. But why was she talking as if she were a Demisian?

"This is your future, your fate." Tess's words rang out and carried in the wind. "Open your eyes and see the truth before you. Open your ears and hear the cries of death. Open your heart and listen to your people. Today, you must choose the path you will lead them down. Do you choose the beginning or do you choose the end?"

Her final word echoed into silence. Why was she giving them a choice? She had the amulet. Why hadn't she just told them what to do?

The troops on both sides began to shuffle, looking around in confusion and at the dead bodies of their former leaders.

Cohl waited, watching the Trakas watching Tess. Maybe the amulet wasn't as powerful as the legend foretold.

She looked so fragile standing there. All she had for protection was that amulet and he doubted that was going to stop a laser blast. She was obviously in no condition to defend herself. Cohl crouched, coiled, ready to leap forward and block any laser fire on Tess with his own body. Then he heard a metallic thunk. Then another. He glanced over as Traka-Nor and Traka-Sou began dropping their weapons to the ground.

One by one, they disarmed themselves and knelt before her, heads hung low until Cohl and his father were the only ones left standing.

The wind died and the ground stilled. Tess's arms lowered as a smile crossed her face.

"You have chosen the beginning. You will need a new leader. A voice that is true, eyes that are clear, a heart that is pure."

She spoke to Nish. "You are the Guardian. It is too late for our planet."

Nish nodded in agreement.

"But you are not here for Demisie. You have the opportunity to save another world. A world you love where our blood runs warm. Will you honor these people until your death?"

He bowed his head slowly. "I will."

Tess addressed the Trakas. "Will you honor your leader for all your people's sake?"

The answer was, "We will."

"Then go. You have a long journey ahead of you." Tess turned and disappeared back into the dark tunnel.

"Now there's a woman who was born to rule." The familiar voice spoke behind Cohl. He spun around to find his father approaching. He looked tired and dirty but well, his restraints removed.

"That's not her," Cohl replied with a deep frown. He glanced up at the Trakas—Nor and Sou—who were slowly surrounding Nish and listening to his quiet orders.

"Come with me," Cohl said to his father.

They found her just inside the entrance, sprawled unconscious on the ground with the amulet by itself several meters from her. Cohl's blood chilled. He knelt down next to her and felt her pulse. Weak but there. He administered his single dose of Aritrox and turned to his father.

"Help me get her back to the transport."

Tess watched Cohl pace the med center before her like a big cat prowling his lair. She smiled. Even through the foggy, happy haze of Aritrox, she knew he hadn't left her side since they had arrived back on *Speculator*. By then she had re-

273

gained consciousness and felt fine, but Cohl insisted she be checked out.

Witley was taking his time examining her and Cohl looked ready to feed on someone. He strode restlessly like a panther circling its domain. God, he looked so good, she thought. So powerful and dangerous and intense. She nearly hugged herself. He was hers. If she had a solid bone in her body, she'd jump him, here and now. The thought sent a giggle through her. What would Witley think of that?

Finally reaching his limit, Cohl stopped directly in front of the medic. "Witley, is she all right or not?"

The medic's head snapped up from his data pad as if he'd just realized they were there. "She's fine. She just needs some rest."

Cohl reached out and scooped her carefully off the med table. "Thanks," he muttered, carrying her out the med center.

Tess smiled a drunkard's smile, happy and feeling fine in his arms as *Speculator*'s ceilings and walls floated by her. The whirlwind settled when Cohl deposited her gently on the bed in his quarters. She watched like a detached observer as he gently removed her clothes and then stripped off his own. He lay down next to her and pulled their naked bodies together. She folded into him with a small sigh, feeling safe and secure and loved.

"I thought I'd lost you." His words sounded so sweet in her ear. "Life without you . . . I can't imagine. I'd die for you, Tess."

So he did love her. He wanted her. She sighed, reveling in love that only he could give her. She should tell him now. Yes, now would be perfect. *I love you, Cohl.* She smiled, proud of herself. She'd finally said it. *I love you. I love you. I love you.*

Funny, he didn't reply. Maybe he was dead tired, too.

Instead, his arms enveloped her, a balm to her scattered senses. His heart pounded in his chest, music to her ears. His breath caressed her, massaging her tender skin. *This must be heaven* was her last thought before sleep slipped over her.

Cohl found them in his office, huddled together like two conspirators, while in the holodeck, Earth glowed blue and white. His father laughed heartily at something Tess had said. Cohl could tell she had already worked her magic on Montral Trae Salle. His blue eyes were twinkling as brightly as ever. Even after all these years, he looked healthy and robust. His full, gray hair was a little shaggy but still regal. He had shaved the rough beard he'd grown during captivity, revealing the stubborn, square jaw Cohl remembered only too well.

They glanced up in unison as he entered.

"Cohlman," his father started with a booming greeting. "About time you showed yourself. This remarkable woman has been filling me in on your adventures in coming to my rescue."

Cohl cast Tess an inquisitive look as he walked up behind them. She batted her eyelashes innocently.

His father continued with a shake of his head. "I must say, I'm most impressed by your efforts." He winked at Tess. "And by this ravishing woman. She was just telling me about her home planet. Sounds a lot like Yre Gault."

Tess laughed. "You're just saying that because I said Earth is so beautiful."

"Of course," Montral replied. Then he leaned in close. "But Yre Gault has better-looking men."

Cohl shook his head and dropped into a seat next to Tess. "Remind me never to leave you two alone for very long."

"So where have you been?" Montral asked, folding his arms over his chest.

"In communications," Cohl said, leaning forward over the table to address them both. "Trying to find out how the Trakas are reacting to their tentative peace agreement."

"And?" Tess prompted.

Cohl glanced at her. "So far, Nish is holding everything together. The battle was between the brothers, not between the people. However, if it had carried on for more than a generation, it would have become the people's battle, too. Luckily, they want peace. Demisie left quite an impression on the troops that landed there. They seem genuinely determined to escape that fate."

"So there's hope," Tess sighed.

Cohl nodded. "There's hope." He looked at his father. "They could use some financial and humanitarian help."

Montral smiled. "They'll have it."

"Nish has promised general elections as soon as things have settled down," Cohl continued. "I expect it to be soon. He realizes that his time is limited but until then, he's the appointed leader."

"He'll be a good one," Tess added quietly. "At least, there was one candidate for Trakas in that bunch. The little girl showed Nish to me. When I wore the amulet, I could see a clear light around him." She smiled at Cohl. "Like you and your father. All the others were dull."

She tilted her head and frowned. "But whatever happened to the amulet? Did you give it to Nish?"

Cohl shook his head. "We decided it was too dangerous in anyone's possession. And we couldn't put it back in the cavern. It wouldn't take long for someone else to steal it. So I dropped it from the transport into the middle of Demisie's largest ocean. Right now, it is lying buried in a few thousand feet of water and silt. There isn't a sensor built that can locate it through Demisie's magnetic interference."

Tess gave him a little smile. "The Demisians would be pleased that their amulet is safe."

"And no one will ever wield its power again," Cohl added grimly.

Tess shifted in her chair. "It never held any power."

"What?" Cohl and his father said in near unison.

She looked from one man to the other and shrugged. "There was no power in the amulet. It only amplified voices and cast light."

"But we saw you use it to bring peace to the Trakas," Montral blurted out. "They were ready to battle."

Tess shook her head. "It was only words. They believed the words because they believed the amulet had power."

"You can't stop a planetwide war single-handedly with a few words," Cohl said in disbelief.

She cast him a long look and tapped her chest. "It's here, in your heart." She tapped her head. "Here, in your mind." She held out her hands. "Here, in your hands. That's all the power you ever need. If you follow your heart, you will not fail."

Cohl stared back at her in amazement and admiration. She had saved a planet all by herself because that's what had to be done. As usual, she had taken the responsibility because she knew it was the right choice.

His father chuckled low and worked up to a full-belly laugh. "My dear," he finally managed, "you are quite the performer. The Demisians were lucky that you got to the amulet first."

"Speaking of the Demisians, what about the rest of the planet?" Tess asked Montral. "Will it be protected?"

Montral reached out and squeezed her hand. "I'll make sure it is. From what I could see, the archeology is a treasure in itself. And the entire culture, haunting yet beautiful, especially your descriptions of what you saw through the amulet. Those have been documented and will be retained as historical record."

Tess shook her head. "I only saw a small portion of their

lives. Perhaps you could talk to Nish, also. After all, he is a direct descendent of the Demisians. I'm sure he'd be happy to record what he knows so their way of life will not be forgotten."

Montral smiled and patted her hand. "Excellent idea. I'm still impressed about the brilliant way he maneuvered the brothers to a face-to-face confrontation. I doubt it would have ever happened had he not taken the initiative."

Cohl interjected, "Using us as bait, remember. I don't know how much I trust Nish."

"His convictions run deep. If his plan hadn't worked, he would have been executed. He took a great risk to save Trakas."

Montral nodded and added, "She's right. His methods may have been devious but it wasn't his idea to abduct me. That was that idiot Rommol. Nish did his duty for Trakas."

Tess shook her head. "It wasn't duty that drove Nish."

Cohl frowned. "Then what was it?"

She looked at him. "Love. He loves Trakas. It's only duty if your heart isn't in it."

Their eyes locked and Cohl understood. She hadn't stood vulnerable in front of them because she had to. She'd done it because she wanted to. Just like everything else in her life.

Montral looked from Cohl to Tess. "I think everything worked out very well for you two."

Tess gave Cohl a challenging look. "Any more complaints?"

He looked at her, committing every part of her to memory. Yeah, he had only one complaint. She was going home.

Montral broke the silence. "How much longer before we arrive at Yre Gault?"

"About an hour," Cohl replied. "Pitz will rendezvous with us there."

Cohl glanced at Tess. "Pitz did try to send a warning that Gothyk was tracking us." Then he pinned his father with a glare. "Because security was so bad on the Yre Gault docking station, Gothyk's men were able to plant a tracker beacon aboard *Speculator* while it was being repaired. That's how they followed us to Demisie."

"Pitz," Montral slapped a palm to his forehead in mock drama, clearly ignoring Cohl's reference to the infiltration. "Imagine my surprise when I thought *he* was abducting me. I may have to tighten up our security."

"What security? I told you ten years ago that your security net was too lax. If you'd listened to me then, none of this would have happened. Instead, you trusted Logen, of all people. Do you know that he's the one who planned your abduction? And Tess's. He nearly killed her."

His father looked at Tess in concern. "I apologize, my dear. I had no idea."

"But I didn't have much choice," his father said to Cohl. "You were gone."

"I wouldn't have left if you'd listened to me," Cohl said, unable to stop the bitterness from his words.

There was a long silence before Montral nodded. "You are right. I didn't listen. I didn't do a lot of things I should have." He looked at Cohl. "Did you take care of Logen?"

"I did," Tess said in a small voice. "He's dead."

His father gave a sigh. "Then I am doubly sorry." He leaned back and raised his hands. "What do I know about security? I want to be accessible to my people, not live in a prison."

"If you don't want to end up in another prison, you need to implement a real system and I'm going to set it up," Cohl stated flatly. "I can't spend all my time coming to your rescue. Besides, Mother has already agreed."

Montral frowned deeply, a look that Cohl had seen many times. He braced himself for the inevitable battle. Too bad. This one was his. This time his father was going to listen.

"Went over my head, did you?" Montral said seriously. Then he turned and winked at Tess. "Now you know who really runs Yre Gault."

Cohl sat stunned while Tess grinned and said, "I can see why Ad is so anxious to have you back."

Montral wiggled his eyebrows. "She's crazy about me, you know."

Tess tilted her head back and laughed. Cohl couldn't believe it. He had never seen his father crack a joke or make anyone laugh or care enough to even try. What had happened in the past ten years? And who was this man impersonating his father?

Tess caught Cohl watching his father and her eyebrows went up. She pushed back from the table. "Well, if you'll excuse me. There's something I need to do in the VirtuWav."

She looked directly at him, and there, in her green eyes, was love. It was the most beautiful thing he could ever recall seeing and the memory of it would surely haunt him forever.

Tess stood up and he watched her disappear out the office door. When he turned back, Montral was looking at him.

"Don't let her go," he said succinctly.

Cohl groaned. The last thing he wanted to discuss with his father was Tess.

"She has a life on Earth. One that I rudely yanked her away from to save your ass. She belongs there."

Montral harrumphed. "Is that what you think? With the way she just looked at you? You won't find another woman like her," his father continued. "Not anywhere else in the universe."

"You don't understand," Cohl explained, staring at the Earth hovering in the holodeck. "She already postponed her dream to help her parents. Then to help us. She deserves her shot."

"Even if it hurts," Montral prodded.

Cohl glanced over at him. "Yes."

"And she feels the same way?" Montral asked, tapping his fingers together under his chin.

There was a long silence.

Montral leaned forward and came nose-to-nose with his son. "She feels the same way, right?"

Cohl took a deep breath. "I don't know."

"You didn't ask her?"

Cohl shot out of his chair and began pacing the room with all the extra energy he had suddenly acquired as frustration gnawed at him.

"If she loved me, she would have said something by now. Obviously, she doesn't. Or if she does, it's not enough to give up her old life for."

"Did you ever think that maybe she might want to make that choice herself?" Montral said. "It can't hurt to ask."

Cohl stopped in the middle of the office and hung his head. "Yes. Yes, it could hurt to ask. Especially if she says no."

"More than losing her forever?"

Cohl glanced up at his father. The man was relentless but he also had a point. Nothing could hurt more than losing her forever.

He dared to hope and just that little glimmer was more than he should risk. He had taken worse chances in his life. Risks that nearly got him killed. But this was the first time he'd ever wagered his heart. Only for Tess would he take such bad odds.

Cohl turned and headed for the door. "If you need me, I'll be in the VirtuWav."

Tess breathed in the pine scent, so familiar and sweet. A cool breeze rattled the thick forest around her. These were the mountains she had visited as a child and loved as an adult.

This was what home felt like, smelled like. This was Earth.

She wrapped her arms around herself and gazed out over a body of water that could be any lake in the Adirondacks. A blue heron cruised by in slow motion and made a perfect two-point landing in the shallows not far from her. Earth's yellow sun cast its brilliant path across the gentle ripples of waves.

A single tear slid down her cheek.

This was one of the places she would miss but as long as the VirtuWav could replicate it so perfectly, it would always be just a virtual world away.

It was all so strange, these new worlds with their aliens and customs. Yet at the same time, exciting and wonderful. But not like home. They would never be Earth, never come close.

She'd go back for Griz. He belonged with her. The hardest part would be giving up her family. Tough to replicate a human being in here. Maybe Cohl could bring her back for a visit every Christmas. That would be enough. Enough time to visit, not enough time to be smothered. She nodded her head absently. Yes, Christmases would be fine.

And the career would hurt. A lot. But what good was success if her life, her love, was here? Who said she couldn't write songs and sing on Yre Gault? Her one stint there had been an unqualified success. It couldn't be any worse than trying to make it on Earth.

Still, it was hard saying good-bye. The little things. Chocolate, lasagna, a good romance novel.

The decision she had been avoiding for weeks was at hand.

She brushed the tears aside. It was a simple choice, really. There wasn't a thing on Earth worth giving up Cohl for. Nothing. Life without him would be unbearable, unthinkable. She could not ask him to give up his destiny for her. He belonged to Yre Gault and they desperately needed him. No, she would not hold him back when he finally realized that. He'd said he would die for her. He loved her, she knew that now. But he wouldn't ask her to give up her life. It would have to be her decision.

So there it was. Simple. Painful, yes, but better than a life without him in it. If she wanted him, she'd have to leave Earth behind. She looked out over the lake and bade a silent good-bye.

Standing in the thick brush by the Earth lake, Cohl watched Tess brush the tears aside. A cold, hard hand squeezed his heart. He should have realized that it would be too much to ask of her to give up everything for him.

There was no way he could ask her to forsake her very roots, no more than he could forsake his own. Yre Gault needed him and he couldn't trust anyone else to protect it. They needed *him*. On Yre Gault.

Cohl turned and walked away. Tess deserved her chance to shine, to reach her dream her way. She deserved a real home, a safe place to raise children and sing her songs. All the things he couldn't give her. He knew what was waiting for him on Yre Gault. Responsibility, long hours, commitment. He couldn't ask her to give her dream for his.

Inside, the fist around his heart tightened until he could barely feel it beating. Silent and still and cold. Perfect. He could only hope it would stay that way forever.

"Exit program," he said softly.

Within seconds he was back in the VirtuWav tube, floating down as Sahto powered it off.

The small man glanced at Cohl in concern. "Did something go wrong?"

Cohl stepped out of the blue circle and walked toward the door. "No. Stay with Tess."

283

He turned once to look at her one last time as she floated gently in the VirtuWav tube. Her hair floated around her like a halo that matched the angelic look on her face. He wished he could see her eyes one more time. Then he turned away.

As he walked down the long corridor to the bridge, it occurred to him that Tess would never forgive him for what he was about to do but his heart simply couldn't take any other way.

He entered the bridge to find Pitz at the helm with his father hovering nearby. Yre Gault sat squarely in the viewport.

Montral glanced up at him and frowned. "Where's Tess?"

Cohl tapped Pitz on the shoulder. "Prepare the transport for departure." Then he addressed his father. "I'll take you down to Yre Gault myself."

Montral crossed his arms over his chest and eyed his son. "What about Tess?"

Cohl felt the fist squeeze the last bit of warmth from his heart. "Pitz is taking her back to Earth."

Tess exited the VirtuWav feeling positively buoyant and giddy, her decision made. She gave Sahto a brilliant smile. "Thanks for waiting so long."

Sahto fidgeted nervously with the control panel, refusing to meet her gaze, and muttered some sort of "you're welcome."

Tess frowned but before she could speak, the door opened and Pitz scooted in.

"Come with me, please," he said flatly.

Tess glanced at Sahto, who was still avoiding her gaze, and back at Pitz, who addressed her as if he had never met her before, and wondered what the hell was going on.

In silence, she followed Pitz out of the VirtuWav room and down the corridor toward the bridge viewport. They were still in hyperspace. Pitz turned sharply into Cohl's office. Tess stepped inside and the door slid shut.

She folded her arms over her chest. "And it's nice to see you too, Pitz."

Pitz's head swiveled around. "Greetings. Cohl has instructed me to inform you that I am to return you to Earth without delay."

Everything froze around her. The words barely formed. "Where's Cohl?"

Pitz's lights blinked feverishly. "He took his father back to Yre Gault in the transport."

"We've already been to Yre Gault?" she asked in a voice that sounded far, far away.

"Affirmative."

It was like being poleaxed. Now she knew precisely what the term meant. For a few minutes, her brain didn't function at all. Then emotions surfaced one by one.

First, panic. Her heart lurched. Oh God. She would never see him again. Light-years away. Different worlds. Impossible obstacles. Unbearable.

Second came disbelief. How could he do this to her? He didn't even ask. Never talked to her. How could he decide her fate without so much as a word? She clenched her fists. She knew what happened. He had blocked her out like his obligation to Yre Gault and the horrid dangers of his chosen occupation. *Just like that.*

Hot on the heels of disbelief was anger. It set in slow and hot and merciless. Damn him for doing this to her again. For deciding her fate without her input. For not trusting her to know what she wanted. Not even caring enough to ask. Damn him.

Her chin went up. Fine. It was clear to her now that his only interest in her had been for the amulet. She'd been used and used good. She didn't need him. She had survived just fine without him up until this point. There was a career to think about, a whole goddamned happy life on Earth.

Pitz blinked and waited before her. She spun on her heel and strode to the exit.

"Thank you, Pitz. Tell me when we get there."

Chapter Twenty

Cohl pushed back from his father's desk and rubbed his tired eyes. After three months, the new security system he had designed for Yre Gault was almost fully implemented. Working on the project single-handedly had made progress slow but he'd had no choice. He was the only one he trusted to do it.

He shook his head. Thank God he was here. His parents had played around like young lovers since their reunion—kissing, holding hands, necking. It was almost embarrassing. There were things a son did not want to see his parents doing.

Much of Yre Gault's day-to-day responsibilities had been left up to him but it hadn't been as bad as he'd expected. In fact, there was something very fulfilling about making sure that his people and his planet were safe and cared for. He had already picked competent advisors to delegate duties to, many of whom jumped at the opportunity for more responsibilities. In all, it was much like running an adventuring business except you didn't go through so much Aritrox.

It's only duty if your heart isn't in it. She had been right, he thought. He loved Yre Gault. It was no longer duty that kept him here. Cohl leaned back in the chair and had to admit, it felt pretty damn comfortable. It was hard to believe he hadn't done a single acquisition in three months. He didn't miss it. He would never have thought that possible. He could say he was too busy or that he had needed a break after the amulet mission, but the reason was simpler: He could not bring himself to face the next one alone. Without Tess.

Cohl stood up, rolled his tight shoulders, and walked to the balcony. The sweet, heady aroma of midnight flowers filled his senses. He shoved his hands into his pockets and gazed up into the night. The two moons were on opposite ends of the sky tonight. Worlds apart.

He wondered what Tess was doing right now as he did whenever time moved too slowly for him. Sometimes, the not knowing ate at him like a slow death. The choice had been made. His choice. He could only imagine her reaction when Pitz told her what he had done. Pitz's recounting of the discussion with Tess left much to be desired.

Cohl shook his head. For ten years, he'd sidestepped his duty to pursue his dream. She deserved her chance. It had been the best decision for her, he argued to himself. So why did that little voice in the back of his brain keep screaming at him? After three months, you'd think it would have shut up already.

Behind him came a familiar humming. Cohl didn't turn around. "What is it, Pitz?"

"I have an audio message for you, sir," Pitz responded.

Wearily, Cohl looked up at the moons. "I'll listen to it tomorrow."

"It is urgent," Pitz prompted.

Cohl let out a long breath and rubbed the back of his neck. "Play it then."

It started slow with a wailing arrangement, played on a simple, single instrument. He knew the singer even before the first line was uttered.

> *Will you smile for me?*
> *Soothe my heart and make it whole*
> *Coax buried hope free*
> *Wring laughter from solid stone.*

Cohl's heart nearly stopped beating at her voice, so clear and close. He reeled under the flood of memories. Her name rolled from his lips in one, long sigh. *Tess.*

> *Once so near, your breath could be mine.*
> *Now so far, fading into time*
> *Through the gaping hole*
> *Light won't reach the hollow of my soul*
> *Where shadows dance in bitter cold.*

Cohl squeezed his eyes shut as a solid wall of anguish crashed and broke across his entire body. So much sadness in her voice. He'd hurt her. He could hear the heartache and the grief. It was the last thing he had meant to do.

And the words, they could have been his own. The pain was the same, the sorrow, the hunger, and the loneliness.

> *Breathe for me, grieve for me*
> *Damn the pride that kills our dreams*
> *And builds the worlds between.*

His eyes closed tightly. *Breathe for me.* The same words she had uttered when she was terrified on the cliff. *Grieve for me.* He had done this to her. Brought her to such sorrow. It was unbearable. He had no idea. She should be happy by now.

Will you come for me?
Through the cage of endless night
Pluck me from this scream
Lead me out into the light.

The words rang through his mind over and over again. *Come for me.* She wanted him to come get her? After all the pain he'd caused her, she still needed him. He couldn't believe it. Couldn't imagine why . . .

Then his head dropped back as relief swept through and eased the suffering. She loved him. Why hadn't she told him? If he'd known . . . He stopped. Hell, why hadn't he told her he loved her?

He knew the answer. They were both too afraid to ask each other for such a sacrifice. But all they'd sacrificed was love. What a couple of stubborn fools they'd been. He could almost laugh at the irony. Almost, except that it hurt too much.

The final chorus ended and there was silence again. Painful and gut-wrenching silence without Tess in it.

For a long time, Cohl studied the formal grounds of his home, the solutions running through his head. He couldn't leave Yre Gault. He knew that now. Tess would have to live here but would she want that? Would she be happy here without her Earth family and friends, without her career? Was it right to ask that much of her after all the sacrifices she'd already made in her life?

He took a deep breath. There was only one way to find out. He would ask her and live with whatever decision she made. Stay on Earth without him or come back to Yre Gault with him—those were her choices. Hope sparked fresh energy within him. He had seen worse odds. He suddenly needed wings.

"Pitz, is *Speculator* operational?"

"Yes, sir. And the crew is also available."

Cohl eyed Pitz, wondering how he'd assembled the crew on absolutely no notice. Pitz simply blinked back. Cohl shook his head. There was no way a robot could understand human emotion, not even one as sophisticated as Pitz. It didn't matter how. He had to get back to Tess before it was too late. The utter desolation in her song worried him.

"Inform the crew that we leave in the morning."

Pitz hummed lightly, almost melodically. "And the destination?"

Cohl smiled up at the millions of stars. "Earth."

"Yes, sir." Pitz turned and slid toward the door.

Cohl narrowed his eyes at the departing robot. "Pitz. How did you capture Tess's message?"

Pitz stopped and spun just his head toward Cohl. "From the radio transmissions from Earth, of course."

"Uh-huh," Cohl said, crossing his arms over his chest. "And since when have you begun monitoring Earth's transmission?"

The robot blinked innocently. "It has rather become a hobby of mine."

"Interesting hobby, Pitz."

Pitz spun his head back toward the door. "And highly entertaining as well."

Tess shoved her hands deep into her winter jacket as a sharp, bitter wind buffeted her, its path broken only by an occasional bare-leafed shrub along the sidewalk.

It was a cold, gray November evening in upstate New York, much like yesterday and the day before and the day before that. In fact, Tess acknowledged as she pulled her coat collar tightly around her neck, every day looked gray to her. When was the last time the sun had shown?

Beneath the circle of a streetlight, the last of the fallen leaves skittered and danced around her feet in their autumn death dance. Aimless, they had long ago lost their purpose, shriveled and brittle and too blind to simply lie down and die.

Tess took a long deep breath and blew it out, watching the vapors disappear with the wind. By now, she should have slipped back into her old life, but somehow, it felt so strange. As if she no longer belonged or felt welcome.

Long days and longer nights dragged into an endless circle of light and dark. She had never known heartache could hurt this bad or last this long.

Even returning to her singing—her one salvation—didn't swallow her up like it used to. The hole was just too big and too deep. Although she had to admit, her blues had never sounded better.

She kicked a rock with the toe of her boot, sending it skipping down the sidewalk in front of her. Then it was quiet again but for the howl of the wind. Even the streets were empty tonight.

Her new CD was doing well, getting the kind of attention she'd always hoped for. The gigs were once again lining up and Bill was beginning to smile again. New songs poured out of her. Things were great. Too bad she didn't care anymore. She was just going through the motions, doing her duty.

It's only duty if your heart isn't in it. Now she understood what Cohl had felt about Yre Gault. Her heart was no longer in it. Her heart belonged somewhere else.

As she had a hundred times in the past few months, Tess cast a look up at the night sky. The stars twinkled back at her, bright and crisp in the cold country air. Millions of them. One of them belonged to Cohl.

She felt the tight squeeze in her chest and accepted it, knowing it was useless to fight. After all this time, the anguish hadn't lessened. In fact, it seemed to grow daily. She had hoped that he would have heard her song by now. The one with her heart and soul in it. The one begging him to come back for her. Her one and only hope for happiness. But there'd been no reply. He either would not or could not reclaim her. He probably wasn't even listening.

Tess bowed her head into the wind as she turned up the little walkway that ran along the back of the house she rented. Ascending the creaky stairs to the second-floor flat, she wondered vaguely where Griz was tonight. Probably playing with his kitty friends. Seemed only right that one of them should have a social life.

Tess unlocked and pushed the door open. Inside, it was dark but she was in no hurry to turn on the lights only to see how empty her life had become. She tossed her heavy coat on a chair and made her way into the bedroom by the light of a nearby street lamp.

As she walked through the doorway, a huge hand clamped over her mouth. The other arm pulled her firmly back against a warm, hard body. Her blood froze.

"I got your message," the attacker whispered in her ear.

The voice. *Cohl*.

For long seconds, her body, mind, and soul hung suspended in disbelief. Finally, she shook her head beneath his grip. *No, no. It couldn't be.* However, her body responded automatically to his scent and his heat. Every nerve ending welcomed him; alive in a way they had not been in months. A hard wave of turbulent emotions rolled over her, thrashing through her system one after the other. It felt as if her heart would come right out of her chest. Then her brain kicked in.

A deep, violent shudder tore through her and hot tears streamed down her face and across Cohl's hand. In one movement, he turned her into his arms; his fingers went to her face, his lips to hers. He entered her mouth deeply, plundering and demanding more. She moaned low and gave him what he asked for. As if she could ever resist. He groaned at her surrender, leaning into her with his entire body.

She broke free and laid her forehead against his chest. He was here as she'd asked. So now what?

"No tears, Tess. Please. I'm here for you."

"Don't leave me again," she sobbed softly, desperately. "Don't love me and then fly off."

Cohl stroked her hair. "I'm not leaving without you."

She rolled her head from side to side, self-preservation giving her strength. She shook from the effort of voicing her worst nightmare. "How will I know you'll come back when you leave the room? How do I know you won't send me back here again?"

"Not this time, Earth girl. I've changed."

She pushed back and looked into his eyes. He sounded so convincing. It was hard to see through the tears but he looked the same to her. She needed more than his words. She needed to know without a doubt that she could trust him.

"Prove it," she said so softly, and it almost sounded like a thought. There it was. The challenge. It was now or never. She had to know.

It was amazing how those two little words had the power to stop time. There was a long pause as Cohl stared back, obviously stunned. Then he stepped away from her and stood in the center of her bedroom, his hands on his hips. He looked grim and she nearly lost her mind. Hope fizzled. He had not changed enough.

In the glow of the streetlight, he began to move, motions that looked familiar to her but completely alien on him. She frowned for a moment, trying to figure out what he was doing. Then her breath caught. Her eyes widened in disbelief as he strutted before her.

Tess covered her mouth. *Oh my God.* He was doing the chicken dance. For her.

Pure joy swept through her. For the first time in months, she could breathe deep and feel it.

He did love her.

He had changed.

She launched herself at him, driving them both into a heap on her bed. Cohl grunted as she landed on top of him. The springs of her old wrought-iron bed creaked woefully.

Holding his face in her hands, she covered him with quick kisses while a deep laugh rumbled through his chest.

"Satisfied?" he asked as he captured her hands and kissed the palms.

She looked down into his eyes. "I love you."

He smiled. "I love you, too. But if you ever tell anyone that I did that stupid dance, I'll deny it until the day I die."

Tess laughed aloud for the first time in months. In a flash, she was on her back with Cohl's big body pressing her into the mattress. His hands roamed over her and his breath deepened. Tess sighed at the sensual pull as her body responded to her lover's call. He kissed her deeply, slowly, as if they had all the time in the world. Then he pulled back and took her face in his warm palms. "Don't suppose you've ever given any thought to ruling a planet."

"What?" With a burst of energy, she gripped his arms as he grinned at her.

"I've decided to rule Yre Gault. My parents are ready to step down," he explained and brushed her tangled hair from her face.

A proud smile slid across her face. "You're going to rule Yre Gault. I knew you would. You could never allow anyone else to take your place."

He laughed at that. "I suppose you are right." Then he turned serious, tracing her lips with his thumb. "It'll be your life too, if you come with me. A lifetime job. And it's not all celebrations. Long hours, little freedom, and the only time people come to you is when they have a problem."

Tess gave him a lopsided smile. "Sounds like the story of my life."

Cohl narrowed his eyes. "I'm telling you the ugly truth, Tess. I want you to understand what you are getting yourself into. Once you commit, there is no turning back and no escape. Are you willing to take on that kind of responsibility?"

She realized he was telling her the truth, the whole truth. She slipped her fingers through his silky hair. "We'll do it together."

He gave an audible sigh. "I'll take that as a yes. What about your career?"

She looked him in the eye. "I don't care if I'm rich or famous. I just want the opportunity to sing. It doesn't matter where."

He nodded as if understanding completely. "I'll try to get you back to Earth to see your family."

"Christmas every year," she suggested. "That would be enough."

"Deal." He paused. "And I want children, Tess. More than one. But only if I can spend time with them."

She warned him, "Then you'll have to learn to delegate."

He reached out and touched the buttons of her blouse. "True. I should start practicing now. Take your clothes off."

Tess looked up and laughed. "Miss me?"

He grinned wide and wicked. "You have no idea. I've been one miserable bastard. Everyone within a thousand meters of me is going to be thrilled when you come back to Yre Gault for good."

She frowned slightly. "And adventuring?"

He nuzzled her neck and worked his way down. "Maybe an easy one once in a while. You don't want me getting bored."

"What happens when you get bored?" Then she gasped as he deftly worked the buttons of her blouse. She could already feel him hard and ready against her thigh. He exposed her breasts to his scrutiny and she saw his eyes darken at the sight of her black lace bra. He dipped his head to suckle one taut nipple through the sheer fabric.

Through the heat, he murmured, "You wind up in bed for a very, very long time. I've been extremely bored for the past few months. I hope your bed can take it."

His gaze raised slowly to hers, filled with more than just humor, more than just desire. They held all the truth she could ever ask for. Those golden eyes were hers forever— every morning, every night, every day for the rest of her life.

She could hardly wait for the adventure to begin.

Epilogue

From the raised platform in the central plaza, Tess watched another laser firework burst over the Great Kings of Yre Gault as thousands gasped and cheered. Laser-etched flowers emerged, unfolding their colors against a black velvet night sky. Music blared as it had for hours. Around them people danced and children squealed in the sultry heat. On the platform, Adehla and Montral stood together pointing and clapping. Some of the crew had joined them—Figalee, Beckye, and Sahto. Even Pitz seemed amused, his lights doing a little dance of their own. Caldara was celebrating.

"Now *this* is a party," she heard Rayce say to Cohl. "Too bad you only become king once."

Cohl laughed. "Once in a lifetime is enough."

Then he nudged Tess and hitched his head back. She turned in time to see Beckye give Sahto a giant hug and a sound smack on the lips. Sahto was grinning from ear to ear.

"Hey, Zain," he said surreptitiously. "I think you're off the hook."

Zain nodded, watching another firework burst over them. "I noticed. You never told me what a brave man Sahto is." Then he clapped Cohl on the shoulder. "Congratulations. I think Yre Gault is in very capable hands."

"I'm going to do my best," Cohl replied with conviction.

She smiled up at him, handsome in his royal uniform with the giant kings in the background. A purple flower exploded above them, flooding the white statues in lavender. Her eyes were drawn to the daunting monuments and she wondered if they were ever intimidated by their responsibilities. Although her coronation gown was stunning, she felt the weight behind its beauty.

She leaned against Cohl and whispered, "You've joined the Great Kings. Are you nervous?"

His eyes reflected the fireworks. "No. I figured out how the Great Kings did it. Their secret."

"What secret?" she asked.

He looked down at her. "They all had great queens. I have you by my side. I'm fearless." Then he paused, gazing at her with concern. "Are you nervous?"

She felt his strength, his resolve. "No. I'd follow you anywhere," she said, batting her eyelashes. "Except into the mist of beasts, of course."

He squeezed her hand. "In that case, I think we're good."

A pink flower burst across the sky and Tess nodded. Yes, they were good. She had Cohl and he had her. Together they could do anything.

The celebration was still going strong as Tess stood alone hours later on the balcony overlooking the royal courtyard. Moonlight spilled onto the many balconies overhanging the gardens. Even the most brilliant flowers were subdued tonight, giving up the spotlight to the dark beauty of the night. So dreamlike in its perfection, she wondered if it would ever seem real to her. A soft breeze caressed her bare shoulders in sweet fragrance. Music wafted through the heat and she swayed to the distant beat, lyrics forming in her head.

This was her home. She loved it, felt loved.

She was still amazed how easy it had been to leave Earth behind. She'd told her family and friends about her and Cohl moving overseas; she just didn't mention that the sea was on a different planet. But her promise to call frequently and come back at Christmas had quieted any protests. The band would find another singer and go on. She'd left them her songs and promised to send them more. Bill should recover in a year or so.

From Earth, she'd brought back a year's supply of chocolate and coffee, her favorite music and her cat. Griz had adjusted surprisingly well to life on an alien planet and terrorized Pitz at every opportunity. Only today, she noticed a tuft of fur stuck in his metal armor. Tess laughed to herself. Poor Pitz. Outsmarted by a housecat. God help his poor hard-wired brain when they had children running about.

Tess hiked the blanket around her shoulders and smiled up at the moons riding each other across the midnight sky— cosmic coupling. It was a night for lovers.

She started at a noise behind her and turned to find Cohl leaning one broad shoulder on the doorway to the balcony. In the moonlight, he stood naked, a perfect statue of flesh and bone, muscle and man.

"Did I wake you?" she whispered.

"You stole the blanket," he murmured in a sexy, lazy voice.

She giggled. "Oh. Sorry. I didn't want to walk out here naked. What would people think?"

He ran a hand through his hair and yawned. "They'd probably think I'm one very lucky man."

There was a short silence.

"Are you?" she asked softly.

His golden eyes fixed on her with the kind of intensity

that told her he was waking up. "I'd have to say that I'm the luckiest man alive."

Tess cocked her head. "Even with all the new responsibilities?"

"A wise woman once told me that it's only duty if your heart isn't in it." Cohl's gaze roamed over her wrapped body as he smiled the devil's own smile. "As a matter of fact, I'm taking the task of producing an heir especially to heart."

Tess's eyebrows went up. "Is that so?" She cast a glance at the cosmic coupling show above her. "I believe this is your cue then."

He shoved off the door frame and slowly approached her—a panther to its prey. "Never let it be said that I shirked my royal duties."

Tess was trembling even before he touched her, before he tugged the blanket away, baring her skin to the night.

"Out here?" she gasped as he pulled her against his chest.

His eyes never left hers. "It only works under the moons."

Tess gave him a skeptical look. "Are you sure?"

"Positive. I've done a tremendous amount of research on the subject."

"I didn't realize there were specific parameters attached to this process."

Cohl nuzzled her neck, nipping as he went. "Trust me. As ruler, it's my job to know details. There's timing to think about, positions, duration . . ."

"Huh," Tess whispered against his throat as the heat began to rise within her. "I had no idea it was so complicated."

He cupped her chin, lifting her face up to the moons. "It could take a lifetime to get it right."

Her smile grew bigger as her hands slid around his waist, pulling him close. "Well, then. Never let it be said that I shirked my royal duties."

He ran his hands down her back and whispered in her ear, "I love you, Tess." She hummed to the beat of his heart and the harmonious cadence of their love.

No song ever sounded sweeter.

THE
STAR
Prince
SUSAN GRANT

Ian Hamilton considers himself a typical guy, a finance major who finds all the excitement he needs in the stock market and his Harley. Then his stepfather offers him the crown to an empire and the reins of a mission critical to world peace. What can he do but go for the ride?

In a daring bid for autonomy, Princess Tee'ah flees her world for the freedom to fly. Both her husband and her life will be of her own choosing. And when a handsome stranger offers her a job piloting the *Sun Devil*, she chooses the romp of a lifetime—with the one man she should avoid at all costs.

From ocean-dark skies to the neon-drenched streets of L.A., Tee'ah and Ian find that true adventure is learning some rules are made to be broken . . . and some loves are written in the stars.

THE STAR King

SUSAN GRANT

Careening out of control in her fighter jet is only the start of the wildest ride of Jasmine's life; spinning wildly in an airplane is nothing like the loss of equilibrium she feels when she lands. There, in a half-dream, Jas sees a man more powerfully compelling than any she's ever encountered. Though his words are foreign, his touch is familiar, baffling her mind even as he touches her soul. But who is he? Is he, too, a downed pilot? Is that why he lies in the desert sand beneath a starry Arabian sky? The answers burn in his mysterious golden eyes, in his thoughts that become hers as he holds out his hand and requests her aid. This man has crossed many miles to find her, to offer her a heaven that she might otherwise never know, and love is only one of the many gifts of . . . the Star King.

___52413-9 $5.50 US/$6.50 CAN

Dorchester Publishing Co., Inc.
P.O. Box 6640
Wayne, PA 19087-8640

Please add $2.50 for shipping and handling for the first book and $.75 for each book thereafter. NY, NYC, and PA residents, please add appropriate sales tax. No cash, stamps, or C.O.D.s. All orders shipped within 6 weeks via postal service book rate. Canadian orders require $2.00 extra postage and must be paid in U.S. dollars through a U.S. banking facility.

Name_____
Address_____
City_____ State_____ Zip_____
I have enclosed $_____ in payment for the checked book(s).
Payment <u>must</u> accompany all orders.☐Please send a free catalog.
CHECK OUT OUR WEBSITE! www.dorchesterpub.com

CONTACT
SUSAN GRANT

A BEAUTIFUL CO-PILOT WITH A TERRIBLE CHOICE.

"After only three novels, Susan Grant has proven herself
to be the best hope for the survival of the futuristic/
fantasy romance genre." —*The Romance Reader*

A DARK STRANGER WHO HAS KNOWN NOTHING BUT DUTY.

"I am in awe of Susan Grant. She's one
of the few authors who get it." —*Everything Romantic*

A LATE-NIGHT FLIGHT, HIJACKED OVER THE PACIFIC.

Shadow Crossing
Catherine Spangler

Celie Cameron spent her youth as a smuggler, skirting the law. But though she's given that up, she misses the adrenaline rush of danger. Then a routine delivery goes haywire, throwing her into the arms of a handsome pilot—an android, or so she thinks—and Celie suddenly finds herself embroiled in a galaxy-spanning intrigue and deception.

Rurick is a miracle creation. But though he attracts her as no human ever has, his secrets threaten all Celie has ever believed. She resists his allure . . . until she learns to trust her heart. Then they will challenge the evil that threatens the Verante quadrant, and love will bring light to the dark expanse of space known as Shadow Crossing.

Shamara
Catherine Spangler

In a universe of darkness and depravity, the Shielders battle to stay one step ahead of the vengeful Controllers, who seek the destruction of their race. Survival depends upon the quest of one man. Jarek san Ranul has found evidence of a wormhole, a vortex to another galaxy; an escape. But when his search produces the most intriguing woman he's ever met, he finds he wants something more than duty and honor.

On the run from a mighty warlord, Eirene Kane has to protect her identity as an Enhancer, one of a genetic few with a powerful gift. Then her flight hurls her into the arms of Jarek, a man who steals her heart and uncovers her perilous secret—and though she knows she should flee, Eirene finds herself yearning for both the man and the one thing he claims will free them forever.

___52452-X $5.50 US/$6.50 CAN

Dorchester Publishing Co., Inc.
P.O. Box 6640
Wayne, PA 19087-8640

Please add $2.50 for shipping and handling for the first book and $.75 for each book thereafter. NY and PA residents, please add appropriate sales tax. No cash, stamps, or C.O.D.s. All orders shipped within 6 weeks via postal service book rate. Canadian orders require $2.00 extra postage and must be paid in U.S. dollars through a U.S. banking facility.

Name_____
Address_____
City_____ State_____ Zip_____
I have enclosed $_____ in payment for the checked book(s).
Payment **must** accompany all orders. ☐ Please send a free catalog.
CHECK OUT OUR WEBSITE! www.dorchesterpub.com

SPELLBOUND IN SEATTLE

GARTHIA ANDERSON

With enchanted blood on her carpet, a house full of Merlin-wannabes unable to clean it up, a petulant cat, and houseguests scheduled to arrive momentarily, Petra Field needs a miracle. She gets a wizard, a whole lot of unwanted sparks, and a man-sized hole in the middle of her living room—a hole into which her feline promptly disappears.

Vorador hasn't felt so incompetent since his days as an untried sorcerer. The girl who leaps after her cat and into his arms causes his simplest spells to backfire—quite literally setting his hair ablaze. And though she claims to be no conjurer, he knows that he's never felt so bewitched, for Petra has a mesmerizing energy of her own: love.

THE BLACK ROSE

JAN ZIMLICH

Though Lucien Charbonneau was born a noble, he's implemented plans to bring about galactic revolution. He wears two faces, that of an effete aristocrat and that of someone darker, more mysterious. He has subtle yet potent charms, and he plays at deception with the same skill that he might caress a lover. And though Lucien is betrothed, he swears not even his beautiful fiancée will ever learn his heart's secret, that of the Black Rose.

Alexandra Fallon has of course heard of that infamous spy, but her own interests are far less political. When interplanetary concerns force her to marry, the man who comes to her bed is in for a rude awakening. But the shadowy hunk who appears lights a passion hotter than a thousand suns—and in its fiery glow, both she and Lucien will learn that between lovers no secrets can remain in darkness.

THE
SHADOW
PRINCE
JAN ZIMLICH

Adrik should be an honored prince of the Median Empire. Instead, he is sacrificed at birth to his father's lust for power. He becomes the property of a great demon, and is taught the ways of sorcery. Someday he will enter the Shadow Realm, trade places with his master, and be damned for eternity.

His black fate keeps Adrik from others. There is no solace for a man like himself. Then he meets a woman who streaks into his life like a dying star. The Arizanti priestess is everything he's ever dreamed of, and she sparks in Adrik a terrible desire for freedom. For the first time, he dares to hope that their love might overcome the darkness.

CHRISTINE FEEHAN
SUSAN GRANT
SUSAN SQUIRES

THE ONLY ONE

They come from the darkest places: secluded monasteries, the Carpathian mountains, galaxies under siege. They are men with the blackest pasts—warriors, vampire monks, leaders of armies—but whose passions burn like dying stars. They have one purpose: to find those women who fulfill them, complete them, and make them rage with a fire both holy and profane. They seek soul mates whose touch will consume them with desire, yet whose kisses will refresh like the coolest rain. And each man knows that for him there is only one true love—and in finding her, he will find salvation.

SEP 17 2010